THE CONQUERORS OF TRITON

"All things must abide by the laws of the dimension it's within, or be utterly destroyed. Such is the nature of existence."

—Isaiah, Former Overseer of Venus

The Conquerors of Triton
First edition ISBN: 979-8-9864688-2-2
E-book edition ISBN: 979-8-9864688-3-9

All rights reserved
Published by Cleere House Press LLC
www.hbnuttallwriting.com
First edition: November 2025
Published in the United States of America
Cover design 2025 by Hayley Nuttall

THE CONQUERORS OF TRITON

H.B. NUTTALL

Dedication

To my children, who I hope can conquer whatever the world throws at them.

To both my sisters who listened to every word before it was written.

To my husband who stuck with me through this writing endeavor, never giving up on me.

And to my mother and Mimi, who taught me that Eve wasn't tempted by the devil, but outsmarted him.

Table of Contents

Part I: Excitatio

Prelude: Ode to Life

Not everyone gets a second chance. Undeniably, most are not given any beyond that.

I knew this was mine. Not my second, but the one that comes after. So precious and rare such a thing that there is no word to describe that opportunity allotted after you've burned your previous..

Never in life did I see beyond it. And yet, it stands to reason that if I were reborn once before—figuratively speaking—one could be reborn again, could they not?

After what felt like an eternity of gelid non-existence, I felt warmth fill my body. I thought I was dead, but if surely one can think, then it mustn't be so—stasis, more like it. The literal stasis that held my body melted away, and I opened my eyes for the first time since my fall into that ocean a millennium ago.

I floated, suspended in the liquid that surrounded me, disoriented. Gravity makes no difference when you're suspended in dark water. The rules of your brain's orientation abilities were actual here, too, on this foreign world orbiting Neptune. But as I twisted, trying to find my bearings, a glimmer caught the corner of my eye.

I turned to see a spectrum of warm colors above me, shimmering beams piercing the liquid surface. Below me was only cold blue and darkness. I reached up to the colors above, feeling the organic warmth they emanated. Before my fall, I only felt artificial warmth for so long.

The liquid resistance around me told me to swim. It had not occurred to me that I should want air in my lungs. Something was within them, and I felt no desire to breathe as you do when holding your breath submerged. I shed my outer shell — my gear — whatever weight was keeping me suspended. I kicked fiercely, treading upward toward the colors, and pushing warmth into my stiff muscles. I knew that familiar heat was the sun, and as soon as I broke to the surface of this water body, I knew too. . .

... I'd be reborn under the sun.

Chapter 1:Emergence

've awakened. . .

Evie's thoughts stumbled into clarity as she broke the surface. For ever so long, her thoughts were chaotic, a dream state of nonsensical reality: no beginning and no end to the cryogenic stasis that held her.

I've emerged. . .

She returned to consciousness, to actual physical reality. Hibernating instincts came alive once more, and she took little notice of her surroundings; only that she was in a body of fresh water..

Swim—swim—SWIM! the voice in her head screamed. She kicked, propelling herself despite the disorientation. Arms stiff from her long sleep felt as though they'd burst.

She treaded, taking in what little she saw—a fuchsia horizon and the dark outline of a shoreline.

Go, a voice in her head ordered. *To land.*

As she swam closer, her vision cleared. The horizon banded into strips of saffron and violet, meeting a bank of tawny weeds.

She felt no desire to breathe. Her lungs were filled stiff like hardened clay, making it laborious to keep her body afloat. Her head bobbed between surface and submergence, her sight flitting between her determined shoreline and the deep she swam through.

A wave of fatigue flowed over her. In a moment of rest, her feet brushed against something soft.

The familiar sensation of cool, lakebed soil curled around her toes.

Home, her thoughts whispered. She closed her eyes.

Its vision filled her mind. The smell of fresh soil and lilac bushes after a summer rain. A field of soft green surrounded by trees. A white framed house with Williamsburg blue shutters, set against a gray, clouded sky. She stepped onto the front porch, loose floorboards creaking as she approached the red front door, wanting to see the person on the other side of it—

—*No.* Her thoughts barricaded the vision, forcing her back to the present. *Don't remember—don't think—don't feel. Survive.*

The surrounding water was up to her shoulders, warm around her floating arms, and chilled from the chest down. She wanted to feel a sense of urgency, but oddly enough felt calm wash over her. The shoreline was close, and her determination resumed. She trudged through the shallow water, her feet digging into the lakebed with each step.

Lakebed? She thought. *Maybe a pond?*

The surface line sank beneath her waist. Her wet, ivory colored bodysuit stuck to her like skin. She stumbled as the lakebed filled with jagged rocks, the weight of her clay lungs making it impossible to stand straight. She stepped out of the water, over the tawny weeds, and fell forward onto dry land, dragging the rest of her body out of the water.

Then the urge hit.

Like an unsatisfied itch, her chest shivered against her lungs. She lunged on her hands and knees. Dark, wet hair slapping her face as she shoved weeds aside. She coughed profusely, uncontrollably, to the point that her vision blurred.

And she felt it come up.

Like ice drawing up her esophagus, she retched out the liquid in her lungs. The liquid, a stark cerulean, poured onto the ground, its tingling cold numbing her mouth as it passed. It felt never-ending as it continued to pour out of her mouth, her chest heaving and pushing the substance from her body.

Finally, she spat out the last of the horrid substance. The overwhelming sensation to breathe hit her like a gunshot, and she drew in her first wheezing breath.

Relief, that's what it was. Although painful, the feel of her lungs expanding and collapsing was a relief; she felt alive. She fell to her back, cushioned by the overgrown weeds around her. She whimpered and groaned, but continued with labored breaths. With each breath easier than the last, and the pain lessening as muscle memory took over the movement of her lungs, she no longer had to think about it.

The rustle of the vegetation drew her eyes up, tips of elongated grass bouncing in her face. The warm breeze had a sweet, young smell as she looked up at the cloudless sky, which blended into an ombre of red, fuchsia, and yellow, like a desert sunset. The sky radiated the same warmth as the breeze, and she felt comfort as it saturated and dried her body.

What is this paradisal place? She wondered, never having seen the sky so wide with these colors, and not fading to dark as sunsets do. She peered to her side and noticed wisps of steam, the blue substance she had coughed out evaporating.

The warmth from the sky relieved the pain in her stiff muscles, and she rolled onto her stomach.

I can do this, she thought. *I made it out of the lake; I can do this, too.*

She pushed herself onto her knees.

She didn't think it would be so hard to stand after swimming across the lake, but the weight of her own self worked against her. Taking deep breaths, she pushed from her knees onto her feet, stretching her back and standing straight.

Before her was a sea of grass and weeds, a plain stretching for miles against the red sky.

And what a sky it was now that she was standing! But it wasn't a red sky emanating the warmth that dried her body—it was the sun, bigger than she had ever seen it, filling all the heavens with its scarlet glory.

She turned away from it, looking behind at the lake she emerged from. The edges of the red sun faded, and another celestial object floated in the sky, reflecting in the lake beneath. A moon, glowing a cool green against the yellow and orange that surrounded it, a sore thumb among the beauty of celestial skies.

Moon? She thought. *No, it's too massive for that, it's not the moon, it's... it's... my god, I never left!*

The horror of that day came alive as memory allowed her to relive her fall. She and the rest of team 4020-A, in full space gear, standing on a plain of ice and waving to the rover, back to loved ones on Earth, when they all heard it: the thunderclap from beneath.

It all happened fast, the unprecedented geyser bursting through the surface, breaking the nitrogen ice crust to pieces, and falling into the ammonia ocean beneath. Her last view of the surface world as she fell was of the pale blue-green ice giant; of Neptune looking down upon them, seemingly laughing at the trespassers facing their fate.

And it was that exact Neptune that floated above her now, but its pale blue was gone, completely giving way to the present cool green.

Evie knew where she was. She never left that ice world from long ago.

She stood on Neptune's largest moon: Triton.

Chapter 2: Not Just a Moon

In all technicality, Neptune's largest moon, Triton, isn't a moon. It indeed orbits Neptune, but its unique features leave it in a conundrum: neither planet nor moon.

In 2006 CE, Earthkind reclassified celestial objects in its system to better track data on planetary objects. Although their understanding of what makes a planet a planet is minimal at best, Earthkind realized, quite frankly, that the celestial objects in their system are more diverse than they could've ever imagined. They finally wanted to answer for themselves, what makes a planet a planet?

And thus was born the idea of a dwarf planet.

The first reclassification was Pluto, the largest celestial object in the Kuiper belt. Flybys by probes further reinforced the idea that Pluto, along with Ceres and Eris, is something more than an oversized asteroid. Still, they are too small to amass a gravitational force to clear their orbits of other objects. Therefore, dwarf planets.

This introduces the conundrum of Triton. Matching Pluto in identity and formation, it, by all means, should be a dwarf planet in its own right. And, its creation alongside Pluto and Triton should've been crowned the largest celestial object within the Kuiper belt.

But the greediness of Neptune's gravity pulled Triton away, propelling it into an orbit around the ice giant instead of the warm sun. Its orbit forever destined to serve the gelid heart.

These were Evie's thoughts as she stared at the incredible green planet above, reflecting on the lake's surface, the water stretching to another faraway, unseen shore. Like looking into a photo negative, Neptune was in the same position it was the day she fell, though the red sun changed everything.

She fell to her knees, shaking her head. *How could this have happened?* How long has it been? And how was the timing so precise that Neptune was exactly where they left it?

It hurt her head to think of such things so soon after waking. She turned her face to the red sun. *Yes,* she thought. *It's the red sun. This is not the sun I know. My sun is a yellow dwarf star. Not this one; this one's a red giant. That means Earth—oh god no—*

The pieces came together as she imagined a time-lapse: a bright, beautiful yellow sun dimming, then expanding as patches of orange and red scatter its surface. Growing larger and more crimson as its circumference swallows the inner planets one by one, their surfaces burning to a crisp before the sun engulfs them whole.

And Earth. Oh, beautiful Earth, she couldn't bear to imagine its fate.

People knew it was inevitable. They wouldn't have stayed. There have to be others out there who left. There have to be others—others—

Others. Team 4020! She was elated, remembering that some people had fallen with her, but she couldn't picture their faces. *My team.*

She came to her feet. Surely she couldn't be the only one on Team 4020 to survive. If she made it, maybe they did too.

She scanned all around her. Nothing in the direction of the lake. Just water.

The grassland only presented itself with endless plains.

I can't stay here, she thought. *I should, but I can't.* The protocol for missing persons was to stay put so that the search party could find you.

But what if *she* was the search party?

And she needed resources.

Number one priority: survival.

Although there seemed to be plenty of water and simple plant life, there were no signs of other resources: no food, no evidence of fish, no signs of edible plants or fruits.

It was strangely quiet. No chirping of insects, no sounds of beasts or fowl. Just the scraping of wind against the weeds, the gently pushing of still water against the bank. Although Triton felt alive, she existed as the only animal life-form.

How? she thought. How is this possible? She knew all the symbiotic connections lifeforms provided to support the environment around her. *How does this place exist?*

She felt the tension to move her body, to go forth. The eras of cryogenic sleep created an uneasiness within her, that any waiting would make her explode from the pent-up potential energy wanting release.

She looked to the red horizon and began to walk.

Then stopped.

"What?"

It wasn't clear, not at all, with the sun glaring at her.

But it was there. A silhouette–

A person!

Thank heavens! She thought and ran toward it. *Another survivor!*

"Hey there!" she called. Her voice felt fresh, newly born. Satisfying to use it once more.

And stopped again.

Although she could make out no distinguishing features, she saw that this was no one from team 4020.

It was a man–or what she thought could be a man–none like she'd ever seen. So pale that his body blended into the white clothes that flowed in the wind.

The man in white.

She'd not felt this kind of paranoia of strangers since she was a child. She'd outgrown such a notion. But she felt like a child again, looking at the man in white, standing still in the distance. He didn't even look real; a humanoid blur against the red horizon—a white stain floating above the grasslands.

Then she heard gurgling.

A paroxysmal cough—just like the one she had when she emerged—sounded from the direction of the lake—splashing accompanied the persistent cough.

She turned and saw weeds moving by the bank. A man wearing the same faded ivory bodysuit as her—*UNSF 4020* printed and bolded across the back—stumbled out of the lake and into the vegetation.

She glanced back at the sun.

The man in white was gone.

Although taken aback, Evie pushed aside thoughts of the man in white. Her teammate needed her now. She ran to the riverbank and found him on all fours, hacking just as she did. She knelt beside him.

I know this man, she thought, but her memory was slow to remember him. She put a hand on his back, and he continued to hack violently.

"It's alright," she said comfortingly, "it will come out."

A name, she thought. Cold water droplets from his wet bodysuit splattered her face as she patted the middle of his back to help ease his retching. She knew it did nothing physically, but her inner bedside manner reminded her that it gave comfort.

He has a name. Why can't I remember it? She observed his thick head of coiled curls, so tight they didn't move as his head bobbed from the vomiting, splashing the ground with the cold cerulean substance that filled his lungs.

An image appeared in her mind.

That's right, she remembered, *he was bald then.*

Her vision erupted. A thin Australian man, bald with umber skin, pushing a set of goggles to his face. Smiling with glee as he poured liquid samples of that same cerulean substance into beakers, a hearty laugh bellowed from deep within his chest.

Asa, she thought. *You're Asa.*

Asa spewed the last of the cold substance, spitting it to the ground. Evie helped him sit up as he panted, heaving in his first breaths as she did. The cerulean substance steamed and evaporated as the light of the sun met it.

Asa took a deep breath. "Thank you," he heaved another breath, "you."

"Of course," Evie said, looking him over. She instinctively put the back of her hand against his forehead.

"Temperature is cool," she said to him. "But not concerning." She grabbed his arm and turned his hand over. She placed two fingers along the fold of his wrist and waited. She closed her eyes, waiting to feel it.

And there it was, a pulse.

She mentally counted. Such an intrusion of personal space should've made him back away, but he didn't. He let her. And she felt no qualms in invading his space.

Why was she here? And why did she feel that was acceptable?

Asa narrowed his gaze. "I know you."

Evie opened her eyes. "Yes, you do."

"But I can't think of your name—or even mine."

"You're Asa," she said. "It's alright. It takes a little time for it to come back — your memory, I mean. I think it's because we were asleep for so long."

"Asleep?"

"Yes," Evie said. She looked into his pupils. They were dilated at normal capacity for daylight. "Pulse is normal. I need you to take a deep breath for me." She shifted her fingers on his wrist slightly to get a better grip of the pulse. "Good, now inhale and exhale normally." She counted his breaths while feeling his pulse.

A thought kept tugging at her mind.

I'm not just Evie. She dropped Asa's arm. *I'm known by another name. A title, a job. . .*

"I almost forgot what a talented astromedic you are," Asa said.

"Astromedic," Evie smiled and nodded her head. She couldn't remember anything unless she matched a word to it, as though words were the only thing that connected her to a conscious state of being. But as coherent words continued to realign within her mind, so did her memory. 'Astromedic' initiated a part of her thoughts that dug deep into her memory. Years of nursing school and certification exams. Hours of studying for practicals and eventual med school. She felt the heaviness of the strenuous hours she spent, unpaid, at her residency.

Suddenly, like a dagger to her mid-chest, she felt regret. It twisted, reminding her of the time siphoned from the person she loved most; the sacrifices she made to be successful. The satisfaction of accomplishment, and the resentment she received in retaliation for her dedication to her med program.

Unable to contain the pain, she numbed it with her mind, forcing it to the back where it belonged.

That's why I'm here, she thought calmly. *I'm the mission's astromedic. I have responsibilities. I'm supposed to keep them alive.* She felt a bitter taste in her mouth. A *fine job I've done at that.*

Asa rolled his shoulders and stretched. "You're right, about both things—the memory and who you are." He had an accent —or what sounded like one to Evie. She was sure she had an accent in his perspective as well, even though they both spoke English. Australian — that was it — but not the Australian most foreigners associated with.

"The substance," Asa nodded to where he had spewed; the cerulean substance had evaporated entirely. "That stuff may have something to do with it, too, if it was in our system for any substantial length of time."

"You know all that?"

"Just guessing," he said. "Feels natural."

"It should," she said. "Because you're a chemist." And then 'chemist' triggered another name. "Dr. Baramba."

He looked up and grinned. "Yeah, I am. *Ha*—this is weird. Knowing and not knowing? Fascinating really. I wonder what other side effects that stuff had on our bodies."

"Not the first thing I'd expect someone to think of in our situation," Evie said. "But I don't think the substance has anything to do with our memory—it only preserved us."

"Time." Asa glanced up at the green planet in the sky. "Are we still—"

A flash in his eyes; a hope that it wasn't true.

"It worked!" he said. "By god, it worked, and we're alive. The mission didn't fail. But that means—" His countenance sank.

"Yes," Evie said. "We're still on Triton. Pretty sure, given we still see Neptune in the sky. Albeit a different color."

"How long?" Asa's eyes widened. *How long?"*

She gestured to the red sun in the opposite direction. "You tell me."

Asa stood, looking into the horizon in awe. Evie stood beside him, scanning his face, his expressions. Was this how she looked when she discovered the red sun and realized what it was? He looked astonished, amazed even. And all the while, hidden deep in the wrinkles on his forehead, fear and grief rippled. He held his breath. Unspoken words yelled a thousand sentiments at once, screaming what the red sun meant. Were they the only survivors? They knew the inevitable was to come eventually, but living to see it with their own eyes was never even an afterthought. Fortunate? Miraculous? None of those things spoke to them.

But one word did: *marooned.*

"No," he breathed. "Impossible!"

"We're people of science," Evie put a hand on his shoulder. He stood a good eight inches taller than she. "Nothing's impossible."

"Charlie!" he yelled, followed by a heart-wrenching moan. The name echoed across the vast grasslands and to the sky above as he fell to his knees, hugging his arms around his chest.

"Asa," Evie knelt to his level. "I-I'm so sorry." She put a hand on her friend's shoulder.

He didn't speak another word.

They sat in mourning silence at the loss of their home world. Earth was gone; there was no denying it. They both felt its loss —a severed connection to the planet that gave them life. Evie thought of the loved ones she hoped to see again: parents, siblings, friends. All those she risked not ever meeting again by going on this mission. She accepted that risk and felt loss before they even arrived at Triton. She managed it, handled it, just as she was trained to. But Asa hadn't. Out of the time she'd known him, he'd not felt loss as she had. He had someone he loved dearly, just as she once did. Was this his first time dealing with grief? He rarely spoke of his personal life.

"I don't know what to say—there is nothing to make this better," she said. "We're alive, and that's a miracle in and of itself. But everything's going to be different."

He put his hand over hers. "You're right. I don't know, but all of a sudden, I don't feel much of anything. No fear—nothing. Not even joy that I'm alive—nothing. "

"That's normal," she said. "Shock. Just be careful not to let it all come crashing down on you at once. Process it."

"Ha-ha, you certainly haven't changed!" Asa shook his head with a friendly smile for her. He dropped his hand, and she did in turn. "No tears from you, Evie, never from you. We can count on that."

"I'm sorry?" Evie said.

"Don't be," Asa said. "I count on your strength. I need it right now."

"We also need to find shelter," Evie continued. "And food. First steps of survival."

"And processing? You want me to make time for that while we make shelter?"

Evie smirked. "And you're the same, you heckler." She elbowed him. That's right, he was not just a colleague, but her friend. "I was thinking we could circle the lake," she pointed to it, "see if there are any other survivors. Find a good spot for shelter before nightfall."

"Nightfall?" Asa said. "Do we even know if Triton has a nightfall at this point? And I don't know about you," he stretched his arms high, "but this weather feels paradisal."

"It does, doesn't it?" Evie looked into the distance, where she saw the man in white. Nothing but grassland, stretching to the red horizon.

"What are you looking at?" Asa asked.

Evie shook her head. "I'm losing my mind. I thought I saw another survivor before you, but he disappeared."

"Maybe," Asa pondered. "But you're the expert in keeping us alive. I'll follow your lead."

The warm breeze dried their body suits as they walked the edge of the lake, the temperate weather keeping them comfortable. Evie searched for more signs of survivors, but none were to be had. The lake's water gently pulsed, sending subtle waves lapping against the shore in a comforting rhythm. Before long, everything darkened, the red sun dipped beyond the horizon, and Neptune glowed brighter.

Fatigue did not haunt them.

And neither did any other people—the emptiness of a lone planet.

"Best make shelter," Evie said as they continued to walk along the lake shore. "Before it gets too late. We have no idea what kind of weather the night will bring."

"Agreed," Asa said. "I'd say find food, but do you not notice? I don't feel hungry. Do you?"

"The thought didn't even cross my mind," Evie said. "And I hate the idea of having to sleep. Nevertheless, we should follow protocol. Obtain food, make shelter."

"And stick together," Asa said. He stopped and pointed ahead. "What do you think of there, where the land is raised?"

"Could work." Evie squinted her eyes to get a better look. "As long as we go further inland. Don't want a tide surprising us in the middle of the night."

And so they made camp. Simple but effective for at least one night. They wove matted reeds and flattened grass into a clearing. No fire, for all the vegetation, was too moist to catch fire. Inconsequential as the temperature was, it caused no discomfort. They foraged for food, but soon abandoned their efforts when nothing edible was readily available, and their stomachs had not yet begun to beg for sustenance.

They sat across from one another in their clearing, watching stars appear above; unfamiliar constellations on a foreign world too perfect to be their own. They did not sleep, only waited as the world continued to darken, waiting for day.

"What's the last thing you remember?" Asa asked.

"What do you mean?" she said.

"The last thing before we awoke here on Triton," Asa said. "I keep thinking, if I keep going back to the last thing I remember, it will make it easier for my memories to return. But it's hard. The dreams are the last thing I remember. Did you have them? Those horrid dreams?"

Evie listened. She wanted to remember, but her head strained when she tried.

"Like living infinite lifetimes," he continued. "At first, I wondered if this was a dream. But this feels different, being awake. That's how I know. No matter how real those dreams felt at the moment, they still don't feel the same now.

"Problem is, memories start to feel like dreams. So it's hard to sort the real from the fantasy. I have memories of Earth, life before the mission. But I can't tell which parts are real and which are dreams. It's all mixed up. Maybe it's because I haven't been awake long enough; still trapped in that between state because we were asleep so long.. Or maybe I'll never be able to tell. Who knows?"

They were silent for a moment.

"How long do you think the night is?" he asked.

"Hard to say," Evie said. "Couldn't tell even if I wanted to. Not my expertise. That was always... always. . ."

A name nagged at her mind. There was someone who could tell them. But he wasn't here.

The name slipped from her mouth. "Michael."

"Hmm?"

"I remember Michael," she said, the corners of her mouth smiling. "He's the first thing I thought of when the memories started coming back. Asa, do you think–" Evie's throat turned dry, and she could feel the salt of tears welling in her eyes. She suppressed it; *I will not cry.* She saw the vision of her approaching the red front door again. Reaching out to open it, hoping that Michael was on the other side.

"Oh, Asa, if we're alive, do you think he could–" she stopped herself as she choked up. If she kept it up, she would cry, and she couldn't do that. She never cried. She wrapped her arms around her knees, grief silencing her.

Recognition crossed Asa's face, and it saddened. He remembered too.

He stood and walked over to her. Evie stayed silent as the numbness took over. She looked into Neptune, refocusing her emotions. This was not the time to dwell on the unresolved.

Asa sat beside her, crossing his legs. He took a deep breath.

"It's alright to feel something about him," Asa said.

"You've said that before." Evie refused to look at him. "A long time ago."

"Hmm," he shrugged. "I guess I did."

"Yep," Evie smacked her lips.

Asa sighed. "I think we're both hurting. I know we aren't fatigued, but I think we should try to sleep. If not for our bodies, then for our minds. Our minds need rest from today. *Your* mind needs rest."

"We fell," Evie said. "Asa, we fell. Into the ice, into the darkness, into that ammonia ocean. And we're awake. We're alive. Michael fell too — he was the first to fall through the ice. He fell long before we did. That blue substance, if he was exposed to it just like we were, then do you think there's a chance? Just a chance?"

Evie's heart raced. What if Michael were alive just like them?

"No, Evie," Asa shook his head. "Don't go down that road. We all mourned when Michael fell through the ice crust. But that happened long before our accident. There's no telling if he—"

"Then there is a chance," Evie tore her gaze from Neptune and bore her eyes into Asa, the soft green light of Neptune casting a sickly shadow on them. "He could be here and alive! He could be. He has to be!"

"Shh, we can't get ahead of ourselves," Asa put up a defensive hand. "But we have to do as you said, remember? Mission protocol: survival. We can't help anyone else if we don't help ourselves." Asa's eyes welled, his lips quivered. "I can't stop thinking about Charlie."

"It hurts." It took all of Evie's strength not to let her eyes swell. "It all hurts."

They took each other's hands, friend comforting friend.

"We'll make it through this," Asa said. "I promise, we'll stick together and make it through this."

"We will," Evie said, keeping her face steady. "I will not leave your side. I'll stay strong and do my job."

Asa smiled through his grief. "Ah, your friendship is not a job, but it is always welcome."

Evie felt a rush of comfort as they released hands, both looking into Neptune, filling the night sky, forever, how long the night would be.

Chapter 3: A Dreamless Night

Evie sat under the green light of Neptune. A pounding pain surged through her mind as she tried to remember Michael's demise. Steady and resolute, Evie, who took pride in never shedding a tear in her life, fought against the mental barrier guarding the memories of the one person who ever stirred her emotions, threatening her composure. She refused to succumb to that vulnerability again. She *would not* lose control.

Yet, despite her efforts, her mental wall remained impenetrable.

But Asa remembered, she thought. Not only did he remember her, Michael, but he also remembered his family and a loved one named Charlie back on Earth. He spoke of comforting memories of Charlie as he fell asleep —or at least pretended to. She couldn't do the same.

Why?

I must remember. She thought. *It's key, it's essential to why this is happening — I know it is. I need my memories. Why aren't they coming back like Asa's?*

Something ebbed in her mind.

Not yet, a soft, tenor voice said.

"Uh, hello?" She glanced at Asa. He was breathing heavily, a sign of deep slumber.

"How are you sleeping?" Evie huffed, with no sensation of fatigue whatsoever.

More mental tricks, she thought, just like seeing the man in white. *There's no telling what kind of damage our minds have undergone.*

She pressed her fingers to her temples. *I will remember.*

She felt a wall build in her mind, thickening; the past disappearing, fading. There was only the present.

"I have to remember," she fought the amnesia. "I can't do this if I don't remember."

The ebb in her mind continued. *Not yet, it will hurt if you push it.* The voice that spoke was clear and song-like. *Careful.*

She stood startled. "Who's there?"

She turned, looking all around.

No one. Only the green light of Neptune shone across hauntingly silent grassland. Her voice echoed far, the only sound of life for endless miles. They were alone.

Have to focus, she thought. *Remember what's real and not real. What did Asa say about Michael?* She pushed against the mental wall and felt a metaphorical crack. A glimpse of Michael, his kind smile, his hazel eyes glinting at her. *Brilliant mind, brightest of us all. And my... my... Argh!*

A sharp pain suddenly shot through her head, making her fall backward.

The pain swelled, pulsing through her body, all emanating from the sides of her head. Was she shot? No, there are no guns in this world, and no one to shoot them that she knew of. She writhed on the ground, trying to scream but unable, as though her voice were muted. She grabbed her head and clenched her jaw.

I warned you. The strange voice spoke. *Your memories will come, but you cannot push them. Sleep and the pain will cease—this time. Next time, well, let's not find out.*

No! She tried to yell, but her voice remained muffled.

Sleep and awake healed.

Maybe it was the writhing and the unbearable torment that caused fatigue to suddenly flood her. Her eyes blinked slowly as she stared up at Neptune. Her vision faded, as well as the pain in her body, as she fell unconscious.

*   *   *

They awoke to splashing.

Dew settled on them, cooling their skin. The warmth of the red sun stretched grassland shadows to the lake.

A familiar hacking cough accompanied the splashing.

Without a second glance, Evie and Asa leaped toward the lakeshore from their makeshift shelter.

"Over there," Asa pointed to the right of them.

Pushing aside reeds, a man wearing the same UNSF 4020 bodysuit dragged himself to shore, coughing the same as Evie and Asa had. They rushed over to him, displacing vegetation that blocked their way.

"Here, I got his right shoulder, grab this left," Evie directed Asa as she propped the man's arm around her. His lean body spasmed from the coughing. "Let's get him to a clear spot."

They pulled him through the brush to a patch of packed clay along the shoreline.

"Let him down easy," she said. They set the man down into a sitting position, both of them supporting him as he leaned forward and continued his productive cough. Evie patted his soaked back as she had for Asa. "There, you got this. It will pass, cough it out."

The man heaved forward out of Evie and Asa's support, catching himself before hitting the ground. His cough escalated as he gasped for air.

Evie grabbed his shoulders, holding him up. "Stay on all fours," her voice firm and authoritative. "Don't lie down. I know it's hard—but you can do this. You need to cough it out. Do *not* give up."

The sudden retching of cerulean blue liquid poured from his mouth, steam leaving it as soon as it hit the ground, evaporating.

The man sat back, leaning against Evie. His mop of thick black hair whipped water into her face. He breathed fast and heavy, his almond, monolid eyes closed.

"Here, Asa, help him," Evie said, wiping the water from her face. "I need to take his vitals."

Asa knelt beside them, supporting the man comfortably in a half-reclined position. "Is that comfortable?"

The man nodded, eyes still closed and breathing heavily.

"I'm taking your wrist," Evie said, picking up his hand and placing two fingers on his wrist. "Try to pace your breathing."

She began to mentally count when the man chuckled.

She glanced at Asa, and he shrugged.

"You want to know about the last person who told me to stay on all fours?" The man smirked and opened one eye at Evie, as though to see her reaction.

Evie ignored the comment and continued to count his pulse, this time mouthing the numbers not to lose place.

"She counted too, but that was before she—"

"Behave yourself," warned.

The man opened his dark eyes and looked up at Asa, winking. "I know your sense of humor is in there somewhere. And come on, you have to admit," he stretched his arms, pulling his wrist away from Evie mid-count, "you love having my stinking wet head resting on your lap." He shook his head, whipping droplets onto both of them. "Ah, refreshing."

Asa shoved the man off of him. "You immature dick. Sit up on your own."

Evie grunted, frustrated. "Trying to take vitals here. And now I have to recount your pulse. Thanks for making me lose count!"

"Success," the man's sly smile spoke all as he sat up; he was trying to make Evie lose count, mess up her vital routine. "Chill it, sister, I'm obviously fine. No vitals for me today."

"No," Evie reached for the man's hand. "You're getting your vitals taken."

The man pulled his hand away, feigning a look of offense on his face. "My goodness, someone has forgotten patient consent.

However," he mused to himself, "there are other *things* I'd rather consent to."

"You are a dick!" Evie stood up. "Asa, let's leave him here."

"Whoa, whoa, what did you think I was talking about?" The man stood, but swayed, catching his balance. He looked around, beyond the lake at Neptune, then turned his gaze further to the sky, to the red sun. "Oh shit, what the hell's happened to us, sister?"

"Don't call me sister," Evie crossed her arms.

"But I always call you sister."

The man looked to Evie, smirk gone, his eyes wide with genuine apprehension.

Evie knew this man too.

But his name escaped her.

This wasn't Michael, that much she knew. She observed this dripping-wet ensemble of a man, one who looked — and apparently acted — more boyish than he actually was. She wanted to hate him for his remarks, for botching her vitals routine, but she couldn't. That was just who he was, and somehow she understood that. She was fine with it? No one in their right mind should tolerate such a man. Yet, she did, and what's more, she embraced it. Why?

"Ren?" Asa stood, eyeing the man, like a long-lost sibling. "Ren, is it really you?"

"Well, of course it's me." Ren swung his arms frustratedly in the air, looking at Asa. "Why wouldn't it be?" He pointed to himself. "Just because I can't remember my own name till someone else says it."

He turned his gaze back to Evie. "Please tell me you remember me. Of all people, you must remember me?"

The mental wall weakened, and she felt memories of Ren slip in. Memories he was tied to. She saw flashes of him, carefree and charming with any and everyone he met. Making her laugh in a time she refused to laugh.

Come on, sister, where's your sense of humor? Everyone has one. His voice echoed.

"Everyone has a sense of humor," Evie repeated.

"Yes, that was me," he said.

Evie felt elation. Ren! It was Ren Tanaka!

"We found you," she said, and approached him with open arms. "You stupid dickhead we found you."

Ren accepted the open arms and they pulled into a welcoming hug. "Eh, glad you remembered that nickname. For some reason, I remembered that name first before my actual name. Speaking of which," they dropped their embrace, "why can't I remember stuff?"

"It will come back," Asa said. "Just not right away. We're still not sure, but it seems we've been out of commission for a long time." He pointed at the red sun. "Longer than expected."

"Huh?" Ren said curiously.

"Huh, that's all you really have to say?" Evie said.

Ren nodded. "If that big green monstrosity in the sky is what I think it is, then yeah, huh is all I have to say. I hope my memories come back."

"I don't know," Evie said. "I can hardly remember anything. Asa's getting it a lot faster than I can. We came out of the lake yesterday, just like you did, and he can already recall his family, Earth, home..."

Evie trailed off, remembering the night before, the pain that caused her to writhe on the ground from trying to remember her life before. Should she tell them? Warn Ren if he tries to remember too much? Asa didn't have that reaction, who's to say Ren would have the same?

"I can't recall much of anything," she said.

Ren shrugged. "Some minds work differently, I guess. I don't know about you, but I'd like to find some civilization if there is any around these parts." He scanned the landscape. "And I'm assuming that's few and far between."

"You'd be right on that assumption," Evie said. "We made a quick shelter yesterday, but it was only for one night. Nothing that can hold up long-term. It's strange; there are no living animals or signs of them. No sounds of insects, birds, or splashing of fish. Just miles and miles of plants."

"How?" Ren looked skeptical.

"We know as much as you," Asa said. "For now, we're the only living creatures here."

"Alright, I see," Ren nodded, putting his hand under his chin. "Well, folks, best get to it then."

"To what?"

"Finding others," Ren said. "Surely we aren't the only survivors? If I popped up, then there's going to more. We need to make preparations. And I don't know about you, but after however bazillion years we were out for that to happen," he pointed up at the red sun, "I want to move around and revel in the joy of being alive. Where's this shelter again?"

Evie and Asa pointed toward their shelter.

"What are we waiting for?" Ren started walking.

They made their way to the makeshift shelter. When they arrived, Ren's face spread with disgust.

"Where's the shelter?" He asked.

"This is it," Evie said.

"You said you made a temporary shelter," Ren said. "This looks like a squished bird nest."

"We waited till dark," Evie said. "It was hard to see."

"You made your shelter in the dark?" Ren raised an eyebrow. "God, did you forget all your survival training too?"

"Food took priority," Asa cut in. "But when we couldn't find any and weren't hungry, we gave up and focused on the shelter."

"Note to self," Ren continued, counting down on his fingers, "we aren't hungry, thirsty, or tired. Are you sure we're not dead and living in some strange afterlife?"

"I'm sure," Evie said. "Or I would be if you'd let me take your vitals!"

"Just saying," he said.

Asa eyed Ren.

"Um, you okay there, sir?" Ren said.

"I'm alright," Asa crossed his arms. "But I just remembered something." He nodded toward Ren's left side. "How's your leg?"

"My leg?" Ren looked at his left leg quizzically. "Oh yeah, my leg." He shook it. "Wow, thanks, man. I remember all that now, too."

Asa smiled and put a hand on Ren's shoulder. "Don't mention it."

"What's with the leg?" Evie asked.

"I broke my leg," Ren said. "But look, it's not broken anymore! Like, it was just about healed before we—you know—fell into that awful ocean. Ha-ha, look what I can do." He hopped on it. "Doesn't hurt."

"Broken leg," Evie said to herself. More memories leaked through the mental crack. Ren had indeed broken his leg. An unprecedented accident involving machinery — Ren Tanaka, flight and machine engineer. He was supposed to operate their energy source, their drills, and perform surveys to determine the best drilling points on Triton. But when his leg broke, he couldn't perform his duties. There wasn't another transport coming for months, and no one could do what Ren did. Someone else took up the charge, standing in as Ren directed from their home base.

And that someone was. . .

It was—

"No," Evie shook her head. "No, no, no."

"Uh oh," Ren looked at Asa.

The memory started to fade.

"No, no, *no!*" Evie held the sides of her temples. She wouldn't let this one slip away.

She imagined herself grabbing the memory before it could slip away, and pushed.

Careful, an inner voice warned, the same soft one from the night before. *Remember what happened last night.*

I have to remember, she thought. *I have to remember him!*

She dug into the memory of Ren's injury. Of his accident, his boyish antics at play once more.

I'll do it, someone volunteered in Ren's place, the lead physicist. *He was under my jurisdiction. It's only right that I go in his place. We can't let this mission fall behind.*

Someone else responded — she couldn't picture who. Their commander, maybe? *I cannot let you go.*

This mission means too much to fail. I insist.

Against my better judgment. . .

Lead physicist.

Michael.

Evie felt all her anger and grief build within her once more.

She saw his memory bright as day. Michael, her Michael, looking at her in his Triton survey gear. His warm hazel eyes and his light brown hair brushed against her fingertips. She wanted her lips to touch hers just before he put on his helmet. Watching him enter the survey vehicle, and her following behind in the emergency vehicle.

And cracks in the ice… Michael's vehicle crashing… watching helplessly…

"No!" Evie screamed.

Pain surged through Evie's temples, and her vision blurred.

She fell to the ground.

"Oh god!" Ren exclaimed. "Oh god, Evie, I'm sorry, I'm so sorry. What do I do? Oh god, what's wrong with her?"

Let it go, the inner voice said to her. *The past is the past. Let it go. I cannot help you if you hang on to it.*

She felt the memory fading, and the pain starting to recede.

That's right, let it go.

But that memory had Michael, and she didn't want to forget.

"No!" Evie shouted. "Shut up! Shut up!" She grasped for the memory, but, like slick oil, it continued to slip through her fingers.

And her memory of Michael faded along with it.

"No," she cried out. "Don't leave me–come back! *Come back!*"

"Asa w-what do we do?" Ren's voice shook. "She's all contorted."

"Working on it," he responded.

And with the memory gone, so was the pain.

Evie's vision focused. She was on her back, the light of the red sun in her eyes. Ren and Asa's faces were looking down into hers.

"What happened?" Evie asked weakly.

She tried to sit up, but felt Asa's hands holding her head in place.

"Sorry," Asa said. "I couldn't let you hurt your head."

He released his grasp, and she sat up. Nausea spread to her mouth, and she dry-heaved.

"Easy there," Ren said. "What happened? You looked like you were having some kind of seizure."

"I'm not sure," Evie said. "I–" she looked at Ren, pinpricks of the memory tugging at her. "He was in your vehicle–*you're why he's gone!*"

Ren bit his lip. "I know. And I'll never forgive myself."

"Evie, you cannot blame him," Asa said. "What happened to Michael was unprecedented."

"He's dead," Evie shook her head. "Asa, he's dead! Michael, he died before we fell. I wanted him to emerge like we did, but I think–"

She didn't want to say it. She'd felt enough grief. And they already knew the answer.

"Ren, I'm sorry," she said. "I know I'm not supposed to blame you."

Ren said nothing.

"I know we're treading on some sensitive things," Asa said. "But your seizure was not good. What happened?"

"You mentioned Ren's leg," Evie explained, "and I remembered something. But instead of just remembering, I felt it. I heard a voice in my head telling me just to let it go, but I couldn't. I had to remember. Just like last night, I pushed to remember, and the episode just started."

"Last night?" Asa's jaw dropped. "You mean to tell us this happened last night, too? Why didn't you say anything?"

"We've been a little preoccupied," Evie said, looking to Ren. He avoided eye contact.

"This is serious," Asa said. "What if one of these seizures happens again? What if they get worse?"

"We can handle seizures," Ren said, still not looking at them. "Our darling astromedic can instruct us how to handle them. I'm more concerned about her hearing voices."

"It's just my head playing tricks," Evie said. "It's nothing."

"Nothing?" Ren looked at her, concern filling his demeanor. "Nothing? Hearing disembodied voices in your head is never nothing. You know this. Doesn't it concern you?"

"You don't need to worry," Evie said. "I didn't do what it said."

"What 'it said?'" Ren gestured to her. "You ended up with a seizure, banging your head into the ground."

"I'm okay." Evie was adamant. She didn't need anyone fussing over her. She'd figure it out like she always did.

Ren pressed his hand to his forehead. "And this is what we call denial."

"I agree," Asa said. "You almost hurt yourself badly if we didn't intervene. As much as I hate to say it, I don't think you should be pushing yourself to remember if it's going to hurt you. You could seriously injure yourself."

Evie looked between Asa and Ren.

Oh god, they think I'm crazy, she thought. *And that I can't handle myself.*

"I know seizures look scary," Evie stood up. "But they aren't half as bad as they look. I don't need anyone to worry about me. That's my job."

"You look out for us," Asa said. "As is your duty. But who is going to look out for you?"

Evie didn't want to answer. "Are we going ahead with our survival plan or not? Maybe you two can build a proper shelter? I'll forage food for when we inevitably do start to feel hungry." She headed toward the lake. "And I don't need you to follow me."

"She's not going to listen, is she?" she overheard Ren say.

"Has she ever?" Asa said.

Evie made it to the lakeshore.

What do they know, she thought. *I'm perfectly alright. It will heal given time.*

I'm glad you listened to me this time, the soft voice spoke to her mind. *You could've died.*

Evie tried to ignore it. *You're just a nasty side effect.*

It's all just beginning, the voice continued. *Keep looking, and you will find.*

"Find what?" Evie picked up a pebble and threw it into the lake. "I'm talking to nothing–there's nothing here. What's the point? What can I possibly find?"

Everything you ever wanted.

More splashing, but not from the pebble.

It was quiet, as though from afar. Evie looked further down the shoreline and saw movement.

Nothing was certain on this strange new world. There were no answers as to why they were here, how it happened, or why her memory was fighting against her. No answers to why they felt no hunger, thirst, or fatigue.

No absolution for anything happening.

But one thing was sure when she saw movement down the shoreline.

There were more survivors.

Chapter 4: $2H_2(g) + O_2(g) \rightarrow 2H_2O(l)$

They emerged. Like a primordial awakening, hands reached out of the waters, bodies dragged themselves onto land, and mouths took their first breaths as they disgorged the cerulean substance from their lungs. Steam wafted around them, the substance evaporating rapidly, creating a warm haze. Familiar faces looked in awe at the world around them as their shaking legs brought them upright—all barefoot and in 4020 jumpsuits. Water dripped down their faces, mixed with the tears of those savvy enough to know what this place was and the realization of Earth's fate.

Evie dashed toward them, her feet pounding the clear stretch of shoreline, avoiding sharp pebbles and rocks as much as she could. The surge of her medical instinct propelled her forward, her mind immediately assessing the situation. Were there injuries? Illnesses?

Any potential hazards nearby that could endanger them or herself? She mentally rehearsed the range of possible interventions she needed to undertake.

"What's going on?" Asa shouted from behind.

Evie paused and looked back. Asa and Ren stood on the elevated land next to the shore.

"Survivors!" She shouted and pointed at the haze, writhing with human activity. "Come—*quick.*"

Asa and Ren jumped onto the shoreline, and Evie picked up her pace again. Although she could hear their rapid steps behind her, her focus narrowed to the haze of people ahead, their coughs, cries, and moans growing louder with each step that dug into the ground.

And Evie remembered her oath:

I will maintain the utmost respect for human life, from the time of conception, even against the possible violation of the law. I will not carry or create tools of harm, and will maintain and complete an unbiased view of preserving life. I, a UNSF medic, must practice pacifism for the good of all humankind.

On Earth, the UNSF expanded the Hippocratic oath: it forbade all medical professionals working for them from using tools of harm. It did not matter who was friend or foe; her job was to preserve life in all its forms. It was this strict law that saved the lives of many medical professionals who found themselves in hostile territory. Any sensible hostile persons would spare the medical professional who posed no threat; only a helping hand—the ultimate neutral party, known to all Earth peoples as pacifists, obligated to help all.

The haze suddenly enveloped her, the shoreline sizzling with the cerulean substance. A person drenched from the lake and in the UNSF bodysuit crawled to her, coughing and weeping.

Female, late thirties, Evie thought as she knelt beside her. "I'm here, let me help."

Evie lifted the woman to a sitting position and brushed sopping dark curls from her face. She took her pulse.

The haze continued to build as steam gathered and mist thickened.

"W-what's happening?" The woman asked meekly. "W-what was that stuff I coughed out? It hurt, oh, *it hurt.*" The woman buried her crying face into her hands.

Pulse and temperature regular, Evie mechanically thought. "Wait here, others are coming to help, but I have to check for more survivors."

"Survivors?" By the time the woman lifted her head from her hands to ask, Evie was gone.

She ventured further into the mist, but the density grew thick, and she saw nothing beyond three feet.

"Shit!" Evie spun around. Where was she? She lost her bearings. She heard the cries of people all around her, their paroxysmal coughs, and panicked exclamations of loss and confusion. A foot brushed past her, too quick for her to catch who it was. A hand here and there, people wandering blind and helpless in the mist.

She stepped in a puddle of retched cerulean substance, its cold sinking between her toes. She shook it off, disgusted.

"It's me, Cunningham," she called out. "If you're out of the lake, stay where you are, and I will help you."

Additional voices arose from the mist.

"What's going on?"

"Oh god, why?"

"Am I dead?"

"Help me!"

"It can't be, no!"

The people's cries overwhelmed Evie's efforts. She was alone; no other medical staff to assist. Dismay surged through her. What if they panicked? Dealing with Asa and Ren individually was one thing, but facing a frantic crowd presented a whole new challenge. There was no predicting the actions of a mob in such a situation if they gave way to animalistic instinct.

Evie paused.

From the mist emerged an indistinct humanoid figure, clad in flowing white.

The man in white.

His arm lifted.

There, go, said the soft tenor voice in her head. *Hurry.*

Evie blinked.

He was gone.

She turned in the direction his arm pointed, and she saw movement, water lapping the shoreline.

No—not the shoreline—a body!

She ran to the body, face down in the water, wearing an UNSF bodysuit. However, this one read *4020-CMD* along the back. She immediately placed a hand on the body's shoulder and hip, gently rolling it toward her and lifting the face out of the water. She tried to pull her inland, but the body was too heavy for Evie's strength.

Female, mid-forties, she thought. *Unconscious.*

She propped the woman gently on her left side, the water shallow enough to allow the woman's face to breathe. Light red hair clung to her clammy skin.

Cooler than average, she thought. *Not good.* She checked for breathing.

"Goddamn!" Evie swore when no breath left the woman's lips. She pushed her onto her back, tilted the woman's head back, and swatched a hooked finger through her mouth. *Nothing obstructs the airway.* Evie pushed compressions on the woman's chest, the beat of the water lapping the shore in time with her.

"... twenty-eight, twenty-nine, thirty!"

Still nothing.

Goddamnit, wake up! Evie strained during the compressions. Evie should've broken or cracked one of the woman's ribs with how hard she pushed compressions, but her chest cavity didn't budge. This woman's strength was something else.

"One, two, three. . ."

And nothing.

Don't give up, the soft voice in her head said. *Almost. You need her right now to survive.*

"... twenty-eight, twenty-nine. . ."

Suddenly, the woman's back arched and her eyes flew open. She rolled herself over onto all fours, coughing out the sickly substance, cold steam emanating as she spewed it from her mouth.

"Thank god." Evie leaned back, a sweeping relief that the woman was alive and conscious. Warm lake water continued to lap against them, washing away any substance that hadn't evaporated.

She reached to take the woman's pulse, and the woman made a stopping sign with her hand. "Wait," she said.

She spat another glob of the substance and breathed steadily. She stared at the steaming substance she spat out, face still and steady.

"It's going to be alright," Evie said. "I just need to take your vitals."

The woman shook her head. "Not yet."

She took another deep breath, then stood, no struggle whatsoever. Her emerald green eyes locked in the mist. "How many?"

"Not sure," Evie said, also standing. The woman towered over her, undoubtedly the tallest woman Evie had ever encountered. How could this woman stand after such an ordeal? How could she speak so assuredly? "They're all panicking. I can't get them together."

Evie wasn't sure why she answered her. She just felt the impulse to obey, a sacred duty of obedience.

The woman's eyes narrowed. "We'll fix that."

A breeze off the lake picked up, carrying away the mist.

And revealed a grotesque sight.

About a hundred people, all in UNSF bodysuits, wandered aimlessly, shaking and confused. One man, no more than twenty, bumped into another, a terrified expression as he swung a protective punch. Others did the same, but fought back with crazed, hungry expressions. Minds sick at the loss, reasonable thought thrown aside. Many more ran to no place, going back and forth, repeating the exact phrases over and over again: "What's happened? Who am I? Why am I here?"

The woman's face snarled. "We'll have none of that."

And she walked straight into the heart of the chaos without a single flinch.

The final banks of mist cleared, and Evie saw the woman more clearly. As she passed, people stopped their chaotic struggle and looked up to her. Despite her broad shoulders and thick arms, she maintained a distinctly feminine physique, boasting curved hips and an hourglass figure. Her piercing green, angular cat eyes exuded a perpetual air of seriousness, silently commanding the attention of everyone she passed. Streaks of stark blond intertwined with her strawberry hair, accentuating the sharp angles of her face and effectively silencing any chatter in her presence. Yet, it wasn't just her sharp features that commanded respect; her reputation preceded her.

The people murmured as she walked through them, their memories coming into focus as they looked upon her. "The Antarctican."

The mere mention of her origin struck people dumb with intimidation. Three words invoked in Evie's mind when she heard Antarctican: *Stronger. Better. Smarter.* Words long since written. Many media tabloids touted how the cold transformed Antarcticans after generations upon generations of adaptations, strengthening their bodies, but deteriorating their minds due to inbreeding and winter quarantines. How true that was, none could say. Clearly, the woman was a perfect specimen of Antarctican civilization, than the other survivors.

And yet Evie's amnesia wouldn't let her place the woman's name—not yet.

She reached the center of the dying chaos, looming over everyone. She threw her arms in the air, waving for attention. More people hushed one another, and the turmoil died down.

They respected her more than their natural instinct to fight or flight.

And Evie couldn't help but continue to gaze in awe at the Antarctican who commanded such regard from those around her.

"Listen up, Triton team 4020," the woman's deep voice boomed. "We've survived a great ordeal. You are confused, as am I, but there's no need to fear. We will sort this out. Cunningham, come here."

Evie's heart skipped as the woman called her last name. This was familiar. And it seemed this woman's memory was intact.

And she felt the urge to obey again—it was her duty.

People parted and allowed Evie to step beside the Antarctican.

"Cunningham will look you over, take your vitals, and assess you for ailments," the woman continued. "But we are civilized scientists; we will not mob her. Line up there," she pointed to higher ground, "in alphabetical order, by last name. Don't look at me like that, I know that you know your name. Talk amongst yourselves and you'll figure it out."

She turned to Evie, looking down at her.

"Cunningham, grab your first assistant on your way there," she said, green eyes narrowing. "Send members of 4020-A to me as soon as you're done looking them over. Make sure 4020-B is in good health. And keep a count of how many are here. I want to know how many more we must search for. Got that?"

The sliver of memory slipped through. 4020-A, the administrative team, and 4020-B, the research scientists sent to live in the Triton hab unit. Evie tended to both.

Evie nodded. "Yes, Commander, it will be done."

The woman's thin lips smiled. "I can always count on you."

I can always count on you. A phrase she often heard this woman say to her.

Evie's blood raced as the woman's name screamed in her mind. Lilith Amulius.

And a longtime astronaut for the UNSF, specializing in ice worlds, and the legendary base commander for Triton hab unit 4020.

And Evie saw a vision of Lilith in the past, garbed in thick astro armor blanketed in white, bearing the insignia of Antarctica: a seal swirling into art deco—a thrill of honor and anticipation in meeting her. Past Lilith removed her helmet, holding out a hand and grasping Evie's in greeting—their first meeting. *Commander Lilith Amulius* smiled a thin smile at Evie. *Glad to finally meet our astromedic.*

"Commander," the word slipped through present Evie's lips.

"Ah, yes?"

Evie shook her head. "Nothing. I will get right on that."

"Good," Lilith nodded.

"Right," Evie said to herself. "First assistant. I have an assistants?" Her mind went blank.

"Um, who's my—" Evie tried to ask Lilith, but the commander was already preoccupied kneeling beside a sitting man, tears filling his face as she gave him a reassuring pat on the shoulder.

"Holy shit, what the hell is happening here?" Ren's voice carried over.

Evie turned, relieved to see Asa and Ren approach. They both looked bewildered and uneasy toward the other survivors.

"And is that who I think it is?" Ren pointed at Lilith, who still tended to the teary-eyed man. "Damn, she doesn't even look like she was out."

Asa facepalmed his forehead.

"Very observant, Mr. Tanaka," Lilith said, helping the teary man to his feet. "Go ahead and line up over there, Bowman."

"And she remembers all our names," Ren snapped his fingers, "just like that? Antarcticans never disappoint."

"I remember everyone," Lilith said, dismissing the teary man, Bowman. "My mind and body are well accustomed to handling harsh conditions and adjustments. And given your memory may not be as accustomed to adjustment, I'll remind you to address me properly as your commander and will be spoken to with respect." Lilith stood imposingly in front of Ren. "I won't need to remind you again?"

"Yes, commander." Ren straightened his shoulders.

Evie felt tension in her chest. She wanted to say something; Ren meant no harm or disrespect. She looked at Asa; he said nothing. But his eyes were serious, and he gave a slight shake of his head that only she noticed—a silent communication between the two of them.

Don't interfere, his eyes screamed at her.

"Good," Lilith cracked her thin-lipped smile at Ren. "You can help Cunningham find her first assistant and get the rest of these people in order for her. Not much else for an engineer to do presently. Dr. Baramba," she turned her sharp gaze to Asa, "walk with me. We have much to discuss."

Asa nodded. "Of course, Commander." His voice had an air to it, as though the response were memorized and well-practiced.

Lilith paused a moment. "And Mr. Tanaka, do try not to offend any poor souls. It won't help Cunningham's cause."

Evie and Ren watched them walk down the lake, away from listening ears.

"I remember, she doesn't like me much," Ren said. "And what do they possibly have to 'discuss'?" He gestured with air quotes, exasperated. "I'm also a part of 4020-A if I remember right. But I don't have doctor in front of my name like everyone else."

"Neither do I," said Evie. "Or her. At least I don't think so."

"Yeah, but she has a title," Ren said bitterly. "And you were supposed to get doctor in front of yours after the mission."

Evie shrugged her shoulders. "Someone's got to gather our people, and I don't remember who my first medical assistant is." She glanced at the survivors, already gathering into cliques and discussing fragments of memory. "I can't do it alone. Will you help me?"

She looked at Ren, searching for something, anything, to reassure him.

He cracked a half smile. "Only because you asked. Not because she told me to."

"Sure, that's why."

*   *   *

Evie made space on the high ground, and Ren ushered everyone into an organized line.

She went through medical procedures as best she could. With nothing to write with and still no recollection of who her first assistant was, she kept track of by way of pebbles. Ren brought her handfuls of pebbles from the shoreline. She carved fist-sized holes into the ground, sorting the pebbles as she saw each survivor, the size and color of each representing the survivor's health condition.

Everyone felt the same—no hunger, no thirst, and no immediate fatigue. Her pebbles for shock also formed a larger pile than the others'. Minor memory loss was the most common condition. However, after prodding questions, each survivor seemed to remember Evie; some more savvy candidates even brought up past visits they had with her. Evie's memory block was more apparent than before, seeing naught but strangers. She kept a friendly bedside manner, doing her best, trying to sound familiar and comforting. But the wall in her mind was impenetrable. She felt no kinship to these people who all called her friend.

Until one.

"Next," she called after Ren led another survivor of 4020 away. He directed them to a clear spot 100 feet away and assisted with building a temporary shelter.

Evie was halfway through her lineup.

A woman with stark white hair approached.

She was older than most of the other survivors, a face mature with the experience of a woman in her mid-sixties. She stood a good four inches shorter than Evie, yet her lanky demeanor made her seem tall.

Of all her features, one stood out above all else: violet eyes ringed with red, set under alabaster lashes, with a complexion to match. The complexion of someone with albinism.

Those eyes had borne into Evie before.

The memory seemed to snake around her mind, though she couldn't catch it. She knew this woman better than others.

She held out her hand to Evie. "Ready for my pulse?" Her voice was deep, with a heavy Eastern European accent, and her lips pouted.

"Yes," Evie said, taking her wrist. "You seem to know the procedure."

"I think I should," she said. "By the way, my pulse is currently seventy-five bpm. And I believe my temperature feels normal."

Evie verified. "So it is. Alright, I have a few questions to ask."

"Ask away." The woman's brilliant eyes stayed steady on Evie.

"Tell me your name," she said. "Then birthdate."

"Name?" Her brows furrowed. "Dr. Olena Solovyóva. You do not remember me?"

"It's not about what I remember," Evie said. "It's about verifying what you remember."

"How can you verify it, or anyone's?" Olena gestured to the survivors working on the temporary shelter with Ren. "If you cannot remember it yourself."

"Who says I can't?"

"Oh, please," Olena rolled her eyes. "I see how you are with the others. Cordial, perfect bedside manners. The same with every single person. Too mechanical if you ask me. You don't know them, not like you used to. And you certainly don't remember me, I can see that. I'm not as blind as I used to be."

"You were blind?" Evie asked excitedly. "And you awoke with vision? That's a first for conditions."

Olena rolled her eyes again. "Not from this mission, no. My eyesight was fixed long before I accepted my position on the Triton hab unit. But you would know that if you remembered me."

Olena smirked at Evie's mistake. A test, and Evie failed it.

Evie grinned her passive smile, the one she used to prevent herself from losing her temper. "Alright then, Dr. Solovyóva, could you tell me—"

"I'll help you with the rest."

"What?"

"The rest," Olena nodded to the rest of the line. "I can take the vitals and you can do whatever it is you're doing," she disgustingly confused at the pebbles, "and diagnose as you see fit. It will help things move along quickly. Commander Amulius will want us both to report to her sooner rather than later."

"W-why?"

Olena crossed her arms. "Do you not recognize your own first medical assistant?"

"Oh," Evie felt her chest sink. She mentally grabbed at the slithering memory, but it kept slipping through her fingers. "You didn't need to keep that from me."

Olena raised an eyebrow. "Who said I was?"

She called the next survivor, and they continued, with Olena taking vitals a few feet away as Evie followed up on their conditions.

Evie's next patient was a young man, no more than mid-twenties, with wide eyes.

"And have you noticed any major changes in your health?" she asked. "Any long-term ailments that have disappeared, or the appearance of another one not present before?"

He pulled back the right sleeve of his body suit. "My stitches are gone."

Evie picked up a pebble, about to drop it into her piles.

He looked confused. "Aren't you going to look at it?"

"I see nothing there," Evie said, collected, emotionless. "How long did you have that scar before it disappeared, not counting the time we were asleep?"

His wide eyes somehow turned wider. "Um, you put them there. When you stitched up my arm, remember? You said I'd probably have a scar the rest of my life."

"Oh," she dropped her pebble, dumbstruck by his response.

"Why are you being so cold?" he asked. "Did I offend you? If I did, I'm so sorry."

The wide-eyed man's face sank, hurt, wounded even.

"No-no," Evie said, recollecting herself. She couldn't allow another suspect of her condition. "You did nothing. I'm just recovering like everyone else."

"I guess?" he said, unsure.

Evie smiled her plastered bedside smile. She had to distract him. "And how do you think the blue substance affected your lungs?" she asked.

Olena called over from a few yards away. "It's not called blue substance." She was placing her hand on a young blond woman's head. The young woman blinked uncomfortably.

"This is supposed to be private," Evie called back to her. "Move further away with your patient so you can't hear us."

"I think privacy went out the window when we found ourselves here," Olena chimed. "And it's not called blue substance. That's just silly. Any well-educated astromedic knows what we're dealing with."

"You can step over with the other survivors," Evie said calmly to the wide-eyed man. An inkling of fear pierced her. She covered it with a frustrated huff and marched over to Olena. She gestured to Olena's patient to go to her space. "I'll meet you over there."

The women, still looking uncomfortable, scurried away.

The rest of the survivors in line groaned, seeing the delay.

"Okay, let's make this quick," Evie said. "People are waiting, and since I sound so uneducated, enlighten me."

She had enough. Whoever Olena truly was, Evie wasn't going to let her assert any authority over her. Evie was the lead, not the assistant.

You're in charge, a past memory echoed—Lilith's voice, from a past council. *Assert yourself. Her seniority does not trump your appointed position.*

This was not the first time Olena did this.

I don't have time for this, she thought. She felt the tension building in her chest, and it screamed for release. *I have to end it before it becomes something more and upsets our patients.*

Olena had no authority—no right—to speak to her in this way. No right to take advantage of her.

"Go ahead," Evie said, level-headed and steady, feeling the sweet release of her tension as she manifested her authority. "Tell me, what am I supposed to be calling it?"

Olena looked alarmed, as though she'd never seen Evie like this. "I—you—"

"Go on," Evie ordered. "You're welcome to share."

She leaned in close to Evie. "Evie, are you alright? You truly don't remember what it's called?"

"You got me," Evie slapped her hands to her sides. "I don't remember what it's called, I can own that. Tell me."

Olena swallowed. "Vita-8."

Vita-8. Life infinite.

And Evie grabbed the slithering memory, squeezing it until it exploded in her mind in a vision of blue.

Olena reached to catch her. "Watch it!"

Evie couldn't answer, for she fell and was lost in the memory that enveloped her entire being.

Chapter 5:Visions of Vita-8

Vita-8.

Life infinite.

Or so coined by Earthkind.

Years earlier before 4020's doomed mission, the UNSF confiscated samples of a cold, liquid nitrate from the Space Intelligence Corporation, also known as SIC. The substance was found within their decommissioned Venus laboratories. SIC had been secretive about their special discovery, but with the UNSF watching, secrets only last so long.

The miracle substance. The Vita-8.

A new campaign launched —one to restore the public image of SIC and to prove the strength of the newly empowered UNSF. The preservative power of Vita-8 enabled advancements in medical practices and, more importantly, business practices. Chiefly, it became the solution to the truth that world leaders could no longer hide from the public: Earth was on borrowed time.

The icy world of Triton was both an impossible and a promising mission for Earth. Scientific equations and reflective color spectra collected by probes indicated that Triton's tholins held the key to obtaining Vita-8.

With funds from SIC and the power from the UNSF, they sent their best and brightest to the only system known to contain the eternal giving substance. All led by the hero of Antarctica.

And Evie remembered the day they found it.

They were in the cramped, central drilling center of the Triton habitation unit. Unlike the clean and slick space stations, the UNSF hab units were in constant repair. With Triton's volatile surface, hab units never stayed put for long. They were easy enough to move when the time came, but it meant sacrificing aesthetics for practicality.

That day, Asa bellowed a deep and joyous scream.

Evie jumped. Quiet, calm, Asa rarely spoke out. She was nearby, typing into a small interactive screen for medical inventory and orders for the next payload from Earth. In the confined space, his voice was louder than usual. It bounced, resonating from the metal and carbon fiber surroundings.

This was monumental if quiet and collected Asa was this exuberant.

Olena came running in from another section, Ren following. He slumped in with his right leg bound in a medical boot, supporting a break he suffered just months before.

"What's wrong?" Olena asked, her voice low and steady, even for as startled as she looked. "Asa, *you* yelled?" She looked like she didn't believe it. "Goodness, have we hit something?"

Ren looked worried as well, a flare in his dark, hooded eyes.

They continued in panicked questions, adding further to the tumult of sound.

"What's going on here?"

The room silenced when Lilith entered, adorned in her white Antarctican leather jacket.

"Has something happened?" she asked in a perfect American-English accent. Those who heard her could only speculate about her origins. She was a natural in English — and her Spanish even more so — sounding native to anyone she encountered. If she so chose, she could fit into any region she pleased, in whatever language she spoke.

"Ah-ha, we've done it, *commander*!" Asa threw his arms in the air. "We've found it! We've found it!"

Asa suddenly looked anxious, as though realizing how loud he was. He immediately quieted himself.

Lilith's eyes widened. "What?" She ran over to Asa. "Let me see!"

Asa held up a petri dish. "Look what the drill brought in this morning."

Although Evie refused to join in the group overlooking Asa's sample, she could see it from where she sat. How could she not? It glowed a brilliant cerulean blue. He'd found it. After all this time, Asa finally found the life-preserving Vita-8.

"This is cause for celebration," Lilith said. "We'll break out the long-awaited champagne tonight. Good work, officer!"

"Ah, but we all can't have the champagne," Asa said. "We still have work to do staying alive in this hab unit."

"Damn, guess that's why we left it on Earth," Lilith laughed. "I owe you a celebratory drink when we get back. Now that we can finally go back!"

Everyone cheered, except Evie. Finding Vita-8 meant their hopes and dreams could come to fruition. They could return to Earth. And arriving with the substance would make them heroes and memorialize their existence in humanity's memory.

And it also meant leaving Michael behind on Triton.

Evie dreaded this day. She didn't care for any kind of glory she'd receive upon their return to Earth. Just an empty promise to her.

She grabbed a pen and pad beside her, profusely writing nonsense onto it, looking like she was busy at work. She both loved and hated the thoughts that haunted her.

Evie, did we really mean everything? Michael's past words echoed. *Maybe—just maybe—there's still something... maybe we could still work out whatever this is?*

Hope is painful. Because all hope is false hope, or so she'd come to believe. Wishful thinking for an absolution that would never come. She felt a chill and placed her warming suit mouthpiece in her mouth. It was always cold on Triton, and the team had grown accustomed to it, especially wearing warming suits, inspired by gear worn by those native to Antarctica. A dull gray padded suit that used a series of conductors beneath the padding to use the body's natural heat to warm the wearer. Sophisticated technology to conserve and preserve energy. Breathing into the mouthpiece further helped circulate warmth throughout the suit, staving off the chill. But even the warmth of the suit could not keep out the chill she felt when she thought of Michael, trapped beneath the ice forever after his accident..

"Ha-ha," Olena laughed. "I know you all won't be missing this place, but I'm going to miss not having to constantly cover up from the sun."

"We need to inform 4020-B," Ren said

"I'll call it over the intercom myself," Lilith said.

They all started talking at once, excited to finally call the mission a success as they all patted him on the back, showers of congratulations.

And Evie remained where she was, pretending not to watch.

She was truly happy for Asa, her friend. But how could she allow herself to be part of that happiness when Michael was still on her mind?

She looked at Asa—all of them. They found that place she couldn't get to; the ability to be happy and move on. Even Ren, in his nature, was as exuberant as the rest of them. She could only imagine the praises and rejoicing once all of 4020-B found out they had Vita-8.

Within the excitement, Asa's dark gaze wandered, his thick brow curled. And for a moment, his gaze turned to Evie, and they locked eyes.

She wanted to tell him. She was dying to tell a friend.. But she stayed in her place. She thought of what she wanted to say—why she couldn't possibly feel joy at this discovery, how numb her mind had become in the past weeks, and how Michael's memory haunted her even in sleep.

And his eyes spoke to her the same phrase he said aloud so many times. *It's alright. You talk when you're ready, my friend.*

She smiled slightly in response. A silent thank you.

"What's all the excitement down there?" a gravelly radio voice said. All their attention was pulled to the omniscient sound coming over the hab unit's intercom system. Tomás, their pilot, was currently in extended orbit above Triton in the transfer station.

"Sorry," Olena smiled innocently at them all, holding up a transmitter. "I tuned him into our cheering. Thought he'd want to be included."

"We found it, Tomás, we found it!" Lilith said. "We're goin' home."

"Woo-hoo," Tomás's voice radioed. "4020-B will be happy to hear that. They were starting to get frustrated with this wild goose chase."

"Thank you," Lilith said. Her eyes glanced at Evie. "Actually, Olena, can you do the announcement for 4020-B? I've some other matters to attend to."

Olena's face beamed. "Oh, would I!"

"Wait," Ren jumped in. "I wanted–"

"Wanted to what?" Lilith looked at him with her full composure, an unchanging expression.

"Nothing," Ren shook his head. "I'm happy we found Vita-8."

Lilith nodded to Olena, and she scurried to the communications center.

Asa and Ren continued talking excitedly about Vita-8 and going home to Earth.

Lilith approached Evie.

She put her hands on her hips. "How does the ancient saying go? All work and no play?"

Evie tittered. "Not really sure. I never cared for rhymes."

"Don't know if it rhymed." Lilith took a breath. "May I?" She pointed to the space beside Evie.

"You're the boss," Evie said. "Of course."

Lilith sat, leaning close to Evie.

"I know with everything that's happened, it hasn't been easy," she said. "You most of all. You and Solovyóva are closer to everyone on this mission than anyone else. You see a side to them that no one else gets to see. I envy that. I wish I could be that close to everyone. I know, especially for Michael."

Evie sniffled. She would not look at Lilith, nor would she cry.

"What I'm trying to say is, well, it's okay to enjoy yourself." Lilith folded her hands. "I'm not saying be happy. Hell knows forcing yourself to be happy never works. But I get it."

"No," Evie continued to jot nonsense onto her screen. "No one does."

"I lost someone too," Lilith said. "And I don't mean Michael."

Evie paused. "Who?"

Lilith put her hands in her pockets. "My dad. A great man he was. I never had a lover or a spouse, but I had my immediate family. My dad was my hero. And he was just gone one day. No reason, no why. And the worst part, I didn't say bye. Left on a mission immediately after."

"That's horrible," Evie put her screen down. "I'm sorry you couldn't say goodbye."

"People rarely get to say goodbye," Lilith said. "I've learned to be okay with no closure. Which learning to do that, that is closure, don't you think?"

She nudged Evie.

Evie looked up at her. Lilith didn't smile, nor did she frown. She was sincere.

"Well, I've got duties, but please, enjoy yourself while you can," Lilith stood. "After all, we're the team that's going to save Earth with Vita-8."

The memory dissipated, Lilith's past eyes fading into the current ones.

"She's waking up," current Lilith said, looking into her face. "What happened?"

"I don't know," Olena said. Evie felt Olena's hand clamp on her wrist. "We were talking about Vita-8, and she just fell over with a seizure."

"Damn, we can't lose our head astromedic, not now," Lilith's face moved, and Evie saw the sky above.

"I'm also a perfectly capable astromedic, thank you very much," Olena snapped.

"This is not the time to discuss it," Lilith said.

"Oh no, not again," Ren's voice sounded above everyone.

Lilith did not sound pleased. "What do you mean *not again*?"

Evie's head cleared, and she sat up.

"Slowly, slowly," Olena said beside her.

"I asked, what do you mean *not again*?" Lilith leered over Ren.

He cowered. "I guess what I mean to say is—"

"And what is going on over there?" she pointed to the survivors building shelter. "I didn't say to do that."

"I did," Ren said. "I'm the administrative engineer, so I figured it was my duty–"

"Your duty is to do as you're ordered," Lilith's voice rose. "And it was to assist Cunningham. And look what's happened; this is on you."

"No, it isn't," Evie stood, still slightly dizzy. Olena helped steady her.

"I told you not too quickly," Olena complained.

Lilith turned her gaze to Evie, her flaming eyes softening. "Please, continue, explain."

"Ren's right, this happened before," Evie said. "There's nothing he could've done to prevent the seizure. This is all me."

"Has anyone else shown these symptoms?" Lilith asked.

"No," Evie swallowed. "Only me. But it's alright. Seizures aren't life-threatening if handled properly."

"Hmm." Lilith didn't sound like she believed her. She turned back to Ren. "I still have not directed for a shelter to be built yet."

"Sorry, that was me again," Evie cut in. "Asa and I tried to make a shelter last night, and quite frankly, Ren noticed it needed a lot of work. He's just having them finish what we started."

"I'll remind you, Mr. Tanaka," Lilith continued, ignoring Evie, "that you take orders from the commander, not the astromedic. She has her hands full already. That's two reminders already today. Don't make a third."

"Yes, ma'am," Ren said.

Lilith faced the three of them. "Asa filled me in about yesterday, however, he conveniently left out your ailments, Cunningham. Your assistant will take over your duties for now."

"I can–"

"Clearly you can't," Lilith propped her hands on her hips. "And your safety is a priority. You're our head astromedic, and your skills are essential to our survival."

She nodded to the line of people still waiting. "See to them Solovyóva, grab a couple more med assistants once they're looked over. And stay close, Cunningham. Mr. Tanaka, we are moving the area for temp shelter. There is a much more suitable space that Dr. Baramba and I agreed upon. I've also asked him to gather a group of survivors to forage for anything edible. Your engineering expertise will be needed for the new shelter."

"My expertise?" Ren perked up. "Really?"

"Of course," Lilith gave a crooked grin. "Come, we mustn't hold up our astromedics. Cunningham is in capable hands."

"Sit," Olena ordered Evie as Lilith and Ren departed.

"Has she always been that hard on him?" Evie asked.

"How is that hard?" Olena looked confused. "She's just being a good leader. He should've done as he was told and not wasted energy on building something that has to be moved. She has to be stern or he gets into trouble. Or do you not remember that as well?"

Evie hugged her knees. "You know I don't."

"Oh well. Stay put while I finish examining everyone."

"Never mind what she said," Evie said. "I can still talk and diagnose sitting down."

"And stretch the brain that is so stressed it has amnesia and seizures?" Olena shook her head. "No, thank you."

"Come on," Evie lifted her head. "Who's to know if I'm sitting beside you. Plus, it's efficient."

Olena exhaled sharply in displeasure. "We'd be breaking orders."

"No," Evie said. "She said for you to take over my duties for the time being. And you are. I'm just helping. She didn't say I couldn't help."

Olena rolled her eyes. "Fine." She pointed at her. "But the moment you start signs of a seizure, *bol'she ne nado,* no more. It's not worth your mind."

"Agreed."

"Good," Olena said, a look of victory on her face. Until she bent over with a dry cough.

"Are *you* going to be alright?" Evie asked.

Olena pulled herself together and glared at Evie. "Just the excitement. I can handle it."

"But we have no asthma inhalers," Evie said. "We can't be down two astromedics."

Olena grinned. "Ah, finally something you do remember. Glad for that. I'll be strong. Don't worry about me—you have enough of yourself to worry about.

Chapter 6: Sickness of the Mind

One hundred forty research scientists in total, all sent to live in the Triton main habitation unit in search of Vita-8. The best and brightest of humankind. Human computers, incorruptible unlike artificial intelligence, or so the UNSF argued when they sent the researchers to Triton. A human touch in making humanity's decisions. Only one fell before his time; Michael perished.

Evie and Olena counted all 139 survivors.

The rest of the day went uneventfully.

Or as uneventful as things could be in a new world.

Asa returned with no success.

"Nothing seemingly edible," Asa reported to 4020-A's meeting.

Lilith called the members of 4020-A together, away from the temporary shelter. With the vegetation partially cleared, they sat in a circle: Commander Lilith Amulius, head astromedic Evie

Cunningham, head chemist Dr. Asa Baramba, head engineer Ren Tanaka, and first medical assistant Dr. Olena Solovyóva.

Olena wore a brimmed headband woven from lake reeds to shade her face from the sun.

"Disappointing," Lilith shook her head. "But not for lack of skill or trying. Thank you, Dr. Baramba."

"I can report that–" Ren started.

"I apologize, Mr. Tanaka," Lilith interrupted, "as much as I would like to hear your report, we need to hear from our medical staff first."

"Of course," Evie said. She eyed Ren across the circle. His face was stoic, showing no offense at the interruption.

But she knew better.

"139 members of mission team 4020 are accounted for," Evie reported. "All are in generally good health, despite some of the obvious conditions after emerging from the lake. I don't know if I'd call those conditions negative for the time being, just concerning."

"Concerning how?" Lilith rested her elbow on her knee and leaned her head on her fist.

"To begin with," Evie continued, "Dr. Solovyóva and I observed that everyone has a degree of memory loss; however, that seems to cure itself given time and reminders. But we also observed the lack of appetite, thirst, fatigue–things that one would suspect after any significant length in what we believe was a kind of naturally induced cryogenic sleep."

Lilith raised her eyebrows. "Naturally induced cryogenic sleep?"

"It seems so," Evie said. "Our bodies preserved by what we think is Vita-8."

Lilith lifted her head. "Dr. Baramba, this falls more in your realm of expertise. What do you make of Cunningham's and Dr. Solovyóva's conclusions?"

Asa brushed a hand over his head, thinking. He always took a moment in times like these before speaking. "Hard to say. We're here and alive. Injections of diluted Vita-8 could theoretically preserve pieces of living tissue, given how the oxygen particles within it reacted during tests. We could've done this with an entire living organism, but the UNSF wasn't even close to that stage. There's no telling how long it could preserve an entire organism. And given the state of the sun, it's been a long time, longer than our minds can comprehend."

"Give it to us," Lilith said.

Asa held his breath.

"Well?"

"At a minimum, five billion Earth years," he sniffled. "Probably more."

Silence.

Evie looked at Asa, his head low, dripping with salted tears.

"I'm sorry," he wiped his eyes with his sleeve. "It's just that–it means that everyone we knew on Earth–oh god, I can't even think about it."

He buried his face in his hands, tears leaking through his fingers. Beside him, Ren put a hand on Asa's shoulder and patted him.

"We were ready to go home–*I was ready to go home*–ready to see them again," Asa wept through his hands. "And now I'll never... we'll never. . ."

He turned mute, tears the only evidence of his distress.

Lilith gazed at him, her eyes widening in compassion. "We all feel it too."

Even Ren wiped a silent drop from his face.

Olena wrapped her arms around her stomach. "The sun is clearly a red giant, but is it possible that Earth could've made it?"

"There's no way," Evie shook her head, refusing to cry. She couldn't while everyone else was on the verge of falling to pieces. She was obligated to be strong, with no sign of weakness. "The inner planets wouldn't have survived the sun's expansion from a yellow dwarf to a red giant. It's a miracle in itself that all of 4020 survived, with all the changes Triton's gone through. Frankly, I don't know how we all survived. Michael could tell you that too, if he were here."

The mention of Michael's name suddenly turned all eyes to Evie. Asa straightened his back, composing himself.

"What?" Evie looked at them, thoroughly confused. "Am I not allowed to say his name?"

"No," Olena squinted. "It's just that we didn't expect *you* to say something about Dr. Smith, not at a time like this."

"Why not?" Evie said. "He was just as much a part of 4020-A."

"Oh, for god's sake," Olena held her temples, shaking her head. "Have you completely forgotten who he is, too?"

"Hey, don't be so hard on her," Ren glared across the circle.

"Michael was special to me," Evie said. "But he was special to all of us, and–"

"Your husband! He's your husband," Olena shouted. *"Chort voz'mi!* That Vita-8 scrambled your brain! Who knows what else it's done to us! What if our minds are next!"

"Now wait," Ren furrowed his brow. "You heard what she and Asa said about Vita-8. There's no proof that it had anything to do with–"

"Proof? Proof?" Olena stood. "Unbelievable! Look at her! It's like I'm not even talking to the same goddamn person. She's living proof of the extent that stuff can do to our minds. We already have memory loss–"

"Temporary memory loss," Ren corrected, "that's fixing itself."

"–what if it turns to full-blown amnesia like hers? Hmm? What then?" Olena fumed. "We're screwed, I tell you, screwed!"

"That's enough!" Lilith asserted authoritatively. "That's *not* what we're going to tell 4020-B. Solovyóva, I hear you, but this outburst isn't solving anything. Please sit down."

Olena's eyes flared red, all violet drained as she sat. They seethed, ruthlessly glaring at all her fellow teammates. But a shutter along her lids told Evie something more was behind this burst of rage–fear. Olena's mask couldn't hide, much to her chagrin.

And Evie felt a tug, a flash of emotion she did not expect. Pity and gratitude, for Olena gave her something beyond measure of repayment. She reminded Evie of Michael — her husband.

Husband, Evie thought excitedly. The word danced in her head, light as a feather. *Michael is my husband. I shouldn't be so happy to know I have a late husband, should I? But I am–*

And memory came to the forefront. It wasn't painful, nor did she have to strain to retain it. A feeling more than a picture in her mind. The feeling of Michael's arms wrapping around her from behind, his warm touch as his soft voice whispered in her ear.

She replayed it in her mind, the vision pushing through.

Come to bed, his words slipped into her ear, slicker than melted butter. *You shouldn't force yourself to stay up so late.*

She was in the memory, sitting in her worn chair within their home office. Wood-paneled walls reflected the green light of her emerald desk lamp. Michael's careful steps crept into the room while she ruminated over the desk, intrusive thoughts keeping her occupied. And yet, she welcomed his embrace, his head resting on her right shoulder.

She reached up and brushed her fingers through his light brown, damp hair, freshly washed and sweet as petrichor.

"I have a lot on my mind," she told him.

He kissed her neck. "Then let me help you think of something else."

A rush of excitement that she quickly suppressed as she thought about her ruminations. "I don't know if we can do this, Michael. I don't know if I can. Everything we have here, we'd have to give up. How long did it take us to get this far?"

"Not forever," Michael reassured. "We'll be back."

She smiled incredulously, shaking her head. "It's not like going to another country. Another planet, Michael–

"Moon," he corrected.

"–*another world in the outer system*! It's not like we can manage a home here and be there. And they won't put our livelihoods on hold. We'd have to give up everything for this. I haven't even finished my residency. I'd have to quit, and that'd put me back so much."

"I thought UNSF promised that their outer-world hours would take the place of your residency hours." Michael's embrace no longer felt natural. "And you told me you hated your residency anyway. You want to be an astromedic."

"I do," Evie sighed. "That's not the point. We've spent so much time coming this far, it just seems wasted if we gave it all up for this, don't you think?"

"Or," Michael dropped his embrace and pulled up another chair beside her, "this puts us right where we wanted to be in the first place. We're finally getting to do what we always wanted to do. You don't have to talk about wishing to be an astromedic–you'll be one."

Evie looked at his reassuring face, his hazel eyes, so calm and confident in this opportunity. The UNSF taking them on a mission —the most improbable circumstance they could possibly find themselves in. And yet, it was happening. Years of hypothetical chatter, dreaming, and it was finally happening.

Nevertheless, Evie couldn't shake her reluctance. This was what she always wanted, right? And it was being handed to her on a silver platter. She wanted this opportunity more than anything, didn't she?

"I still don't know if I can do this," Evie's voice shook. "And I don't want to stop you from chasing your dream, but I don't want to be—"

Alone. She should've said alone. But to admit such was weakness. She held her tongue, eyes locked on the desk drawer she threw her lap computer into. The UNSF's offer letter was on it.

Michael bit his bottom lip. "Evie, I don't know what to say. I thought this was what you wanted."

"Well, it is," she said. "But wasted years are also not something I wanted."

"Wasted?" he looked confused. "None of it's wasted."

Michael frowned, but not in a sad way. He leaned over and wrapped his arms around her again. "We'll figure it out, my love. I don't know how, but we will. I promise."

I promise.

The memory closed.

Evie's thoughts returned to the present as she looked at 4020-A gathered together.

The flush of affection grew as she looked at Olena's flaring eyes. She did this — she reminded Evie of something she loved.

Evie's wave of gratitude overflowed as she placed a comforting hand on Olena's arm, a small consolation in repayment.

"Don't touch me!" Olena shook her arm off. "What? I remind you that you have a husband, and you get all weird. We are *not* friends. We just work together."

"That's enough," Lilith's jaw tightened. "What we need to figure out is the long term. We clearly aren't going anywhere, no matter what this place is. Anything we had, technology-wise, is inaccessible. Even if it was preserved like us, there's no way of knowing. We will come up with further plans as we go along, but what I currently need is something to tell 4020-B."

"Tell them the truth," Asa said. "There's no use in hiding that we're marooned on Triton."

Ren coughed. "Yeah, that will go over well. You saw them earlier—you want another Donner party?"

"I'm just saying that if we keep things from them, it won't end well," Asa said.

"There are ways of being honest without causing panic," Evie said. "Yes, be honest, but avoid 'marooned.' We can't have them lose hope, not at a time like this. Even if there is none, they can't know that—not yet, at least. Focus on survival and rebuilding. Give them a goal, and that should distract them from how desperate our situation is."

Olena raised an eyebrow. "All gloom and despair with you—that's the Evie I know. And the one I prefer."

Despair? Is that who she was? A pessimist? She didn't feel like a pessimist. A realist, maybe, but not a cynic.

Lilith nodded an approving smile. "A goal, yes, I like that. And we need to make clear that our line of authority has not changed. Keep things normal as much as we can, but also accept what's changed. Our new norm for the time being. We will remind 4020-B who is administrative, meet with our respective team leads, and align them with our goals. We need their help in enforcing order."

"When you say 'enforce,' what do you mean?" Asa asked. "We literally have the smartest scientists Earth has to offer."

"Had," Olena added cynically.

Ren made a look at her. "The only reason they're not in full mutiny is because they're smart enough to want order as much as we do. They probably already figured out there's no real line of authority anymore."

Lilith looked as though something distasteful had entered her mouth. "Is there?" She stood. "Evie, you're right. We must give them something to hope for, or we won't make it. Our goal is to create long-term shelter and resources until we make contact with other survivors off-world. And we will continue in our respective roles until we know otherwise."

The group was silent. The red sun's light dimmed, a cloud cluster covering its face, Neptune casting a cool glow in its place.

"Do you think there are other survivors?" Ren brushed hair from his face. "Off-world?"

Olena grumbled. "Obviously not, Ren."

He looked at them all, a boyish innocence about him. "But that would be lying."

"No," Lilith held up a finger. "We don't know anything. And we will tell them we don't know. They're smart enough to think for themselves and draw certain conclusions for themselves. They certainly can hope other survivors will turn up just like us. Until then, we help ourselves."

Ren didn't look convinced. "But, what if—"

"We all need to be on the same page," Lilith looked to the group. "Supporting one another."

"We can't have this morning happen again," Evie said. "That will only happen if we're all aligned. I trust Commander Amulius, and I'll do what it takes for this to be a success."

Lilith smiled at her. "Well said, Cunningham." She turned a sharp gaze to Ren. "That's why *we're* a team. We hold together and survive."

A wave of guilt flushed over Evie. It felt cathartic seeing Ren's comments shut out by Lilith, and hers favored. But Ren was her friend; she shouldn't take pleasure in his distress.

And yet, something in her demanded recompense.

A slight ebb scratched at Evie's consciousness. A soft, almost sing-song voice hummed in her mind.

That was necessary, it said. *And justified. When you remember, you'll understand why.*

Evie stiffened. They were not her own thoughts.

Ignore it, she thought. *Just ignore it.*

Ignoring will not unmake me, the voice said. *I'll still be here.*

Evie held her composure, dismissing the voice's presence.

Lilith smiled. "Thank you. Alright, I want each of you to set a specific goal for your team leads and carry out a seven-day plan. Then a general monthly plan, one week at a time, or what we can count as a week on this moon. Today is day 1 on new-world Triton."

*   *   *

They came together, setting a seven-day plan. Lilith, the mission commander, but also the lead of the scouting team. Their goal? Scout the landscape, work with Asa's chemistry team, repurposed to a facilities team, to create clean water, scavenge for edibles, and create a space for human waste.

Ren's team—the physicists and engineers. Goal: plan the long-term shelter and create a temporary shelter until the long-term shelter can be established.

Evie and Olena pulled additional individuals to their team—health and wellness. Their members were to assist in gathering the daily check-ins and see to the well-being of 4020. The extra hands were a godsend, even the ones without a background in astromedics. They needed data to report to their fearless commander, tracking the changes to their bodies. A perfect niche for the astromedics.

As the sun began its descent, 4020 settled into a temporary shelter. An encampment of lean-tos woven from local grass and reeds. And a fire pit was dug in the center of it.

Two members of Evie's team sat around her lean-to, helping her pull the fluff seeds from bulrush-type plants; a moderate replacement for cotton balls. Neither one of them was thrilled about being pulled from their respective teams. One in particular, a young auburn-haired man named Dennis, delighted in grumbling about the differences between the engineering team and the health and wellness team. His counterpart, Luis, was much more experienced in years, his skin spotted with age and hair salt and peppered. He focused on the task at hand, with only an occasional polite nod.

Evie tried to make conversation, but any medical procedures she tried to explain went through empty ears, or were shut down.

"Careful not to mix any soil in the cotton," she directed. "I know it can't be completely sanitary, but I want them as clean as possible."

"Maybe if they had all hands on the engineer team, we'd be able to expedite tech for sanitation," Dennis said spitefully, rolling his r's smoothly through a distinctly Scottish accent.

"Hmph," Luis shrugged, pulling another fluff seed and placing it carefully on their makeshift grass bowl.

Evie huffed. Dennis was getting on her last nerve with his grumbling. "Well, you're part of health and wellness, so they'll just have to manage without you."

Dennis smirked, as though he'd won a game from her frustration.

"Hey Dennis, lay off, will you?" Ren called from across the encampment space. He and three of his team members were fifty feet away, making the final touches on the lean-tos before Lilith's inspection.

Dennis rolled his eyes, swearing under his breath.

"What was that?" Ren's face popped over one of the shelters.

"It's fine, Ren," Evie called over. "I've got it. But thanks."

"I'm not a child," Dennis said, crossing his arms. "Please don't talk like you're babysitting me."

Luis shook his head while piling a handful of fluff. "El hombre niño ha hablado. No le hagas caso, todavía es joven." *The man-child hath spoken. Pay him no mind, he's still young.*

"Then stop acting like one," Evie said to Dennis. "And thank you Luis."

"De nada," he answered.

"People had to come over to health and wellness," Evie continued. "Olena, the med assistants, and I can't do this by ourselves. Commander Amulius knows what she's doing."

Dennis furrowed his brows. "You sure about that?"

Evie picked up another bulrush. "Yes, and we shouldn't question it. She's Antarctican—who knows better than her about survival."

"That's a different tune, I say it is," Dennis clicked disapprovingly.

She paused. "Different?"

"My last wellness check in the hab unit, you advised me to question everything," Dennis said. "Including the Commander. Quite a change of heart you've had."

Quick, tell him something or he'll know, the soft voice pulsed in her head.

I don't need you to tell me that. Evie tried to push away. *I'm not scared of someone like him finding out about the amnesia.*

Your emotions say different, the voice cautioned mockingly.

It was true. A strike of fear, like a paper cut to her heart, slivered through her. Dennis, no matter how young or naive he was, was still smart. He'd easily figure out her amnesia wasn't leaving like everyone else, then surely say something to lower 4020's confidence in her.

"A million-year sleep will do that to you, I guess," Evie said. "Just like your irritability."

A frustrated voice floated over to them. "This isn't going to work if my hair keeps going in my face!"

Everyone's attention was pulled to the fire-pit.

Three middle-aged female physicists leaned over the pit, sweat beading along their foreheads. They'd been profusely rubbing hardened reeds to make fire, twisting the elongated sticks between their palms to no avail, and shredding tinder.

One with tangled hair in her face arched her arm back and hurled her reeds away from her. "I hate camping! I didn't sign up for this!"

The reeds hit Dennis on the back of the head. "Ow!" He rubbed the place where they hit. "Watch where you're throwing those."

Ren approached, picking up the reeds she threw. "Serves you right." He walked to the pit. "Rita, I'm sorry you hate camping. But this isn't camping, it's survival. The sooner we get a fire, the sooner we can advance our tech and do the things you like doing."

"New orders—no fire." Lilith also approached, putting her fists on her hips. "At least not right now. Not till we are in a safer location for burning."

"It's plenty safe," Ren assured. "We cleared—"

"Beautiful job, ladies," she said, nodding her head at the three physicists. "Very sturdy shelters for such a short amount of time."

Ren scurried closer to Lilith. "Thank you, I—"

"But of course we'll need to abandon them as soon as we find more suitable grounds." She continued, not acknowledging Ren.

He crossed his arms uncomfortably. "Um, yes, of course, Commander."

Evie felt something build in her chest; pressure to say something. Her jaw muscles spasmed to speak. Ren just put Dennis in his place for her. Could she really let Lilith keep chastising him like this? The guilt from earlier resurged.

That familiar ebb pushed against her mind. *I know what you're thinking of doing. Don't. I told you, Lilith's ire for him is well deserved. It's not your place to involve yourself.*

You're not real, she said in her mind. *You're just my subconscious, manifesting itself.*

Keep telling yourself that.

Leave me alone!

Evie stood. "Excuse me, commander?"

Everyone around the fire pit paused. Ren looked surprised.

Lilith raised an eyebrow. "Yes, Cunningham?"

Evie's mind blanked.

You're on your own. Good luck.

"Commander," Evie composed herself. "I think you should reconsider Mr. Tanaka's need for fire."

Lilith's towering figure took a step toward Evie. "Should I?"

"Yes." Evie's guilt pushed her to continue. No backing down. "All the teams need fire—heat. Health and wellness need it to sanitize if injuries occur. It's an essential need."

Lilith said nothing.

"Facilities will also need it when the need for food comes," she continued. "I don't know how long the lack of hunger will last, and I'm sure you see the need to cook for our continued survival."

Lilith still said nothing.

"And—" Evie searched for the words. What else could she say? Ren stared her down, begging her to continue.

Lilith dropped her shoulders, smiling generously at Evie. "I understand. I truly, completely do. But tonight, we can't. I hope you can trust me." She turned her gaze to all of them, green eyes glimmering. "There are some mitigating circumstances that prevent us from making a fire tonight. And ladies," she looked at the physicists, "I think you've earned a well-deserved break, don't you?"

The physicists smiled and nodded.

"Wonderful." Lilith patted Ren on the shoulder. "Mr. Tanaka, we'll discuss a plan to expedite thermal energy technology at our next meeting," Her emerald cat eyes burrowed into him. "I promise you."

"Yes, of course, Commander." Ren's voice hinted at relief; all strain had dissipated.

"And Cunningham," Lilith's slick smile directed to Evie, and it felt like a knife to the throat. "Come report in when you're finished there."

Evie's chest tightened. "Yes, Commander."

Lilith walked away, heading out of the encampment.

"Enjoy that little chat," Dennis smirked at Evie.

Evie sat to finish her task. "It's my duty to report in every evening."

Luis picked one last fluff and dropped it carefully on his pile. "You should be careful with your words." His Latin accent trilled as he spoke.

Ren ran over. "Oh my god, Evie, I can't thank you enough!" He plopped down beside Dennis. "Like seriously, I thought she was going to lop off my head after everything today."

"Don't worry about it," Evie responded. "You were right, we need heat. I don't know how Olena and I are going to do anything if there's an emergency. No meds and no sanitation—we really can't start anything without fire."

"Still, I needed that," Ren grabbed some bulrushes. "I'll finish this. You probably shouldn't keep her waiting. You know how she gets."

Evie sighed. "You're right about that, too."

As she walked away, she heard Dennis's grumblings begin again.

"Ah, shut it, Dennis," Ren said. "Stop being such a stick up the ass. That's my job."

*　　*　　*

Evie saw Lilith's silhouette knelt atop a dark mound; ripped up vegetation and earth leftover from building the temp shelters.

She didn't flinch as Evie approached, her gaze focused on the horizon.

"Join me, will you?" Lilith patted on the open space next to her, still focused on the horizon. "There's plenty of room."

Evie climbed to the top of the mound and sat.

"See there," Lilith pointed to the dim horizon. "Do you see it?"

Evie squinted. The dimming evening made it difficult to see anything out of the ordinary.

Lilith traced an invisible line in the air. "That thin line, just over there."

Evie saw it this time. Faintly, blending into the darkening atmosphere, a thin, smoky line steadily gathered like a swarm of insects. Easily mistaken for typical clouding.

"Looks like we're not alone." Lilith looked trepidatious. "Campfire smoke. Small, far, but no doubt human-made."

More survivors? She thought apprehensively. *Not from 4020.* "Are you sure?" Evie kept her emotions at bay. She couldn't bear false hope. "How can you tell it's not naturally occurring?"

"The smoke pattern is too uniform," Lilith said. "There are people over there, oh, most definitely. We'll see their firelight by the time the sun fully sets. Always harder to tell at dusk, and this goddamn red sunlight."

Evie felt that flicker of hope scratch in her chest. She undoubtedly thought they were all that was left of Earth. But what if others escaped while they were in their strange cryogenic sleep? What settlements did humans create further out in the system? How long had they been on Triton? Her head spun with the possibilities.

Lilith frowned.

"You don't look overjoyed about it," Evie said.

Lilith eyed Evie curiously.. "Neither do you."

"Well," she shrugged, "if evolutionary history, or this morning, has taught us anything, it's that deep down, people only think of themselves. They'll do anything to survive."

"How right you are," Lilith cracked a smile. "This is why I like you, Cunningham; you get it. But I'm surprised—*you* didn't mention anything about this."

"Survival?"

"The fire smoke," Lilith said. "I just thought you would've understood its significance enough to tell me about it when you reported in."

"I–I," Evie wasn't sure how to answer. Had she noticed, of course, she would've said something. Then her heart sank—Lilith didn't think that.

You just validated what she thinks, that ebbing voice in her head spoke. *That was foolish.*

Stop it, Evie snapped at the voice with her own thoughts. *I'm not crazy, and I'm not speaking to you about this.*

No one said you were crazy.

I'm not talking to you anymore!

The voice went silent.

Lilith continued to eye Evie curiously. "Cunningham?"

Evie realized she had paused too long in the conversation. Lilith already suspected her of withholding information; she couldn't give her more reason to distrust her.

"Sorry, I was just thinking of anything I saw last night," she said thoughtfully, earnestly. "But we saw nothing. I was—" she couldn't tell Lilith about her fits, how severe they were. "—I was preoccupied with the situation at hand. Still foggy from awakening."

Lying. The voice brushed against her mind. *A good idea if the time calls for it. Too bad you're inept at it.*

Evie ignored the voice. It had no business giving her unsolicited advice or belittling her.

Lilith didn't look convinced. "We?"

"Asa and I, I mean," Evie corrected. "We found Ren early this morning, right before you."

Lilith's stern face softened. "I guess if Asa didn't notice either, maybe there wasn't anything."

Evie forced herself to smile encouragingly, but it felt false. Just like the smile she gave all the patients, she didn't remember.

If you're trying to win back her trust, the voice sounded amused. *That certainly isn't working.*

Evie continued to ignore it.

Lilith relaxed her posture as she went back to observing the smoke in the distance.

"I'll watch it tonight," she said. "Don't feel like sleeping anyway."

"Everyone's like that," Evie said. "The only ones who want to sleep are doing it out of comfort, not fatigue."

"We've got a lot ahead of us, you and I," Lilith said. "I'll look out for 4020 in my way, and you'll look out for them in yours. They need us more than ever. And I need you of all people, my head astromedic, to trust me. I can't always give a why to my orders, but I need you to support me. You understand what I mean?"

Evie nodded. "Yes."

Lilith looked pleased. "Do you understand why I don't want fires tonight?"

"You don't want us found by whoever is over there," Evie nodded in the direction of the spoke.

"We have to protect our own," Lilith said. "I want to investigate tomorrow, in the daylight. Approach them first, give us the upper hand if they're less than welcoming. However long that is until tomorrow comes. My sense of time is a bit off."

Lilith looked up to Neptune, as if speaking to the planet. "When we first arrived, one day here was six Earth days; tidally locked to that nasty bastard of an ice planet. A goddamn seventy-hour night. Not so different from my home. I got used to it. But I don't think I can ever get used to this. Everything's different. I feel it in my bones."

"Things are," Evie said. "Night and day rotations like this shouldn't be happening on a moon like this, but it is."

"It's unnatural," Lilith said, sinking her head into her hands. "And I don't like it."

Evie gave a resigned chuckle. "Who's to say what's natural anymore?"

Lilith lifted her head. "Come with me."

"What?"

"Tomorrow," she said. "I'm taking my team to investigate. I want a medic with us in case anything happens."

"What about the people here?"

"Solovyóva will cover," she said. "But I want *you* with us; someone who knows what they're doing. Someone who *gets* it."

Evie understood. A badge of respect to join an excursion party— a sign of trust.

Good, the soft voice in her head said. *You need her trust.*

"It must be a surprise," Lilith smirked, but not unkindly. "Me asking you to come. After all, I should blame myself, but I did it for you."

Evie did her best to hide her confusion. She had no idea what Lilith referred to. Surely, a past experience she had no pleasure in remembering.

"You did what you thought was best," Evie said. "You always do."

Lilith sighed. "You're just saying that, but it's justified. Please know I had Solovyóva come on the other excursions because of everything that happened on the last one we did together. Your feelings matter and I couldn't put you through that again... not after. . ."

Lilith suddenly stopped talking and looked away, her face unnaturally stoic.

After what? Evie screamed in her mind. *Please just let me have this one.*

And then she saw it. Lilith's overly stoic face was the same as it was when they both saw Michael's fall. Evie was there that frigid day, she and Lilith following in the surface vehicle behind Michael's. He drove the survey transport, scanning for drilling points.

And he found the perfect drilling point.

And then the unprecedented. A weakness beneath the surface undetected by their scanners. Cracks erupted beneath Michael's transport. The survey transport and he fell into the bitter ammonia ocean deep beneath them.

On that day, and despite Evie's screams, Lilith kept her composure, saving them both from the same fate as her swift maneuvers drove them to safety.

Lilith saved her life.

And Michael's sacrifice gave them the new drill point for Asa to discover Vita-8.

Present Evie finally understood why she felt so compelled to please Lilith.

"You saved my life that day," Evie in the present said. "I'll always be grateful, no matter what."

"But I couldn't save his," Lilith said. "Not even for you could I save him. And I'll never forgive myself or Ren for that. No. I can never do that."

Chapter 7: Orders and Oaths

The scouting party gathered at sunrise.

Lilith pulled Asa and three scouts from the facilities team in addition to Evie. They met beyond the flameless fire pit, along the edge of the encampment, making preparations.

Unsettled grass brushed against their ankles as they prepared to leave. Evie observed Asa, his face pallor, as though he'd retch at any moment.

"Asa," Evie put a hand on his arm. "Are you up for this excursion?"

Asa bit his bottom lip, dry and cracked. "I'll be fine." He brushed his hand nonchalantly through his curls. "Really, I'll be fine. Just last night, I thought I was alright, but I couldn't stop thinking about it. Earth—Charlie—all of it."

He looked away, trying to hide it. But Evie knew her friend, even with the loss of her memory. The swelled, bloodshot eyes couldn't hide the tears he spilled throughout the night. Precious tears that took much-needed hydration from his body.

Noted, Evie thought. *Lack of thirst is temporary until the body overexerts itself. I wonder if this is true for satiety as well? How long do we really have?*

"You're dehydrated," Evie said. "And not going anywhere in this condition."

"No, I want to—"

"I'm ordering you," Evie cut in, but not unkindly. Asa was her friend, probably her most loyal friend, that much she knew. But the same tension she felt with Olena built her chest again. Medical decisions were her area of authority, and she would not be challenged.

"Doctor's orders," she continued patiently. "Your health and well-being are important. You're not fit for an excursion. Please, Asa, go drink water. If not for yourself, then for those who need you. And allow me to prescribe a day of rest for you. You've already done more than your fair share."

She pointed toward the lake. Asa's team built a water filter, woven grass baskets filled with layers of pebbles and sand. Although charcoal was ideal for the filter, the no-fire order forced them to make do with what they had. When dirty water was poured into it, the layers filtered, allowing clean water to drip beneath it to the drinker. Unsophisticated, but better than drinking straight from the lake until they could boil it. Although no one felt thirst as of yet, they wanted it on the ready.

Asa nodded. "Don't tell Lilith why."

His face begged, a silent communication between friends—*don't let her know I cried all night, causing this.*

"I wouldn't dare," Evie mused. "I only have to report you're unfit."

He smiled. "Thank you."

"You there," she pointed to a passerby, an adult woman. "Escort him to the lake, please, and make sure he gets plenty of clean water."

As he ventured toward the lake, Evie felt calm again, the tension in her chest alleviated. A sense of gratitude to a friend who listened to her.

Something ebbed against her mind. *You're getting to know yourself again. Keep acting on it.*

Evie refused to respond to the voice.

You can't ignore me forever. Or yourself, for that matter.

It was right. She hated anyone who challenged her or questioned her. She couldn't refuse whenever the tension developed in her chest. It felt as though it went against her very being were she to sweep it aside. She felt that more than ever before.

I won't lose it, she thought. *I want to be me, I want to remember who I am.*

"Scouting team ready?" Lilith approached, the sun rising behind her. "I looked ahead, and we are in the clear for now. Beyond that, be on your guard. Anything could be out there."

Her dark silhouette against the rising sun cast a shadow that stretched across the encampment.

"Take these." She pulled from her back a handful of long reeds, hard as wood. "And do try not to nick yourselves with them. Sharpened them myself last night."

Her towering self handed one to each of the team. Evie took one, turning over Lilith's sleepless night's work. Two-foot spears, made of reed shoots hardened like solid wood, a rock blade proficiently cut and tied to the end. Evie pulled on the blade. Lilith not only bound it with plant twine, but also glued it with clay from the lake bed. Creating such a tool was no easy feat for one evening.

She slid her finger across the smooth blade, checking its sharpness.

"Ow!" She slit the tip of her right index finger, no finer than a paper cut. The edge of the blade stained a dark scarlet. Blood pooled, coagulated at the site of her injury, and she quickly sucked the precious drops before they ran down her hand, the taste of salted copper filling her mouth.

"Really, Cunningham?" Lilith chortled. "Don't trust my craftsmanship? Here." She slid her finger steadily opposite to the blade on hers, caressing it like a favored pet. "Against the blade, not with it, to test the sharpness. You should feel finesse. Anyone else need to test?"

The rest of the team shook their heads.

Lilith looked at them, confused. "We're one short. Where is Dr. Baramba?"

Evie stepped forward. "He won't be coming today."

"Not coming?" Lilith stroked her spear. "Why in the hell not? And why didn't he tell me himself? He's quiet and all, but not telling me? That's not like him."

"Oh, he would've," Evie said, holding her spear low. A flush of anxiety ran through her, and she gripped it tight. "Had I not given him a medical disqualification. He's not fit for service today."

Lilith's slanted eyes pondered, staring at Evie. "Well, I trust your medical judgment. Anyone else showing signs of ailments?"

"The rest of us are ready and up to par." Evie gestured to her fellow teammates.

Lilith nodded. "You're hand's still bleeding."

Evie looked down and saw a steady stream of blood dripping down on her spear. Why was she gripping it so hard?

"Before we go," Lilith continued to the rest of the team. "These are tools, and tools only for an emergency. Not the solution. Remember your hand-to-hand defensive training if you can. If it comes down to it, leave it to me; my body is designed to take more than yours. I don't want heroes."

"You really think we'll have to fight something?" said a middle-aged man on their team. "What's out there?"

Lilith raised her eyebrows. "No idea, which is why we must prepare to protect ourselves. And we're going to find out for the sake of those staying behind. I know this isn't easy to accept, and I'm grateful, so infinitely grateful you agreed to scout with me. I chose all of you for this excursion because you are the most physically fit to handle a challenge if it comes our way. And Cunningham graciously agreed to attend to you if anything were to happen. I won't lie, I don't know what will happen, but remember the goal: information. Find what's out there and make it back to the encampment to report. You're not soldiers, and I don't expect you to be. I have every confidence in you. If you don't want to do this, I won't force you, and I won't hold it against you."

Silence. No one answered, and Lilith waited.

The middle-aged man perked up his head. "We got your back, Commander." He held up his spear, looking at the entire team. "We all do."

The others followed suit, lifting their heads and holding up their spears.

All but Evie.

Careful what you do, the voice ebbed in her head. *This is not the time to challenge.*

If this is merely scouting, do we really need weapons? Evie hesitantly asked the voice. *Of all the things we created first in this world—spears? Weapons?*

As well as water filters, medical supplies, and shelters, the voice urged.

Necessities, Evie responded. It was strange holding a conversation in her mind. She hoped no one noticed. *Things to heal and help, not harm. Preserve life.*

And weapons—also a necessity to preserve life.

Evie's oath came to the forefront again. *I will maintain the utmost respect for human life, from the time of conception...* So ingrained in her, it pained her to even conceive of breaking her oath.

"I'm with you, Commander," Evie said. "Always with you." She held out her spear, blade down. "But I cannot carry this."

Lilith stepped toward her, her towering shadow shrinking. "I understand." She took the blood-stained spear from Evie. "But please, Cunningham, if it comes down to it, take it. Protect yourself. Your medical expertise is worth preserving." She eyed Evie. "If not for yourself, then for those that need you."

*　　*　　*

They ventured across the seemingly endless grassland. Patches of dirt began to break up the monotonous landscape, becoming more numerous as they distanced themselves further from the encampment. Although the red sun beat down, the temperature was pleasant enough to only break a slight sweat from the hike.

As dirt patches grew, so did rock formations. Starting as mere pebbles, not unlike those washed ashore from the lakebed. They stubbed toes upon small clearings of gravel and dodged bits of cobble that arose like blemishes. The soft soil only protected their bare feet so long as they avoided these formations, but the land became more formidable.

Looking to the skies, no sign of fowl. Looking at the land, no sign of pests or crawling creatures. The lake still stretched long beside their route, also an avenue to no end. No splashing or any sound of aquatic life caught their attention. Just the lonely whistle of the wind, howling from its isolation.

No one dare speak, keeping their steps light. Essential to maintain an advantage of mystique. They spread, but not so much that they couldn't make eye contact if needed.

Eventually, the encampment they left behind could no longer be seen. Evie wondered at such a phenomenon. For on Earth, the curvature allowed humans from ground level to see three miles beyond standing point. Surely the smoke they saw the night before couldn't have been more than three miles away?

But this wasn't Earth. It wasn't even a similar world. This was a world trapped in the forever twilight of the red sun, only to be contradicted by a green ice giant at night. This was a moon, and significantly smaller than Earth. Not even close to that of Mars. The curvature surely affected how far they could observe the distance.

What mountains and other formations do we not see because of this? She wondered.

The rocks around them grew in size, quicker than expected. Before they knew it, the rocks were boulders, tall as an average human. Scattered as they were, like a rock forest, Evie still kept her compatriots in the corner of her vision.

Light sweat beaded upon their brows. Evie now wished she had said something about Asa's dehydration; what if they became dehydrated? None of them felt it, but it was to come.

That was not a wise choice, the voice brushed against her mind.

Patient confidentiality, Evie thought. *And he's my friend.*

Your strange ethics will be the death of you.

Evie chose to ignore the comment. After all, this voice was just her, a manifestation of her own insecurities. That's what they always were in the case studies she read. She wouldn't let it run her mind. She was in control.

Evie stopped. She looked either way.

Where was everyone?

Only boulders and gravel scattered the earth.

Damn, she thought. *The voice distracted me!*

She felt a tug on her arm.

And she was pulled behind the nearest boulder.

Lilith crouched low, her enhanced height making it difficult to conceal them both behind it.

She made the 'shush' motion with her finger, then pointed to the ground across from them.

Evie held her gut.

Holes. Dug too perfectly, unnaturally. They weren't in a rock forest; they were in a quarry.

A human-made quarry.

And not alone.

From the holes, footprints of shoes tracked away from them.

Lilith pointed to her ears. *Listen.*

Evie did.

Soft stepping. Not that of bare feet from their teammates, but that of padded shoes in sand and gravel.

Lilith pointed to her eyes. *We're being watched.*

She pulled Evie's hand open and placed Evie's blood-stained spear into it.

No. Evie shook her head. Her oath forbade her.

Lilith motioned her head toward it. *Take it.*

Evie shook her head again.

Lilith's nose flared.

It was an order.

The sound of footsteps quickened toward them from the other side of the boulder.

Before Evie could refuse again, Lilith forced the spear into her hand and ran around the boulder to face whatever was coming toward them.

Stronger. Better. Smarter. The UNSF Antarctican catch-phrase repeated in Evie's head as she looked at the spear. Lilith's genetically enhanced body was better suited for this, not Evie's small, weak one.

This UNSF doesn't exist anymore, the ebbing voice slashed quickly in her mind. *Your oath is meaningless.*

Only if I allow it to be meaningless, Evie struck back with her thoughts. Visions of mercy paid to medics, and the consequences if they did not abide by the oath; chaos.

Your oath is paradoxical, the voice argued back. *No one can follow it without dying. Have you not taken life for your own survival from the very food you eat? Do not think that the very plants you stole life from yesterday did not cry out in their own way when you harvested their bodies for your shelters and tools. Your oath is meaningless.*

No! Evie heard the footstep's swift approach. This was happening too fast.

And Lilith was ready to face it alone. No other teammates were in sight to assist.

No heroes she said. Evie told herself. *No heroes.*

Anything to alleviate your guilt, the voice mocked *when your leader is dead. Good job preserving life.*

Evie heard something whistle and something sharp hit the boulder, shards flying in the air.

Something was shooting at them.

Shooting!

Oh god, Evie thought. *This is worse than we thought!*

"Retreat!" Lilith yelled. "Go!"

But Evie couldn't run. *I will maintain the utmost respect for human life... even against the possible violation of the law...*

She couldn't follow Lilith's orders, her law. Running meant letting Lilith die, and thus defying her oath.

Evie pulled herself to the top of the boulder, spear in hand. She could keep her oath of no harm if she created a distraction so Lilith could escape her attacker. Evie stood above them. Lilith directly below her, spear in hand and in an attacking attack position.

There was a person across from them, hooded in woven burlap. The person aimed a strange contraption, a cross between a gun and a crossbow.

Evie saw the damage it did to the boulder, the shattered mark it left above Lilith's head.

This thing was deadly.

And there was only one Lilith—one leader who could lead their people to survive.

Flashes of the awakening the morning before filled her mind. The panic, the near and utter destruction of themselves. The murderous look in the eyes of those she was supposed to help, their fear making them scream and gnaw at themselves. Her heart pounded in terror, for she never imagined such a spectacle could ever happen. Those she worked with became nothing more than wild animals with no leader.

That couldn't happen again.

Only Lilith stood between them and total destruction.

If Evie sacrificed herself, Olena could easily take up the mantle of head medic.

She prepared to create a distraction, sacrifice herself.

And the reality of death stared her in the face.

The idea of nothing; of existence, thinking, being oneself, over and gone. Was she ready for that? Was she ready for that possibility, for her death to end all that she was?

It terrified her

She didn't want to die.

Take a life to save many lives, including your own, the voice said. *Your oath is meaningless otherwise.*

The voice was right. She preserved more lives, including her own, by killing this thing that would end them.

I want to live!

And Evie felt something she had never felt before.

Bloodlust.

Remembering the awakening, she no longer wanted to distract. She wanted to kill whatever thing that would cause such chaos again. The thing that would unjustly take the life of another. Unjustly take her life.

I want to live!

Evie yelled as she jumped from the top of the boulder. Her vision turned red, all color leaving it as she screamed. Her jump forced her to lunge over Lilith and onto the stranger who aimed the deadly weapon at the only hope for humanity's survival.

As Evie landed on the stranger, he fell backwards, his weapon flying from his hands.

He?

Evie knew this was a man.

She held her spear over his covered face. Her other hand ripped at his hood. Instinct took over, and her bloodlust didn't just want to kill; it wanted to see the face of her victim before it died. The animal that would see her dead.

She tore the hood away.

And froze.

She dropped her spear.

All bloodlust melted away, and her mouth quivered. This man she pinned to the ground was supposed to be dead.

One word slipped between her lips: "Michael."

Chapter 8: Lightning

ightning struck.
She saw it as she looked into his eyes, a memory as quick as the blink of an eye. It hit her mind, a jolt of electricity sparking it to life. Her mental wall shattered as she looked into the shocked face of her late husband.

Michael is alive. He's here.

My Michael. The memory came to view, as though a framed painting. Evie remembered seeing lightning strike through the café window. Their café, the site of many a date they attended. More strikes bounced over the lake in the distance. A spectrum of incandescent amethysts, strewn apart into fingers of glowing indigo and porcelain, dancing rapidly through the rainless storm. Although too far to hear the thunder, all still felt its presence from the blinding light unveiling details worthy of a mannerist painting. Unique in majesty, it was a common midsummer sight for residents in Ithaca, New York.

"It's like lightning," Evie said, referring to the fourth dimension. She and Michael were discussing fourth-dimensional phenomena when the lightning struck outside.

"I guess it would be," Michael said, also glancing at the spectacle of lights.

They sat across from one another, decompressing from a day of stress. Although the café had all the modern conveniences of augmented reality menus and waitress bussers—a sleek black cuboid contraption coded to carry orders to paying customers, and a slot for throwing away uneaten food—it took the aesthetic of classical diners. Checkerboard floors and bright scarlet upholstery for stools and booths. Projections of local news and sports floated in empty spaces for patrons to watch, but the storm outside dominated Evie's interest.

"And really, when you think about it," Evie continued, turning her attention back to Michael, "we as humans have electrical currents running throughout our bodies as a fourth-dimensional phenomenon. Which truly makes us fourth-dimensional intelligences, existing and perceiving a three-dimensional plane."

Evie had gotten used to saying intelligence instead of animal or creature when speaking with Michael. It was a word he and his colleagues often used when talking about extensional subjects, things that brought boredom to most people when discussed. But Evie loved it. A biologist at heart, she loved anything that explained life.

"Ha-ha, fallen intelligences," Michael smiled his gentle, thin smile. "And much of it science fiction. Seriously, why aren't you an astromedic yet?"

Evie shrugged. "Not my calling." She'd given up on the idea of astromedicine long ago; the love child career of physics and medicine. She accepted being an earthly medical practitioner and was content with it. "And that's your thing, I just like to talk about it. If I had to do it as a job, well, I wouldn't like talking about it so much with you."

Evie paused, thinking.

Michael's smile fell. "What? Did I say something?"

"Yes and no," Evie said. "At residency this morning, I saw a patient suffering from hallucinations; she said she was haunted by ghosts, and she was hurting herself from the anxiety of seeing them. We couldn't find any reason why. No medications, drugs, or mental health history. Even the AI analysis couldn't find anything. The head practitioner had her transferred to specialists, but it still had me wondering. What if what she was seeing wasn't in her head? What if, for brief moments, she was peering beyond our plane of existence and was seeing something we couldn't perceive? Is that even possible?"

Michael chuckled. "Now you really are getting into science fiction."

"I'm serious," Evie narrowed her stern gaze. "With everything we know about reality, couldn't it be possible?"

Michael sighed. "It's not impossible." He took a breath. "There are theories, but the physics community is careful with them. Nobody wants to be known as a crackpot. There's evidence that suggests the possibility of fifth-dimensional intelligences existing in a fourth-dimensional plane. It's nothing new—great thinkers have theorized about it for centuries. Ancient Greek philosophers wrote about it; maybe that's where they got their idea of gods. They weren't wrong. The math explains it all."

"Why avoid it?" Evie said. "It sounds fascinating."

"Because even with the evidence, it still isn't *sound* evidence," Michael said. "Any physicist worth his mind doesn't touch it. All who have gotten into it, well, to put it gently, become abnormally eccentric and ruin their reputations. No one wants to be ostracized or put their PhD on the line for it. Not with the stigma attached–too many con artists using the theories to sell useless crystals and trick people into meta spiritual cults."

"Sound's pretty harsh."

Michael nodded. "It is."

"Hmph," Evie felt that tug in her heart, the one that made her want to push the subject. She hated not knowing.

The hum of their waitress busser approached, and scooted right next to their table, a tray on top full of fried comfort foods and bubbling beverages.

"Still, what if my patient did truly see something?" Evie reached for her order. "Is it possible for these supposed intelligences, her ghosts, to take an interest in us?"

"Maybe," Michael said, also reaching for his order. "Here, I got it." He grabbed the remaining contents, gentlemanly handing Evie the rest of her dinner. He leaned toward the waitress busser. "Thank you, we'll page when we're done."

"Most welcome," the waitress busser chimed with a deep female voice from unseen speakers. "Thank you for your patronage." It glided smoothly away from their table, toward the café kitchens.

"But it'd be like us taking an interest in insects." Michael took a bite of food. "We'd be nothing more than pests to them."

"Yes," Evie sipped her drink, feeling relief as she drank the contents. "But plenty of zoologists do that for a living."

"Either way," Michael continued, "if there are intelligences beyond us, I wouldn't think them benevolent. Given how the universe always gives way to domination and survival, it's a bad idea to make ourselves stand out. If human history has any bearing on how the universe works, one thing always conquers another. The conqueror lands on top, and the conquered are snuffed out."

All the projection screens across the café suddenly flashed red, 'Breaking News' blinking across them. Frustrated customers slammed utensils on tables, their precious sports games interrupted.

Breaking News, a sternly professional male voice bellowed. Visuals of suited professionals being escorted by UNSF officers played across the screens. *The Space Intelligence Corporation CEO and members of the board have been indicted under Article 304.* The screen switched to a video stream of a winged space transport being evacuated. *All travel through SIC transports is suspended indefinitely, per United Nations Space Force officials.*

"Damn it!" Angry exclamations echoed across the café as people pulled up personal AR devices, looking up more information.

"There goes my vacation!"

"No refunds? Who the hell do they think they are?"

"That's my job on the line!"

UNSF committees are working to subsidize necessary travel to those currently residing on Moon Orbiter Armstrong, Venus Station, and the Ares Mars Project. Recent UNSF raids on the Venus station labs brought to light a rare substance, coined Vita-8, that SIC allegedly failed to report to the UNSF and illegally tested on human subjects.

'SIC again," Evie shook her head as she stabbed a piece of fried potato with her fork. "They're always in the news these days."

Michael's eyes zeroed in on the closest screen. "Not so breaking really."

"What?"

"Oh," Michael's attention turned back to Evie. "The suspended transports and the whole raid, I already knew about it."

"What?" Evie dropped her fork.

"You said that already."

"How did you know?"

"From work."

"From work?" Evie took a deep breath. "How long have you known? You didn't think to tell me?"

Michael nervously rolled his shoulders into perfect composure.

Great. Evie thought. *He's getting that way. I hate it when he gets like this.*

"I found out two days ago," he said patiently. "I was forced to sign a confidentiality agreement when I was told, which means I couldn't even tell you. But the cat's out of the bag with it going public, so we can talk about it now."

Evie eyed him.

"Don't look at me like that."

"I get it with the confidentiality agreement," Evie said. "Doesn't mean I have to be happy about it."

"I know." Michael was still holding his perfect composure, not touching his dinner.

Evie matched the composure.

"What else?"

"What do you mean?"

"I mean, what else are you not telling me?" Evie said. "You're getting in that way again when something is going on. Why would you get confidential information on UNSF affairs at *your* theoretical lab?"

"I didn't want to trouble you," Michael said steadily, "especially with how stressful today's been for both of us, but there's something we need to talk about."

"Okay then," Evie said as she sat back and crossed her arms. "Let's talk."

"Evie, don't do this." Michael's shoulder twitched, his perfect composure starting to break as he rolled his head. "Not here."

"Why not here?" Evie said. "Better communication. I thought we agreed on that. You said you wanted to talk, so talk. Communicate with me." She didn't mean for it to sound sarcastic; it just came out that way, second nature to her. She truly did want favorable communication, but the resentment within screamed to manifest.

"Fine," he said through pursed lips. "I knew because the UNSF told me when they extended a contract to me."

"Contract?" Evie's mouth dropped. "Oh my god, Michael, that's—"

She lost the words.

"Remember when we submitted our names for consideration into their program?" Michael continued. "Well, they liked the paper we published. With all the new information coming to light, they contacted me—and extended an offer."

"Offer?" Evie's stomach dropped. It'd been almost three years since they applied to finish their post-grad education through the UNSF. When they never heard back, they made other plans, bought a house, and settled their lives in the quiet countryside.

"Yes," Michael said. "They want me to be the lead physicist on a mission to Neptune."

"Lead physicist," Evie breathed. "For an outer reach mission! That's—wow—that's a lot to take in. UNSF."

Michael smiled. "Yes, lead physicist. Me? Can you believe it?"

"Yes," Evie said indifferently.

Michael's smile disappeared. "Why aren't you happy for me?"

"I am happy for you." Evie's voice was too level, too stoic. She always had a bad poker face. "And I'm assuming they won't want an AR avatar of yourself calling in from your Cornell lab..."

"No."

"United Nations," Evie swallowed. "That means New York City."

"No," Michael shook his head.

"Switzerland?"

"Ah, no," Michael said. "The lead physicist doesn't stay in the lab. The lead is needed directly on the mission; off Earth, extra planetary."

Evie felt the tension in her chest, the panic starting to set in. She masked, hiding it from Michael.

"But that's for astronauts," she said. "You're not an astronaut."

"Where do you think they pull astronauts from?" Michael said. "They don't just send anyone on these kinds of missions."

Alone. He's going to leave her alone.

"How long?" she said bitterly.

"How long till what?"

"How long will you be gone?" Evie crossed her arms close to her chest. She felt like her chest was going to fall out if she didn't hold it in. "It's not like going to the moon or Venus. I'm well aware of how far Neptune is. We're looking at years, right? That's how these things work. Kind of hard to start a family if dad isn't there to contribute."

"Family?" Michael's lip twitched. "Really? You want to talk about 'contributing' when you're the one who's always absent and changing your mind all the time!"

It cut, ice to the heart. Evie felt it stab and it hurt. Her eyes welled, but no tears came as she forced herself to feel numb—it was better than feeling pain. They'd spoken of raising a family; they both desperately wanted it, but it was never the right time. Michael's education and career were demanding, but not nearly as much as her medical endeavors. After all, he wouldn't be the one who'd have to sacrifice and put everything on hold. He'd be able to carry on in his professional passions while her body changed, and she dedicated her body to keeping another human alive. How could she do that and become a medical practitioner? Timing was everything. They were almost there with her residency nearing its end, and now he wanted to leave it all.

Michael dropped his head into his hands. "Sorry, that was unfair. I just mean, you can't put this all on me, okay?" He picked up his head. "And I wouldn't be leaving you here. You'd come too."

"How?"

"We both wrote that paper," Michael said. "They want us both." He sighed. "I'm not supposed to tell you, but the UNSF is going to reach out to you any day about your application for astromedic."

"My application?" Evie shook her head, thinking. "It's been *three* years. A lot has changed."

Michael looked at her, his expression disheartened. "It certainly has."

The rest was a blur to Evie, hard to remember. Her memory block shoved back into place, blocking any former pain of the moment. But one thing would never be forgotten:

It was the first night they slept in separate rooms.

Chapter 9:Abrupt Emergence

Evie's memory faded away almost as fast as it came. Michael's disheartened, disappointed face from that day at the café. So different compared to the present. She looked down at his wide eyes, a mix of disbelief and surprise. A hint of terror as they glanced at the blade Evie threw aside.

Evie jumped off him, stumbling backward, unable to stand. "No-no! It can't be! Who are you?"

Michael stood, draped in his burlap cloak. His once clean-shaven face was rugged with poorly cut facial hair, his chocolate hair overgrown. His bright hazel eyes were still the same as ever beneath his strong brow, as he reached innocently with one arm. "Evangeline, it's me. I promise it's me."

Evie felt her heart flutter at the sound of her full name; something she did not dictate to anyone but those closest to her.

Her limbs shook, too shocked to move. "It can't be! I saw you fall. You fell! Through the ice."

"Yes," he nodded, still holding up an innocent hand. "I did fall. And I didn't make it out, not for a long time. I was frozen–asleep. But I woke up, and I'm here. I'm alive."

Too good to be true, Evie thought. *Another mind trick, just like the voice. I can't let it take hold of me.*

"Can't be," her voice shook. "It can't be."

She felt arms support her from the back. Lilith pulled her to her feet. "It is him, Cunningham. My God, it is."

"I apologize, Commander," Michael hung his head. "I didn't see it was you when I shot. That was reckless of me. I was lowering it when, um, Evie jumped on me."

"Thank god you're lousy shot." Lilith held Evie, supporting her under her arm. "I guess I can forgive you."

Evie took in the entire situation.

In her mind, she approached her mental wall holding back her memories like a dam. She imagined gripping a sledgehammer, pounding into the wall, cracking it. But every crack repaired itself quicker than the blink of an eye.

Let me! She screamed at the wall, hitting it with the hammer.

A single drop penetrated through a crack.

All that time, mourning, weeping alone after his death. She worked hard to let him go, to build the wall in her mind against the trauma of losing him.

And yet here he was, standing, breathing, living in front of her.

More drops leaked into her mind, and she felt it. The warmth she felt every time she looked into his face. It was familiar, comforting.

Although no specific memory came through, she felt them. Felt the affection she had for this person she loved more than anything she'd ever known.

A vision of a red door on a white farmhouse. Her hand reached to open it.

No. Something warned in her mind. *Don't.*

She let the cracks repair before anything else came through.

"Michael," Evie breathed, finding strength in her stance. "It *is* you."

She left Lilith's supporting arms as she and Michael fell into one another's embrace.

His affectionate arms wrapped around her. Although her amnesia begged her to feel nothing in the embrace, it was too familiar to ignore. As though muscle memory knew what to do, they wrapped around him, around his waist, as she rested her head against his neck, taking in his scent, still the same.

This was no trick—it was Michael.

He uncomfortably backed out of the embrace. "Sorry."

"Sorry for what?" Evie asked, confused. This seemed right. It felt right.

Just as quick as he backed out of their embrace, so did the rest of the scouting team appear from their hiding places, behind other boulders.

And a fire sparked inside Evie. "You all, you were here all along?"

None of them responded.

"Look," she said excitedly. "It's Michael. And you all—" a fire in her flickered, "—you all just stood there, watching. You saw the commander in trouble and just hid? It was Michael!" She didn't know why she felt the need to point it out. Danger or no danger, they all hid, just to watch the worst happen. And even now, when clearly it was someone who wouldn't harm them, they still hid away until all hint of danger dissipated.

Did they not care if Lilith lived or died?

"Cowards!" Evie yelled, stepping aggressively at them, flailing her arms angrily. "You just hid there, and it was Michael! Cowards, all of you!"

Lilith grabbed Evie's arms. "That's enough, Cunningham. They were following my orders."

"How can you just stand there!"

"Okay, you're coming with me." Lilith pulled Evie away from them.

"Wait!" Evie looked at the team. They frowned, refusing eye contact, pure shock struck across their faces.

And Michael, who looked neither ashamed nor surprised. But his mouth slightly parted, his eyebrows upturned, and his overall expression tense.

He was afraid.

Afraid of her.

"Wait, I didn't mean—"

"Come on," Lilith pulled at her. "Over here. The rest of you all get reacquainted."

She continued to pull Evie, though she did not fight it. Was she afraid of her, too?

Lilith led her between boulders until they were just out of earshot of the rest of the group.

"Don't even think about running back to them until we discuss this." Lilith dropped her grip from Evie. "Seriously, what the hell, Cunningham? You're their medic, not their mother! How dare you talk to my crew like that!"

"I-I—" Evie kept glancing back as Lilith towered over her. Could they really not hear them from here? "I just saw my dead husband alive again! How do you think I'm going to act?"

"You, my god, you," Lilith gripped her fists, tense, then reached up and rubbed her temples. She took a deep breath. "You saved my life. Again. Thank you."

Evie nodded.

Choose your words carefully, the voice in her mind spoke. *Better still, don't speak.*

Lilith sighed. "That jump, from the rock. Holy shit, I haven't seen anything like that in years. And from you? I never thought. I swear I saw red in your eyes when you landed on him. You scared the shit out of me."

Evie swallowed. So Lilith was afraid of her.

They all were.

"Look," Lilith put a hand on her shoulder. "I am grateful, beyond grateful. That's twice you've saved my life, and not even a full day apart. But the way you were just now, that red I saw. It was still there when you yelled at our people—*your* people. And I get it, more than anyone. When you turn it on, the fight, the rage, it feels impossible to turn off. It's how we survive. But Cunningham," she pointed in the direction of their team, "those people aren't the enemy. They aren't trying to kill you; they aren't fighting you. They need you. They look up to you, goddammit. And you just terrified them. And Michael, I don't think he was going to make the shot when he saw it was me. I really don't. But you sure as hell scared the shit out of him, too."

Evie bit her lip. She wanted to speak up.

Say nothing.

"I'm worried," Lilith crouched so that she was more level with Evie. "I've never seen you like this. You're my level head on this mission. Never saw you shed a tear, ever. Reserved, yes. Grieving, yes. But not this. This is something else."

My dead husband is alive! Evie screamed in her mind. *I don't know who I am, I don't know how to be! What if this is the real me?*

"I don't know," she shook her head. "Shock does strange things to people."

Lilith pursed her mouth, nodding in acknowledgment. "You're not a soldier, Cunningham. I don't need more of those. I need my astromedic. I need my level head." She looked Evie in the eye. "I need you. Can you handle it?" She pointed in the direction of the others. "Can you handle seeing *him?*"

Him being Michael.

Evie breathed. "I'm calm. I can handle it."

"Are you?" Lilith's emerald eyes narrowed. "Because we go back there, 4020 will eat you alive if you yell at them like that again."

"I get it," Evie said. "I'll be calm."

Lilith dropped her hand and gaze. "You know what they used to call it in the ancient days? Shell-shocked."

"You mean post traumatic stress?" Evie corrected.

"Whatever you call it, that's what they're going to believe," Lilith said. "It's what we're going to have them believe. I swear, we all have PTSD from this whole thing. Come on, let's get back to them before they wonder if one of us has killed each other."

As they started back, Lilith paused. "And Cunningham, from now on, I want you to check in with Solovyóva. I don't want that shell shock getting the best of you again. And don't worry, I'll have her report to me directly to make sure she is staying in line with you."

Evie had the strangest feeling that those reports were not for Olena.

*   *   *

It was after midday when 4020 regathered.

The scouting team returned to the temporary shelters, directing leads to run the camp while all administrators gathered at an undisclosed location. Olena stayed behind to finish the daily medical check-ins.

Thank goodness, Evie thought. The last thing she wanted was to deal with Olena when she was still swallowing Michael's presence.

Beyond the quarry, they went, Evie, Asa, Ren, and Lilith. Flat land rose in elevation and overlooked the lake. Winds picked up at the higher elevation, lashing loose hair around their faces, and sending a chill through the warm air. Waves ruptured against a ledge wall, the roar of its pounding heard all the way inland upon the wide plateau. In the center of the plateau rose a waist-high structure; a wall made from carefully placed skull-sized rocks. Behind it were the roofs of burlap tents.

And a man donned in beaten burlap-type clothes waited for them in front of the wall. His hooded cloak whipped around him as he watched them approach.

Michael.

Asa paused and grabbed the side of Evie's arm. "No—is that who I think? No, it can't be."

A tingle of giddiness spread through Evie. "It is him. I knew there must've been a way after we emerged that he could, too. It's him. It's Michael."

Ren stopped beside them, crossing his arms. "Well, I'll be damned. And here I thought we came all this way for a new encampment. And we get a whole entire person with it."

"We're here to inspect a new shelter location," Lilith said from behind them. "As well as Dr. Smith."

Ren crossed his arms. "As much as I love surprises—birthdays, bachelor parties, a surprise chocolate left on my pillow—a heads up as to whom we'd be seeing would've been nice."

"We didn't want to shock anyone with the news," Evie said. "Best we deal with it first before letting everyone else know. Who knows how an entire hab unit of people will react without preparation? We all had to deal with his parting when he fell. In our own way or another."

Lilith narrowed her green cat eyes at Evie, a reminder of her reaction to Michael.

And a reminder to keep quiet.

"The rest of 4020 is being prefaced right now," Lilith said, proceeding ahead. "You lucky ones get the delight of discovering him in person."

Asa reached and squeezed Evie's hand reassuringly, a gentle smile for her, a silent comment. *I'm happy for you.*

Evie returned the gracious gesture and felt a sudden sickness. A hollow poison that made her mouth taste bile. Remembering Michael's quick release from their embrace earlier, his unashamed tense face. *Sorry*, leaving his unapologetic lips. A refusal to individually acknowledge her when the scouting team made plans. Turning his back to her as though she were any other member of 4020.

Just another colleague.

This was not how a husband was supposed to treat a long-lost wife. Why was he being so cold?

This was not how she remembered him treating her, as far as she remembered. Her mental wall wouldn't allow her to see more.

As they approached, Evie saw that Michael had shaved away some of his facial hair, making him more recognizable. He looked neither ecstatic nor anxious about seeing them.

He's doing it, Evie thought. *That composure, that face, when he wants to be unreadable. When he wants to appear professional, appear strong.*

A flicker of wrath in her chest, a fit of pique. Her jaw tightened.

Why did that irritate her so?

"Dr. Smith," Lilith opened her arms wide as they came close. "A pleasure and a relief. We came as directed."

Michael kept his steady expression. "I hope it wasn't difficult finding this place."

"Not at all," Lilith said. "And I think in the end it was better to meet you here. It was hard enough getting the scouting team to be discreet when they returned to the encampment."

"Of course," Michael smiled. "I, well, I can't tell you enough how happy I am to see you all."

Michael clenched his fists.

He's breaking his composure, Evie thought. *He hates doing that.*

"I–I–" Michael suddenly burst. Tears streamed down his face as he slammed into Ren with a bear hug. "You have no idea. I'd hoped you'd all awake like me, but I also thought—"

"Oh buddy," Ren awkwardly patted Michael's back, "if you saw us yesterday morning, I think you'd be wishing for isolation again."

Michael released Ren and pulled in Asa for an embrace, as well as Lilith.

But not Evie.

What the hell! She screamed in her mind. *He won't hug me in front of them?* Michael was never one to show public displays of affection, especially to those who weren't family. His isolation made his unusual outpouring of emotion forgivable.

He'll hug Lilith! Not me! That wasn't justified.

He released them. "Sorry, Commander, that was out of line. I won't do anything that's inappropriate again"

Lilith slouched to meet Michael's eye level. "It's perfectly all right, Dr. Smith. Don't be embarrassed. We're here. You're not alone. And no, hugging long-lost friends is not inappropriate."

Michael shrugged.

"Michael?" Evie came close.

He took her right hand, cupping it between his own.

"Evie," his warm smile, but not the one he reserved for just her. His formal one that he used for work and pleasantries. "I'm truly happy to see you. Please don't think otherwise. I'm just so relieved."

Her fit of pique began to surface again. "Relieved?" She ripped her hand away. "That's all you have to say? *You're relieved!*"

Michael's mouth twitched, leaning his head close. "Um, I'm trying to respect your boundaries, like you wanted."

Evie shook her head. "What I wanted?"

"We probably shouldn't talk about this here, in front of everyone."

"And why the hell not?"

Asa and Ren looked at one another uncomfortably.

Ren coughed.

"Did you need something, Mr. Tanaka?" Lilith cut in.

"Oh, no," he said, clearing his throat. "Oh my, we should get out of this wind, blowing up dust and plant debris. So windy." Ren coughed over-enthusiastically. "Just so windy."

"Of course," Michael pulled in his composure, releasing Evie's hand. "There's an opening to my encampment over here. Follow me."

Michael led them. No second look at Evie, not even an acknowledgment.

That was worse than if he did.

He led them to a thin opening in the wall, two feet at most. As they entered, they came to an unexpected sight.

It was evident that Michael had awakened long before they did. His encampment was roughly a hundred-foot radius, unfinished on the northern side. He built up three tents of the same burlap-type fabric as his cloak, open-faced on one side. The open sides all faced a center fire pit. The pit, five feet wide and built up with dry stone, slightly smoked from the previous night's embers, the roasted scent filling their nostrils with a string. A primitive canopy made of the same fabric floated above the pit at approximately ten feet, supported by poles made from hardened lake reeds and bound by string. A gaping hole in the center tunneled, simmering smoke through it.

They passed one of his tents. "The cattail-like plants have been most helpful," Michael said. He plucked one of the supporting strings, and it droned. "Made string from their fibers, and their tubers are not unlike potatoes. Their stems harden like wood if you let them cure."

"Our spears," Lilith pulled out one she had tied around her waist. "Too bad they're small."

Beyond the unfinished part of the wall was tilled ground, rows upon rows of black earth containing plants just beginning to sprout. Enough to grow food for one man.

"This way," Michael gestured as they passed the tilled ground. "I want to show you something."

On the eastern side of the encampment, facing the lake, was a bed of cool gray slate rock, rising up from the ground. Revealing an opening into the earth below.

A cave.

Michael led them to the opening. "In here."

"You're not going to murder us, are you?" Ren pointed uneasily. "You know, and do some kind of cannibal party trick so that you can survive. Because inviting us into a cave seems a bit murdery."

Michael chuckled, though he didn't smile. "Ah, no. You're more useful alive anyway."

"Wait, w-what?" Ren said, caught off guard. "I mean, yes, exactly what a cannibalistic murderer driven insane from isolation would say."

No one said anything.

"What?" Ren looked at them all. "It's called a joke. Geez, can we please lighten the mood? At least he gets it. No one's going to survive if we keep acting all cloak-and-dagger serious."

Lilith sighed, rubbing her forehead.

Asa put an arm on Ren. "Not the time, Tanaka, not the time."

Michael gestured for them to enter again. "After you. Watch your step, it's dark, but there is some light at the end. Keep going till you get there."

"Where?" Asa asked.

"You'll know it when you see it," Michael said.

They went in, one by one, into the small opening.

Evie followed last behind her party. As she approached, Michael reached out and put a hand on her elbow.

"Evie," he breathed. "I'm sorry, I wasn't trying to embarrass you. Can we talk? Not now, and not in front of them—later. I think we need to clear the air on some things."

Her chest tightened. She wanted to yell, scold him for being so cold and uncaring to her. She held her head high, ready to face him.

But his head was low, his hazel eyes looking at her, softened. Not the look he gave the others. One only for her.

It felt like static running through her arms and fingers.

"Fine," Evie said, feeling her shoulders sink. "After you show us whatever it is you're showing us, when we head back to camp. I'll stay and catch up with the others after."

The corner of his mouth smiled. "I'd like that."

Evie smiled in return.

No, she screamed in her mind. *Don't you dare give him the satisfaction! He treated you like shit back there. That's not how a husband treats a mourning wife who thought he was dead for months—for a millennia—but that's beside the point!*

"After you," he let go of her elbow. "Watch the step."

Evie stepped into the cave, a wall of cold air hitting her face, and darkness enveloping her vision.

It took a moment for her eyes to focus. She was in a tunnel, not more than five feet wide, at most six feet tall. Lilith's figure crouched ahead of them, Ren and Asa barely clearing the cave ceiling.

Drops of cool moisture tapped her exposed skin. She bumped into something hanging on the wall, knocking it over.

She picked it up. Although she barely saw it, she felt a round object the size of a dinner plate. Water spilled onto her foot from it.

"This should help," Michael's voice carried. A sudden flash of heat, and flames erupted from a torch, blazing beside him. It filled the chilled void with its warmth and light.

Ren's mouth dropped. "Where did that come from?"

"This?" Shadows danced under Michael's eyes as he glanced at his torch. "Had it all along, just needed to light it."

Evie blinked. "You could've led with that."

"Didn't want to burn anyone by accident," he said. "And do you mind hanging that back up? It's part of the water supply."

Evie looked down at the round thing she picked up. A woven bowl glazed with clay and strung with a string. It matched a series of them hanging along the tunnel wall, all collecting runoff water.

"Of course." Evie found a jutting rock and hung it.

"Thanks," Michael nodded ahead. "Shall we continue? It's not far. You can see it lighting the end of the tunnel."

"See what?" Asa asked.

"The antechamber," Michael said. "Keep going."

They continued down the dark, dank path. The drip dripping of cavernous water echoed around them, the crisp cold air crawling across their skin, the taste of petrichor nipping at their tongues and tickling their sense of smell. A hint of salt stung, but not unwelcoming. The pressure of gravity pushed upon them as the tunnel inclined, going deeper underground.

There indeed was an opening at the end of the tunnel, a human-sized entrance. A light emanated from it, bright enough to guide their path with the assistance of Michael's torch.

As they approached, Evie's eyes adjusted, drinking in the details. Rock patterns, bands of limestone cut by colorful granite. Green, rust, and earthy yellow tones mix together in playful swirls. Crystals glittered in the bands that stretched across the tunnel wall.

"Igneous intrusions," she muttered to herself. *Volcanic activity long ago left a band of granite like this.*

More importantly, it meant Triton was alive far beneath its surface. Plate movement, a phenomenon not just unique to Earth. A feature of life-supporting worlds.

"Asa, what can you tell us about the intrusions?" Evie asked.

"Hmm?" Asa's hand brushed against the tunnel wall. He didn't answer right away. He was like that sometimes, when asked on the spot. Waiting to give an answer.

"The colors I can tell are evidence of sulfur-rich deposits somewhere or at some point in time," he said thoughtfully. "That much I can identify—I'm not a geologist."

"We can have one of them look at it later," Lilith said. "Find some useful minerals to mine."

"Oh, there's a lot," Michael said. "More than you imagine."

Evie's eyes adjusted further as they crossed the threshold at the end of the tunnel.

She entered a room. That is to say, an underground room, carved by thousands of years of erosion. A high ceiling drew them in, fissures above them revealing the surface world above and flooding the room with its light. The room was rounded out, looking to be fifty feet in diameter to the naked eye. In the center was a rock slab, smooth and flat like a dinner table, but jagged along the edges.

"Don't worry about flooding," Michael's voice sounded around them, the cavern singing to his timbre. "I created guards above so that run-off drains around the fissures, not into them. Not perfect, but we'll have light and air with no fear."

Michael stepped before all of them, holding his torch high.

"This is the antechamber," he said. He went and slipped his lit torch into a wall crevice. "Come, sit at the table. Let's talk. "

He gestured for everyone to join him at the rock slab in the center, a gathering table. As he did, his eyes locked with Evie's. "How much do you remember?"

Chapter 10: An Unlikely Council

Evie didn't want to answer Michael's question.

His hazel eyes turned to everyone as they gathered around the makeshift rock slab table. It was just high enough for them to sit without chairs, the cool, smooth rock beneath them, the sensation seeping through their bodysuits. Although imperfect, it was circular with no head, everyone sitting equal from one another.

Michael sat beside Evie, Lilith across from them. Asa and Ren fit in between.

"Fragments are returning," Lilith said, responding to Michael's question. "Most everyone can piece together what happened. When we first awoke, it was chaos until people started to remember. It's only a matter of time until all of it returns."

"And you?" Michael placed his hands on the table, drumming his fingers together. "Our fearless commander? How much do you remember?"

Lilith cracked a smile. "All of it."

Michael nodded.

Evie felt the stroke of a memory. Slithering, like a slippery eel, swimming in her brain, leaving traces of what happened. She held her temples, as though doing so would slow down the eel's path. Flashes of the geyser erupting, breaking the surface. The horrid, wretched screams as everyone fell beneath the surface, the sloshing of solid ice against the ammonia ocean as all of 4020, including the hab unit, sank.

And then it shifted.

Ice cracked along the surface. But this time, she wasn't a part of it; she was a witness as she watched Michael's vehicle sink, and Lilith held her back. Her heart raced, panic setting in, reliving the moment.

Two separate events, so similar, and both ending in a fall into the ice world beneath, into a cryostasis. Michael's fall, and theirs that happened months later.

"Evie, are you alright?"

She felt a soothing hand clutch her shoulder. Michael's hand.

The slithering memory faded. He wasn't dead. He was here, alive and well, sitting beside her once more.

"Sorry," Evie let her hands drop. "Just a headache."

Eyes around the table looked concerned.

"Really, nothing to worry about," she emphasized. "What I want to know is how you are here? We saw you fall—we saw you die."

Michael took a deep breath. "How are you here?"

"We fell too," she said. "Months after you, when a geyser burst the surface. It took the entire hab unit down."

"Then I'm here the same way you are," he said. "It seems we all fell and slept."

"You did first," Asa said thoughtfully. "And given what you've built here, you also awoke possibly months before us. Curious, quite curious."

"Sorry, but why does that matter right now?" Ren said skeptically. "Shouldn't we be worrying about survival before getting into semantics of how we're alive?"

"It does matter," Evie said. "We don't know what side effects the cryogenic sleep will have on our survival. Michael is our first case study."

"I'll tell you this," Michael cut in. "The absence of thirst and hunger doesn't last long. Whatever Vita-8 in your systems kept you alive will be expelled. You'll all be feeling it within a few days, if not sooner. It starts small, but the appetite continues to grow each day."

"That's going to be a problem." Lilith leaned into the table. "We need to figure out how to feed 140 people. Michael, you've already started some kind of agricultural project?"

"I have," he said. "But obviously, I wasn't expecting all of 4020 to suddenly appear out of nowhere. I've only prepared a long-term surplus for myself."

"What food sources have you found?"

"Plant-based sources," he continued. "I've attempted to fish for aquatic animals. They're there, but I've been unsuccessful. They migrate, leaving this part of the lake desolate for long periods."

"How big is this lake?" Asa asked.

"Don't know," Michael said. "I haven't been able to travel much further than my encampment because of supply limitations. Wouldn't surprise me if it was something like the Great Lakes on Earth, but it's only speculation."

"We can get a team to start on figuring out the fishing," Asa said. "Even with plant-based food, people will still starve if there isn't enough protein and fats."

As they continued talking about food sources, Evie eyed Michael. She knew him. He wasn't telling them something.

"What else?" she interrupted.

"What?" He didn't act surprised by her request.

"What else?" she said. "What aren't you telling us?"

Everyone was silent, waiting for an answer.

Michael shifted uneasily and sighed. "As relieved as I am that you're all here, that I'm no longer alone, I fear that your coming has spelled out all our deaths."

Lilith's eyes pierced. "What's that supposed to mean?"

Michael stood and reached to the ground. He took a fistful of dirt and sand in one hand, and a smooth rock in the other. He spread the dirt and sand on the table, tracing out shapes and figures into it with the rock.

"Nice drawing," Ren jested. "But I think we're beyond elementary shapes and lines."

The corner of Michael's mouth smiled. "Ha-ha, real funny." But it didn't last. His face turned grim as he continued to draw, adding numbers and symbols until it was clear he was writing equations.

Ren leaned over, looking at Michael's diagrams. His face dropped. "Oh shit, that's not good."

Everyone else stood and leaned over to closely observe Michael's drawings. Two spheres, one large to represent Neptune, and the smaller one for Triton. A half circle on the side represented the sun. All around were a series of trajectory arrows and parabolas. A language telling them something more sinister was coming than they ever imagined.

Evie's chest grew cold. She knew what was coming. The trajectory of Triton was directed behind Neptune.

An eclipse.

Hidden from the sun, from warmth.

From life.

"Our time may be more limited than we think." He pointed to his equation. "Triton is no longer tidally locked; it can rotate independently, creating the day and nights we experience, slowing its planetary orbit and allowing the sun's radiation to warm the entire surface. However, we're not on a planet. We're on a moon, which means we live by a moon's orbit. According to this, we are more than halfway to the eclipse."

Evie glanced at her team. Everyone looked just as confused and worried as she felt.

"Look here." He traced his finger from Triton and around Neptune. "We are here." He made a dot. "Living day and night as we would on Earth, however," he carved another trajectory. "It's going to be cold. Colder than anything we experienced on Earth, even for you, Commander. Cut off from the Sun, albeit temporarily, but long enough that it will kill much, if not all, of the surface life."

"Surely not everything," Ren shook his head. "The atmosphere must hold some of the warmth."

"Triton's too small," Michael said. "It can't hold enough warmth like that to sustain surface life. Beneath, yes, some may survive, but nothing too complex."

"That explains a lot," Asa said. "The absence of land-bound creatures. It has to start over from the inside out every time an eclipse happens."

Evie wasn't convinced. Life doesn't just 'start over.' It persists, somehow and somewhere. The evolution of the organisms they'd seen so far did not match any geological timeline. What were they missing?

She strained to think. What was *she* missing?

"Just think, Earth's poles were desolate," Michael continued, "just from being a few degrees off from direct sunlight. And that was when the sun was considerably hotter. This is going to be a total eclipse with a red giant."

Ren's eyes flared. "So you're saying we've come back just to die again!"

"No," Michael said. "I'm saying that if we don't prepare and advance 4020 into a sustainable colony before Neptune's eclipse, we won't survive."

"And we didn't die," Evie cut in. "We weren't dead that entire time; we were frozen. We were alive, evolving."

For a split second, Michael looked pleased, proud even. "She's right."

She felt a flutter when he said it.

"Haven't you noticed?" he continued. "The gravity? We don't move like we used to. For all intents and purposes, we should be bouncing like we were outside the hab unit's artificial gravity. But we're not. That means our bone mass has changed."

"The hair, the nails." Evie thought back to her medical checks of 4020. She hadn't thought it was as significant as the other conditions she observed, but it connected. "They didn't stop growing. Our bodies were growing, aging, and slowly adapting over a millennium, or eons, who knows. Even if Earth were still around, we wouldn't be able to go back."

She looked at Asa, who gave her a silent side-eye. The loss of Charlie still hung over him. His split-second glance, their silent communication told her everything: he hated this. All of it, more than anyone else in 4020. And yet, no one else seemed to take notice of his maximal sentiment.

Likely, he didn't want them to know.

"We can never live on any Earth-like planet again," Evie said. "We're bound here by our own mass and Triton's gravity."

"Marooned." Asa brushed the hair on top of his head. "I guess I do like having a warm scalp for once."

Ren crossed his arms. "We might as well be dead."

"We survived," Evie said. "And that's something. You can't bring back the dead."

Lilith looked ahead, beyond all of them. Her eyes were as though they were in a mist, looking to a future that none of them could see. Lilith was envisioning something that only her eyes could perceive.

Evie wondered at her envisioning. What could she be thinking? What was she seeing?

"Tell me," Lilith said. "What would you do with humanity's second chance?"

Everyone looked to one another.

"I, for one, Mr. Tanaka, don't plan on wasting it with death." Lilith's faraway gaze came to the present. "My friends, my team. We are survivors. We were all hand-picked for the Vita-8 mission because we proved we could survive in the harshest conditions known to humankind. And now we're faced with conditions unknown, but not impossible. We must reframe our minds if we are to survive and conquer this new world. For in tragedy lies promise. We've been given something that no one in the history of humanity has ever been gifted. When we fell so long ago, it was not to our detriment. It saved us from the inevitable.

"Earth is no more. There's no dancing around that fact. But we didn't just survive, we were spared. The best and brightest minds of humanity were saved for this moment. A fortunate accident? Maybe. If we view this with purpose, we *will* have a chance to make it through the eclipse."

"You really think it's possible?" Asa asked. "Can we make it? Or should we make the most of what time we have?"

"Do you have to talk like that?" Ren shook his head. "Like seriously, I'm already freaking out enough."

"You're the one who said we might as well be dead," Asa shrugged. "If I'm alive, I'd rather be happy, instead of feeling miserable all the time."

Ren looked at Asa skeptically. "Yeah, because someone like you is going to be such an upbeat, merry fellow in our last days before destruction. "

"Come on, I'm not like that," Asa said. "I just don't like to be a loudmouth. I prefer being a realist."

"Yeah, and realistically speaking," Ren continued, "we'd be better off dead than dealing with all of this."

"You do want to live, don't you, Mr. Tanaka?" Lilith asked. "Because I have no doubt we can survive, if we do this right. Dr. Baramba, it is possible. But we have to make 4020 believe it's possible. Dr. Smith, you said the surface life won't survive the eclipse?"

"Most assuredly yes," Michael said.

"Then we adapt," Lilith said. "We go beneath the surface. If this is an antechamber, what's beyond it?"

Michael walked to the wall and pulled out his torch. "Let me show you."

*　　*　　*

He led them deeper into the cave.

The path was harsher, not well-worn. They squeezed between crevices, but Michael assured them of the safety, that it was direct. He'd visited this place on various occasions.

The light of the antechamber shrank from their sight, only the guiding torch of Michael. They continued onward, uncertainty at every shadow and every corner. Echoes deepened, and yet their voices did not travel. Silence was a comfort as they delved further underground.

"Watch your step," Michael said as stalagmites interrupted their way from above, stalactites reached to touch their speleothem companions beneath, like lovers just out of reach, just out of connection.

Evie searched for words to say to Michael. But her heart found none. Her memory block stopped her, the fragments of their life together like puzzle pieces not quite matching. No words aligned to all things she wished for him, for them. She followed behind him, and he awkwardly kept inches away from her, as though to avoid physical contact, even by accident. Strange it was, though, that she caught his eyes glance at her so often, beckoning her to stay with him, but to also watch her step.

The mouth of their path opened.

And they stood in an enormous sight to behold.

A cathedral chamber.

Walls curved high, dripping water, sparkling from the speckled stalactites. A cathedral of natural stonework, as though a god whispered into the cave and created the masterpiece. The endless darkness dissipated from the torchlight, deepening into the spacious chamber. Ribbons of rock told of ages long since past, the life of a planet embedded into its very stone, the body of its existence. Cold air swiftly moved, interrupting the stillness, breathing the life of the cavern. A palette cleanser to their nostrils, the scent of mildew and other unpleasantries wiped clean from their faces. Metallic scented, a slight taste of copper on their tongues. Glistening stalagmites disappeared into a bottomless pit that rippled from the dripping ceiling above.

A subterranean pond.

"Feels c-cold enough to freeze down her," Ren shivered through clanking teeth. "There's plenty of fresh water if we're to use this place."

"This is warm compared to what's to come." Michael held his torch above the edge of the pond. "And I wouldn't drink this if I were you."

From the moment Michael held the torch above the water, the warm light turned cool. Shadows of the ripples reflected off the light, the deep cerulean of the liquid beneath them.

Vita-8.

Asa's eyes grew in awe. "An entire reservoir! More than we ever dreamed."

"Not only that," Michael picked up a small rock, no bigger than his palm. He dropped it into the liquid.

Holding the torch close, they watched the rock sink slower than it should've.

"It's concentrated," Evie said. "More viscous than water."

"Yes," Michael pulled the torch back to the group. "I've experimented with pieces of living vegetation. It's the reason why this chamber is so cold, yet nothing freezes solid, not even the water dripping from above. Unfortunately, none of the experiments proved beneficial; it's just too strong in its concentrated form. I had no way of containing its effects without hurting myself. It defies the known states of matter, making it all the more puzzling."

"Puzzling, but also a possible solution," Asa said.

"Solution?" Ren raised an eyebrow. "What, you want to throw everyone in to cryogenically freeze again?"

"That's not what I'm suggesting," Asa said. "Even if we wanted to, the conditions in which we froze are completely different. Unprecedented and impossible to replicate. And there's no telling the effects a concentrated Vita-8 solution would have on us. The possibilities of more harm than good are too great. But there's a solution here. I just can't see it."

Although Asa spoke, Evie focused on Michael.

"You said you couldn't contain it," she said. "What happened?"

"See for yourself." Michael pulled back the covering over his left arm and held the torch over it.

A scar, right in the center of his forearm. But not like any Evie had ever seen. It was shaped as though something splattered on it, six inches in diameter. Silvery, glittering like frost, as though delicate ice crystals were tattooed into it.

"May I?" Evie asked.

"Go ahead." He held his arm closer to her.

She brushed her fingers over it, inspecting it. Rough and frigid to the touch.

"Does it hurt?" she asked.

"Not anymore," Michael said. "But it's been cold as ice since the day I got it. I was experimenting with Vita-8, and well, one thing led to another. One wrong move, and I thought my entire arm was going to freeze off. I was able to warm it, but it left this behind. I–um–I didn't have the stomach to cut it out. I thought it would spread and cause frostbite, but it never did. My arm works fine, and it's not harming anything. No way to tell why the scar stayed, and the rest dissipated from my arm."

Lilith's lips pursed, her gaze darting between Michael's arm and the pool of Vita-8.

"Sometimes there isn't a direct solution," she said. "We know virtually nothing about Vita-8. Any expert beyond us died with Earth. This is far too dangerous to tamper with, and we have other priorities. Sometimes the old-fashioned way is the best way."

"Old-fashioned how?" Ren said. "I know I'm asking a lot of questions, but you know, when we're talking about not dying, it gets my attention."

"I mean," Lilith continued, "we do what we would if we were stuck in the wilderness, anywhere. We create a surplus of supplies and ration. We make shelter down here, preparing for the worst."

"Is there even enough time?" Evie said. "The eclipse is not that far off, according to your drawings. We won't even have enough food by then."

"Fortunately, we have a head start," she nodded to Michael. "Even if it's only enough for one for now. There are 140 of us, 140 of the best and brightest." Her gaze turned far away again, just as it had in the antechamber, but this time it was somber. "This happened to my people in Antarctica. Scientists stranded, left to die by the world. But they made it. They survived. Maybe this place is not so different as we thought. Half a year of cold and darkness. We made it work before, and we can make it work again."

"A community of minds," Evie said. "Humanity's second chance."

"The Community." Lilith's eyes returned to the present, looking at all of them. "That's what we'll call ourselves.."

"Has a ring to it, doesn't it?" Ren said. "The Community?"

"Yeah," Asa nodded. "I like it."

"We'll need to plan," Michael said. "Count the days, prepare."

"And we will," Lilith said. "But first things first. We'll move 4020 to Michael's encampment, rename it the Community. Given he's alright with that."

"The more the merrier," he said.

"Good," Lilith continued. "Our respective teams each take on tasks for the long term. But I do ask for one thing: stay away from the Vita-8 pool and keep your teams away from it. Not till we are stable enough to learn more. It's too dangerous, and curious minds will experiment." She gave Michael a warning look. "We see how that fared."

"I'll create a barrier," Michael said. "Block the way and redirect the path elsewhere."

"Good." Lilith reached for Michael's torch, and he handed it to her. "We will make this work. I know we can. Neptune above, I know we can."

*   *   *

"Think it'll catch on?" Ren asked as they left the cave. "The Community? Neptune above?"

"Hopefully," Evie said. "We need some unifying jargon to keep people together."

They walked as a group, leaving Michael's encampment.

As they did, Lilith picked up her pace. Asa and Ren matched her pace while Michael slowed.

Leaving Evie awkwardly in the middle of their marching order.

I heard much of that, the voice ebbed in Evie's mind. *A quaint little name you came up with, the Community.*

You're back, Evie darted her thoughts at the voice. *Kept pretty quiet, huh? Thought my mind was finally rid of you, but that's wishful thinking. Especially if you're just a figment of my own insecurities.*

You still truly believe that?

And Lilith came up with the name, not me.

And you'll continue letting her take credit for your ideas, the voice said. *Good to know.*

Evie scowled, ignoring the cheeky comment.

"Hey, um, Evie?" Michael came up beside her. "Can you walk with me for a bit?"

And that was why the others walked ahead. Typical.

Although Evie couldn't hear it, she felt it, the voice laughing. *This should be good.*

Shut-up.

The voice went silent.

"So, um, it's good to see you," he said, his voice slightly cracking. "And um, I just wanted to make sure we were good, and um."

"You're doing it again," Evie smiled. She couldn't help but feel flattered at his stumble of words.

"What thing?"

"Your ums," she said. "You've done it a few times today. It's cute and I missed it." As natural as flowing water, she reached to hold his hand. "I missed you."

His warm hand, despite the rough, unfamiliar cracked calluses, still held the sense of intimacy. Forming around one another like pieces of broken ceramic, once again reunited.

She stopped, tugging his arm for him to follow suit. She leaned to kiss him.

He let go, dodging her kiss.

"What's wrong?" she asked.

"Nothing." Michael hung his head, eyes averted

"Clearly not nothing." She tried to find his hidden eyes. "Why aren't you happy to see me? I don't get it. I thought you were dead."

"I thought you were dead, too."

"Then why aren't you, I don't know, more ecstatic?" Evie felt like she was begging. "This is the single most wonderful thing to happen in a situation like this. What's going on?"

If the others heard them, they pretended not to, continuing to walk further ahead.

Michael lifted his head and looked at Evie. She half expected a look of reasonable assurance; that he loved her and wanted this as much as she did. That she was as much the love of his life as he was to her.

But that didn't happen.

Instead, he looked concerned, as you would at a dying patient. An expression she all too mastered during her former residency.

He sighed, cupping her right hand gently between his.

Not the gesture of a soulmate, but that of a friend about to deliver something unpleasant.

"Evie, be honest," he kept his voice soft. "I implore it. How much do you remember?"

"Enough," she said nonchalantly.

"I know you better than that," he said. "Please, be honest with me. This once, tell me the whole truth on what you're thinking, what you're feeling. Your life could depend on it."

This once? When had she ever hidden anything from him?

She bit her lip. She didn't want to admit it. Everyone else had the entirety of their memories back in a matter of hours. And for her, only fragments remained, fractured nonsensically and causing seizures.

Maybe her life did depend on being fully truthful this time.

This time? What other time was there?

"It's hard," she said. "At first I thought it was coming back to me, but there are gaps—I'm not getting it back like everyone else. I remember objectives, the mission, you know, things I was trained to know. Muscle memory. And emotions." She peered deep into his concerned eyes. "Like how a baby remembers being loved, but no details as to why."

He nodded. "I see."

"But please, Michael, no one can know," she gulped. "They're already on the verge of anarchy as it is. They can't lose hope in their head astromedic as well."

"And us?" He let go of her hand and placed his over his heart. "What do you remember about us?"

Evie paused. What was he talking about?

"I... I..." her lip trembled as she stuttered. "U-us?"

The red door flashed across her memory.

And the pain began in her temples.

"No," she shook her head, closing her eyes. "Not now."

"Evie, I think there are things I remember that you don't." He sighed. "We really shouldn't be affectionate, like kissing or touching one another."

She felt a flare in her chest. Pain? No—*anger!* She was angry with him, more angry with him than any other person she knew. Angry enough that it was as though acid was eating her away from the inside out. But why? She couldn't think of why she was so angry with him—the man *she loved*—only that she was. She felt her nose flare as she breathed heavily. And the red door, persistent in her mind as she felt her vexation at him grow.

"You did this," she spat quickly. She suddenly felt herself in the past, repeating words from quarrels in an age distant past. "It's because of you!"

"So you do remember?"

"No!" She was still angry. "I don't remember. I just know it was because of you that it happened. It's your fault!"

Michael looked both hurt and relieved. "You've said that before." He took a deep breath. "I know you don't want to hear this, Evie, but we need to have boundaries to protect ourselves. We agreed before we left on the mission."

Her eyes felt hot. Would she cry? They felt too dry to cry.

You don't cry, her memory of him spoke to her. *You never did. And you won't now. Not even for me, and that hurts.*

"Boundaries?" Evie couldn't understand. "But I'm your wife, we're married."

"Evie, I'll just come out and say it." He looked pained as he spoke. "We're not together anymore. I'm sorry. I'm so sorry."

The shock shook her. "What?"

"Lilith told me her suspicions about your amnesia after you, to put it gently, attacked me with a spear."

"You tried to shoot us!" Evie felt the heat in her head surge. "With your stupid slingshot gun thing!"

"Warning shots," he said. "Before I saw who you all were. I thought I was alone, and I assumed the worst when everyone approached hidden. But Evie, the way you attacked. I've never seen you like that. I almost didn't recognize you."

"But—" she lost the words.

"Lilith told me that 4020-A agreed to let your memories come as naturally as possible to avoid more seizures," he said. "They're all worried too."

"She said that!" It wasn't a question. She stated it, her throat tensing. How could Asa and Ren agree to it? Olena, she understood, but them? Her colleagues, *her friends*. And Lilith, she trusted her, and she said that.

"I can't do this with you," he said. "I have to set things straight. We're not together and we haven't been for a while."

"But we're still married."

"Yes," he said. "But that's because the mission came before we could finalize that kind of thing."

"How come you remember it and I don't!"

"I don't know," he said. "I've also been awake longer than you."

"That's not it," Evie shook her head. "I should remember more."

"I think you remember more than you realize," Michael said. "Or want to admit to yourself."

Irritation flickered in Evie. "What's that supposed to mean?"

"Feelings can be memory too," he said. "Just like you said. I think you remember more about us."

"There you go again," Evie's irritation spilled over. "Explaining everything to me like I couldn't possibly understand. Like I'm some kind of emotionless prick while you aren't even showing a single iota of disappointment that we have no relationship."

Michael closed his eyes. "And why are you angry with me?"

"I'm—I don't know why!" Evie turned and stomped away. She had no reason to be angry with him. He just helped them establish order and a mode of survival. He didn't lose his calm while speaking to her, being honest. She couldn't fault him for being so honest, for not taking advantage of her. And yet she felt more irritated and agitated with him. The words repeated in her mind, a distant past. *It's his fault! All his fault! I h—*

Hate. Even now, she couldn't bring herself to say the word, let alone think it. She didn't hate him. She wanted to, but couldn't. He did something, something unforgivable that her innermost subconscious would never forget. Hammering at her memory wall did nothing to show her the vision, but the emotions overfilled her.

And yet she didn't cry. Not for him, not for anyone.

"I won't tell people about the amnesia," Michael caught up behind her. "I promise you that."

"Hmph," she scoffed. "You've made promises before."

"And kept them all."

"Except one."

She didn't know why she said it. Even as she picked up her pace and left him to grieve her words, she knew one thing was certain.

It was true.

Chapter 11: The Matriarch's Challenge

The coming days were procedure upon procedure. 4020 adjusted Michael's encampment and created the Community. Much like the hab unit they lived in previously, they sectioned off sleeping quarters, workstations, and a food preparation area for when hunger would eventually arise.

The first days were hard. Creating stable shelters and expanding their team's efforts. The mild bickering among conflicting personalities and the delegation of duties made the smallest tasks astronomical. Lilith's solution? Keep them busy. Task upon task assigned to individual team members ended many of the quarrels.

While running the health and wellness team, Evie had no time to think about Michael.

Lilith still insisted on everyone completing a daily medical check-in, which took the greater part of Evie's time. Overall, she found everyone in superb health. For some, they claimed the best they'd ever been. No signs of disease, no viral or bacterial infections. All seemingly healed of Earthly ailments and new surges of energy made each person a powerhouse for their respective teams.

Most of all, Evie got to know them again.

She'd forgotten there were things they told her.

Awkward at first to have her patients all speak candidly with her. After all, to her, they were strangers. They whispered secrets and told off-hand jokes not to be heard by others. Far too familiar for her comfort, but she never showed it.

An odd thing, she thought, *that people should let their boundaries down for healthcare. To trust inexplicably for no reason other than you're their medic.*

They weren't just her patients. They were people.

And the foreign voice that ebbed in her mind left quiet whispers, easily ignored when she didn't want its unsolicited advice.

But all good things don't last forever.

It started with thirst. People worked themselves to dehydration. Asa's team kept the clean water coming, especially with the ability to boil it. Evie found that more and more people came to the health and wellness tents with dry lips, headaches, and dizziness.

"You have to drink," she insisted to all her patients.

"But I don't feel thirsty," they always claimed. "How can I know how much to drink if I'm not thirsty?"

"Drink anyway," she directed.

And the surge of dehydration did not help other matters of animosity.

Especially one such morning when Dennis paid her a visit to the health and wellness tent.

"Will you just convince 'em already?" Dennis was desperate, trying to get his say between patients. "It's easy for you. Just say something on my behalf."

"I have," Evie said, exasperated. Dennis was on again about transferring to another team. "But it's the same every time. Everyone's got to do their part. Including you."

"Load of shite that is." Dennis looked like he could spit. "I should be on the engineering team, not checking everybody for scrapes and bruises."

Evie swallowed her displeasure. "There is no engineering team anymore; everyone's been reassigned to what we need for survival." She busied herself, sorting her limited medical supplies. "Why do I feel like I'm repeating myself?"

"I should be out there, designing boats and searching for the migrating fish," he waved his arms. "But no, I'm stuck day to day fetching for you astromedics when there's nothing wrong with anyone."

"Dehydration is nothing to scoff at," Evie said. "And—"

She winced.

Ache slapped her across the stomach. Like indigestion, it flexed, making her pause until it passed. The stress of constant evaluations and building up surplus medical supplies took its toll. She'd started thirsting like the others, and the pains of skipping rests and breaks were catching up.

"Conversation done," she said, saving face as she spoke.

"Done?" Dennis gawked. "Just like that? Done?"

"Yeah, just like that." Evie reached up and tightened the tent strings, pulling on them, masking her pain. "We have more people waiting for their check-ins."

"But—"

"You heard her," Olena's deep voice slid from the tent doorway. "You've got a lot to do today."

She stepped in.

Dennis sighed. "Of course, *Dr.* Solovyóva." He glanced at Evie as he emphasized 'doctor.'

Another jab at your authority, the voice whispered in her mind. *Your lack of title. What will you do?*

She did not react, ignoring the voice and Dennis.

As he left, a look of triumph stretched across Olena's face. "Still trouble with that one?"

Evie waved it off. "He'll get over it like the rest did."

"He doesn't seem to be." Olena crossed her arms. "I should think that the lead astromedic would see to her own team's mental health and well-being."

"Is there something?" Evie put bundles of reed cotton into a basket, hoping the distraction would further mask the ache. "I know we're being run ragged with the dehydration flux, but we've got to focus on our tasks before anything else."

"First case of hunger," Olena said. "Be prepared."

Maybe it's hunger, she thought, thinking of her indigestion pain. *Hunger and stress, that's all.* She shook her head. *Please don't be—*

"With hunger will come other things," Olena continued. "Disease, whatever is present in the land."

"Yes, yes." Evie handed Olena a basket of cotton. "Take this, tent two is short. Stat." *And for god's sake, get out,* she thought as the pain in her stomach increased. She didn't mean to dismiss Olena so harshly, but the pain in her stomach demanded isolation.

Olena nodded, looking annoyed at being dismissed so quickly. "Yes, *head* astromedic." She enunciated it, another jab at Evie's lack of a doctor title.

And then Evie felt it.

Her stomach dropped.

"Oh shit!" She grabbed a handful of cotton from the basket Olena held.

"Shit?" Olena looked confused. "What do you mean? What the hell are you doing?"

Evie pulled open the bottom of her body suit. Although they started making clothing from woven reeds, Evie tried to always wear her body suit, keeping a sense of civility.

"It's nothing you haven't seen before, *doctor.*" She reached in with the handful of cotton.

She pulled out the cotton. Tell-tale scarlet streaks tainted the white fluff, like a river bleeding into a desert.

"I'll be damned." She folded the cotton, hiding the shame of it. "This is the last thing I need to deal with."

Olena's gaze went impassive. "It's not like we didn't know this would come eventually."

"I just didn't expect it," she said. "Not yet, so soon."

"No," Olena set down the basket. "You didn't expect to be the first. Congratulations, you're officially a woman again."

"Thanks," Evie said sarcastically. She searched through other baskets stored in the tent. She anticipated bodily functions such as menstruation. They prepared hygiene products and stored them until use. But her being the first to show was unprecedented.

Evie found the basket with hygiene products.

"This is a good sign." Olena sounded too pleased, acting amused by this. "And more work for us."

"Just say what you mean, please," Evie said, frustrated.

"Means humans can repopulate," Olena said. "Both a blessing and a curse, don't you think?"

"Damn," Evie swore again. Another stake and a new problem to solve. The most complex of medical matters. For ages, it brought women close to death all for the sake of giving life. 4020 already had scarce enough resources to support them through the eclipse. And now she had another to resolve.

Maternal and infant care.

*   *   *

It was near sundown when 4020-A gathered for their administrative meeting. Evie, Olena, Asa, Ren, Michael, and Lilith. They gathered in a circle within the center tent of the Community, using the last of daylight. They kept the tent flaps open wide, welcoming reports from their respective teams.

Evie and Michael did not speak, nor sit near one another.

"It was there, the entire hab unit," a stern-looking woman with short hair stood before them, giving the latest scout report. "Heaped up upon itself, parts of it turned sideways. Most of it collapsed, but some were intact enough to look around."

"How?" Ren looked astonished. "The whole thing? That'd be almost impossible."

"Impossible?" the stern woman shrugged. "But it's there."

The scouting team reported finding ruins. Upon closer investigation, they discovered the ruins were the Triton hab unit, sunken long ago with them.

"Us and our body suits were preserved," Olena said thoughtfully. "Who's to say what kinds of materials were preserved by Vita-8?"

"Hence the almost impossible," Ren said. "None of us were wearing our outer Triton gear when we awoke. Why wasn't that preserved?"

Lilith held up a hand. "Questions better left to a different time." She turned her attention to the stern woman. "How far?"

"A day and a half by foot," the woman said.

"I see," Lilith said. "This is an incredible find. We'll put together an excursion team. Good work."

She dismissed the woman, and Lilith turned her attention to 4020-A.

"Game changer," Michael said. "I had no idea it was out there."

"Let's not count all our eggs yet," Lilith said. "We don't know what's usable or can be salvaged. We're looking at a minimum three-day excursion. We'll head out day after tomorrow. Mr. Tanaka, Dr. Smith, I want one of you and one member of your team to join the investigation. And Evie," she turned thoughtfully to her, "I want medics to join as well, given the state of the hab unit and multi-day traversing. I'd like you and one assistant."

"Yes, Commander," Evie said.

"Good," Lilith continued. "Then, if there are no more matters of interest to discuss…"

"Actually, there is one," Evie said. "There are some medical developments we need to report."

"If it's the case of hunger, Dr. Solovyóva already reported it," Lilith said. "Rations are at the ready."

Olena smirked. "Yes, the Commander and I discussed it while you were preoccupied."

Of course she did, Evie thought. "Well, there is another development of interest."

Lilith nodded. "Please, go on."

"There's no delicate way to put it," Evie said. "We've spent our physical and mental energies preparing for survival that we haven't thought ahead as to repopulation."

"Isn't it a bit early to discuss that?" Ren said. "We don't even know if we can make it through the eclipse, let alone populate."

"And what of unplanned pregnancies?" Evie said. "May not be the first thing that comes to mind for those who don't bear children, but it is vital all the same. We have no plan for maternity or infant care. It's bound to happen whether we're prepared or not. Humans will act like humans, and Murphy's law says what can happen will. Along with hunger, we've had our first case of menstruation, which means women are ovulating. We have no way of preventing unwanted pregnancy, not to mention those who may want it."

"Want it?" Ren looked scared. "Hope that's no one I, well," he gave a shy grin, "you know."

Asa rolled his eyes. "Too much Ren, too much."

Lilith rubbed her temples. "She's right." Disgust crossed her face. "And he's right too."

"Don't be too thrilled I'm right for once," Ren winked.

Lilith blinked slowly, then sighed as she addressed the rest of the team. "There is an answer, albeit temporary. But being scientists, I think we can all logically agree that bringing children into this world at this point in time is not the best use of our resources."

Evie felt a stab in her mind; a memory trying to break through. She looked at Michael, who made no motion to return her gaze.

It's not the best time.

It's never the best time.

I hate waiting.

I hate you making me wait.

I thought you wanted this.

Who said what? She couldn't place the voices in the past conversation. It was undoubtedly Michael and her on Earth before the Triton mission. Was this what caused their estrangement? She felt both yes and no. There was more to it, but she couldn't get the mental wall to let up. She strained to try. She pictured herself at the wall, surrounded by mind-numbing fog, chiseling for the memory.

And it disappeared just as fast as it came.

"We don't have much choice," Lilith said. "But to practice a level of self-control. We cannot support a mother and an infant. The answer, for now at least, is abstinence."

The circle went silent.

Too silent.

Ren coughed uncomfortably. "Yeah, good luck enforcing that."

Lilith's eyes shot darts at Ren.

"I hate to say it," Evie said, "but I agree with Ren on this. There's no way you can enforce abstinence, not with consenting adults, and when we're living in such close quarters. Human nature. That's why I have a job in the first place."

Lilith closed her eyes, shaking her head. "What other choice do we have? I want solutions, not 'what ifs.'"

"We prepare," Evie said. "Just as we're doing with everything else."

"I, too, disagree—" Michael spoke up. Was he really going to speak against Lilith? Evie's heart quickened. She needed all the support she could get. She wanted to count on him.

He avoided eye contact. "—with Evie."

Everyone looked astonished.

Lilith's eyes lifted, a glimmer within them. "Go on?"

"Yes, please go on." Evie bit her lip before she said anything else.

"Think of who we're working with," Michael said. "Other scientists. Logical, reasonable thinking people for the most part. I know how they were when they first awoke; anyone would give in to their instincts in a situation like that. But look how fast they've recovered, how quick we've all been to create our Community. More so than the average person. I'm sure if we explain the sense and the dangers unexpected pregnancies currently pose to survival, they'll understand. It's only temporary till we're strong on our feet. We have to save ourselves before we save others."

Evie blinked in disbelief. "So you think everyone will just obey because we explain it nicely?"

"Oh, this is good." Olena leaned in, captivated, clearly savoring the spectacle.

"Is my suggestion that surprising to you?" Michael asked Evie.

"No, not at all," she said curtly. "Not from you."

It hit her as soon as she said it. This was not the first time Michael made such a suggestion.

We can't, his past voice rang in her mind. *Not with the mission coming, with such an opportunity. And we're not ready.*

No one's ever ready, her past voice told him. *You're the one uprooting everything we've worked so hard for. Our house, our home, all of it.*

You made this choice too, his past self argued back.

I thought this was what you wanted, past Evie said. *With me.*

We knew what we were sacrificing when we agreed to this, past Michael snapped. *This is hard for me, too, but be realistic.*

I am being realistic, past Evie yelled back.

I can't talk to you when you're like this.

And I can't talk to you when you're like this.

The words hurt as much as the day they were said. And yet, even as she and Michael looked at one another across the circle, and everyone's faces anxiously flitted between them, Evie felt no urge to tear.

I never will, she thought.

"I'd like to add, please?" Asa's voice wavered.

Lilith looked to him. "Of course. You always say the right things at the right time."

"As long as we're showing a voice of reason, I know our colleagues will understand," he said calmly. "But reason alone will not convince them of anything. We must demonstrate trust. It's been trust that's helped us this far. They trust us, and we will reciprocate." He stood, gesturing to Lilith. "They trust our commander."

Asa sat back down, and Lilith smiled with a nod. "Thank you, Dr. Baramba."

He nodded in acknowledgment.

"I will speak to 4020 and demonstrate our trust in them," Lilith said. "As leaders of your respective teams, I expect you to reinforce."

"And if not?" Evie cut in. "What then? It's not like we have any kind of, I don't know, penalty for not following directives. Nothing to enforce. What if one of them were to assault someone? What will we do then?"

"Do you not trust our people?" Lilith asked evenly. "And assault is a far cry from consenting adults getting pregnant."

"It's not about that," Evie tried to keep her cool, but felt her voice falter.

"Exactly," Lilith said. "You don't have to trust them. But you still need to demonstrate it, show it, if you're to get anywhere with people. You won't go far if you can't do that. They, under no obligation, have followed all procedures and laws we established before we fell. Why? Any one of them could've easily chosen to forget their humanity, go unrestrained. And yet they haven't. Like a machine, they're functioning, working for the good of our survival. But why? We'll face what comes, but demonstrate trust, and more than likely your outcome will be the one they lean toward."

Evie bit her lip again. She wasn't going to win this, no matter what she said. She knew people, how cruel they could be. She'd seen it first hand, although she couldn't remember. Their awakening was merely a preview of what 4020 could turn into. Altruistic motivation wasn't enough to keep people from being foolish.

She knew Lilith knew this. Why was she entertaining the thought?

"We must consider these are colleagues," Michael continued. "People whom we've established," his hazel eyes glinted at Evie, "boundaries long before coming here."

Evie felt a feather of consciousness touch her mind. *Ruthless.* The ebbing voice was back, seething condensation. *You could learn a thing or two from that.*

"Definitely some things to think over," Lilith said. "Time is short. Let's dismiss and return to the subject at a later time, and work together for a more detailed plan."

As everyone arose to leave, Lilith put a hand on Evie's shoulder.

"Stay," she whispered. "Let's speak."

Asa threw a warning look, a silent reminder. *Tread carefully, my friend.*

Evie acknowledged the look.

As soon as the tent emptied, Lilith closed the flaps, darkening the inner room.

"Necessary?" Evie asked.

"Not yet nightfall," she said. "We can still see."

"I mean this private conversation?"

Lilith's tall stature barely cleared the ceiling of the tent. She slightly hunched so as not to tangle in any supporting twine. Even in her hunched state, she still towered over Evie. Domineering, trapping her in.

"I have a favor to ask," Lilith said.

"Of course, Commander," she said. "Anything."

Lilith's professional tone wavered. "Watch your words."

"What do you mean?"

"I mean," she began. The dim light from outside barely breached the inside of the tent, and the warm glow turned cool into shadows under her eyes. "Some things are more delicate than they appear. As an astromedic, you understand. All those things you brought up, you are absolutely right to think. But it's not as forward or easy to implement as we wish. You probably think I'm dense not to instill law and penalty, to think people are purely benevolent. We're alike, we know this isn't the truth. If we come in with a heavy hand immediately, we'll have a mutiny on our hands within one breath of enforcing it. They have to want it for it to work."

"There's no way people will ask for it," Evie said. "The only thing keeping people in line is the memory of their past commitments, which they're bound to forget once their lives are at stake."

"Our lives are already at stake," Lilith said. "It's that thinkings that's kept them in their roles. Believe me, they'll be begging for law and order. It's already started."

Evie thought about it. So far, there hadn't been any serious incidents that couldn't be solved by a team leader. People like Dennis and Olena complained, but overall, they were harmless. Still, she couldn't shake the feeling that complaints were bound to boil over and individuals would lash out.

"I've done this before," Lilith sighed. "Antarctica. It was cut off for so long. We made our own way, our own sovereignty. But not without mistakes, *costly* mistakes. Force only goes so far. When the people want it, they will make it happen. Our job is to guide them to it, ease them into the new norm. And they're already on their way." She put a hand on Evie's shoulder. "Trust me, there's more happening, more cogs turning."

"I do, Commander," she said. "But not all members of my new team trust me."

"How so?"

"Morale's low," she said. "Some were not prepared to bear medical burdens."

"Some?" She raised an eyebrow.

Evie didn't want to say. It made her feel weak to even mention it. Dennis and Olena's disrespect clouded her thinking. "Who do you think?"

Lilith shook her head, her hands on her hips. "I thought you were equipped to be lead astromedic."

It hurt hearing Lilith say that. She was equipped. Even with Olena's seniority, the UNSF chose Evie to be head astromedic on the mission. And did so knowing she hadn't completed her Earth residency hours. They promised her the title of *Doctor* if she completed the Triton mission. Olena was placed as first assistant, co-running the team, but Evie always had final say if it came down to it. If the UNSF trusted her, why couldn't others? "I will handle Solovyóva and Dennis."

"How?" Lilith approached the tent doorway and pulled open the flap. "How will they trust you if you do not show it in them first?"

Opening the flap meant they were done. Evie walked out, the last of the warm light sinking into the horizon, the radiance of the center fire pit heightening with the oncoming darkness.

"You still have someone to choose for the excursion," Lilith said passively as Evie left. "A brimming opportunity to demonstrate it."

*   *   *

Evie did not know it, but as she walked away, Lilith thought back to Earth. To a place where she wasn't the odd one out for her increased height or escalated strength. A place where many were like her, but also few in number compared to the rest of the world. A place she called home and primed her for this once frigid world.

Antarctica.

Chapter 12: The Antarctican

There are no people native to Antarctica.

It was only a matter of time before that changed.

For centuries, the uninhabitable landscape was not home to any human. Only temporary research facilities housed people. None stayed.

Until some did.

Wars and rumors of wars made people afraid to claim nationality or citizenship. The world, trying to destroy itself, was at the forefront. And the state of living in Antarctica was forgotten.

Along with the people left behind to freeze.

But humans are strange in that they always somehow manage to survive.

Lilith Amulius was a descendant of those survivors.

Young fifteen-year-old Lilith watched through the rifle scope. The crosshairs centered on a fat fowl, black and white, and highlighted with gold. A Snares-Emperor penguin; a genetic hybrid of the extinct Emperor Penguin, and its more muscle-massed cousin, the Snares Penguin. A relic of early DNA editing practices and reversal extinction technology.

We shall eat well tonight, she thought. It'd been long since they tasted fresh food. Migration season was upon them, and the fowl colonies finally moved to the more suitable coastal regions. The time of long days and short nights was drawing to a close. March marked the end of Antarctic summer. Although the oncoming autumn promised colder temperatures and lengthening nights, living creatures instinctively migrated to the coast before the bitter grip of winter's perpetual darkness confined them inland without sustenance or refuge.

Laws of survival bid hunters kill only during spring and autumn migration. To kill during mating season was a sin and spelled destruction for the Antarcticans; resources were only renewable if given time to recommence. Furthermore, the central regions were the most deadly to humans. Hunters could only survive a maximum of thirty minutes in the extreme subzero temperatures, given they had the resources to even make it that far. Transports had limited fuel supply, and the ancient fortresses, research facilities of a bygone era, were long buried and gave no refuge.

Lilith took a deep breath to steady her aim. *I never miss.*

She felt a weight push on her rifle barrel. The crosshairs went out of focus.

She angrily glanced up at her father, Chomar Amulius, unrecognizable in his goggled Antarctic gear.

He held up a thick gloved finger to where his mouth should've been, his face covered by a snow-colored balaclava. He made the silencing motion.

Her image mirrored in his goggles, her snow gear matching his. How did he know she was about to yell a string of obscenities at him?

He made the silent motion again and pointed across the cove where she'd been aiming at the penguin. He signed one word to her, and her chest tightened.

Poachers.

She looked through her scope again, except this time in the direction her father pointed.

Hidden just under the ice shelf across the cove was unnatural movement.

Within the shaking crosshairs, she saw them. Three poachers donned in immaculate white snow gear stood out starkly against the blue-tinged ice. Their attire, too pristine and clean, made them conspicuous from afar. It was no surprise that her father spotted them without the aid of a scope at such a distance.

Wealthy poachers, Lilith thought. Outsiders weren't permitted to hunt, as they took more than their share. No doubt these poachers were here for the penguins, to stuff and sell their skins to the highest bidder.

She let her rifle rest on the tripod and signed to her father. *Do you want me to do it, or wait?*

Over time, they developed a sign language, one that transcended the many languages spoken by Antarcticans. The language of the hunter, they communicated with ease and in silence.

He looked across the cove, assessing.

Can you make the distance? He signed.

She huffed. *This is me—I never miss.*

Check.

She positioned her rifle. Unobstructed sunlight and still air; nothing to affect the shot. A perfect day for hunting.

She nodded.

Good, he signed. *Wound only—trial needed.*

Poachers plundered their resources, exacerbating the challenge of securing sustenance for prolonged periods. Sure, routine trade transports brought goods, but it was useless without anything to trade.

The moment she took the shot at them, it'd be over. The penguin colony would dive into the bay beneath the cove and would not return. She'd be out a kill.

Shoot for food, or defend against invaders.

Both options spelled starvation.

I never miss.

She took a breath.

Air thundered around them.

Crimson blood marred the snow.

And so did the corpse of the largest penguin.

Like a foot stamping out insects, the rest of the penguin colony scattered, braying maniacally as they dove into the bay.

Lilith's shoulder ached from the kickback, and her ears rang.

She and her father remained motionless. She'd clearly given away their position. Would the poachers retaliate? She held the high ground, making it challenging for the poachers to take any action from their position.

Lilith turned the scope to the ice shelf.

They were gone.

She felt a tug on her collar.

And found herself abruptly flung into the snow bank behind her.

"*Damn you! Damn you!*" her father's deep voice bellowed. "Have you any idea what you've done!"

Lilith sat up, brushing off chunks of ice and snow. "I provided us food."

"No!" He pointed at her, his face still veiled behind his goggles and balaclava. "You've ruined us. The UN transport's going to be here tonight! We were finally going to have proof of those saboteurs. I cannot appeal or hold their nations accountable without them!"

Lilith stood. "Then send a drone to seek them."

"We don't have the resources for that!" His arms shook. "Or time before they arrive. Do you really think it's that easy to find them? You've single-handedly undermined our opportunity to finally prove who they are."

"I did what I had to," Lilith argued. "I will always do what I have to."

She didn't want to concede, but he was right. Poachers had become savvy, or at least their patrons did. They employed EM wave technology to knock out Anarctican drones, and countermeasures through deflection devices to evade satellites and other image-capturing technology. Even heat-detecting monitors were rendered ineffective by their sophisticated tools. To the world, they were ghostly stories from paranoid Antarcticans.

Her father tossed her pack, and she caught it. "Back to base," he barked.

She angrily threw her pack down. "I need to retrieve my kill."

"It's not a request," he said. "It's an order."

"I'm not one of your lackeys you can boss around," Lilith stomped her foot. "I want my kill!"

He looked up at the sky, swearing a string of Anarctican obscenities. "South-poles frostbite—we don't have time for this."

"I didn't spend all morning tracking the colony just to—"

"You want to die?" Her father pulled down his goggles and pointed to the cove. His dark eyes, beneath thick brows, scowled. "Because that's what's going to happen if you go down for it. Those poachers are just waiting to grab and go. We go down, they'll kill us."

"We can fight them off," Lilith said. "I'm capable, stronger than they are. I'll handle myself."

At fifteen, Lilith was already the size of an average man. Her father more so. Outsiders dwarfed compared to him.

"No!" He snapped. He closed his eyes and sighed. "There are some things you just don't understand."

Anger. Hatred. Vexation. Her memory of the moment blurred into a concoction of adverse emotions. She'd been told often that her father was a good man. She knew it, but it didn't stop her from hating him all the more in that moment. She didn't just want him to be good... she wanted him to be better.

Never forgive. Her mantra.

Chapter 13: Wreckage

Please don't make me regret this, Evie thought.

They walked as a group, pushing overgrown, waist-high grass aside in their wake.

"I've been waiting to get out and stretch my legs," Dennis's voice floated to her, his accent somehow thicker as he spoke quickly. He chatted away with former members of the astrophysics team, also reassigned to their new roles. "Yeah, I missed Jenny's jokes too. Kept things light when things were heavy. Heard she's not too happy with her reassignment either, but she's real good with figuring out that kind of stuff, with the fish and all."

Evie felt relief.

Relief at finally hearing Dennis display something other than total disdain. Maybe there was still hope to mend their professional relationship.

"You just had to bring him." Michael walked up beside Evie. "Out of everyone you could've chosen."

"It was the right thing to do," she said. "Despite any personal grievances he or I've had."

In truth, Evie felt like it wasn't her idea at all to choose Dennis to investigate the hab unit ruins with her. As she prepared to delve out the task, Lilith's words haunted her:

How will they trust you if you do not show it in them first... You still have someone to choose for the excursion. A brimming opportunity to demonstrate it.

It was an opportunity. One to give Dennis what he'd been asking for and gain some favor. And another to leave Olena in charge within the Community, an appointment she more than heartily took. But not without remark of her efficacy.

A win for both of them. And hopefully a win for Evie to get them out of her hair.

"I agree, he's brilliant," Michael said. "Saw that when he was under my charge. But people skills are much too be begged for."

"Seems to be getting along with his former team," Evie said. "He's just immature. Were we really that different at his age?"

Michael sounded like he choked. "I'd like to think so."

She nervously picked at her nails, something she felt in her heart she hadn't done since they first dated, although the memory didn't emerge. It felt good to speak with him so friendly. Strange, but still a sense of comfort. Something she missed.

She thought of last night and coming to that emotional place with him.

She had stayed awake, well after most of the excursion team retired for the night. They walked all day, keeping pace to arrive at the hab unit in time and keep their mission within the three-day window. She sat on the ground alone, tending the meager campfire. She watched its blaze, the stems of flame lashing at one another, dancing, yet not touching.

A tease.

"Who'd ever thought we'd watch visible gas for entertainment?" Michael's voice jovially carried behind her.

She didn't look at him.

His footsteps approached. "Just like early homo-erectus. Do you think they watched like we are?"

Michael sat beside her, resting his arms on his knees. He was in his 4020 body suit, the first Evie'd seen since they organized the Community. He'd worn his handmade clothes, an example to those creating their own. Not only that, his facial hair was trimmed short, and his overgrown hair was cropped.

"Looks like the suit's held up," she said.

"I've been saving it," he said. "Preserving it for my sanity. To look back whenever I felt like I was going to lose myself. It was weeks, before the rest of you awoke from the cryostasis. I didn't even imagine anyone else was like me. I thought I was alone."

"I can't imagine," Evie still watched the flames, "what it was like, being solitary for that long, and thinking it would last forever. What it takes to drive you to survive."

He shrugged. "That kind of stuff doesn't bother me as much as I thought it would. I'm used to being alone."

Evie felt the sting. Being alone, even when he was with her.

Michael must've noticed as he dropped his arms defensively. "No, not that way. That was in no way a slight toward you. I just mean—"

"It's okay," Evie said. "I got what you meant. Even if I can't remember, I know that you're a loner. An introvert. Lots of time to think about time and space."

He smiled, warmed by the firelight. "That's good to hear. You're memory I mean. Um, not the part about me liking being alone."

He continued to stumble over his words.

Evie darted her gaze to him. "What are you doing?"

He paused his fumbling. "What do you mean?"

"What is this?" she motioned her hand between the two of them. "Because I was under the impression that we were supposed to have boundaries."

He nodded. "Yes, boundaries."

"And I asked for them?"

"You did."

"Then what are you doing?" She tried not to sound exasperated. She wanted them to connect, but not at the expense of her well-being.

"We have boundaries, yes," Michael said, resting his arms on his knees again. "And I've tried to give you time to adjust before talking again."

"About?"

"Our relationship," he continued. "It wasn't hostile."

Evie tried to gauge him. He seemed sincere, but was that enough?

"Actually, it was quite amicable," he continued. "You know, despite everything."

She racked her brain. Was this true? Michael wasn't the type to outright lie that she knew of.

The type not to say everything, she thought. Why did she think that?

He sighed. "I don't want us to fight. We've both been rather cold toward one another as of late, and I don't think that's good for us, or the people that look up to us."

Evie nodded. "You have a point." She had patients, and he had a team of people who sought his guidance. They couldn't afford to appear antagonistic toward one another, not with their very survival riding on the line. He was right; they had to get along.

"Fine," she said candidly. "Friends, it is." She held her hand out for a shake. "It'll be good for 4020."

He chuckled and gripped her hand. "*And* good for us."

"Yeah, for us."

Don't get your hopes up.

She couldn't tell if that was her or the invasive voice.

Her thoughts of the night before came to a close, retreating to the present.

"Who am I to judge who you pick for excursions?" Michael continued as they furthered their trek. "You're the one who has to work close with him if someone's injured."

"Oh, let's hope it doesn't come to that." Evie didn't delight in any idea of working with angsty Dennis when she needed to focus on a patient. Bringing him on the excursion may have toned him down, but it didn't mean she looked forward to it.

All conversations suddenly halted.

"Unbelievable," Michael sounded astonished. "There it is. All of it."

Evie's apprehensions flushed away when she looked at the sight ahead of them.

Waves crashed in the distance, splashing against the foreign surface. Like a beached shipwreck, the remains of the ancient hab unit grew into view. A stack of heaped material, once designed to withstand the extreme conditions of Triton's ice landscapes. A mixture of polypropylene polymers and metal alloys, bent into rounded shapes. Once upright, corridors twisted into gnarled designs, while other sections were completely collapsed. Aging discolored the silver and white materials, evidence that it washed ashore from its preservative cryogenic state far before they did. The red sun cast a warm glow across it, as though setting into the evening.

They all felt it, the twelve explorers. A ghost of nostalgia at the place they once called home, all set to ruin. Speechless mourning at the thing that was but a remnant of what it once was.

The grass cleared as they crossed onto the rocky beach, hand-woven shoes doing little to protect their feet from the sharp pebbles that pricked their path. Splashes of waves hit the shoreline as the wind picked up, chilling. Clouds above the lake gathered.

"That's the first I've seen," Evie said, looking at the oncoming storm. "Has it stormed at all since you awoke, Michael?"

Lilith came up beside them, also observing the rising tempest.

"No," he said. "Clouds have gathered, but never beyond the lake. I assume the wind currents are blocking them somehow. Taking them downwind further than I've traversed."

"Maybe there's rainfall on the other side," Evie said. "Worth exploring?"

"Hmm," Lilith grunted. "Yes, but not any time soon. That's a long way, and we have no supplies to sustain a group going that far, especially on foot. This excursion's been more than enough with our limits."

They continued the approach, and the state of the hab unit became more apparent as they closed in. Lilith's scouting team previously reported parts intact enough to explore, but it didn't seem to be the case.

"Whatever lake storms wracked it onto the shore sure did a number on it," Dennis commented.

They entered its shadow, the mound of damaged materials rising twenty feet. Waves continued to pound upon the side bordering the lake, the spray of crisp water sprinkling on them like needles..

"Search for a suitable entrance," Lilith shouted above the crashing waves. "If we can't, we'll salvage what we can from the outside. Dr. Smith, a moment?"

Michael and Lilith stepped away from everyone as the rest of the excursion team busied themselves looking for an entrance.

What could she want with him? Evie tried not to look suspicious as she watched them. The depths of the lake swirled behind them, violent breakers concealing their voices. But she saw their lips move, Lilith clearly saying, *You know what to find.*

Find what? Evie wondered. Did Lilith have ulterior motives for salvaging? What warranted such discretion with their lead astrophysicist? Evie pushed against her mental block, trying to remember why she and Michael were on their mission in the first place. Something he'd done... something she wasn't supposed to know about... something *she* did. . .

Do not go in there.

Her mental wall fortified, pushing her away. The foreign voice echoed through her mind, repeating it: *Do not go in there.*

"Get out of my head!" she told the voice aloud, hoping the others were too busy to notice. "This is my mind."

Heed my warning, the voice foreboded. *Do not enter that structure.*

"Kind of hard not to," she said. "I have a job to do."

I cannot protect you in there, the voice urged. *You'll be vulnerable to any and all harm, physical and emotional. I cannot go with you.*

"Hmm, unable to come with me?" Evie pondered. "And my head my own again? How ever will I cope?" She smiled sardonically.

Do not go in there!

"Oy, over here, a way in!" Dennis and the woman he spoke to earlier were on top of one of the bent corridors, waving down to everyone. Water continued to splash against the structure, their heads dripping like sap.

Lilith, Michael, and the others ran over.

"How goes it up there?" Lilith called.

"There's an opening into section C," Dennis yelled. "No flooding either."

Lilith's face radiated with excitement. "Section C, we couldn't ask for better luck!" she beamed. She elbowed Michael. "This is perfect!"

"I'll take Rami with me," Michael said. "He knows the signs."

Lilith nodded. "Alright, everyone, gather round."

Those who climbed the ruins slid down, while all the others came together.

"We're going to play this safe," Lilith said. "I don't want everyone going in all at once. Six in, six out." She pointed to the two most fit of her scouting team, one of them the woman Dennis sought the attention of. "You two, Benson and Theo, you're coming. Rami with Michael. Medics—" she looked to Evie, "—one in, one out. Who's it going to be?"

"I found the entrance," Dennis piped in. "I'll—"

Lilith's sharp eyes cut to Dennis. "That's not for you to decide."

Dennis bit his lip, his desperate eyes on Evie. A moment of pleading, begging for trust. He wanted this more than anything, she could tell. His discovery, his moment of glory.

And yet the prospect of finally being free of the voice was much to be desired.

Evie swallowed.

Do not go in there—heed my warning!

"I'll go," she said. "You'll need an astromedic if something goes awry inside. Dennis is still learning the ropes."

Evie turned away from Dennis, his lethal gaze more murderous by the second.

"It's settled then," Lilith said. She pointed to the sky. "If we're not out by the time the sun reaches that point, move forward with emergency procedures. Shouldn't come to that, but you all know what needs to be done."

"We sure do, Commander," Dennis said, eyes locked on Evie. "Anything you say."

Chapter 14: We Are Xyelex

Sometimes you work hard your entire life.
And receive nothing in return.
Such was the sentiment of Dr. Michael Smith.
Although it wasn't always so.

He and five others stood upon the ruins of their beloved hab unit. Waves from the freshwater lake sprayed like ink, splotching them. The creaking and groaning of the wreck sent a protest to their presence. The twisted remains piled beneath them, and more stacked above.

They prepared to descend into what was left of section C. They untangled handmade ropes and warmed up their arm strength. The crude opening over section C did not reveal any far drop into the ruins, but it was enough to warrant caution. Those staying behind watched with bated breath.

Michael glanced at Evie. She hadn't said much since arriving at the hab unit. But neither had he, knowing what he had to find.

And couldn't tell her.

Out of those who came on the excursion, only Lilith knew why they were really there.

There's no telling what will happen, Lilith had warned him before they left. *Not with that kind of power. We can't get their hopes up or tempt the more ambitious ones. Find it if you can. If it works, we're saved. If not, well, there aren't many options, are there?*

No one truly knew how dire their situation was with the oncoming eclipse. Even if they prepared and did everything they set out to do, it wouldn't protect them. They'd either freeze or die from starvation.

Which was why he had to find it. *It* was the only solution.

If only he could tell Evie.

Her amnesia kept her from remembering all he did. He made that mistake before, and it ruined them. She was finally friendly with him. Their conversation this morning made things feel like they used to.

Before he had to do what needed to be done.

Nothing can ever happen between us again, he told himself. *I don't want to hurt her again; I can't hurt myself like that again.*

Not good enough. Never good enough.

Husband—wife, they were words that described what they once had on Earth. But they weren't on Earth. They were on Triton, fighting to survive, rebuilding a society, fortunate enough 4020 hadn't devolved to killing one another. No governing bodies enforced any previous obligations or promises of loyalty. Only God prevented it, if there was a god.

Friends were all they could ever be.

It was better this way.

Safer this way.

Lilith descended first through the opening.

He looked down. He saw the top of her head as she lit a torch.

"Commander," he called down. "Did you make it safely?"

"All clear," she looked up at Michael from below with her cat-like eyes, glistening from the gloomy depths. "Lower the rest."

The dark corridor they lowered into dripped with moisture.

Dim, grey light peeked through cracks, speckling deteriorated walls. Cool moisture exposed the sour scent of chemical decay, rotten synthetic materials. Only hundreds of Earth years could break down the materials of their hab unit this much. There was no telling exactly how long it'd been since washing ashore, but clearly hundreds of years before Michael emerged from the cryogenic sleep. The ices and Vita-8 of Triton preserved it for millennia, only to become this within mere centuries.

They lit torches that sizzled and crackled from the trickling humidity, steaming the corridor with their heat, and burning away the unpleasant smells. Although water dripped, it didn't pool, leaking to sections below.

"Groups of two," Lilith said. "Find what you can, drop pebbles to follow back."

"We know this place like the back of our hands," Rami said, the one assigned to go with Michael. "We'll be fine."

"Still," Lilith continued. "There's no telling how convoluted our path will become. I know it's hard to keep time, but estimate it, and try to come back before the sun reaches its mark."

Michael looked down the dark corridor. He seemed to know where they were, as long as he didn't get turned around.

And had a good guess where *it* was.

"We'll go this way," Michael said, pointing his torch down the corridor. "If this really is section C, medical quarters must be that way," he pointed in the opposite direction. "And if you turn left, inventory. It'd been good to look into those if there was anything worth salvaging."

He looked at Evie, her dark brown hair reflecting red in the firelight. She was completely stoic, no emotion, no expression. Like a mannequin, unreadable.

Which irritated him to no end.

And continued to irritate him as they parted ways.

I have to find it, he affirmed to himself as they traversed the slick path. *I will find it. Even after hundreds of years, it should still work. Our lives depend on it. Just have to find it.*

And he knew *it* would work.

Because he made *it*.

*　　*　　*

Evie enjoyed the sweet relief of her mind being her own, despite the company with her.

The woman Dennis had given so much attention to was partnered with her to find the medical quarters. Theo, a very fit young woman on Lilith's scouting team with sharp features.

They parted ways in groups of two. They turned corners and lost sight of both Michael and Lilith's teams.

Evie led the way. The corridor seeped light from their torch, cracks and holes filled in with rubble. Water stopped dripping, but the air still remained humid, warming as they delved further.

Familiar, Evie thought. *This way is familiar. I know it.*

Their path continued, taking a sudden downward slope.

They stopped before the slope.

Evie held the torch forward. It was gradual, not anything difficult to traverse.

"Looks like part of C has sunk," Theo said. "We should turn back."

"No," Evie shook her head. "It's supposed to descend downward."

Evie started down the sloped path, the torch providing a small radius of light around her.

"I don't remember medical quarters being down in a place like this," Theo caught up to Evie. "If my memory serves right."

"It's okay," Evie said. "This is the way. I remember it."

And she did. Evie imagined a sledgehammer and pounded it against her mental wall.

And broke a hole through it.

She was back on the hab unit before it sank beneath the piercing icy depths. She descended down the corridor lit with artificial white light, the rounded walls smooth, clean, and metallic. She breathed dry, cool recycled air, anticipation making her heart race. She was getting closer to *it,* the thing she sought. An electrical buzz reverberated through her body as she neared an entrance, feeling the power within.

But the mental wall only allowed so much through the hole she made. All she remembered faded.

The electrical buzz dissipated, along with the light. The walls around her darkened, and the air turned warm and musty. The scent of charred vegetation from the torch she held made her nostrils itch and burn.

And their path stopped, blocked by a solid barrier.

A sealed entrance.

"I don't think I've ever been in this part of C," Theo said, eyeing their surroundings. She tugged at the torch, pointing it closer to the wall. "This—this place—it's restricted! This isn't section C. We've gone down into area E."

"It would seem so," Evie said, shining the torch over the sealed entrance. "Or at least the entrance to it anyway."

Any paint that indicated words was long gone. Just a large engraving, well-worn that looked as though it once read *AREA E*, but was eroded away.

"We shouldn't be here," Theo panicked. "What if the commander finds out? She'll, oh she will—"

"Calm down," Evie said, irritated by the overreaction. "We'll be fine. It's not like this place is up and running with something to hide. We didn't know we'd be here."

"You did," Theo said. "You said you remember this place."

"I remember walking down a passage like this," Evie said. "It's barely recognizable; it's a shambles."

"But the commander—"

"What's she going to do?" Evie asked. "Scold us like children for doing what she said to do? We'll be fine."

The firelight flickered in Theo's eyes. "Do you even know the commander?"

Evie laughed nervously. "What kind of question is that?"

Her eye suddenly caught something behind Theo.

"Are you okay?" Theo asked.

Evie pointed at the sealed entrance. "What's that?"

Theo turned, taking the torch from Evie and holding it up. "The entrance?"

"No," Evie waved her hand for Theo to lower the torch. "I thought I saw something glint when your shadow blocked the torch."

Evie stepped closer to the sealed entrance.

She saw it again.

A wisp, a line of iridescent color, glinted off the entrance.

And disappeared as soon as firelight touched it.

"I think I saw it," Theo said, holding the torch closer to it.

Evie grabbed the torch.

"Hey, what are you—"

Evie threw it to the ground and stomped out the light.

But they were not drowned in darkness.

From the cracks of the sealed entrance branched thousands upon thousands, thread-like veins, branching along the corridor, further than either of them could see. Tendrils that glowed cool iridescent colors: azure, cobalt, turquoise, and silver. They pulsed, like neurons to a brain, their light living and breathing. No thread was left without connection, no vein strayed. They twisted and danced around one another along the walls and ceiling, though none touched the floor beneath their feet. They looked to grow upwards and escape from the hab unit. Where the ceiling was worn, they bunched around small cracks and openings, spilling into unseen areas. A living organism in its own right.

Evie stood in awe at it's beauty. As she breathed, be it her imagination or not, she saw the light of these tendrils pulse brighter and dimmer, matching her breath.

From her knowledge and the way it grew, this stunning organism was a fungal colony.

"My god," Theo gasped, stretching a hand to it. "It's the most beautiful thing I've ever seen!"

"Don't!" Evie grabbed Theo's hand. "Beautiful or not, we have no idea what we're dealing with. It's a fungus. We have no idea what it could do to human skin contact."

"I know it's weird," Theo said curiously, eyes fixated on the fungal tendrils around them. "But it doesn't feel dangerous. You know what I mean? Makes no sense."

Indeed, Evie knew what she meant. The cool, calming light and a sense of comfort emanated from them. She too felt the urge to touch it, tempted to admire its beauty.

She reached out.

"Well, well, well," a familiar voice echoed, each 'well' enunciated carefully. "What have we here?"

Sense knocked into Evie as she tightened her fist and pulled it away from the fungus.

"Dennis," she scoffed. "What are you doing here?"

Dennis approached them, eyeing the site around them. "I thought to light a torch, but it doesn't seem necessary."

Evie took a stern stance. "I asked what you're doing here? Commander Amulius ordered you to stay outside."

"Oh, I just had to come in and ask you something," Dennis said, unnaturally calm.

"Ask me something?" Evie crossed her arms. "You defied a direct order to ask me something?"

His demeanor was too poised, too impeccably polite. So much so, Evie almost didn't recognize him.

"What's so important for you to break the commander's orders?" she said, taking a step back. He seemed off, not his usual hot-headed self. "Is something wrong?"

"Oh, everyone's fine," he smiled a saccharine smile. "It's exactly like I said, I have to ask something."

"Then ask," she said. "And go back to your post."

Dennis chuffed through his nose, shaking his head.

"Um, I think you should answer her," Theo said timidly. "She's technically our superior."

"Really, Theo?" Dennis shook his head, approaching closer still. "I thought better of you. Oh well."

The fungus continued to pulse their light, brighter, then dimmer. Was it Evie's imagination? Were they quickening their pulse, just as her heart was?

"Theo," Evie said calmly. "Go retrieve Commander Amulius. I would like a private word with Dennis."

"Oh no," Dennis said coyly, taunting. "A private word? Boy, I'm in trouble."

"Please let her know we found area E," Evie continued to speak calm and authoritative. "And that I'm having words with Dennis. Apparently, he needs me to answer a question."

"Oh dear," Dennis continued to speak coyly. "Don't tell the commander."

Theo looked between the two of them, confusion stretched across her face.

"Just go," Evie said, irritated. "Now, please?"

Theo darted down the passage.

Dennis crossed his arms. "You really know how to make a mountain out of a molehill, don't you?"

Evie glanced to make sure Theo was out of sight and hearing, knowing Dennis would probably make a fuss if she didn't respect the privacy of their conversation.

"Molehill? That's what you have to say?" Evie said. "How about failure to follow orders? Insubordination?"

"Will you just shut the hell up for once?" Dennis uncrossed his arms, his voice beginning to shake. "What orders? What insubordination? As if any of it matters. Don't you get it? Earth is gone." His voice was still. "UNSF is gone. There is no order, no enforcement, no justice. When will you stop pretending like there is? What will she do to me? Ground me? Lock me in a poorly woven cloth tent?" He pointed at Evie. "It was my discovery, my idea on how to get in here. All this," he motioned to the glowing fungus, "is rightfully mine."

"Yours?" Evie kept her voice steady, rolling her eyes. "Dennis, do you hear yourself? Be reasonable."

"Reasonable?" His voice cracked. "You, talking about reason. That's a laugh! You're going to steal credit for this discovery, that's what people do. Where's the justice in that? Who's going to stop *you?* You're only alive because of the people's good graces, but some of us have had enough. You hear me? Enough!"

The fungus continued to speed up its pulse.

And suddenly a calm came about them.

Like a fog, it surrounded them, quieted them. The beauty of it all, the light of the fungus beckoning. A silent call to touch and revel in its elegance.

Evie resisted the urge, turning away from the temptation.

But Dennis's eyes fixated on the wall, the glow reflecting in them.

He reached a hand out to touch it, the pulse of the fungus quickening as his hand neared it.

"Don't touch it," Evie warned. "It's some kind of fungal growth. It could be Infectious."

He paused, the tip of his index finger an inch from touching it.

He took a deep breath, eyes still fixated on the fungal veins. "You don't get to tell me what to do. No one does—not anymore."

Oh my god, he's lost it. Evie rubbed her forehead. *Cracked under the pressure. I should've left him.* "So you're going to do the singular most stupid thing anyone has done since awakening just to make a point? Grow up. I'm telling you this for your own good if you'd just listen."

If you'd only listen, a past memory spoke to her. *Just for once, listen instead of doing asinine shit just to prove a point.*

Evie felt the pain growing in her head as the memory grew. A fight she and Michael had, but who said what? The image of the red door blared louder in her mind, louder than any siren, as she saw herself grabbing the bronze doorknob... turning it... pulling the door open...

"No," she tried to snap herself out of the memory, but it was more vivid than it was before, as though she were there again. "Don't go in there." Her face turned hot, and panic made her blood surge through her. "Don't go in there." She begged her past self not to do it, not to look at what was on the other side. "You know what will happen. You can't live through that again. Stop!"

"Listen, you," Dennis turned and aggressively approached Evie. "You're nuts! You think that just because Lilith made you my superior, that puts you over me, doesn't it?"

"No," Evie said. Not to Dennis, but to her past self, reliving and watching her open the red door. "I said don't! Don't touch it!"

But Dennis was not the kind of person perceptive enough to realize for whom her words were directed.

"Shut the hell up!" Dennis continued stepping closer. "I'm done listening to the likes of you!"

Evie listened for the voice in her head. It came at times like this, right? Even if she believed she was insane, that it was only a figment of her own insecurities, the voice helped her, guided her. The voice would stop her, stop the memory from proceeding. Stop her from opening the red door again.

But only silence filled her mind.

Evie breathed.

She was on her own.

If she couldn't fight it, then her only option was flight.

She backed away from Dennis, also forcing the memory of her past self to back away from the red door. She realized how close to the sealed Area E door she was. She couldn't allow herself to touch the fungus, no matter how tempting.

She glanced to the side, searching for a means of escape.

Dennis noticed.

"Oh no!" He grabbed her arm.

"What the hell?" Evie tried to shake off his grip unsuccessfully. "Are *you* crazy? Let go!"

"You're not running off," he said, "to go be Lilith's little lap dog."

Evie glared.

"That's right, I said it," Dennis gritted his teeth. "And everyone knows it. You make it seem like you're friends with us, like you care about your patients, but you don't. You always go crying to your master like the little bitch you are. I know your secret; you don't remember anything, and you're nuts. Your mind is sick and you've been pretending."

Evie tried to break her arm free. "Don't make me do something we'll both regret. Last chance, let go."

"Or what?" He put his other arm up, blocking escape. "What can an UNSF pacifist astromedic do? You're going to listen to me for once, all of you will, and stop dismissing me, *silencing me*. I will be heard!"

The memory of her opening the red door dissipated as training and muscle memory took over. Past training surged through her; break free of his hold, a weak spot between his index finger and thumb, then push back while sidelining him. Escape with little to no injury inflicted. An astromedic's path to defense without causing harm.

But Dennis let go.

"No!" he gasped, cradling his left hand, backing away. "What's happening?"

Evie froze in horror.

Dennis's hand had touched the wall behind her.

And one of the fungal veins.

Like splinters on his fingertips, iridescent azure and turquoise tendrils burst from them, burrowed under his skin, then broke to the surface, growing up his hand.

"Oh god no!" Dennis squeezed his wrist.

He tore at this sleeve as it seeped up his arm. "Stop it! *Stop it!* Oh god, it hurts!"

Evie's reflexes urged her to help, her medical training bidding her so. *It needs to come off before it gets to his vitals.*

She looked for something, anything to sever his hand. *I will maintain and complete an unbiased view of preserving life.*

Her duty to help. Her passion to preserve life. Despite everything Dennis was, she wouldn't lose herself, who she was.

There was nothing to sever his hand here. Not anymore. Anything useful in the hab unit was long gone.

And she couldn't touch him, or risk infecting herself.

Her worst nightmare came to life as she watched him rip off his shirt, skin writhing and voice whimpering. Having the knowledge to help, but none of the means to do so.

Forced to witness, helpless to stop it.

The pulsing fungus spread, an iridescent firestorm across his body.

"It burns!" he screamed. "Make it stop. Make it st——"

He fell back as the fungal tendrils spread on his chest and up his throat, drawing out his voice and silencing it.

So instantaneous as it overtook his head, Evie had no time to react. Time felt like it slowed as she watched. Her thoughts blanked, and no signals reached her limbs to move. Nothing to say, no words of comfort or assurance.

She became the thing she detested most: a bystander.

Dennis's eyes rolled back, the iridescent fungus overtaking the sclera, darkening to pitiless black.

And he became still as ice.

"Dennis," Evie gasped.

His body lay motionless and stiff.

"Dennis," Evie said more assertively this time. "If you can hear me, do anything, show any sign of life."

No response.

"Oh god," Evie clenched her fingers up to her face. "What've I done?"

She hated this. Losing life was always pointless. He was young, ostentatious. And yet, she couldn't feel angry with him.

Because he was right about her.

You're going to listen to me for once, his words haunted. *I will be heard!*

"Damn it!" she clenched her teeth. It was her job to de-escalate, to prevent things like this from happening. With her mind as sick as it was, she only exacerbated and delayed the inevitable.

He was dead. Because her mind was compromised, someone under her purview died.

Because of *her.*

She was no longer of use to 4020. High time she accepted it.

Light-headed, she felt blood flush from her head and nausea grip her stomach.

She failed him. "Damn it, Dennis!"

Yet, she shed no tears. Because if she did, she'd be too weak to continue.

All of a sudden, his body flailed.

Evie would've screamed if not for the sudden dryness in her throat.

He sat up, hanging his head low, his face shadowed.

"Oh, thank god." Relief rushed through Evie, warmth as she felt blood return to her head. "You're alive."

The iridescent fungus shimmered. He curiously inspected his hand where he had infected it.

"I can't touch you, but I can still help you," Evie said, stepping closer, his face still shielded from her.

"Help me?" his voice was just above a whisper.

"Yes," she said, cautiously coming close. She wanted to do something, anything to relieve herself of shame. "I want you to feel heard. I'm so sorry we made you feel that way, Dennis. Let me help you."

He stood, facing away from Evie. The pulsing of the fungus quickened.

"Dennis-s-s?" A voice emanated from him, slurring his esses. Ethereal and polyphonic, like a thousand voices spoke with him. "This is a Dennis-s-s." He inspected his other hand and arm. "And not *a Dennis-s-s.*"

Evie froze. "What?"

"We are not a Dennis-s-s."

She held her breath.

He turned around, facing her. His eyes were black as pupils, his lips shriveled and blue, the fungus on his body, and on the walls pulsed fast, rapidly flickering.

His chest did not move to breathe.

His mouth hung open, not moving to speak.

And yet, a thousand voices still spoke from it.

"We are not a Dennis-s-s," it repeated. "We are Xyelex."

And reached to touch her with its fingertips.

Chapter 15:Parasite

Nowhere to run. Nowhere to hide.

The glowing, parasitic fungal tendrils grew, encasing Dennis's body further, making him unrecognizable. They continually grew, layering upon him, but keeping his humanoid shape. He truly was no longer Dennis, but the namesake that slipped from his gaping, motionless mouth: Xyelex.

"We are Xyelex," the ethereal whisper of a thousand voices said. "Join us-s-s."

The Xyelex's hand was inches from Evie's face, and the decrepit finger drew close. Her heart was pounding as it neared her cheek. One touch and it would own her body and soul. Of this she was sure.

In an instant reaction, her mind shut down. She became mechanical, relying only on instinct and muscle memory. A training from Lilith long ago on basic defensive and escape maneuvers. Ones she never thought to use on their peaceful Triton mission, but required of all UNSF staff.

She ducked before the Xyelex's hand touched her.

There was space between his legs, barely enough to clear. But it was more than if she dodged to the side, where she'd hit the wall and be taken by the Xyelex all the same.

She dove.

Slipping ever so quick and careful, she slid past him untouched.

The dark tunnel ahead grew in light, the fungal tendrils that stretched down the corridor gleaming, changing colors. Red hot in frustration at Evie's escape.

The Xyelex turned, a screech leaving its hollow mouth.

"We know you, Evie Cunningham," its ethereal voices screamed. "We see into this vessel's memories. You cannot escape us. Join and be at peace. You cannot hide from us-s-s or yourself. Join—join—*join!*"

Evie ran, not daring to look back. The fungus on the wall growing brighter, hotter, and thicker. Writhing like tortured worms. The Xyelex's voices echoed throughout the entire hab unit.

"We see you, Dr. Smith. We know what you seek," the Xyelex ringing in Evie's ears. "We know your greatest achievement, your greatest secret, *your greatest regret!*"

All was as though it were on fire, the Xyelex's fungal tendrils spread.

"Shit!" Evie looked down and saw it slowly closing in from both sides on the floor beneath her.

"Commander Amulius," the echo of the Xyelex continued. "We know you too. So headstrong, so powerful, *so fragile!* You'll never escape your past. *They'll all find out!*"

"What the hell is going on!" Lilith came running with Theo.

One short.

"It took Benson, the bastard!" She yelled. "Evie, thank god. Where's Dennis? Theo said—"

Evie shook her head.

"Damn!" Lilith snapped.

"Don't let it touch you," Evie said. "Make for the entrance. Michael will meet us there. Go!"

They all ran, single file, as their path continued to close on them. Like magma, the Xyelex's tendrils stretched and glowed with strains of ochre, turning their desolate hab unit into a vibrant inferno chamber.

Evie had no assurance that Michael would meet them at the entrance. But she said it—she had to say it—someone needed to make a decision, and she did, or they'd lose all chance of escaping the Xyelex. She trusted Michael. He would make it there. He'd know what to do, wouldn't he?

But she trusted him before.

And it didn't work.

"He left," she murmured as she ran.

Stay, the memory of her begged. *Stay, don't leave—don't leave me! Stay!*

And she saw it again, the red door. The back of Michael's head walking away, not turning back.

And his fall, sinking into the depths of Triton.

*Evie no! T*he memory of past Lilith's voice yelled, holding her back from trying to get to Michael. *Don't!*

Evie, past Asa's mournful voice rang while comforting a friend. *He's gone.*

Oh god, Evie, forgive me, past Ren's voice cried in contrition. *Forgive me!*

You'll be vulnerable to any and all harm, she remembered the voice warning. *Physical and emotional. I cannot go with you.*

She heard them, all the past memories looking to her, seeing her weakness, calling her name repeatedly: *Evie... Evie... Evie. . .*

She stumbled on her feet, barely missing the Xyelex's fungal tendril as she caught herself on the floor, the voices in her mind continuing to scream her name: *Evie— Evie— Evie—*

"Evie!"

She felt a hand under her arm to support her as she stood.

Michael.

He made it to them without Rami.

"This way," he waved for the group to follow.

Light beamed in from the ceiling entrance fifty feet from them.

As well as the Xyelex's fungus closing in on it.

"Before it seals it," Evie yelled. "Go!"

"Ahh, no!" Someone screamed.

They all looked.

Theo was half engulfed in the Xyelex, the fungal tendrils penetrating her skin and growing up her torso and neck.

"Join us-s-s," the Xyelex's voices echoed around them. "Dearest Theo, join us-s-s. You wanted to join with the one called Dennis, and he's here with us-s-s. Join!"

"No, please no," she cried as she completely submerged into the Xyelex.

Lilith pushed them forward to the entrance.

They huddled under the opening, just out of reach of even the most feeble jumper.

The Xyelex continued to close in on them, creeping ever closer all around the floors, walls, and ceiling.

"Rope, rope," they cried. "Send down the rope."

Their cries were heard as faces of fellow 4020 members peered down at them, lowering ropes.

"Shit!" One of them bellowed.

And the rope coiled nimbly, falling to their feet as the end was dropped from above.

"We could throw it," Evie grabbed the rope in a panic. "Toss it back."

"Or you." Lilith squatted and positioned her hands at a waist-level boost. "Hurry!"

Evie stepped a foot onto Lilith's boost.

"Three, two—" Lilith shouted. "—one!"

Evie felt Lilith's raw strength surge through her as she jumped. Lilith's arms boosting her upward with no struggle. The momentary airborne weightlessness exhilarated her, and a sense of admiration at Lilith's Antarctican power. Had Lilith not thrown her toward the opening, the tenacity of it surely would crack the skull of anyone unfortunate to hit the ceiling from the sheer force of it. A true leader, putting their charge before themselves, and giving all their might. And a reminder of Evie's own debilitated mettle.

As Evie emerged through the opening, she grabbed for the edge. Although a look of startle filled the faces of her peers, they reacted quickly, grabbing her before she fell downward.

The spray of fresh lake water flecked her face, and a cool breeze met her. But she was not yet relieved.

"Look out!" Lilith called as soon as Evie cleared the opening. Michael appeared next, also thrown by Lilith.

"Commander," Evie called down. "We'll pull you."

She barely saw from the shadow of the opening. But Lilith's determined face glared upward, the Xyelex an inch from touching her feet.

"Commander!" Evie yelled.

Lilith crouched, eyes locked on the opening.

The Xyelex closed in.

She swung her arms behind her.

As the space below her filled with the Xyelex Lilith swung her arms and sprang upward in a high jump.

Right through the opening.

And slammed on the edge as she grabbed it.

"*Pull me up, pull me up,*" she ordered, and everyone scurried to do as she ordered.

"My god, Commander," Michael said as he helped her out. "That jump!"

'No time!" Lilith got to her feet. "Everyone off this thing, now!"

They slid down the side of the hab unit. Onlookers looked confused, their alertness giving a worried urgency.

"This way, hurry," Evie said, splashing into ankle-deep water, pointing to dry land. "Before it leaves the unit."

All ran for high ground, well away from the hab unit ruins.

Upon reaching it, they stopped, looking behind.

Crashing waves continued against the wreckage. All else was silent. Nothing emerged from the unit.

"It's not following," Evie panted next to Lilith. "Why isn't it following?"

"Not following," Lilith also panted, "or waiting for an opportunity."

"What's not following?" One of the scouting team asked.

"What did you see—"

"What's supposed to come out—"

"What happened—"

Evie looked at the surviving members. "You didn't see it when you helped pull us out? The Xyelex."

They all nodded no. They looked confused. "A Xyelex? What's that?"

Lilith turned to them. "The hab unit is off limits unless you want to face certain death. We put as much distance as we can between that thing and us until we reach nightfall. And then I want double watch on the camp, ready to move at a moment's notice."

One of their team approached, a young, wide-eyed male. "Commander, what happened? Where's Benson? Theo? Rami? What happened to Dennis? He went in, and we couldn't stop him."

Lilith shook her head. "I don't know how to tell you."

Loss of words. Evie'd never seen Lilith in such a way.

"We have grim news," Evie said solemnly, empathetically. She stepped forward. "4020, the most unfortunate has happened. I can barely bring myself to say it." She gulped her shock, her disappointment. "We've—we've lost four people in our excursion."

Some held their chests. Others cried out. "No, they couldn't. Not them—this can't happen!"

Michael watched Evie carefully and steadily.

"We witnessed it," she said. "The details—it's too soon to tell. But we'll debrief all tonight when we make camp. We will mourn. But we need to be alive to mourn. The Commander's right; we must put as much distance as we can between us and our hab unit if we're to preserve our lives."

Worry.

Anxiety.

Sorrow. All the words blared across their faces. But Evie noticed something else.

A small spark arose in their eyes as she spoke. A glimmer just in the corner as they teared for those they lost. They'd not yet lost motivation to continue as they turned to journey forward. No one smiled, and no one spoke. But their eyes screamed louder than words as Evie watched them, amazed that her oration gave them tenacity beyond their shock and fear.

Traces of hope.

A heavy hand lay on Evie's shoulder.

"Good work, Cunningham," Lilith said, her eyes slimming, narrowing in on her. "Good work."

Evie breathed. "I hardly feel like accepting praise at the moment."

"Praise?" Lilith said thoughtfully. "Praise? Interesting way to put it. But I wonder, you said we'll debrief tonight. How exactly are we going to explain this formidable fungal parasite?"

Lilith's words filled Evie with unease. "I guess just like how we've explained everything else that we have no idea about."

You have that right. The ebbing voice in her mind pushed against her thoughts. *You have no idea what you've done.*

*   *   *

They were still half a day's walk from the Community when they stopped for camp. Hardly anyone spoke other than to communicate the necessary. The loss of four team members at once was unimaginable, people they lived in close quarters with, worked with, and survived with. How could it have happened? After all, they made it this far, reestablished order, and survived a planetary apocalypse. Surely that meant they could weather anything they faced.

But this loss proved they couldn't.

That night, they sat around the campfire, debriefing the day's events.

Explaining the Xyelex to the remaining five members wasn't a simple task. This recent challenge was well beyond logical sense. Some argued hallucinations, while others took it with a grain of salt, refusing to accept the deadly challenger.

"How do we know you didn't murder them?" One member challenged. "We know how certain members *felt* about other members," nodding to Evie.

"What kind of accusation is that?" Lilith defended. "There are three of us alive who witnessed it. And those of you who kept watch over the entrance. Don't go around yelling such accusations without sufficient evidence."

"Evidence or not," another interjected. "There's an obligation to investigate what happened. It's protocol."

All five joined in, interjecting their voices:

"Respect the dead."

"Follow protocol."

"Duty. Protocol."

"Justice!"

"Justice for the deaths!"

Evie and Michael stood on either side of Lilith as she put a hand up, listening and waiting for everyone to settle.

"Everyone, please, the commander has something to say," Evie said. "We should hear her out."

All eyes looked to them, the firelight dying, closed mouths masking unspoken demands.

"I apologize," Lilith said when they calmed. "You're all right. The dead will have justice, and they deserve better. That is why I've decided to do as the people will it. You have a right to be suspicious; you have a right to know if things could've been done better.

"You have the right to run an UNSF inquiry."

Evie's blood flushed, her hands sweated. An inquiry. Not just any, but an UNSF inquiry. They were bad, awful for those on the investigated end. It always ended in dismissal of some kind, a blacklisting, or a relief of duty. Never a matter of guilty or not-guilty; that wasn't the point. They only ever sought equal justice for the offended parties, never context or fairness. Satiation of the masses.

"Commander?" Evie felt her jaw drop as she quietly prodded her. "You can't be seriously thinking this is a good idea."

"We'll follow protocol," Lilith continued, speaking over the top of Evie. "When a tragedy strikes, it is our duty to have it recorded and investigated. We don't know what could've been done differently unless it is fully investigated to prevent future tragedy. We will honor our fallen by giving them that. I will have the remaining members of 4020-A not involved in this perform the official inquiry when we return to the Community, including myself. I know I'm not perfect, and if they find that my and the others' judgment was not sound, leading to the deaths of our fellow team, we will face consequences to appease justice. We will step down if necessary. I do this for you. Always for all of you."

Nods of acceptance spread among the group. Whispers of their wise and fair commander, always doing right by them.

Seeming pleased with Lilith's words, they dispersed.

"I guess that ends our debrief," Lilith said. "Rest, please. Be ready for tomorrow. First watch, you're up."

Evie's heart sank. Why was Lilith acting so lightly about this? What could 4020 possibly think of to do to them? People often go heavy-handed when affronted.

"Commander?" Evie pulled Lilith aside, voice low for others not to hear. "What are you doing? They're going to destroy us if you allow this inquiry. Why would you put that in their minds? Aren't you thinking of Michael and me?"

Lilith looked indignant. "Of course I'm thinking of you, but I'm also thinking of the whole of 4020. About doing the right thing." Lilith said, holding her head high. "Like we always do. Duty and protocol. Maintaining order to survive."

"We did nothing wrong," Evie entreated. "They died of their own accord. This is going to become a witch hunt, and you know what they're capable of. They love you, respect you, and may let you out of it with minimal consequence. But it's not the same for me. You know what they'll do. You've condemned us."

Lilith gave a wry smile. "We're not on Earth. And you'd do well to remember that Cunningham."

Evie turned to Michael. "Are you going to really go through with this? It affects you too."

Michael stood beside Lilith. "It's not for us to decide what is right and wrong; that's what an inquiry is for."

"But there's always a sanction, no matter what, in these inquiries," Evie couldn't believe she had to say it. "Commander, you basically told them it's okay to think we're guilty and punish us."

"An outside perspective during the inquiry may see things we didn't," Lilith continued with her wry smile. "I'm glad, Dr. Smith, you see reason in that. Inquiries aren't bad; they make leaders accountable and better. And that's what these people need for their closure."

"Closure? At what cost?" Evie felt her voice faltering. "That's all talk, just to please people. We shouldn't feed into that."

"You're making this worse than it is," Lilith said. "Accept it. Move on. Those dead deserve justice, and as leaders, we're just going to have to take the brunt of the blame deserved or not. That's just how it is."

Evie shook her head. "No, I thought we were building something better here." Betrayal tugged at her heart. She trusted Lilith to protect 4020, and wasn't she a part of 4020 too? "You're doing this to us. I don't want to be their whipping boy."

"So little faith in your own people," Lilith frowned. "Sad really. Baramba, Tanaka, and Solovyóva are the ones who will perform the inquiry. Trust them to do their job."

"By encouraging mob mentality?" Evie fixated on Michael. He stood stoically, crossing his arms. "Say something. I know you think this is wrong, too. It's a trial by rumor."

"That's not what this is," he said. "Unfortunately, the moment those people died, there's no way we are going to make it out of this without repercussions. Maybe the commander's right—the inquiry is the best way."

Evie felt herself begging. "Commander—Lilith—please don't let this happen. Don't let them do this to us."

"It's already done," Lilith said. "We're not going back on our word."

"Michael?" Evie stared him down, entreating. "For us?"

Michael didn't look at her, his face looking into the firelight.

"Unbelievable," Evie couldn't bring herself to it. "This is unbelievable. We almost died, and you're letting them investigate us!"

"That's enough, Cunningham!" Lilith snapped. "Say what you will, but do not draw attention to yourself, especially right now. You've done enough of that already.

Evie felt her face drop. "What?"

"Answer me this honestly," Lilith put her hands on her hips. "Do you truly think you did everything right by those who died? You made every decision perfectly without any bias? You believe none of your decisions of late had absolutely no bearing on what happened to those people? That you are completely and perfectly guiltless? If you can honestly say yes, I'll get you out of this, happily."

Evie took pause.

Her conscience weighed on her.

You're going to listen to me for once. Dennis's words haunted. *I will be heard!*

Flashes of him begging her to be the one to go in and her taking his place, the Xyelex taking over his body, how it contorted, and he cried in pain. Her tripping and slowing them down, Theo being taken, and the terror in her eyes as she pleaded with them to help her.

And Evie did nothing to stop it.

"I, uh—" she didn't know what to say. It's impossible for any human to be completely guiltless and unbiased. There was no way to answer without sounding fraudulent and arrogant.

Lilith nodded her head. "That's what I thought. Let it go. This is happening."

Michael said nothing.

You're fighting a losing battle, the voice in her mind said. *You're not going to win something you've already lost. They've already decided your guilt. Heed my warning this time, please.*

"Fine then," Evie pursed her lips, trying to control her words. "I see. Do what you will. But I do it under protest."

"You have the right," Lilith said. "As do they. We will not deny them theirs. Burden of proof is on them, not us."

Evie's head spun. How could Lilith continue this, and Michael go along? She waved them off. "I need to be alone."

She stormed away, not caring who saw.

*　　*　　*

As Evie stormed away, she did not notice Michael's careful gaze watching her, his stoic face losing composure for a split second.

"Commander," he said in a low voice. "Is this really wise? What if they find out?"

"Find what out?" Lilith shrugged. "There's nothing for them to know."

He breathed deep. "If that's what you say. But what's all this going to accomplish? A useless distraction until the inevitable? We're not going to survive without *it*. *It* was our last chance."

"Stick with the same plan we've always had," she said. "Build up supplies and prepare an underground shelter. It was a long shot to begin with."

"What if *it* caused the Xyelex?"

Lilith looked down at Michael, eyes wide, a menacing aura surrounding her. "Don't ever suggest that again." Her entire demeanor changed, as though she were an animal acting on pure instinct. "Or even hint at it. You hear me?"

He felt like prey to a predator. But he did what he did best, and held his composure.

"My apologies, Commander," he said calmly. "A terrifying phenomenon that fungus, don't you think? Quite formidable."

Lilith seemed to calm at his reassurances. "It is."

Chapter 16: A Trial of Malus

Evie lay on her back under the stars, Neptune ever watching. Its jade green glow, constantly apparent, polluting the skies with its light. She tried to pinpoint new constellations and create familiarity with them. But Neptune's light made it difficult to connect them, fading their light.

Moreover, they became a reminder that she'd never see the familiar connections of Orion, Ursa major and minor, and Cassiopeia. Relative only to Earth, their corresponding myths found no meaning on this alien world.

And Neptune, a repulsive replacement for the silver-lighted Earth moon.

Backward, she thought. *All of it backward.* When the team settled for the night, she watched the last of the warm red light settle beneath the horizon, and Neptune's jade light bleed into the heavens. It felt perverted, off. This world was truly alien, discomfortingly foreign. And not just by its nature, but by the people who inhabited it.

Her mind felt sicker than ever from her amnesia. It ached from the constant searching of memory and not finding it.

It's not for us to decide what is right and wrong, Michael's words repeated in her mind. *Let it go.*

Those she trusted most forsake her. Lilith, her mentor. And worse, Michael. Things were finally good between them, and he buckled to Lilith's authority instead of supporting her.

The inquiry was wrong, she felt it deep inside. It set a bad precedent; a precedent to accuse and turn on one another.

Or a precedent to question leaders and hold them accountable. That isn't always a bad thing, the voice said.

I don't want to speak with you, Evie said. *I have enough to deal with.*

She tried to think of something, anything, to block the voice from speaking to her.

The red door.

She saw the vision of it again. Apple blossoms petals blew across her yard that day, the ones the tree shed before growing fruit. The sweet scent it sent as she remembered her hand reaching for the brass handle, opening it, then——

No! It was too painful.

Her mental wall reinforced itself.

I want to live, she thought desperately. *I want to remember.*

Live.

Remember.

Her conscience weighed heavily. Four members of their team were dead. She knew she wasn't completely guiltless. None of them were. But did they deserve what was coming to them? They were not going to escape this inquiry unscathed.

And her compromised mind only complicated matters. Once the inquiry started, there'd be no way to hide it. They'd all find out, and she'd take the bulk of the blame.

Maybe Lilith knows that, she thought. *That's not like her, is it? Would she throw me under like that? She did just now. Theo was right, I don't really know her. I will be crucified for this.*

She knew without a doubt because she also knew there was more she could've done. There's always more people can do.

Lilith's orders would cause her death in more ways than one.

She looked at the reflection of Neptune creeping over the lake in the distance. The shadow of clouds far away.

Clouds have gathered, but never beyond the lake, Michael had said.

"There's more where that came from," she said to herself.

She'd find it.

And live.

She carefully stood, inspecting the encampment around her.

Finally, relief fluttered in her chest. *They're sleeping.*

She could easily sneak away.

But in the back of her heart, it stabbed. A reminder that their condition of not needing food or water was temporary and time was ticking. Hunger and thirst already began when they left for the excursion, and it was only going to escalate.

One less person to care for. One less person to worry about. One less burden upon 4020.

All the more reason to leave.

She tiptoed so as not to make a noise; not that someone leaving their bed was suspicious. Obviously, people had to relieve themselves. But she wanted no person to even suspect what direction she went, taking a chance of stopping her. She carried only the small pack allotted her with water and dried roots for food once the hunger inevitably hit her.

Where are you going? The voice ebbed in her mind curiously.

Evie continued to use light feet as she avoided the watch, tending to the firepit. She reached the edge of the camp and licked the tip of her finger.

East, she thought as she tested the wind, *to where the rainfall originates.*

She scanned the land before her. Long, wide, and lit in Neptune's jaded light. Nothing beyond the horizon she could see, and would never see until she sought it out on her own, beyond Lilith's influence.

Where are you going? The voice asked again.
She went forward. *Where I need to be.*

Part II: Peccata Mortifera

Chapter 17: Origin of a Hero

Some say Antarcticans are nothing more than relics of the past. Others argue they're an atrocity against humanity, abominations. Remnants of genetic research, once performed on vegetation and creatures to preserve and create life tolerant to the harsh Antarctic environments, only to turn to human trials when the world abandoned them.

Some say humans did what was necessary to survive, but others claim they were not so naive. They knew the eugenics behind the Antarcticans' abilities—stronger, better, smarter—and would forever fight against their endeavors to prevent the rise of tyrannical and fanatic regimes of old.

Such were the contentions fifteen-year-old Lilith Amulius's family faced as the UN did nothing to validate or stop the poaching wars her father—the First Chancellor of Antarctica—fought against.

"I'll never forgive him," Lilith told her mother. It was later in the morning, following her incident with her father and the poachers. "That was my kill, and I could've taken them on."

"Enough," her mother said, condensation leaving her breath as they walked. She, Lilith, and Lilith's little sister Lamesh made their way down the dimly lit tunnel behind the amphitheater. The tunnels were always cold and only held residual heat from the other compounds they connected to. The Ronne Ice Shelf, once only recognized as a region, was now a city of Antarctic compounds connected by above-ground tunnels and solar-capturing materials. Simply referred to as Ronne.

"We have more serious matters to attend to presently," her mother continued.

Lilith endured the cold of the tunnels more than usual. They did not wear their regular rugged warming suits. They all had their hair slicked back and wore Antarctic formal wear. Unisex white uniforms with shoulder pads, and ice blue art deco embroidered into the sleeves, cuffs, and front panels. Like royalty, the uniforms were passed down and only worn by First Chancellors and their families, and only on special occasions. An honor to wear such luxury to represent their sovereignty from the rest of the world.

"Where's dad?" Lamesh asked. "Why isn't he with us?"

Describing Lamesh as a 'little sister' was difficult when speaking to their mother, a non-native to Antarctica. Both Lamesh and Lilith already exceeded their mother in height, despite their ages.

"Your father's preparing for the ambassador and will follow on stage separately," her mother continued, wiping a stray hair from Lilith's face. "He's expecting the best out of all of us today. God above, this better go well."

Lilith felt her muscles tighten. Her mother, a staunch atheist, never said anything involving gods unless she was under immense stress.

Because they all knew the outcome of the war depended on today.

Dr. Gaia Farina-Amulius. Lilith's mother and the wife of the First Chancellor. Considered the sharpest mind in the genetics research community. Responsible for bringing back long-dead creatures through genetic hybrids, artificially combined and edited in her lab with the other researchers. Despite her efforts, she was informally ostracized when her research was deemed unorthodox by the UN. Banished herself to the cold depths of Antarctica, where her work was respected. A place where none of the nasty rumors invented by the jealous could follow her. Rumors of secret experimentation on human fetal young. A place where no one would question her about eugenics research and the perfection of humanity.

Because all those things were alleged.

Lilith heard the audience's voices echo around them as they advanced to the end of the tunnel. Her father prepared a broadcast speech welcoming the arrival of the UN Ambassador, practicing days on end for the family. At this point, she too had it memorized.

A tall, burly man dressed in the Antarctic common wear—a stained, white warming suit—descended down a set of steps from the end of the tunnel. His warming suit was insulated with a series of tubes enwebbed throughout it, making him look thicker and more domineering than Antarcticans already were without the suit. A mouthpiece that the tubing connected to hung freely, dangling from his collar.

"First Lady Dr. Farina," he bowed his head slightly, greeting her. "I am warmed at seeing you and your family arrive."

Dr. Farina's non-native Antarctic slender figure looked frail compared to his. "I'm warmed as well." She responded with the same head bow, her response a picture of perfect Antarctican decor.

Lilith rolled her eyes and scoffed. She hated the old-fashioned "warming" greetings that the aged Antarcticans did.

Her sister did not move.

"Forgive my daughters, they forget themselves." She gave them both a knowing look, one that warned, *Do not do that again. Fix it, now!*

Both Lilith and her sister bowed their heads, resentfully reciting: "We are warmed at your arrival."

The man laughed. "I hope you sound warmer than that when the delegates arrive, ha-ha!" He turned his attention to Dr. Farina, holding a small earpiece to her. "It's already tuned. Once it signals, count to ten, then step up to the stage."

"Of course," Dr. Farina graciously took the earpiece. "And the girls know to follow."

He gave the girls an informal thumbs-up. "Good luck today."

He disappeared through the opening and up the steps.

Breathe. Lilith took a deep breath. *Hold. Release. Repeat. Breathe.*

Music played from the amphitheater. Triumphant and grand, an enduring tune to represent the endurance of the Antarctican people. Cold and icy timbre to the music that brought to mind the vast landscapes of tundra that made up their continent.

Dr. Farina stepped first, ascending through the opening onto the stage. Cheers spilled down the steps to Lilith, and she braced herself.

Breathe. Hold. Release. Repeat. Breathe.

Hand in hand. Lilith and Lamesh mechanically walked up the steps onto the stage.

Bright lights hit her eyes, but she didn't blink. They didn't hurt, nor did they skew her vision. A plastered smile swiped across her face as her free hand habitually rose to wave at the massive crowd that filled the domed amphitheater. Although the stage was elevated, the audience tiered and surrounded them.

Above them was the dome, jewel of Ronne. A massive structure to give the feel of an outdoor amphitheater. Clear as day, sunlight and sky poured in. But it was all an illusion; having a translucent or clear dome invited in too much cold. It was still a compound built to seal in the heat. A digital image made to mimic the current weather and time outside, all run by a simplified artificial intelligence.

Lilith's eyes glanced above for a moment, seeing the perfect mimic. *Just like my smile.* She took her place beside her mother, standing at attention like a soldier.

Chomar Amulius stood center stage at a podium, his family behind him. Her father, she'd just argued with early that morning. His refreshed face with dark features couldn't hide the gloomy circles under his eyes, or the streaks of silver that stroked his hair. The features didn't dim his charm. In a way, they made him more attractive with the sense of him being one of the people, a true Antarctican who fought to survive just like the rest of them.

The assembly turned dead silent, his domineering presence capturing the room. Even the children were silent, eyes locked on him.

"My Antarcticans, family, friends, colleagues," his voice bellowed throughout the amphitheater. "I want to begin by thanking you for all your efforts in preparing for today's historic event. Today will mark Antarctic history, as we finally assert our identity as a nation to the world, stepping from the sidelines and coming to the forefront in foreign affairs that affect our nation.

"Shortly, the transport with the ambassador and emissaries from the United Nations will arrive. Upon their departure, they will escort myself along with selected delegates to Switzerland. There we shall plead our cause and make known the hardships and grief the Poachers War has brought. I've been informed that we will continue to be recognized as a sovereign nation. However, they still do not recognize our plight—our enemies. The extinctions they provoked, the periods of starvation they instigated. We are few, but our identity as Antarcticans is valuable.

"And I will do all I can to preserve it."

Cheers erupted from the massive audience. Dr. Farina looked at her husband proudly. Sincerely? Lilith wasn't sure, but she knew that the audience knew no difference.

Yet, she drank his words, storing them in her mind.

"For our people, our sovereignty," Chomar continued, saying buzz words and phrases that excited the people. "My family... our families... "

He gestured to his daughters.

Lilith, still furious about that morning, suppressed her anger. She smiled proudly at her father, knowing that a supportive grin gave the people the hope they needed.

Because given the events of that morning, and despite the rallying optimism of the Antarctican people to end the Poachers War, there was no telling if this visit would turn anything in their favor.

*　　*　　*

The First Chancellor's quarters were no grander than any other quarters in the homesteading compounds. Everyone lived based on their needs due to the extreme limitations of resources. It was so for all generations that built up the Ronne Ice-Shelf.

Lilith mingled among the guests, being friendly and charming as was expected. Lamesh was too young to mingle among the guests and UN delegates, but Dr. Farina insisted that Lilith be a part of the gathering.

It was easy to pinpoint all who were Antarctican and who were delegates. All the Antarcticans wore warming suits, moving freely and comfortably in the chancellor's communal room. While the delegates, heavily bundled, still shivered and moved like puffed snowmen, bumping into one another, not used to the amount of space their bundled gear took up.

Impractical, Lilith thought as she took a few breaths into her mouthpiece, feeling the circulation of warmth. She laughed inside as they continued to bump into one another. *Bumbling buffoons.*

Something caught her eye. A UN delegate who wore more sleek winter wear and who did not seem to mind the cold, or at least pretended not to mind it. An older, balding man, speaking to her father.

Lilith approached to listen in.

"Interesting clothes you all wear," the man said, eyeing her father's warming suit greedily. "Clothes? My mistake, essential gear."

"Ah, our warming suits," Chomar said. "Good of you to notice, Ambassador Leonno."

The ambassador. *That name,* Lilith thought. *Northern European sounding, along with his accent. So he's the one we need to impress to get what we want.* Antarctica, a mix of many nationalities of the past, prided itself on the people knowing multiple languages and cultures. Lilith, young as she was, could pick out any background to any person just by hearing a few words they spoke. Although considered impressive by those outside Antarctica, it was common practice from a young age for her people.

She continued to listen, trying to look inconspicuous as she took a drink from a passing Antarctican server. A mug of hot mead. No one thought much of someone her age drinking alcohol. It was scarce enough, as most of their alcohol was used to preserve foods never enough for anyone to get exceedingly inebriated unless it was a special occasion.

"I've heard rumors of the traditional wear of your people, garb based in science," Ambassador Leonna said pleasantly. "What a delight to see it in person. Please, do tell how Antarctica came to wear such scientific adornments."

Chomar went into details of the warming suits. "It reduces circulation hazards met from treacherous cold. As well as providing additional filtering for humidity on the body as that would create a cooling effect as opposed to warming. Functions on practicality. . ."

As he explained, the ambassador nodded, fully immersed.

He's not telling all, Lilith thought. *Respecting our secrets, as he should.* A flush of anger coursed through her, remembering his outburst at her that morning. *Why can't he do that for me? Always about the whole of the people, never about me... his daughter... always for the people. One for the whole.*

"Has saved our people from hyperthermia on more numerous occasions than I can count," Chomar continued. "Even in generations before myself."

Leonno, eyes locked, steadily nodded again. "How very fascinating to create something sophisticated as this with limited resources. Begs me to think, though, about the keeping of this technology only in Antarctica. Have you ever thought of exporting such a creation? A good way to bring in revenue for businesses."

"Unless you're planning on living long term in the extreme subzero, they aren't really necessary," Chomar said. "I don't see much demand for it. Most do not choose to live like us. If people had the choice between a beautiful tropical paradise or our tundra, I'm pretty sure they'd choose the paradise."

"Some don't have the choice," Leonno said, smoothing a wrinkle in his sleek coat. "Some also value a paycheck more than location."

"Additionally," Chomar wasn't going to let it go, "given our small numbers and extreme environment, we do not live in a profiteering system like many other nations. We don't seek revenue in the same way other nations do. Exporting our warming suit technology isn't of worth to us. I speak for the people when I say we value our independence and self-sustainability more."

"And yet you seek entry and assistance from the UN?" the ambassador said. "And still depend heavily upon imports. You'll have to clarify your motives first, Chancellor, but please do also consider what your warming suits could accomplish. Truly, you never know what this technology could do for others. Or how others could further advance it for you. Many locations could benefit from such a technology, both on Earth and in outer systems, including ice worlds and planets. Think on that as you seek validation from the UN."

185

If Chomar was anxious or disturbed by the comments, he didn't let it show. Instead, he turned a pleasant grin toward Lilith.

Lilith gulped another swig of mead. *Shit, he knew I was listening.* Nothing ever got past him.

"Lilith, my darling," he beckoned. "Come, I'd like to introduce you to someone."

She set down her mug. *Time to act like a brown noser.*

She came close, her height more apparent next to the ambassador..

"Ambassador Leonno, this is my lovely daughter Lilith," Chomar said, putting a hand on her elbow. He nodded to her. A silent, *you'd better be on your best.*

She screamed inside as she prepared to say it, bowing her head. "I am warmed by your safe arrival to Ronne."

The ambassador bowed in return. "I am warmed as well."

There was an awkward silence between the three of them.

"I must ask," Leonno said. "How did I do with your greeting?"

"Excellent ambassador," Chomar said. "You are becoming well-versed."

Lilith coughed, hiding a laugh.

"Bless you, my dear," Leonno said politely.

"Something to say?" Chomar asked, giving Lilith a warning eye. *Don't you dare say anything.*

"Well, if you want feedback," Lilith started. "I'd say you sounded forced. It needs to be more natural. Not the bow, but your words. It's not just saying them, it's how you say it. You want the person you're speaking to feel warmed by the tone of your voice. Like, emotionally warmed."

"Oh, then give me the pleasure of trying again." The ambassador bowed his head again. "I am warmed as well."

"Better," Lilith said. "But it's still too cold-sounding. Adjust the tone of your voice. It takes practice. Even I don't get it right all the time."

"Charming, absolutely charming, Chancellor," Leonno beamed. "Seems she could follow in your footsteps one day to be the first Chancellor herself."

"Dear god, no," Lilith's words slipped.

Chomar gave a nervous laugh. "Lilith has plans of her own, of course." He gave another subtle look. "Ambassador, you said you needed a statement from those who've witnessed the atrocities of the foreign poachers."

"*Alleged* foreign poachers," Leonno corrected, taking a mug of mead from a passing server.

"Well, my daughter has been a first-hand witness to many of their terrorist acts, as well as their concealment technology." Chomar put a hand on her shoulder. "She is more than willing to give her statement."

The ambassador sipped his mug as though he were drinking from a delicate glass. "If such concealment technology were to exist, the UN would already either have access to it or knowledge of it. And as much as I'd appreciate her statement, I'd prefer to have statements of unbiased views to avoid conflict of interest."

"Are you calling me a liar?" Lilith blurted out.

Those around them silenced, heads turning.

"Now now, Lilith," Chomar laughed. "Let's not jump to conclusions. He wasn't calling you anything. I'm sure the ambassador has procedures he must follow. How about you run along—"

"My ass that he has procedures!" She felt the heat rising in her chest and to her head, just like it did when she got angry with her father. "That pompous asshole was calling me a liar!"

The entire room was now silent, staring at the three of them.

Chomar looked like he would explode. "Lilith—"

"You didn't have any idea about our warming tech, what makes you think you know anything about the tech these poachers use?" Lilith pointed at Leonno. "And yeah, they're terrorists. Isn't the UN supposed to neutralize things like that? Or are they all a bunch of talk and flamboyant spectacles like you!"

Ambassador Leonno's mouth hung open. "My word, I have never—"

Lilith growled, ready to pounce on him.

Until she felt an arm hook around hers.

Leonno's face suddenly softened. "Gaia, my goodness, it has been too long."

"Twenty years, Gabriel," Dr. Farina said pleasantly, her arm squeezing Lilith's. She felt her mother's presence stretch, using the ambassador's first name. "And it is Dr. Farina-Amulius. But most call me Dr. Farina now."

"Gabriel?" Lilith scoffed. "Isn't that like a girl's name or something?"

She knew it wasn't. She just wanted to get back at the ambassador.

Dr. Farina tugged on Lilith. "I'm going to take care of this one gentleman. Do carry on."

"Please, Gaia, I mean Dr. Farina, join us when you're finished," Leonno said desperately. "I'd love to hear about some of the genetic hybrids you've researched here."

It was strange being pulled by her mother, dainty as she was next to her.

"Mom, I—"

"Shh," she simply and peacefully said. "You seem cold, Lilith. Why don't you use your mouthpiece?"

Lilith reluctantly placed her mouthpiece in her mouth.

She glanced back at her father and the ambassador. He was talking, making apologies, while the other guests returned to their conversations.

But Chomar's eyes met hers across the room for an instant, speaking.

Disappointment.

And the anger she felt for him turned to cold resentment in her chest.

Proof, Lilith thought. *He wants unbiased proof; I'll give him proof. I'll give both of them proof instead of dancing around this UN bullshit. I'll get it myself. By morning, they'll eat their words.*

Chapter 18: A World with No Moon

Ancient tales tell of a time when the Earth existed with no moon. The moonless world in a purgatorial wet haze. Mists watered the plants and fungi, and animals gathered the condensation. Including a curious animal called human.

And then the moon came, its gravitational lock forcing the atmospheric water to fall and for the living creatures to run in fear, as great floods and tidal waves abounded. Despite the fear it caused, the moon became Earth's savior. It stabilized Earth's axis to create seasons, allowing food to thrive. It made the tides so living organisms may traverse oceans.

Most importantly, it slowed Earth's rotation. Creating day and night, thus birthing to all living things the illusion of time; circadian rhythms for body systems to run by and function.

The gradual slowing of Earth's rotation brought it to just the right speed. Protected it from becoming too cold, allowing it to absorb the sun's radiation to warm its atmosphere and take in elements only a star can provide a planet.

A fate not granted to Earth's sister planet, Venus, a rotation so slow that its surface became wholly uninhabitable.

The moon, Earth's guardian and protector.

The ancient peoples celebrated the coming of their great protector. Arcadians called the moon Selene and celebrated her as a goddess. They often told of the dark era before their supposed goddess came to them. Colombian Chibcha tribes also preserved oral traditions of their tales, pre-lunar civilizations in the Bogotá Highlands. Early peoples of India passed down their legends of the moonless sky. They named her Chandra, the Hindu god. And Middle Eastern desert tribes immortalized the moonless sky by writing it into sacred psalms; their monotheistic god created day and night, and sent a great flood with rains.

But scientists dare say all such tales are symbolic narratives. That the moon came from a collision during Earth's protoplanet phase, still in formation. Theia, a Mars-sized protoplanet, collided with Earth and eventually became the moon, forming from both Earth and Theia's collision debris.

Ancient narrative or collision theory, there's no way to tell which one is definitively true.

Dr. Asa Baramba believed in both.

He thought about it as he kicked a two-inch rock from the shoreline into the water. It collided with the water, reflecting a sickly green from Neptune above—a typical afternoon on this peculiar moon world.

He remembered ancient Australian Aboriginal tales he was told as a child. Of the time when the Earth was encompassed in a purple haze. His scientific mind told him to believe otherwise.

"Truth in all things," he said. "You can always find truth behind all things, whether they're facts or lies."

He and Ren sat across from one another, binding dried reeds into burning logs and stuffing them with fluff to increase their burning efficiency. They took their supplies and sat near the lake shore, waves concealing their voices. Anyone else could've done the task, but they wanted an excuse to get away from the Community and talk alone about the inquiry. The caves echoed too much for private conversations, and tents were easily eavesdropped on.

"That's just bullshit," Ren responded beside him. "Truth is truth, and it's our job to find it." He changed his voice higher, as though to mimic someone, but Asa couldn't place who. "Snuff out the liars and make them pay," he said bitterly.

"Yeah," Asa raised an eyebrow, "you seem *so* thrilled."

He wanted to say more, but his throat froze. It happened all too often. At least with his friends and colleagues like Ren, he could speak more freely. Years of exposure also helped, but it still happened from time to time.

He remembered his mother's voice from his childhood: *You have to speak up sometimes. You have to fight it, push through...*

What if people get mad at me? He remembered asking her.

He took a breath. *One, two, three,* he mentally counted. He hadn't struggled this much to speak to others since childhood. But the stresses of survival caused his mutism to relapse. He was quiet too often when he should speak his mind. And when he did speak, it was without offense, to calm. To please.

One, two, three, he mentally counted again. *Okay, I'll talk.*

"Don't let your grief speak," Asa warned as he tied a knot. He knew well enough how Ren did things impulsively when he got emotional. He couldn't let his colleague do that this time. "Or the commander will be all over you, and you won't be able to help. We already have Olena to deal with—do you think she'll be impartial? You're not even supposed to be on 4020-A, but Michael insisted you stay administrative after they found him. Watch yourself."

"Yeah, yeah," Ren stood and threw a rock at the lake, further than Asa kicked his. "Whatever. They aren't even out looking for her. And we're just sitting around tying logs." The disgust on his face screamed disapproval.

Her, meaning Evie.

"If any of us leave to look for her, it will be bad for Michael and the commander," Asa said. "The Community isn't taking it well, and we cannot lose all our leadership this close to the eclipse. Who knows what chaos will ensue if incapable leaders take over, if any at all, because this query doesn't go well."

"Inquiries never go well," Ren shook his head. "Believe me, I know. Been through it before. No one likes how they end."

"Then you know you can't let them down," Asa stressed. "The commander, Michael, and Evie. You know what will happen. The Community will never let it go until they feel satiated."

News of their teammates' deaths didn't go over well. The day the excursion team returned empty-handed was grim. From a distance, Asa saw how they walked, like an oncoming funeral procession. No retrieval of bodies, just that they were lost to the horrors found within the hab unit.

And Ren took it the hardest when he saw Evie was not among the returning team members.

"You should've done something," Ren had yelled at Michael when they returned. "Stopped her, protected her from whatever made her leave!"

"Her leaving was of her own volition," Lilith told him. "And does her no service of absolving her or us of guilt. You've got a job in this inquiry Tanaka and you'd better do it right!"

Asa, Ren, and Olena were tasked with running the inquiry and appeasing the righteous anger of 4020.

Asa continued his busy work of tying and binding as he thought it over. Why did Evie leave? Did guilt force her? Or had Michael done something to hurt her beyond reason that she fled from the emotional pain? Either way, their task of appeasing became that much harder with her fleeing.

What killed four of their team in the hab unit? Why couldn't they be saved or helped? Lilith and Michael told them about a creature, a thing called the Xyelex. A fungal parasite right out of a fictional story. Too many questions that needed answers, and no absolute truths to follow. Already, he had interviewed and taken statements, and the witnesses' accounts were hard to match up. Separating fact from emotion —a virtually impossible task during grieving. Even more challenging to judge the exaggerated from the understated.

The fate of the Community was tied to their leaders and their convictions.

"There's a lot on our shoulders," Asa said. "Can you take the pressure?"

He didn't ask resentfully or condescendingly. He paused his task, trying to communicate his sincerity.

Ren slumped. "I have to, don't I?" He chuffed. "Look at the kind of leader I've turned out to be." His head hung low, pulling at twine between his fingers.

"I wish you could understand," he said, not looking up from his twine. "Like you said, I wasn't even supposed to be on the administrative team. I'm just the replacement. And Evie's gone. She's like, you know, family.

"Growing up, I was an only child. As much fun as it was having my parents spoil their little prodigy because I'm me, I never had anyone else. Evie is the first person ever to make me feel like I had a sibling. When Michael died, or when we thought he died, everyone blamed me. I was the one who should've gone on that survey, and if I, *'irresponsible Ren'* hadn't broken his leg, then Michael wouldn't have died. And of all people, Evie should've been the most resentful. But she wasn't. She was the only one who treated me like I was worth anything and welcomed me to my new role. If anything, that's when she went from being a friend to being a sister. And not just any sister, an older one. She looked after me and didn't have to."

Asa, somewhat stunned at hearing this, felt a wave of fondness and respect. Ren, of all people, opened up. Only Evie ever had deep conversations like this with him, and a certain comfort flushed through his mind. He wasn't alone.

Ren needed to know he wasn't alone either.

"Well, that's something we have in common," Asa said calmly. "I was an only child, too. Of course, I didn't earn the pleasure of being spoiled as I would've liked, but I get it; it's hard when you feel like there's no one. There's not much anyone can say to make it better or change things. And Evie, she's a sister. Was always there, talked with me to help me deal with—get through losing—"

He couldn't bring himself to say it. Not the name of the one person he ever fully opened himself to. The only person he felt that he was ever truly just himself around. The person he wanted to have a family with.

Because more than anything, Asa wanted a family.

"Asa, I uh," Ren dropped his twine.

"It's okay," Asa wiped a tear from his eye before Ren could see it. After all, this wasn't about him. "I get too emotional. I'm okay knowing that about myself."

"Yeah, you can be a bit of a crybaby," Ren smirked, but still put a comforting hand on Asa's back. "But I guess that's a good thing."

They both looked at the horizon, watching the waves on the lake, and then up at Neptune, its ever presence bearing down on them.

"So strange," Asa said. "To look up and know that there's no moon. We're the moon guarding that planet."

"Yeah, weird," Ren nodded in agreement. "So hey, just so that we're on the same page and all, because we agree that Evie was like a sister and we were both lonely children, doesn't mean you're like my brother or anything, okay? Because if you were, you'd be like the annoying older brother who's like super smart, and cool, and too responsible, and makes the younger sibling look bad. And I can't have anything else to make me look bad. Alright?"

Asa laughed. "Alright, *brother*, I get it."

Ren brought his knees up, wrapping his arms around his legs. "Just don't let anything happen to you. Not that something will, but, you know. And you have to promise."

Asa tossed a finished log onto his pile of supplies. "I won't make promises I can't guarantee to keep, but I'll try."

"Good," Ren said. "I wonder if Evie's looking at Neptune like us. God, I wish she didn't leave. I wonder where she is, if she's even alive."

Asa shook his head. "I don't know. I hope so. I really hope."

But his mind tangled in a mess of what-ifs. Questions he needed to seek during the inquiry. Why did she flee in the night? What did she know that she felt she had to leave? Who, if anyone, drove her away? Their main objective was to get to the bottom of the deaths and avoid a riot of righteous anger. But he'd do more.

He'd get to the bottom of this. And answer the main question on all their minds.

Where did Evie go?

Chapter 19: The Grove

Sometimes, time has no meaning.

And then there's the occasion when it's everything.

Trudging on, Evie followed the edge of the lake, keeping her distance to avoid anyone spotting her. She doubted anyone searched; she knew the condition of their resources, and Lilith would never sacrifice the group for one wayward soul. No one was looking for her, and no one would.

That was how she wanted it.

Minutes, hours, it mattered not as it all blended together. Gratefully, the hunger did not hit her, and she drank little, conserving her water.

Need to be careful, she thought. *Spread the water intake so I don't become dehydrated. And if I run out, Asa showed me how to make the filter. I'll go to the shoreline and gather..*

Despite the ache in her legs and the exhaustion gnawing at her, she felt a relief at only being responsible for herself.

No rules, no laws to be broken, her thoughts sang. *I am truly free.*

And alone.

It was risky, not knowing how far the lake went or how far it would take to get to where the rains originated. But where there was rain, there had to be other resources. Another way to live on.

She continued, the wide flat lands stretching endlessly before her. She couldn't judge distance as she did on Earth because of Triton's curvature, which made it that more difficult to judge the location of the rains. She saw the clouds over the lake and kept them in her sights.

The voice did not speak as she continued her journey. No mocking quips or unsolicited advice to be had. Had it been only a couple of days ago that she desperately sought to rid herself of it?

She hated to admit it, and despite her reservations about hearing voices in her head, the voice had been helpful. It was right about the hab unit; she never should've gone in there. And everything it told her was always to her benefit. Its criticisms were not to harm, even if they injured her pride. The intuitions it gave her on individuals always came through. And the times she ignored it always ended in her wishing she'd chosen her words and actions more carefully.

"No regrets," she repeated to herself. "This was the right decision. Leaving was the right thing to do."

But she did regret it. She regretted abandoning Ren and Asa, her friends who supported her. She regretted leaving the people in Olena's hands for medical needs.

And most of all, she regretted leaving Michael.

She paused. "He was a jerk back there," she said, reminding herself.

It was midday and about time for a rest. She'd walked most of the first night and all of the first day. She was on day two, and her body felt it.

She took a spot that overlooked the lake, feeling the cool breeze coming off it. The waters reflected the cool green of Neptune and were streaked with the sun's orange-red.

The celestial positions have changed, she thought. That meant she'd changed direction. *I must've reached the end at some point, and I'm making my way around the other side.*

She pulled up her knees and rested her head on her arms. "He'll be better off without me," she said to no one. "And me without him. He left me once, I know that much now. No more distractions. He and I have a better chance of surviving alone. They all do."

Her heart swelled as she thought of him. Of his face... his smile... his touch. . .

"Oh god, this is stupid!" She buried her face. "Why the hell did I have to be friends with him? This is how people get hurt!"

No regrets, whispered in the wind.

"No regrets," she repeated again. "I cannot have regrets!"

Her resoluteness reaffirmed, and she stood.

I will live for myself.

*   *   *

What day was it? How much had she slept?

Pushing forward, she continued to walk. The only constant was the lake, always to her right.

The positions of Neptune and the sun continued to gradually change. The waves of the lake ever being pulled by the ice giant's gravity, and pushed back by Triton's own.

And then it happened. It started as a slight twinge in the pit of her stomach and a watering in her dry mouth.

The hunger.

I can't, not now, she thought. *Not till I find the place with the rains.*

Was this how it started for the others that began to eat again? Whatever was left of Vita-8 in her system must've worked itself through. Cravings took the forefront as she thought about the foods she used to eat on Earth.

Keep going, she reassured herself. *The origin of the rains has to be close.* She looked up to gauge her position. How far on the other side was she? It was getting harder to think as cravings kept intruding.

Little nibbles of her surplus food here and there. It ran out before she was ready.

Her mind wandered, and it was getting harder to focus. Was she hot? Or was she cold? She pushed the limits of her body along the unchanged landscape.

Barren of all but reeds and grass.

She stumbled to the lake's edge. She pulled on reed stems, her feet sinking into mud. Once a task with ease, she felt as though she were pulling lead apart as she struggled against the roots.

Must eat, her mind in a haze. *Need food.* She fell back, taking the reed root up with her. A tuber encrusted with mud, she did not hesitate to bite into it.

Mealy and bitter.

But it did not matter. She consumed it.

Not enough.

She pulled more, each one no more than a few bites. Despite eating her fill, they did not satisfy. Only staved off the cravings.

She continued walking. Each step heavier than the last.

Cannot sleep, she strained to take a step. *If I do, I may not wake.*

Exhaustion.

Hunger.

Thirst.

Such simple things to remedy were defeating her.

Monotony. Was she even awake? Everything looked the same and continued looking the same. The rain clouds grew broader, closer, but still she did not reach them.

Her ears rang, humming in the mental haze.

She fell forward.

Not now, she thought. *Not now, not when I'm so close.*

But was she close? She doubted and relinquished the hopeful thought.

Her ears continued to ring and hum.

Humming?

Those weren't her ears.

A chirp here, and the hum of buzzing wings there.

She lifted her head.

Had she not fallen, she wouldn't have noticed, not with her mind in such a hungry haze. Insects, arthropods, and other such critters fled away from her in the grass.

Living creatures!

"I'm not alone," her voice rasped.

Hope filled her chest, revitalizing her energy.

Arms shaking, blood pulsing through her body, she pushed herself to her feet. *Maybe I'm stronger than I thought.*

She continued forward, seeing the life that surrounded her. The insects, arthropods, crawling things, and flying vermin parted from her path, as though she were parting the waters.

The grass softened, and she noticed other greenery growing with it. Leafy ferns and long-stemmed plant bodies with buds yet to open. Shades of green gradually diversified, a rainbow of chlorophyll stretching around her.

Then she saw it. Like a white dot, one of the buds on the stemmed plants was open. She bent over, holding it in her hand, but not plucking it. No bigger than a dime in diameter, the threads of thin petals stretched forth from a yellow center. It tickled her skin, caressing her palm against the tender breeze, and a sweet floral scent wafted up her nose. Familiar, like a piece of home.

Beautiful.

And though her eyes ached to do so from the joy, she did not shed a tear.

She gently left the flower and continued on her way.

All too soon, the landscape was dotted with white flowers. Patches of yellow speckled among them as they grew more numerous. Then other colors debuted, vibrant violet and pale pink. All the flower heads tilted toward the sun, as though they worshiped it and were trying to grow closer to their god.

The land inclined and dipped as the flowers blossomed in numbers, rolling with hills. Gradually, they became steep peaks of rocks jutting through the greenery. The rocks streaked in color, granites sparkling with feldspar mixed with bands of gray and ocher. Sandstones heavy with oxidized iron cut through with vibrant reds.

The vegetation continued to grow, becoming increasingly difficult for Evie to venture. Ivies and heavy-leaved bushes appeared, starting waist high, but quickly becoming taller than her. Like walking through a living geologic timeline, the plants and wildlife continued to diversify and become more numerous. She saw the flutter of a feathered wing and the scuffle of a small reptilian creature flee from her as she pushed through, tearing down thin branches that blocked her way.

And then she saw it.

Ivy climbing up a tree.

It was a young tree by Earth's standard, and not exceedingly tall. She did not trust herself to climb it without breaking. But seeing its deciduous leaves open to the world filled her with something she could not describe. The slight musical scraping of its branches floating in the wind brought her back to missing something she did not realize she missed. Even before awakening on Triton, it was long since she heard the wind sing through trees. The cold, desolate journey through space had taken her from their song. Although their transport ship had recordings of it to pass the time, it was never the same as standing in the presence. The peace of it, the scent of its dewy bark, and the damp soil it burst from.

Trees like this are sexual in nature, she remembered. *Which means there are more trees that give birth to this one's seed.*

She pushed forward, sharp tips of vegetation scratching her arms. It was too tall for her to see ahead, but all of it was too weak for her to climb. Fortunately, she came upon another tree—and then another—and then more.

They were taller, more numerous, and free to grow as they pleased. As the trees turned more numerous, the undergrowth shrank, and she was able to walk with ease. A grove, bursting with cool shade and life.

Leaves padded her path, and a canopy dimmed the way in a comforting way. Beams of the red sun broke between tree branches, giving the illusion she was walking during sunrise on Earth. The fresh, moist air and dew sitting on the vegetation gave way to the illusion. For the first time since beginning her mission, she felt at home.

A droplet of dew caught her eye as it glinted against something indigo.

A patch of berries grew beneath one of the trees. A treasure in the woods that surrounded her.

She ran to it, the animalistic cravings overtaking her body. She ignored the thorns that pricked her fingers as she pulled the berries from the small bush and hungrily stuffed them in her mouth.

The satisfying sweet and tart flavor caressed her tongue and throat as she swallowed. Nothing in her entire life ever tasted so good.

After eating her fill, she saw a puddle of rainwater beside it.

Kneeling low to the ground, she drank the crystal clear water and washed her hands and face.

She lay back, the cushion of forest floor her bed.

"I made it," she said. "To the place where it rains. I made it."

She closed her eyes, taking it all in.

Paradise. Her own Garden of Eden.

But how did it grow to this level of complexity if the eclipse killed all surface life?

She sat up, taking in her surroundings.

This place shouldn't be here.

The voice had not spoken to her once since she started her journey. She felt a dropping sensation through her body, a sudden anxiety.

Something was wrong with this place.

Movement from the corner of her eye.

She jumped to her feet, reinvigorated from her short rest and fear that suddenly coursed through her.. Her heart pumped, adrenaline pulsing through her.

The Xyelex isn't here, she thought, looking around, remembering how she last felt like this, right before entering the hab unit.

Another movement from the corner of her eye, this time catching the flutter of white cloth.

She turned quickly.

"Who's there?" she called out. "Show yourself!"

No one. Just trees, vegetation, and small creatures expected in a habitat such as this.

Impossible, she thought. She remembered when she saw that flutter of white cloth before. When she first emerged from the lake and looked upon Triton's horizon, she saw him.

The man in white.

"I know you're there," she called. "Stop hiding and making me feel like I'm crazy. I saw you before, and I saw you just now. You're real! You have to be!"

She blinked.

In an instant, no more than ten feet away, a man appeared before her.

The man in white.

Until this moment, lingering doubts told her he was a figment of her mind, a wishful thought. An indescribable figure her mind conjured, looking in the distance.

Yet here he was.

She couldn't look away from him.

"W-who are—," she tried to get the words out, but so strong was the gaze of this otherworldly being that she stuttered, unable to think of the right things to say. She'd seen the man in white from afar, and now up close she feared his reality—that his existence rang in a new truth for this plane. It was a comfort knowing that all life she knew was of Earth, familiar in her mind's eye. But this being's silent presence screamed at her; the first truly intelligent presence not of Earth, for nothing about him seemed Earth-like, even if humanoid in appearance. Although she didn't believe in auras, there was an aura in his presence that told her he wasn't of Earth or Triton. And more importantly, she assuredly knew she did not hallucinate his image.

He had cool, silver platinum hair carefully slicked back, tucked neatly behind his ears. His face was young and fair, with an iridescent quality to his unbelievably flawless skin. But his eyes were deep-set, as though they'd seen a thousand eons come and go. Pupil-less and with irises neither blue nor green, but a muted in-between that reflected a silvery glimmer, like Earth's moon during the pale dawn.

His clothes were loose, sleeves and pants gently floating within the smallest hint of a breeze. Neat, clean-cut, and washed white, with subtle trims of frosted silver.

His gaze pierced through her, and she felt her chest turn cold.

His mouth parted slightly.

And there was music.

Not music she recognized, but a melodic sound and his mouth moving along with it. Syllables? It was hard to tell with the smoothness of his voice.

Evie stood dumbfounded.

The creature stopped speaking in his melodic tones. His eyebrows came together, looking her up and down, a predator inspecting its prey.

Evie tried to move, but fear stiffened her legs. Why couldn't she will herself to move? His penetrating gaze held her in place as he approached.

Move, move! She screamed in her mind, but her body still refused to obey as both fear and curiosity continued to hold her. As real as he was, her inquisitiveness wanted to know more, pushing aside all reasonable thought of danger. Always a trade-off for knowledge, and she always willing to pay.

He came within arm's length, still inspecting her.

A pounding began, a thumping in her ears. She felt each individual breath as her heart beat so hard she thought it would pound through her chest. She kept still as his steps slithered around her, her spine shuddering as he walked behind. She felt his presence come closer still when she felt a warm breath hit her neck, and the light fabric of his clothes brush against her arm.

In an instant, his face was before her, his nose almost brushing against hers. His eyes were wide, filling her entire view.

She felt his hands wrap around her head, covering her ears. For how soft they looked, they were strong, and if she struggled, she knew they could hold her in place.

He's going to break my neck, she thought, intrusive visions of him twisting and snapping her head filled her mind. *I cannot break away.* Why did she always take the risk? Because even when death was a possibility, it never seemed present.

Yet now it was.

I'm going to die, and his eyes are the last thing I'm going to see.

She didn't want them to be. She closed her eyes.

And thought of Michael.

His smile, soft and gentle, the way he used to look at her. She pushed aside the looks of disdain, the loathing he all too often threw at her before their fall. If these were her last moments, she wanted to remember how they were. How his hand felt around hers in their evening walks around their home.

Home. Oh, how she yearned to be home, or have it all as it used to be before she fled their home-world. Just to remember it, not bits and pieces. The Triton mission was only an excuse for her to flee from what happened. She yearned for the times when she felt Michael's snug embrace and tenderly kissed her head. How it used to be before—before he—

No, a foreign voice, authoritative and smooth, ordered within her mind. *You will look at me. Think only of me! You'll hurt yourself again!"*

The creature's hands turned hot, and everywhere they touched, they stung, as though electrical impulses were shooting from them into her mind. She could not pull away, the impulses somehow paralyzing her in place.

The impulse hit her eyes, and they were forced open, ripping her away from images of Michael and home.

His eyes bore into hers.

Yes, said the voice. *Look only at me.*

Her eyes rolled back.

And everything turned black.

Chapter 20: Ghosts of the Past

Night.
Or at least night for Triton.
Neptune glowed its jade green in the sky. 4020 already noticed that nights were shorter on Triton than they were on Earth. It was only a matter of time until the eclipse arrived. For now, the short nights and long days were a blessing, giving them precious daylight to work by.

Michael is so kind, Olena thought, lying back on her makeshift bedroll. *Easiest one I've taken a statement from so far.*

Michael was her latest interview for the inquiry. While other survivors in the excursion party were hostile, demanding justice for the dead, Michael showed her kindness. Something she'd not known for a long time.

Just because I'm old doesn't mean I'm delusional, she'd told one of the people she interviewed, who started screaming at her. *I've performed dozens of inquiries, and I know what to ask at this point and what to look for. Yes, I know Evie's gone, and no, I'm not saying she's innocent.*

The inquiry was getting hostile. When Lilith filled her in on the situation, she hoped the inquiry would appease the people.

But that wasn't the case. She hadn't even scratched the surface.

4020 was getting more antsy by the minute. Complaints were increasing, and accusations of minor offenses were running rampant. She tried to keep those she interviewed on task, but it was becoming impossible. People were no longer demanding statements and interviews. They wanted results and answers to questions she couldn't answer.

Especially after she interviewed Lilith.

Earlier that morning, Olena met with Lilith and got her statement on the events that happened. Simple, straightforward. It was perfect and matched the others she'd previously spoken to.

But something was off. No honest person's stories ever matched that well.

When she spoke to Lilith, she seemed too perfect. Stoic at the right moments, and tearful at the ones people should feel grief for. She took full accountability for decisions and defended her team.

A perfect leader.

That was the problem.

"I just want to clarify a few things, Commander," Olena had said at the end of the interview. They were in Lilith's tent. People were stationed outside to maintain a distance to decrease eavesdropping.

"Anything," Lilith said graciously.

"So, Theo's death, " Olena continued, "she fell victim to the thing you call the Xyelex. The sentient fungus? It just doesn't make sense."

"What doesn't make sense?" Lilith looked confused. "I apologize if I wasn't clear."

"It's the marching order," Olena said. "Evie and Michael were ahead, Theo behind them, and you were in the rear. Wouldn't the Xyelex have taken you before Theo?"

"Did I say that?" Lilith laughed. "I'm sorry, some of the details are hazy since we were fleeing for our lives."

"It just doesn't make sense."

Lilith's face dropped. "Are you insinuating—"

"I never insinuate," Olena said. "I'm just stating facts from what you said."

Lilith's eyes shot. "So you're calling me a *liar*?"

Olena didn't like how Lilith said liar. Disconcerting in a way she had never heard Lilith speak before. "No, no, of course not, Commander. We all trust you. I'm on your side. I want this query to end as much as you do."

Lilith took a breath. "I apologize, the pain of their deaths and Evie's abandonment is still fresh in my mind. Forgive me." She wiped a tear with her sleeve.

"I understand," Olena said. "I *am* a medical doctor. I know how people react to grief."

She waited a moment for Lilith to pull herself back together.

"I just have one more question about the Xyelex," Olena said.

"Yes," Lilith smiled pleasantly.

"So I think I understand the nature of the Xyelex, it's parasitic."

"It seems so."

"Knowing how parasites work, our teammates are their hosts," Olena said. "They could still be alive, and we hypothetically could retrieve them."

"No," Lilith simply said. "I doubt they're alive. If you saw how it took them, they couldn't have survived that. We need to stay away from that hab unit at all costs."

"But logically speaking," Olena continued.

"Logically speaking, that thing is dangerous," Lilith said. "We can't go back."

"But what if it's our fault?"

Lilith blinked. "What now?"

"What if it's our fault that thing is here?" Olena continued. "By what you said, this thing followed Evie and Theo from the restricted area on the hab unit, and possibly originated there. What if we were the ones who inadvertently brought in a contaminant and it evolved to this Xyelex? It basically had a millennium to do so. We're the ones responsible for it."

Lilith held her breath.

Olena waited for answers.

"I don't like hearing that," Lilith said. "I really don't."

"I can't help it if it's true."

"Is it?" Lilith glowered. "This has no evidence, so it's speculation at this point."

"I guess." Olena felt a tickle in her throat. "We would need to go back and—"

Her throat suddenly caught, and she coughed uncontrollably.

"Dr. Solovyóva," Lilith's eyes wide with concern, "are you alright?"

Olena took a swig of water, cooling the tickle in her throat. "I'm fine. Just my asthma acting up. Gets worse with age."

"Careful," Lilith said, leaning over Olena. "Don't let your ailment get the better of you. We don't have the resources to create treatments for asthma."

Olena took another swig of water. "I know. I'll be fine. Been dealing with it my entire life."

That was how the interview ended. She proceeded to interview others and finally Michael. And now, she lay on her bedroll, thinking about all the information she took in during the day.

And asked herself why Evie left.

Wonder why Michael and Evie don't get along? They are married after all. She probably doesn't appreciate him. And does marriage matter anymore? She looked across the encampment, through the firelight, to Michael's tent. *After all, Earth is gone. Does anything that happened there matter here?*

She thought things she knew her long-dead mother would've shamed her for.

I'm old, she thought. *It's useless to think those kinds of things. Need to stay on top of the inquiry.*

She thought about Lilith again. The marching order when Theo was taken by the Xyelex still bothered her, and Lilith never explained.

Something was missing.

Night drew on, and the encampment slept. The firelight dwindled and plumes of smoke piled upon it. A soft breeze made it dance and waft around the sleepers.

As Olena began to drift into sleep,

And heard steps slip by her.

Her eyes flew open.

Olena watched Lilith's figure move to the edge of the colony.

"Now, where are you off to?" Olena said to herself.

She stood, crouching low. Lilith had no reason to sneak away unless she was hiding something. And Olena would find out what it was.

I'll find what you're up to, she thought. *Just wait and see.*

She crept along, trying to keep up with Lilith.

And took a whiff of the smoke.

She coughed.

Blin, she thought. The sleeping area was arranged to be upwind of the fire pit to protect them from smoke inhalation, and she went right into its stream. *I've got to get away before it gets worse.*

She felt the muscles around her lungs tighten, her airways itch and burn as they constricted. This was how it always started: a small itch in her chest to full-on tightening and burning. And there was no inhaler to relieve her. She could calm it on her own if she controlled her breathing in a cool, clean place. But such a thing is easier said than done.

She wandered senselessly from the encampment, coughing to scratch the burning itch in her lungs and esophagus. No sense of direction, she didn't care. Anything to get away from the smoke.

Stop, she told herself, her head spinning. *Stay calm. This is a mild attack. You're clear of the smoke; you just need to relax. Rest your chest, breathe —breathe.*

She started to feel relief, although the irritation in her chest didn't dissipate. She knew she'd pay for it in the morning; there was always a price after her asthma attacks, especially with no medication. Her chest would ache for days, and she'd have to take it easy with physical labor. The lingering cough was the worst.

The commander probably heard me, she thought.

Why did no one else come to her aid? Did they not hear her?

Lightheaded, she sat and took control of her breath. The lightheadedness lessened. Darkness enveloped her.

She realized how far she had strayed from camp. The dim firelight was no bigger than her fist from her position. No wonder they didn't hear her.

Can't go back till that smoke dies down, she thought. *I'll just rest here. It's not like there's anything out here anyway.*

Foolish? Maybe, but she was too tired, too weary to think it through. *There's nothing out here; nothing in this new world.*

And then she saw him.

It was only a moment, far in the distance, opposite the encampment, a flutter of cloth blew in the wind, shrouding a man.

A man in white.

She blinked. He was gone.

Hallucinations, she took a deep breath, holding it in, then breathing out slowly. *Too much oxygen loss.*

And then she saw him again.

From the other corner of her eye, she saw the flutter of white cloth again.

This time, he didn't disappear.

Upon the horizon, he stood, a still silhouette in the glaring mantis green planet light. It was hard to make out details from this distance in the dark, but the bright figure couldn't be hidden. It was most definitely a man from her perspective, so oddly pale even compared to her, that the planet's light made his skin and white clothes a sickly shade of jade.

I don't know this man.

Leshy. Spirit. Trickster. She threw away such superstitions in her childhood. But somehow, the dark of the night and this alien world dug out her old fears. Bedtime tales were for children, and this creature made her feel like one again.

She shied away from his presence.

Quite a sad thing to not believe in people; to not trust them, a distant memory spoke to her. A mentor, a teacher.

Foolishness, she remembered telling her mentor. *You cannot depend on anyone. They will always turn on you, always hurt you for being different. For not being like them.*

And she saw herself as a child again, hiding under a blanket in the woods.

Léshy gónitsya za tobóy! Bud' ostorózhna, léshy poymáet tebyá! She heard the bullies from school taunt when they chased her away during summer camp. *The leshy's coming to get you! Watch out, the leshy will get you!*

A leshy, a forest spirit known to trick and mimic voices. Humanoid, it taunted and led the travelers to become hopelessly lost to their doom.

Léshy poymáet al'binósku, uródku! She continued to hear them taunt in her memory. *The Leshy will get the albino girl, the freak.*

All those years, an irrational fear stayed in her heart ever since the other children chased her into the woods that night. She made it to morning, and desperate adults found her curled in a ball on the ground under her blanket. She told them what happened, how the other kids from camp did this to her. But it was the parents of those other kids who found her, and her words went through empty ears.

Never any justice.

A lifelong mission to prove them wrong—to be better than them. She focused on becoming a medical doctor, researching all she could. Never giving a care in the world to those who looked at her strangely or told her that her poor vision would limit her. She still did it; she got her medical doctorate. And when she had enough money, she used surgery to fix her eyesight. But there were still wounds deeper than surgeries could touch.

And a never-ending resentment toward Cunningham. Younger than her, Evie logged more medical hours because she was born lucky with perfect eyesight. And thus trumped Olena's seniority, becoming the lead astromedic on the Neptune mission, even with a doctor title.

A role that should've been hers. No end to the discrimination against what she was.

You know what you are, a strange voice sounded in her head.

Léshy poymáet al'binósku, uródku! The children's voices sounded in her mind again. *The Leshy will get the albino girl, the freak.*

The man in white continued to stand, watching her. She made out no facial features, but she clearly saw him raise his hand, beckoning her—a colorless, pale hand, more so than hers.

Her anger started as a pinprick and grew. And in that moment, her fear mutated to something far more ferocious. Who was this creature that beckoned her? No, not beckon, *mock*. He was no human, she felt it deep in her. And from the corners of her mind, she heard a laugh, a snide chortle that ridiculed her albinism.

"Who are you?" Olena said, feeling her anger growing. "You think you can scare me? I'm not afraid of you!"

She chased him. The tightness in her chest warned, but she wouldn't have it. Her anger begged her to stop him.

Léshy gónitsya za tobóy! Bud' ostorózhna, léshy poymáet tebyá! The past voices continued to mock. She wouldn't hide like she did as a child. She'd show this thing, whatever it was; she was strong. She was no longer the pathetic little girl who'd hide under a blanket in the woods.

As she grew closer to him, he faded like a mirage.

She made it to the edge of the lake and slowed her pace.

"Where," a huff, "are," another huff, "you!"

Her vision blurred, and she blinked hard.

Damn, she thought. This happened sometimes. Her eyesight ailing her at the most inconvenient times. Even the best surgeries never fully cured her. Regressions still happened momentarily, mainly when her asthma symptoms occurred.

A glow of white flickered ahead, just upon the ledge overlooking the lake.

She blinked, and her vision focused.

There he was, clearer than day—the man in white standing on the ledge.

The pain in her chest tightened. Even this momentary rest wasn't enough to sate it.

She blinked again, and he was gone.

"No!" she rasped.

Despite her entire body telling her not to do it, she picked up her pace. It wasn't far, the ledge. *I can't let this creature escape me,* she thought. Not this daring creature with the audacity to use voices to taunt her. She'd teach it a lesson it'd never forget.

Each step was a brick, weighing her down as she made her way up the ledge. Every movement of her legs added more bricks to her feet, the pain in her chest spreading to the rest of her body as her muscles continued to stiffen. Each breath scratched and forced a dry cough from her esophagus.

Still breathing, she told herself. *Still alive. I can make it.*

And when it felt that she couldn't take another breath, she took one last step onto the edge of the ledge.

She fell to her knees, coughing, trying to control her breath. Her vision blurred in and out.

Not good. She heard the lapping of waves below. *I let my emotions get the better of me.* She forced her chest muscles to replicate the wave pattern, controlling her breath.

Alright, she felt slight relief between coughs as she controlled her breath. *If I can keep this up, I'll be okay. Take it easy—in—hold—out—cough cough—in—hold... "*

As she breathed, she glanced over the edge, down to the lake below.

A reflective pool, a mirror of the night. A shadow of the ledge, and waves distorting the images of the sky and Neptune.

The man in white nowhere to be found.

"Bud' ty próklyat!" Cough-cough. Olena swore, trying to push herself to her feet. She failed and fell to the ground. "Chort tebyá poberí! Pokazhís', kozyól!"

The waves below continued to pulse, and her heart felt as though it would rip from her chest from the forced breathing. *I'll die if I don't force it.*

As her vision blurred, the image of the man in white taunted in her mind. A man with skin paler than hers with colorless hair.

"How dare you," Olena spat between coughs, her voice rasping, "mock me—"

She tried to stand again and fell, holding her chest. "Show yourself," her voice sandpaper against stone. "No right!" Her anger grew to uncontrollable rage. She'd suffocate, but she would not do so silently. She spent too much of her life silent. Her voice would be heard. "No right—" cough, cough "—sozdániye d'yávol'skoye!"

"Every right."

Olena lifted her head.

Lilith was there, making her way up the ledge.

Olena was saved.

Her stiff muscles fought, pushing her down. But she fought it, lifting her arm to her savior —the hero of Antarctica, come to lend aid. With her, she'd surely make it. "Commander," her voice no louder than a whisper. "Co-mman-der, h-help."

Lilith stood over her, her dark outline harsh against Neptune in the sky. Olena's vision was too blurry to see her face.

"I warned you," Lilith's voice was smooth and condescending, patronizing. "Your little ailment will get the better of you if you're not careful."

Olena struggled to take in a full breath, her coughing fully taking over.

"Hel–" she couldn't get the word out. The weight of her muscles pulled her hands down.

Lilith leaned in close. "Do you finally see what you are? A burden, a genetic carrier of weakness. It makes my stomach churn when someone like you can't help themselves."

Lilith straightened her stance. "There is mercy in such ruthlessness. For the sake of our survival. For the sake of humanity's ongoing existence. We've survived to make humanity stronger, better, and smarter.

"You are not a part of that."

All it took was one swift kick. Before Olena knew it, a sharp pain enveloped her side, and the ground beneath her disappeared.

Lilith sent Olena into the lake depths below.

But Olena did not feel the cold sting of the water as she submerged. For she had already coughed her last breath.

Never to breathe another.

Chapter 21: The Wall

hy didn't you run? Someone asked.

Evie was on a cushion of vegetation.

She opened her eyes. For a moment, she thought she was on Earth, looking through leafy branches from under the backyard oak tree in the twilight evening.

"Michael, I—"

She stopped herself. Her vision focused. Those leaves weren't oak, and hints of cool green from the nearby celestial giant showed through the branches. Neptune was looking down on her..

She felt too dizzy to sit up.

Why didn't you run? Someone asked again, smooth and calm, like a father comforting a child.

The voice.

It came back.

"You're here," she said. "You sound different." The voice seemed all around her, but isolated at the same time. She rubbed the temples of her head. They ached.

Why didn't you run? The voice asked more adamantly this time. *I need you to answer.*

Evie groaned. Why was the voice different? It sounded the same, but also not. As though it had a locale other than her mind. It emanated from somewhere near her. Dizzy or not, she wanted to find it.

She sat up, scanning her surroundings.

And froze.

A few feet away on a boulder sat the fair humanoid creature, cross-legged and looking down on her. His facial expression a mask of stone, the stillness of an expressionless statue.

The man in white.

It does take you time to come around, doesn't it? He stared at her with his unblinking, piercing, pale eyes. The pupilless, silvery irises sending chills down her back. The voice was coming from him, and yet his mouth was serenely closed. *I half expected that to happen.*

He was the voice in her mind.

All of Evie's pain and dizziness ceased at that moment. Maybe it was the adrenaline, but she suddenly felt energy to defend. This was the creature that attacked her, grabbed her head, and messed with it, *hurt her.* Numbness spread to her shaking limbs as she snatched a fist-sized rock from the ground and jumped to her feet. She cocked her arm back, ready to smash or throw, whichever would save her from this being.

He tilted his head to the side, as though to express curiosity with his emotionless face. *What do you intend to do with that, young one?*

"It was you! What the hell did you do to me?" she demanded.

The man in white folded his arms mechanically, still not removing his gaze. *Interesting.*

"Interesting? Interesting!" Evie panted from the anxiety. Now she understood. He was piercing her brain telepathically. She wasn't insane like she thought. He made her feel that way. "Get out of my head!"

"Is this better?" He spoke aloud.

"Ahh!" She jumped back and threw her rock at him.

And promptly missed.

The man in white eyed her rock as it hit the boulder beneath him.

"How fortunate," he said steadily. "That wouldn't have been a pleasant experience if you made your mark."

Should she run? Even if she did, she had nowhere to go. At this point, no one in 4020 would help her, and this entire world moon was wilderness.

She was on her own against this thing.

And yet she still stood alive before it.

She thought a moment ago she'd die, but she didn't. Medically speaking, aside from her momentary headache and dizziness, she was not visibly harmed. This being could clearly kill her if he wanted, but refrained.

So far.

"What are you?" Evie asked wearily.

"Do you really want to know?" the man in white asked. "It seemed you were intent on killing me a moment ago. My, your kind is so very indecisive and fickle." His eyes narrowed, once again, the motion looked forced as though he were imitating. "Or is that just you, I wonder?"

"I…" She didn't know how to answer.

He was scanning her with his narrowed eyes. "Very interesting, very interesting," he spoke softly to himself.

"I-is that all you can say? I-interesting?"Evie said shakily. "Y-you still haven't answered m-my question." Why did she have to sound so nervous? She wanted answers, but forward assertiveness was never her strong point.

"In all fairness, I sought an answer to a question and disappointingly haven't received one." He paused thoughtfully. "Why didn't you run? You still haven't fled. Why?"

Was this otherworldly being really trying to initiate a verbal conversation with her? How would she answer? Did he know what she was thinking before she said it? What were his limits, if he had any? These were all things that kept her from taking off. Like staring down a tiger, a desperate attempt not to initiate its prey drive if she showed the slightest motion to run.

"To be honest, I haven't physically communicated for a long while," he forced a sigh. Another action too rehearsed to look natural. "And not in a form like this. Quite laborious. When I came close, you were clearly scared, yet you stayed. Why?"

Did he even know how to act in front of a living thing like her?

And Evie finally grasped what was before her.

The man in white wasn't human. This wasn't even what he was supposed to look like. His colorless features, his forced motions and gestures, he was a photo negative. A pitiful attempt at copying a human.

And realizing this, she no longer felt any sense of endangerment, the knowledge bringing a strange comfort in escaping part of the unknown. But she still felt uneasy about fully letting her guard down. Nevertheless, she relaxed her shoulders. "You're something I've never encountered. In my experience, you don't gain knowledge by fleeing from its source. You seek it." She straightened her stance. "I want to know what you are—I want to know about this world; why it's here and what it is. Although I doubt you're native to it, you're here like I am, but you're not like me."

The man in white continued to sit still. His emotionless expression was alien even to someone like her, who did not cry and disliked showing her feelings.

"Language will no longer be a barrier between us," he said.

"Um, what?" It seemed so random for him to say that.

"What I did to you," he continued methodically. "I did not mean any harm. But humans do not communicate the same way my kind does. I had to learn." His mouth clamped shut. *Note, when I speak to your mind, it's not words you are physically hearing. You feel them. I had to learn how you physically form your language before I could physically speak it to you.*

"So you grabbing my head," Evie pointed to her temples, "that was you learning how to speak like me?"

"Precisely," he said aloud. He stepped lightly down from his boulder, barefoot. "I did not know you would lose conscience as you did. I miscalculated the stress of me absorbing your knowledge would have on your three-dimensional body. It's not often I've run into a kind like yours, and never from Earth."

He approached closer to Evie, and she saw the details of his clothes. Intricate patterns of celestial objects—suns, moons, and stars —woven into the trim and only visible upon closer inspection. The fabric itself looked so light and thin it was as though it floated, and would dissolve into thin air. And yet, it still appeared opaque. His hair floated with it, but still maintained its slicked-back appearance.

Evie stepped back as he came closer.

He paused. "Have I startled you?"

"You can read my mind, can't you tell?"

"I thought it was considered rude," he said. "You told me to get out of it."

"Then yes," she continued. "You startled me. You're just so, well, you're very…"

"My appearance is disconcerting to you."

"Well yeah," Evie said. "I've never seen anything like you."

"I appear colorless to you, more so than your compatriot," he held up an arm, gesturing to the whole of his body.

Is he talking about Olena?

"I will not skirt around it like your Earthkind does," he continued. "I do not have reservations or shame about physical features. I am not like your compatriot—her appearance is due to your kind's three-dimensional genetics."

"I know how genetics works," Evie said. "I'm an astromedic and I tend to human life."

"You are, aren't you," he reaffirmed and took another step closer to her. "I appear almost completely colorless to you because my form cannot completely configure itself to the visible light spectrum within this plane of existence. Were I to completely descend to that, then I would lose all connection to my former dimensions, and probably would suffer a kind of death as you would imagine on this plane."

Dimensions? She was actually speaking not to just another worldly creature, but a being formed from a higher dimension. *How much higher?* She wondered. Science definitively proved four, but theorized more, extending beyond the fifth. Most speculative math.

"How would you appear to me from five dimensions?" she asked. "What would you look like?"

"So concerned about physical appearance." He stated it as a fact, without disappointment or praise as if he expected nothing more from someone like her. "But clever of you to ask specifically about four dimensions. I'd appear as *all* the colors, from your observable spectrum and beyond, for I reflect white light. That is something three-dimensional eyes cannot perceive."

"Wow." Evie took a deep breath. "I think I need to sit down."

"That will do." He immediately dropped down and sat cross-legged.

"Okay then." Evie was not as graceful as she sat across from him.

He watched the trees, the wildlife around them, not seeming to have a care in the world.

"What's your name?" she asked. "You already know mine."

"A name," he said thoughtfully. He turned his gaze to her; it still felt unnerving to have him look at her with his pupil-less eyes. "I can think it to you, but even then I don't know of a word or emotion that would fully evoke who I am."

"Surely you are known by something," she said. "An identity to recognize you by."

"Identity," he said again thoughtfully, once again allowing his face to trail off and observe the wildlife curiously. "My name is Isaiah. Yes, Isaiah, that's what my name would be to you."

Evie thought back to Earth history and such a prominent name; biblical in nature, powerful to those who believed and followed Abrahamic religion. A deliverer of divine messages and a keeper of visions. Was that how he wanted to be known to her?

"That seems rather Earth-like," she pointed out.

"It is the name I find most fitting to my identity," he said. "And how I want you to recognize me, following your suggestion."

Evie felt foolish at him using her own words after questioning him.

"Alright then, *Isaiah*," she continued. Was he even paying attention? He seemed so distracted by an insect creature that flew by, she couldn't be sure. "How did you make this place?"

"Make this place?" Isaiah looked curiously. "So odd you should ask such a thing."

"This was a lifeless moon," Evie said. "And yet, I find you in this grove, and it's abundant with life. How did you create it?"

Isaiah seemed amused, even let out a chortle. The first bit of human emotion she observed. "Oh my dear Earth child, you assume far too much. I am but a humble servant. There are many a thing I wish to do, but even my powers are limited on this three-dimensional plane."

"So you didn't make," she gestured to the grove around them, "all of this."

"Not at all," he continued. "This was Triton going through its natural process."

"But why is it teeming with life on this side of the lake," Evie asked suspiciously, "with you at the center of it? The other side has barely anything."

"Be assured, I cannot create life," he said, his tone trying to be mournful but slightly missing its mark, "nor can I give it back if it's lost. I have *ways*, per se, of manipulating it, guiding it, even speeding up its process. But I cannot make it."

Isaiah went back to curiously observing, this time a small feathered bird above them, one Evie did not recognize. Like a North American finch, but the proportions in its beak and feet are slightly off, looking alien to her.

"The life here looks so much like Earth's." The wind brushed through the leaves and sang a song to them. "But also so different."

"It's exactly as it should be," Isaiah said methodically. "It's Triton's after all. All life is created in the same process, the same patterns, but always takes on its own identity to fit its environment. Maybe something like this existed once on your Earth, and took on similar features for this terrestrial world, but this creature is evolved for Triton."

"And you sped up the process?" Evie furrowed her brows.

"In a way," he said nonchalantly.

"Why?" She didn't like the sound of this ability, even more than his telepathic abilities. Dangerous if abused. "How?"

He blinked slowly, his expression too relaxed. Did he read her thoughts? Her fears and dangers of manipulating life? Would he do the same to her and others she cared about? To Michael?

"You don't need to fear me," he said. "I have no need or desire to interrupt Earthkind's processes. I've done so here because Triton was struggling, and it is my occupation to ensure this world's survival."

"Occupation?"

"Yes," he said, brilliant white teeth peaking through a slight smile. His face was starting to take on a more natural transition to expressions. Was he still imitating what he saw of her expressions? Evie suddenly felt an ebbing in her mind. *That is what my kind do.*

We're called Overseers, shepherds of worlds. We guide planets to flourish with life and prevent the extinction of planet races.

"Overseers?" She felt the draw of intrigue. "There's more of you?"

Yes. But not here.

"Why tell it to my mind?"

So that you with assurance would know I'm not lying, he continued, his still face somehow following his mental words. *That seems to be important to your kind, assurance of truth. In this medium, I am speaking to your heart and mind, your brain interpreting it into the words you will best understand. Perfect communication.* "But if you prefer physical communication, I can accommodate, but I cannot guarantee no misunderstanding as it were."

"Um, talking for now," Evie gritted her teeth nervously, drumming her fingers, not knowing what to do with them. "The mind thing is still a bit weird."

"Understandable."

There was a silence between them. Isaiah didn't seem to mind, patiently watching Evie.

She didn't like it. "You're much nicer than you were before."

"Nicer?" He looked slightly surprised.

"Kinder, I mean," she said. "What happened to all your sarcastic and condescending quips?"

He blinked, the surprise draining from his face. He didn't know how to look. A blank slate.

"You were always talking to my brain and making me feel stupid or insane," she said. "Like an all-powerful being that knew better than an inferior human."

"Oh," he said. "You mean my words are currently more acceptable from your perspective?"

"Sure," she nodded. "We'll go with that."

"You've been through much," he said, his tone somber but his face still impassive. "I know more about you and your kind since probing your mind for language. Do you want me to be condescending? Is that preferable?"

"No, no," Evie put her hands up defensively. "That won't be necessary. But I'll be honest, the lack of emotion is also unsettling to me. I'm doing my best here."

I told you, his inner voice smug. *Physical communication is prone to misunderstandings.*

"There it is," Evie pointed. "The condescending 'I told you so' quip."

I'm still learning; this three-dimensional form is new to me. He forced a friendly smile. "I'm doing my best here."

Using her words again. Maybe he wasn't that much different from her, also a stranger in an unfamiliar world. "Fair," she cracked a slight smile. "Well, we could stay and talk, or we could do something."

"Like what?" Isaiah carefully placed his hands on his knees. He looked like a human business executive, the way he placed his hands, waiting for an answer.

"Before I left the Community, we were preparing for an oncoming eclipse," she said.

"Yes," Isaiah's eyes lingered on the sky above. "That does seem to be an inevitability."

"I should do the same here on my own," she said. "Prepare."

Isaiah forced blinks. "Are you under the impression that you're staying here?"

Evie gave an anxious laugh. "Um, it's kind of the whole reason I left the Community."

"You did not leave your Community because of this place," Isaiah said, mouth straight and tight. "And you cannot stay here. But you knew that already, didn't you?"

"I can't go back," Evie said adamantly. "I left and there's no way I can return, not without, oh god, not without…"

Sudden flashes through her mind. She saw herself in the hab unit, the Xyelex's tendrils creeping around her, the dead eyes of those taken by it, their hands reaching for her—

—the red door from her past, forcing itself into the memory.

"No, *no!*" she shook her head, holding her temples. The ache spread into her eyes, stinging them. Her mental wall cracked, pieces breaking and stabbing her memories.

Allow me, Isaiah's inner voice cut through all of it.

He stood, reaching his arms over to her.

She almost half expected his hands to go right through her. He took her hands from her temples and gently pulled her to her feet. Until this point, she still held doubts about his existence. But he was real, and he was a physical being, with soft hands much like any patient she dealt with.

Her pain was so immense, she did not back away or stop him. She faced him, wanting anything to make this mental pain subside.

Close your eyes, he said.

She did.

Suddenly, she was no longer in the grove. Neither of them was. They were both free-standing in an abyss, fog licking their legs.

And rising from the fog was an immense stone wall. Parts of it cracked, fragments falling like drips of water.

"Quite an immense structure you've made." Isaiah walked up to the wall. He looked impressed at the structure.

"I didn't make that," Evie said. "How did we get here?"

"We haven't moved," he said. He jumped, gliding up the wall and gracefully sitting upon the top. "This is all you—your mind."

"Explains why you're more animated."

He gave a clever smile. "My being is much more suited to express itself through the mind, and I want you to see the true me."

Evie picked up a broken piece that fell into the fog.

"Those are what's causing you pain," Isaiah said from above. "Those broken pieces stab you every time they break from the wall. I can fix the cracks temporarily, stop the broken parts from falling off, but it will only last for so long. It will have to come down eventually."

"This thing?" Evie looked about and saw a sledgehammer leaning against the wall. She approached it. Although it was clearly heavy beyond her own strength, she easily picked it up.

"I wouldn't do that yet." Isaiah looked down cautiously. "Unless you're ready, and given how sturdy this wall is, it won't come down, no matter how hard you hit. You'll only cause more pieces to chip away and stab you."

"How will I know when I'm ready?" She tightened her grip on the sledgehammer. "I want this thing down."

"You can't force it." He stood and beckoned her upward. "Come, I want to show you something."

The wall was easily fifty feet high. "I can't make that."

"It's your mind," he smiled cleverly again. "You can do anything."

Evie felt the weight leave her. The urge to jump filled her very being, and she willed it. Before she knew it, she flew upward and landed gently beside Isaiah.

The wall wasn't wide, only a foot in depth. Yet, no vertigo overcame her. She felt perfectly balanced beside him.

Curiosity compelled her to look beyond the wall, to see what her mind was shielding from her.

She saw nothing but fog.

"I don't see anything," she said, frustrated.

"Exactly," he said, standing beside her, crossing his arms, and tucking his hands into his sleeves. "You won't. It doesn't matter what side you stand on; you won't see anything till your wall comes down. And you've built a very strong one. Yes, there's cracks, but that's not enough. Even I can't penetrate it. It's not going to budge."

Evie shook her head. "All the more reason I shouldn't go back to the Community. My mind's broken."

"No," he said patronizingly. "Guarded. You can bring down this wall at any time, but I can tell you, you won't."

"How can *you* tell?" she said wryly.

"It would've come down the moment you willed it," Isaiah said. "There's clearly a part of you that isn't willing. That's why it's only cracked." He pointed to a newly developed fissure beneath their feet. "Until you come to terms with all parts of yourself, it will stay put."

"Come down," she ordered and stomped on the crack. She knew it was useless, but frustration got the better of her. "I hate not remembering anything."

Isaiah didn't look convinced. "I highly doubt you do. There's a reason the wall is here. "

Evie huffed. All this figurative gibberish symbolism annoyed her. She liked things straightforward, things with a solution. If someone was sick, there was a prognosis. Always an answer, even if it was hard to identify.

This was near impossible.

"Why is this stupid wall up in the first place?" she said. "Like, I get that it's not actually a real wall, but why is it here?"

Isaiah blinked conspicuously. "What are you afraid of?"

Afraid? She wasn't afraid.

"I'm not," she said. "I can't afford to be."

"You're human," he said matter-of-factly. "All humans fear something. Hence," he gestured around them, "your wall."

"I'm practical," Evie said. "I made the most logical decision—removed myself from the situation and gave the Community a better chance of survival and satisfied their justice."

"Satisfied their justice?" Isaiah pulled his hands from his sleeves. He smiled triumphantly. "The lies we tell ourselves. Maybe we'll get somewhere with you."

Just beyond the wall, the fog stirred. Neurological violet lightning shot down from above with a startling crack into the fog, and murmurs sounded from it. A dozen or so voices arose, and members from 4020 stepped from it. Familiar faces shadowed gray, masked with rage, holding torches high as though on an ancient witch hunt. Their murmurs turned to mobbish yelling, all demanding the same: *justice for the dead.*

The mob was led by four translucent beings wearing 4020 jumpsuits, their bodies infected by hot fungal tendrils. The four taken by the Xyelex.

They pointed up the wall at Evie, leading the crowd closer, repeating the same word: *blame.*

Not far behind the mob stood Michael, his face also gray and sullen. He didn't join the crowd, but hung his head in disappointment, refusing to look at Evie.

He walked away, not looking back.

Much like he once before.

The red door appeared just beyond him. He opened it and walked through.

On the other side, he fell, much like he did the day she watched him fall through the broken ice.

Evie's throat tightened. She thought of crying, but didn't.

"Leaving before the pain comes," Isaiah said. "You couldn't escape it before, could you?"

"No," Evie shook her head, looking at the red door Michael disappeared through.

"Twice he hurt you," Isaiah said. "And twice you persevered. Why not face it again?"

The mob gathered beneath them. Their yells carried up with the torches they threw at her, but never reached.

Evie sighed. "I know what it is to hurt, and I hate it. I don't want to feel it again."

" 'Better to love once than never at all.' Is that not a saying from your Earth?"

"No," Evie said. "That's not always true."

"You refuse to acknowledge what happened that day with Michael behind the red door?" Isaiah said. "Is it really that much more painful than when you thought he died?"

"Yes!" she yelped. She clenched her fists, angry. More Neurological lighting struck down, stirring the fog. "It was worse, so much worse!"

Lightning struck them on top of the wall.

The moment it struck, Evie found herself transported in front of the red door.

Isaiah stood beside her. "Do you still want me to fix the cracks?"

She hesitated. She was there again, in front of the same red door, the one to her home, the day it happened.

"Will it stop the pain?" she asked. "If I go in?"

"It won't stop it," he said. "But it will make it manageable. You have to open a wound to clean the infection before it can properly heal."

She held her breath. "Fix them."

"Then allow me in."

She reached for the door handle.

A scene unfolded from the fog, replaying in front of her like a sick joke. The memory was exactly as it was the day it happened. But it included Isaiah just out of the corner of her eye, ever watching.

She hesitated again.

"I can't mend the cracks if you stop," he said, staying just barely in sight. "Let me in."

She felt a twinge of pain in her temples. Another stab. She held her head; the pain she felt in her physical body seeped into her mental being. He was right; it could only be kept at bay for so long.

She lowered her guard. Anything to stop the pain.

She no longer controlled herself presently, the memory taking hold of her being. She was there, not just reliving it exactly as it was. Her last day of residency at the hospital, for she was preparing to leave for the UNSF Triton mission. A promise that the mission would bypass residency and acknowledge her as an astromedic. One where they'd be hailed as heroes, bringing back a miracle substance they knew little about, other than it could save all humankind. Her dream home is ready to close to a new owner, with her and Michael scheduled to leave together for Europe. All disputes resolved, so they would leave as wife and husband, together through it all, to accomplish the greater good.

But opening the red door to her home changed all that.

She pushed it, and Michael stood there waiting with packed bags.

"I almost left before you got home," he said. "But I thought I'd do you the courtesy of telling you so you wouldn't worry and go looking for me."

"What?" Evie was confused. Why was he waiting with packed bags?

"I've made arrangements," he said.

"No," she said. "I thought we decided to look past it. We'd sell the house, I'd leave residency, and you'd leave your lab. We'd go together."

"We will both be on the mission," he said. "I'd never ask you to give up that opportunity, and I know you'll never ask me to. But we won't be together."

Evie shook a melting pot of emotions: rage, disappointment, fury, grief. How could he do this? Why would he do this?

"But that was a last resort, if we couldn't work things out," she sounded desperate. "If we couldn't—"

Michael shook his head. "I can't take it."

"So you're just going to give up?"

"I'm tired."

"But if we love each other."

"I don't love you."

Everything blanked. She couldn't form words; she couldn't move. What did he just say?"

"Evie, I'm leaving," he said, grabbing the handle of his bag. "I don't love you, and I don't think you've loved me for a long time."

"W-we promised," her lip quivered. "You promised to always love me. You promised to always stay with me."

"You broke that promise long before I did," he began to walk forward. "And I don't want to stay in a loveless relationship."

She stepped in front of him, and he side-stepped her.

"Don't make this harder," he said, averting his gaze. He became self-poised, perfectly conducted in his stance and tone. He masked.

And that made her fury boil over.

"Harder?" she said. "You say you don't love me and leave right before the mission?"

She felt tears, but she pushed them back. She wouldn't show weakness, not now when he was hurting her.

But he saw through it, shaking his head.

"You don't cry," he said. "You never did. And you won't now. Not even for me, and that hurts."

"And you pretend," she crossed her arms. "You lead people on to think everything's okay, lie to pacify them, and then do this out of the blue. That's worse."

"Goodbye." Michael walked past her.

And right through the open front door.

Evie looked back, hoping he would too, and show the tiniest hint of remorse for doing this to her. For convincing her to sell their home, to leave her career, to go to another world with him.

But he didn't.

*   *   *

The mental fog enveloped the scene, the memory fading.

All melted around them, and Evie and Isaiah stood upon the wall again, the voices of the mob beneath dying into silence.

"That was more painful than when you thought he died?" Isaiah asked curiously.

She continued looking into the fog where the red door had been. "Yes."

"That seems rather odd."

"Not really," she said, the pain still fresh, the wound reopened. Her heart bled. "I lost him twice. Once, when he said he didn't love me, and again when he fell through the ice. The first time losing someone is always harder than the second. The first time, you're unprepared, unequipped to handle it. The second, you've felt loss. You know grief, you know pain. And you know how to push it away."

The mob beneath was gone, and the cracks in the wall disappeared.

But the wall still stood.

"I still don't remember everything," she said. "That's why the wall is still here, isn't it?

Isaiah nodded. "That was painful, what you just recovered."

"I can't believe I let you see that." She sighed and sat, dangling her legs over the side. "God, I must be stupid to let you in like that. I barely know you."

"But you do know me." He stood over her, like a father looking disconcerted by his child. "We've been communing for some time, haven't we? Do you still feel the pain?"

She rubbed one of her temples.

"No," she said. "It's gone. But I don't get it."

"What escapes your understanding?" he asked, slightly tilting his head. "It all seems pretty straightforward."

She whipped her gaze up to him, brows furrowed. "Why help me?"

He came down to her level, sat beside her, his flowing clothes floating around him like water. "I have reasons."

"It's extremely sketchy someone like you would be interested in helping me," she said. "What's the catch? I'm like a pest compared to your being."

He let out a small laugh. "Pest? Do not your people take interest in things they find inferior?" he said. "Such as those who study creatures and species? Do they not authentically care for them?" Evie expected it to be condescending, but even his use of *inferior* didn't make it so.

He was genuine.

"But I don't want you to think of me like a pet or an insect to study," she said. "I'd like to think I have more dignity than that."

"I don't," he said plainly. "I am genuinely invested."

"I still don't get it," she kicked her legs freely. "But I guess I shouldn't complain when I receive extra help, even if I have reservations."

Isaiah looked at her, eyes filled with concern. "You have every right to be suspicious, to have reservations. No one, nothing gives help freely. There is always a trade-off of sorts, even if it's mutual. There are laws we all must abide by, no matter what plane we are in. All things must abide by the laws of the dimension it's within, or be utterly destroyed. Such is the nature of existence."

Evie froze. "Should I fear you?"

He didn't seem mad, or even hurt by the question. In fact, he seems delighted that she asked.

"Fear is a matter of perspective," he said. "Yes, always have reservations. But I intend you no harm, child of Earth. I hope I've proven that. I have a goal, an objective in mind for Triton. All overseers do. You are a part of that objective. Your medical skills among your people make you worth more than you realize. You need them, but more importantly, they do need you."

"Why do you even care if the humans here survive?" Evie looked into the mental fog beyond them. It swirled and turned into the Community, the people working, growing, and it became something more—a town? A city? No, it grew into a civilization, the second chance for humanity and for Triton.

"It seems you already know," Isaiah smiled, looking at her vision. "Humans are among the most destructive beings I've encountered. But they're also the obverse. They're the greatest cultivators of planets in your known universe. For Triton to succeed, it will need the humans who are here. And they need you."

"They don't need me," she said.

He looked her in the eye. "I'll help you, but will you help me make this vision a reality? Help me learn how to use my physical form?"

A feeling swelled in Evie as she observed her vision of Triton growing into humanity's home world. Isaiah looked at it proudly, glancing sideways at her with his clever smile. This being, this dimensional alien was nothing she ever expected. And yet, she no longer feared him. Instead, she felt something grow; a kinship of sorts. Nothing romantic like she had with Michael, but a deeper affinity than fair-weather friends.

A kindred spirit.

"Yes."

Chapter 22: The Boy Who Grew Up

Young Michael Smith, by all accounts, was a perfect child. All the Smith children were. Well taught, well brought up, smarter than a whip, and inherited the best of their parents' good looks. No one was finer than those Smith children.

Especially the eldest of the lot. The brother Michael never lived up to.

Fat numbers blared off the handheld screen Michael's dad held. "Hundred, good." Mr. Smith's weekly grade check. "Good, another hundred, and yes hundred."

Fourteen-year-old Michael wanted to play sports this quarter. He was more than qualified, but his parents thought otherwise. Extracurriculars never took the place of triple-digit grades.

"Looks like you're doing well so far," his dad smiled, not taking his eyes off the screen. "Maybe sports are in the picture this upcoming quarter."

Michael did not react. He stood still as his dad sat at the kitchen table. He couldn't give any hint of what was coming at the end of the progress report. He kept his hands behind his back to hide the sweat pilling in them. His older brother Benjamin, so called Benji and identical in looks, sat across from them.

Oh, please don't let him see it, Michael prayed in his heart. *It's at the end, so maybe he'll miss it. It's just an elective; he won't notice it. Please don't notice it.*

"I've got to say, Michael, I'm impressed," Mr. Smith looked pleased. "Triple digits in every class, and—what's this?"

And there it was. Highlighted in blue. All other grades were in the green, but this one was piercingly cold blue. *Piano Music Theory*—83 percent.

B-minus.

His heart raced. The anxiety that he suppressed came to fruition as he felt his blood pump, the sweat ready to drip from his palms.

"Ho-oh, little bro," Benji teased. "Drop into the double digits, and a B? You're toast!"

"Shut up!" Michael's fists were at his sides. He clenched the sticky, nervous sweat. "You don't know anything!"

The fury was boiling over, the fear of what would happen next. He knew he'd never hear the end of it, saying 'shut up.' To his parents, it was just as bad as any profane word.

"Seriously, Michael, the yelling?" his father set down his screen, pursing his lips. "And we don't use that foul language in our house."

Oh no, Michael thought as he saw how his father looked at him. *He's making the face.* It stabbed deeper than any physical wound. Hit harder than any punch that could be delivered. 'The face' his father made. The careful controlled one right before bad things happened. Like a feral beast ready to emerge from its lair. Michael felt sick to his stomach, the taste of bile filling his mouth. *I hate it when he makes the face.*

His dad shook his head, a disapproving tsk. "I was impressed, but mark me mistaken, I'm disappointed. Why the 84?"

"It's just an elective," Michael defended. "It doesn't mean anything."

His dad continued to shake his head. "Not good enough, son. I thought I taught you to advocate for yourself to the teacher if you needed help, and to tell us."

Michael huffed. "Dad, everything else looks great, and I *really* want to play this quarter." He begged. "Please just let this one go."

His dad raised an eyebrow. "Can't do that, son. You're all meant to excel, and that's what you're going to do, even for a piano elective. You're momma's going to help you on the baby grand in the music room. And instead of sports, you're going to tutoring until that grade goes up."

"What?" Michel felt defeated. "They don't even have tutoring for electives like this."

"Watch it, little bro," Benji continued to tease, playing on his own personal screen device.

Their dad glared. "Not helping Benjamin."

"And mom's already got enough kids in piano lessons," Michael said. "She doesn't need me added on. I can handle it."

His dad held up the screen. "This proves otherwise. Get your attitude in check. *Now!*"

Michael bit his tongue. There was no use fighting. He knew what talking back meant.

His entire family did.

"Don't just stand there," his father raised his voice. "I said attitude check—NOW!"

He yelled that last word. Michael pushed him this far; he didn't want the next part if he pushed him further.

He composed himself, just as he always should. "Yes, father, I apologize."

Perfectly performed. But Mr. Smith still didn't look fully sated. He waited.

Oh crap, Michael thought. He couldn't say it aloud, never use words like that in front of his family. *Did I forget something?*

His father still waited.

Michael felt the sweat drip down his back, slow beads as time around him stretched. The tick on the antique clock in the corner sounded like a thousand moments as he stood his ground, holding composure. *Everything is fine*, he repeated in his head. *We are a happy family. Do you're best and you will be loved. Never fail, and you will be loved. Don't think about what happens otherwise...*

"You're dismissed, Michael," Mr. Smith said calmly.

A wave of relief. Michael turned on his heel to go upstairs and hide in his room.

Mr. Smith's voice trailed behind him. "I expect not to be disappointed again, son."

*   *   *

Michael stuffed his face into his pillow and cried.

He did everything they ever asked. Best grades in his class, active in all religious activities, dressed as an exemplar, watched after his little sisters, took all the advanced classes, on the road to graduate early, never yelled, swore, or used profanity—*absolutely everything*! And they wouldn't give on this one thing. Just one quarter to play with the other kids like him, one season to be like the others and play. He was a good kid, always the good kid.

But never good enough.

A knock on his door.

He recognized whose knock it was. "Go away, Benji!"

The door flew open anyway.

"I said go!" He threw a pillow at his older brother and missed.

Benji watched it hit the wall and laughed. "You're going to have to throw better than that if you want to play anything, Mikey."

"Shut up, you made things worse." Michael looked away, hoping Benji didn't see the tears. "And don't call me Mikey."

"Really?" Benji crossed his arms and leaned against the door frame.

"Yeah," Michael pulled his blankets protectively around him. "Shove off and leave me alone."

Benji playfully frowned. "That's no way to treat the person who just convinced Dad to let you play sports."

Michael froze, his tears stalled. Did he hear that right?

"Don't mess with me, I'm not in the mood." He let part of his blankets drop.

"Who said I was messing?" Benji came in and sat at the end of the bed. His stature was that of a grown man, fit and ready to take on the world. And he did, having recently returned from a religious mission, as many young adults from Utah did. Nothing like lanky fourteen-year-old Michael, who still felt too short among his peers. Benji was prepared to move out and attend his first semester of college, staying in-state to please their parents.

And more so, it meant he'd be close to Michael.

"You really convinced him?" Michael said sheepishly. "What about mom?"

Benji reached over with a wide hand and ruffled his hair. "Sure did, Mikey, and Mom will be fine. I'll catch her later. But you've got dad's blessing."

"If?"

"If what?"

Michael wasn't so easily convinced. "There's always an if."

"If you get that stupid B up in the next couple of weeks," Benji said. "And if you consider applying in-state."

"Ugh," Michael fell backwards onto the rest of his sheets. "Of course." Although he was the age of a freshman, he was considered a junior in high school. Not only did the school pressure him to start looking and applying, but so did his parents. His mother, never prouder, already saved applications for him to start filling out.

All in-state.

"I hate Utah," Michael stared at the ceiling. "I want to leave."

"Hate Utah?" Benji asked. "Or hate living here."

Michael pulled his blanket over his head. "Both."

He felt a careful hand tug on the blanket. "It's not so bad. Mom and Dad love you, you know. They're just trying to do what's best for my genius brother."

Michael pulled the blanket tighter over himself. "They're doing what's best for them. You don't know, they think you're perfect."

The hand pulled harder, and some of Michael's blanket pulled off his head, Benji's face right over his. "And you know better?"

Michael playfully punched Benji's shoulder.

"Now you've done it!" Benji pulled Michael off the bed, and they wrestled. Not hurtful, but to vent. Michael knew Benji could pin him at any moment, but it was a game. One that neither wanted to end.

It felt good to let it out, the frustration, the angst Michael pushed into his chest. It was wrong to feel anger; it was wrong to feel resentment. Wrong to feel anything negative. And wrestling Benji somehow made it all go away.

With no clear winner, both boys fell on their backs, panting and sweating.

"How'd you," Michael panted profusely, "convince," pant, "him?"

"To let you play?" Benji wiped the back of his hand across his head. "Easy. I told him no respectable college will even look at you without a more *rounded* application. That includes extracurriculars. And since music isn't working out... I let him figure out the rest."

"You're evil," Michael laughed.

"Just a little," Benji jested. "Just enough to get by."

"So I *have* to apply in-state?"

"It's a part of it," Benji said. "And it's not so bad. You can room with me."

"Gross."

"If I bring a girl over, I can tell her you're my kid."

"I'm not that short," Michael said. "Joke's on you, she'll get scared and run away."

"Perfect repellent for the crazy ones, then," Benji sat up. His demeanor changed as he reached a hand over and helped Michael sit up. "Mikey, I know it's hard. But please remember, Mom and Dad *do* love you."

Michael nodded. By all means, his parents never did anything to hurt him, not even a spank as a child. Never a slap across the face, never a flick or poke to teach him a lesson.

But some things hurt more than physical beatings.

"I know." But in his heart, he knew it was only for now that they loved him. As long as he didn't screw up again.

Never good enough.

Chapter 23: Death and Judgement

onversations among the 4020 put Ren on edge.
Where openness was once common, shushed voices dominated. Those he once laughed with scurried away when he approached. Others became too friendly, hidden torments under pleasantries, noses browner than if they rubbed filth on them directly.

And he felt lonelier than ever because of it.

Only Asa spoke to him like he used to before the disaster of that damned inquiry started.

And then true calamity hit.

A cold, misty morning, the first they'd seen since awakening on Triton. Fog rolled in at the shoreline, forcing 4020's anxiety to compound, as though waiting for something to happen. Rays of the red sun peeked through, pushing aside spots of haze, revealing a ghastly sight washed ashore.

"A body, a body!" The final watchperson of the night heralded at the dawn. "A body north of the ledge!"

4020 amassed and ran in a mob. The watchperson was pulled aside and reprimanded for stirring up the Community thus.

Ren got caught in the crowd.

Shoulders pushed and shoved. Panicked voices cried, "Who is it? What's happened? Are we next?"

"Get Dr. Solovyóva!" Ren yelled desperately among the mob, but no one heard him.

Alone again.

Unable to beat the crowd, Ren accepted his fate and flowed with them.

They slowed as they reached the lake's shoreline, the crunching pebbles beneath everyone's feet like gnashing teeth.

Ren pushed through to the front.

"Where is Dr. Solovyóva?" he asked. "Someone fetch her quick, before—"

He stopped when he saw the gruesome scene. Close to the water's edge, they looked down at a waterlogged body in a 4020 jumpsuit, face down.

Lilith hovered over it, and Michael knelt beside it.

"Good God, no," Ren gasped. *Please don't be who I think it is.*

But it was. A puff of fog rolled by and cleared further. A tangled mess of platinum white hair.

Dr. Olena Solovyóva.

Ren stepped forward. "How did this happen?"

Lilith put up a hand. "Stand back," she ordered. Her eyes shot at Ren, as though to pierce right through him. "*Do not* come closer."

"I can—"

"No, you can't." Her voice had a growl within it, like an animal protecting its prey. "All of you stay back."

Michael reached to examine Olena.

"Wait, don't touch," Lilith said. "Asa, fetch two poles. I want to see something."

Asa emerged from the crowd and ran back to the encampment.

Ren turned to face the mob. "Alright, nothing to see here." He waved for attention. "Back to—"

"They do not have to go anywhere," Lilith said. "Stand down, Tanaka."

"I was just trying to help."

"I said stand down." Her authoritative gaze sent a shiver down his spine. "They have a right to know, *to see.*"

Everyone spoke up in agreement, nodding. *"We have rights... we want to know... the commander speaks truth. . ."* Their affirmations continued into jeers at Ren. *"Who does he think he is... who does he get to judge us... he's not in charge... the commander's right. . ."*

He took a breath of defeat. "Of course, commander."

"Commander," Michael stood. "If it's alright by you, I'd like Tanaka to stand by me while we examine. I do use his judgment in many things, being co-administrator of my team."

Lilith nodded and gestured to Ren to join them. "Rest of you, please keep space out of respect for the body."

Ren just about pranced to Michael away from the mob. Lilith backed the crowd to a ten-foot breadth, but didn't push them further.

"Thanks," Ren mouthed to Michael, hiding his face from the onlookers. He didn't want to think about what might've happened—*what would've happened*—if he stayed among them.

Michael merely nodded, as though he could be responding to anything, concealing their conversation.

Ren felt a prick in his right leg. Nothing touched it, but he felt it nonetheless. They all hated him. He knew it, despite their faux smiles, despite late-night soirees, and despite any sort of friendly conversation; they hated him. The inquiry made it more so. They despised what he did to Michael. *'Irresponsible Ren,'* he was to them. There for a good time, but not someone to count on. Not someone to ever be taken seriously. A cheap replacement for Michael after he fell.

It should've been you, he repeated in his head. *You should've died, not Michael.*

And yet, Michael was here, alive and well among them. He held no visible qualms against Ren. *Why,* he asked himself. It drove him insane. He didn't deserve it.

He didn't deserve forgiveness. He never did, and never will. He learned that lesson well when he was young.

All continued to gawk at the body, whispers murmuring. More fog rolled in, and the scent of death with it, bitter and acrid, floated among them. Some in the crowd coughed, and another vomited. Ren averted his eyes, getting sick to his stomach. And yet they stayed, still fixated on Olena's body.

Why is she letting them stay? Ren plugged his nose. This was completely out of UNSF protocol.

But then again, there was no more UNSF.

He wanted to leave, get as far from death as possible, but with the entirety of 4020 there, he felt the pressure. The pressure to feel like he belonged.

Not to be alone.

Asa returned with two poles, no more than three feet in length.

Lilith carefully used two long poles, flipping Olena over.

And that's when Ren saw it: a glimmer of sickly blue-green iridescent veins reflecting off her skin.

And when she was supine, her face was not her face. It was spider-veined with iridescent blues and grays. Eyes and mouth wide open, completely blackened, and as though screaming from oblivion.

"The Xyelex!" someone yelled from the crowd. "It's come for us."

"It's real," another exclaimed. "They were telling the truth."

And it hit Ren. Lilith already knew the state of Olena's body.

She wanted them to see.

Proof that the Xyelex killed their team members in the hab unit.

And absolve her of guilt.

"This is tragic," Lilith said. "There are no words to express what's happened here. No words."

"No words," many repeated among their other murmurs and exclamations.

The sight of the Xyelex across the body made Ren's very innards churn.

And he looked at Lilith. She faced the mob, standing tall. "... her legacy will not be forgotten in this tragedy. Her talents were truly unmatched . . ." along with more words to inspire.

And as convincing as she was, there was something off that he couldn't describe.

Too convenient, he thought. She sounded too good, *too* inspirational. *Rehearsed. I know it when I hear it. I've done it plenty of times.*

But no one else seemed to pick up on it. Tears filled the eyes in the crowd, enamored by Lilith and her presence.

"Can you believe this?" Ren turned to Michael. "Can't you see?"

Michael shook his head warningly, eyes only giving a hint of disapproval. *Do not cross Lilith,* they warned.

Lilith paid no mind, continuing to feed the crowd's grief.

"... and with Evie Cunningham's abandonment. . ."

Evie's name nicked Ren's ears. What did Evie have to do with any of this?

Tears suddenly turned hot in 4020's eyes, the righteous hate of those who not only wanted to, but needed to blame someone.

"Abandoned." The word spread across the crowd. "If only she stayed."

"If only she. . ."

"If only. . ."

"Olena'd be alive. . ."

"They'd all be alive. . ."

"If only Evie. . ."

As if a rush of cold water flooded the mob, they stirred angrily.

And in that moment, Lilith and Michael were completely absolved of guilt.

But Evie wasn't.

"No," Ren shook his head. "This isn't right." He nudged Michael. "You can't let her do this. Say something, they'll listen to you."

Lilith continued on with her emotional speech, the triumph of the human race, how they were all survivors, and how they'll overcome this challenge.

Michael didn't move. He hung his head, his face completely composed.

"Really?" Ren rolled his eyes. "And Asa? You too?"

Asa looked like a scared deer. He didn't move either.

Something stirred in Ren. He no longer cared if they all hated him, because he hated what they were doing. Evie, whom he saw as a sister—*as family*—was becoming their scapegoat.

Disgust filled his mouth, and not from the scent of the dead body.

"Hey," he yelled out.

And Michael put a hand on his shoulder. "Don't." His voice shook, scared.

"I'm doing your job," Ren shook off his hand. "Together or not, you're her husband, and you should be doing this!" He waved his arms, yelling above Lilith. "Hey, listen up."

The riled mob barely noticed him.

"Listen, you're all scientists," Ren yelled. "Be reasonable. We cannot turn the blame on Evie Cunningham. We'll be no better than those who once hunted witches. *Please listen to yourselves! The commander is wrong!"*

Although the mob did not sway in their yells and slurs, some eyes turned to Ren.

As well as Lilith's.

Her eyes darted at him, like daggers stabbing, and murderous. She paused her speech. None seemed to notice as they were so riled in their own griping.

"You dare interrupt me," she said so low only Ren heard. "You'll regret that, you little worm."

And he saw something glint in her hand.

A blade, hidden in her palm.

Blood rushed to his head, and his heart stopped.

Time stretched around him. Lilith grabbed his forearm, her grip tighter than anything he thought humanly possible. Her domineering stance over his slender body, the hand with the blade moving up to his neck.

She twisted his body around. He pulled against her, but he, like everyone else, was too weak against her giant hill strength. She pulled him close in front of her.

"Look at Tanaka!" An older member of 4020 shook a finger at them.

One of the female physicists yelled. "He's going after the commander!"

"Leave her alone!" Another joined in.

Ren's heart dropped. It looked like *he* was the one attacking her.

His outburst at the crowd, and then positioning Ren in front of her with his arms outstretched, onlookers would easily assume she was in defense against irresponsible Ren, acting before thinking.

She'd finally won against him.

And he prepared for the end.

Ren stared up into the crazed, bloodshot eyes.

The blade reached for his throat.

A blood-curdling scream erupted from the edge of the crowd.

And all fell silent.

Lilith dropped her grip on Ren.

He fell backward. "Am I dead?" he patted his neck. He didn't feel anything, not even the slice of her blade.

He looked up at her. Her face concentrated on something distant. Her blade out of sight.

She didn't do it. Whatever screamed stopped her.

"You!" Ren pointed in disbelief.

"Shut up!" Lilith waved for him to quiet down.

"Y-you," Ren stumbled over the words. He knew Lilith didn't like him, but to kill him? "You tried to k-ki—"

"Shut up!"

A piercing, shrill screech sounded through the fog, and everyone plugged their ears.

Ren felt it pulse through his mind. His ears pained. Were they bleeding?

The screech suddenly ended. Something glinted through the fog.

A glint of something iridescent.

They appeared out of the mist. Four massive and imposing humanoid creatures surrounded 4020 and the shoreline. Iridescent fungal tendrils encased their bodies and glowed, layers upon layers of it writhing like worms, extending their limbs and making the creatures stand close to ten feet tall. Their acrid odor was overwhelming, matching the scent of Olena's dead body.

"Join us-s-s," the sound of a thousand voices rang through their gaping mouths beneath eyes with blackened sclera. The fungus on their bodies squirmed excitedly.

They outstretched their arms, the fungus building upon itself, flaring toward those closest to them.

And all order among 4020 was lost.

Screams erupted as people ran, the Xyelex bodies snatching people into their clutches. The extended fungal arms wrapped around those unlucky to be near them, like vines shooting from branches. It grew around those caught, drowning them in its assimilation, creating new hosts.

"We are Xyelex," their voices repeated. "Join us-s-s."

Ren froze in the chaos. He heard it the voices; an echo of familiarity mixed in their clamoring unison. These weren't just any humanoid creatures. His blood ran cold as he realized these were people he knew: Dennis, Theo, Rami, and Benson, infected by the Xyelex Lilith told him about. And now, completely unrecognizable in their new parasitic form.

Running senselessly wouldn't work. They needed direction.

"To the caves!" he yelled, coming to his senses. "Hurry!"

He started to run, but heard a yelp from behind.

He turned and saw Michael still along the shoreline beside Olena's dead body.

One of the Xyelex stood over Michael, its fungal appendage wrapping around his left arm, writhing up to his shoulder.

Chapter 24: To Live or Die

Evie awoke in the morning upon a bed of leaves. Though the red dawn never truly made it feel like morning.

She breathed in the refreshing grove air. *I'm here,* she thought. *I can't believe I'm actually here.*

She sat up.

Isaiah's familiar voice danced above her. "Are you in need of sustenance, child of Earth?"

She looked up to the tree that loomed over her.

He dangled above, upside down on a branch. His colorless clothing floated around him, his silvery white hair feathering.

"What the hell?" Evie stood. "Why are you like that?"

"A different perspective," he said calmly. "Is it odd to you?"

"Yes."

"Alright then." He blinked.

And disappeared.

"Where the hell…" Evie looked around her. "I am *not* ready for this first thing in the morning."

"Are you in need of sustenance?" In another blink, Isaiah appeared right in front of her.

Evie jumped back, holding her heart. "*Oh god*—don't do that! Announce yourself!"

Isaiah's indifferent gaze took on a curious expression. "Don't humans like you need sustenance?"

"Yes," Evie said. "And we also need to not be startled half to death when we're still waking up."

Isaiah nodded. "I see. Do you need sustenance?"

Evie sighed. He wasn't going to stop asking. "Yes, I need sustenance."

"Go look," he raised a hand, gesturing beyond the tree line. "On the other side of the grove.

"Okay?" Evie headed in that direction.

She parted ferns and brush, pushing through until it cleared.

And opened to a wide view.

A water body was before her, the waves lapping as a cool breeze brushed over it.

"Wow, I didn't even know I was still along the lake," she said. She's explored the grove the day before. The grove was immense, bigger than she expected. It went dark before she could finish her roaming. "I didn't even hear waves or anything."

Sweet air rushed to her, the scent of refreshing, clean minerals. A few feet ahead, the land sloped down to the water. Along the edge, it was cleared of plant life, a sandy foreshore. She gazed in awe as the foreshore sparkled, as though diamonds embedded the very land that surrounded the water. Rich crystalized minerals.

This wasn't an ordinary freshwater lake. It was salt water.

"A saltwater lake," Evie said.

"By your standard, no," Isaiah suddenly appeared next to her. It didn't startle her this time. Was she getting used to him popping in and out?

"More like one of your oceans from what I saw in your mind," he continued, "only much, much smaller. Triton is a fraction of Earth;

an ocean here is like an Earth sea. The freshwater lake you followed here drains into it."

"Something like this seemed out of reach at the Community," Evie said. "If only they knew that it was here."

Isaiah eyed her with his expressionless gaze. "Are you not one of the Community? You know, therefore the Community knows."

Evie shrugged. "If I ever go back."

Isaiah did not respond, but turned his gaze to the salt lake.

"Why not take a closer look?" he suggested. "You may yet find sustenance."

Evie felt the hunger pang in her stomach. The feeling wasn't at its full capacity yet, but close. It was only a matter of time before her thoughts turned to only that of satisfying the hunger, losing control, and being willing to do anything to eat.

As an astromedic, she couldn't allow her mind to go there. *I must keep my wits.*

She carefully climbed down the foreshore's slope and onto the mineral beach. Her feet sank into the crystallized sand, granules slipping into her shoe crevices. She took them off. The granules pushed between her toes, and she felt an odd sense of relaxation. She walked to the water's edge. The waves were minuscule compared to the freshwater lake. The sand continued to sparkle into the water's depths.

"Go look," Isaiah called from the grove. "You'll find what you need."

Evie stepped into warm water.

As soon as she did, her shadow swirled.

Wait—not a shadow.

Creatures.

A small school of minnow-like fish, no larger than Earth's tadpoles. The water's warmth emanated around them, and they gathered at her feet.

She didn't feel them, but she saw them. Their heads brushed gently against her ankles and heels.

Eating the dead skin, she thought. *From a human. A first for them. Their behavior isn't that different from Earth fish.*

I told you before, Isaiah's voice echoed in her mind. She could feel him smirk. *Most processes are patterns that repeat throughout the universe, including life. All things can be replicated and repeated. Such is the nature of existence.*

She sighed. "Oh boy."

Continue forward, Isaiah said. *It's not much further.*

Evie stepped carefully, taking in the fullness of the water. The minnow-like fish continued to follow, swirling around her feet with each step. Her footsteps sank into the soft landscape, painting it with the warm diamond glow.

The water stayed clear and warm. When it was waist-deep, she paused, stepping on a rock the size of her fist.

The rock moved.

And a dozen more rocks emerged from beneath the seafloor and scurried around.

Pick one up, Isaiah's voice said to her mind. *They cannot harm you. And you need them.*

She dipped her hand into the water, splashing its salted taste into her face. She almost fully immersed herself, keeping her head above water. Her hair ends lapped the surface.

She grabbed one and pulled it from its sandy home, up to the surface.

The creature had a hard shell on top, rough and rounded. She felt something tickle her palm, and she flipped it over.

Underneath it had ten spider-like legs surrounding a soft underbelly, gills, a small flipper at one end, and a small bulb on the other, tucked into the shell protectively. As soon as she flipped it over, it pulled in its legs and covered its underbelly with the flipper. The scent that wafted from it matched that of the surrounding salt water.

"A crab?" She studied it. It wasn't like any crab she's seen on Earth. The closest she could relate it to was a horseshoe crab, but even this wasn't exactly like it.

"Like the bird, it's evolved for this world," Isaiah said.

He appeared, sitting cross-legged above the water.

"Oh god," Evie almost dropped the creature, startled by his sudden appearance.

"I prefer not getting wet," he said.

"I can see that." Evie prodded the creature.

"Well?" Isaiah tilted his head curiously.

"Well what?" Evie said.

"You need sustenance," he said nonchalantly. "And I've led you to it. Do what is necessary."

Evie felt stunned. Did he mean for her to do what she thought?

"Eat this?" she held it up.

"Ingest the appropriate nutrients, yes," he said. "It has the proteins and enzymes your body craves. Though it'll probably be easier to do so with it dead."

"Kill it?" She looked down at it in her palm. It stayed curled protectively, terrified of her.

It feared death.

"Do you need assistance on how?" Isaiah asked.

"No," Evie held her breath.

"Then what's the delay?"

"I,uh, don't want to kill it."

Isaiah peered inquisitively. "Why? You need its nutrients to survive. Have you not consumed the energies from once living things before?"

"Yes," she said.

"Then what is the difference?"

"I never was the one to take life," she said, thinking back to dishes she had on Earth. She knew the importance of meat and protein for the human body, but always discarded the thought of its source. It was easier that way. "It's silly, I know, but I don't think I can just kill a thing, even this. It's terrified, it doesn't want to die."

"Nothing wants to die," Isaiah said. He clutched at his shirt at the center of his chest, like something was under it. "And yet it still happens. We've spoken on this before."

Evie felt an ebb in her mind and a blurred vision trying to materialize. He was sending her a mental message.

Let it in, he said in her thoughts.

Evie breathed. "Alright."

She let the image materialize.

She saw the day they found Michael at the rock quarry, except she watched from the outside. She saw herself hidden behind a boulder, pelted by the rock shards that were being shot at her.

But she didn't recognize herself.

A savage animal, enraged by fear and guilt, clutching a bloodstained spear, ready to attack whatever came next.

This was you that day, Isaiah's voice echoed. *And will be again if you do not do what is necessary to live.*

The vision faded, and Evie stood with the creature in her hand, Isaiah watching from above the water.

"I will maintain the utmost respect for human life," Evie told herself, "from the time of conception, even against the possible violation of the law."

"That includes yourself," Isaiah said.

A sharp hunger pang vibrated through her.

"I don't know if I can," Evie said. "I'm not strong enough... emotionally."

Pathetic. That was how she felt. Weak and pathetic, she felt guilty for not having the stomach to kill even this mundane creature. It's life literally in her hands, and she couldn't bring herself to do it.

"Do you value your life so little that you will not take life to sustain your own?" he asked.

"No," Evie said defensively. "I value my life."

"Is that so?" Isaiah's gaze didn't blink. "You claim you came here because you felt your life added little value to your Community. And now you hesitate to take the life of an inferior being to sustain your own."

"Inferior?" Evie didn't like the sound of that. "It sounds pretty arrogant."

"But it's truth!" Isaiah no longer sounded nonchalant. His voice changed, taking on a slight authority. "Truth is not fair, but it is reality. You can either accept it, or perish."

Evie looked down at the creature again. She didn't want to die. A human can't live by scavenging alone—all the non-domestic plants in this world couldn't provide enough protein and fats for her to survive in the wilderness. During her Earth residency, it was popular for local people to go on hunting and survival excursions. She treated people who almost starved themselves during these excursions, not because they hadn't eaten enough; they did. They didn't balance the nutrients they needed.

She imagined their starved, emaciated bodies.

"Death," she said. "I hate that it's this way. Always more death."

"You know the truth," Isaiah said. "The universe is a place of energy and matter. Energy and matter don't ever dissipate or disappear. It transfers, becoming something anew, giving into another."

"Kill or be killed," she said. "It won't stop here. I'll keep killing, taking life for my own."

"As Triton grows, so will its challenges," he said. "If you can't do this small thing, how will you face more?"

She thought about animals on Earth, ones more advanced, more intelligent. Mammals she could empathize with that would eventually form here if what Isaiah told her was true. And other intelligent beings she'd possibly have to take the life of to survive. Not just to consume, but to defend against.

Like the Xyelex.

"The Xyelex," Evie said. It'd take life without a second thought. Apathetic. Intelligent, immense, and unlike anything she ever encountered. Not only did it take their lives, but it became more formidable as it did.

And more than likely viewed her as an inferior pest.

"Yes," Isaiah said, nodding in agreement. "I'm properly showing approval, am I?"

"Surprisingly, yes," Evie said. For a fleeting moment, she felt a twinge of fear that he was learning to mimic human behavior so quickly and accurately.

The wind picked up, and the warm water surrounding Evie sloshed around her waist. Strands of her hair blew freely.

Isaiah stood, still floating above the water, his clothes flowing freely, his slicked back hair picking up in the breeze. He leaned over and held a hand out to Evie, as though he sensed her fleeting fear. His colorless, stoic eyes melted in compassion.

Take my hand, Earth child. I will not harm you. His lips did not move as he spoke in his silent understanding to her, the words coming to her heart and mind as they did before. *You know I cannot lie when I communicate like this.*

Was he truly showing concern, or just trying to alleviate her fears through mimicry? Did it matter? He'd not touched her since he probed her mind, nor had he ever made an indication that it was all right for her to touch him. He kept her just beyond arm's length, a certain distance be as it may. It always felt wrong to do so around him.

But now he offered her his hand, his expression determined.

Evie dropped the small sea creature into the water.

And took his hand.

The touch surprised her. It was warm and gentle, but she felt a static deep within as though he emitted electrical energy. It shouldn't have felt so foreign and familiar at the same time. Such a notion was improbable, absurd, or such opposites to be present at once in his touch.

He pulled, and she lifted gently above the water, also standing completely dry in front of him.

"Incredible," she said, looking down. She felt the smooth water beneath her feet, but it did not affect her in any way. Sea creatures scrambled and swam about beneath them, red sunlight spreading across the surface like painted glass, their shadows stretching, long silhouettes side by side and equal.

"Keep hold," he said. He turned and faced the open sea. With his free hand, he placed it on his chest, as though gripping something just beneath his shirt.

"Wait, what are we—"

They suddenly jolted forward, speeding away to the wide blue.

"Oh my god!" Evie almost let go.

Isaiah tightened his grip.

Don't let go, he said. "You're safe." *I won't let you fall.*

Evie looked down and saw her feet gliding across the top of the water. "We're—we're—" There were no words to describe how she felt. The open air rushed around them as they flew across the sea, her hair trailing behind her.

She was free. No rules, no bounds, not even physical laws binding her. She felt his power keeping her afloat, static energy coursing through her, making her limitless.

She glanced at him beside her. He noticed, also stealing a glance at her, a smirk stretching across his face. That same smirk she felt him do so many times in her mind. Further evidence of the growing mastery of his physical form.

They slowed gracefully to a stop. The salted air pricked her tongue, and the waves grew, catching their ankles, and yet they still floated dry. Beyond the horizon, the sea continued, no land in sight.

Isaiah took her other hand and faced her.

"Is this how it is for you?" she asked. "All the time? This freedom?"

His eyes met hers unblinking. They glinted cool silver. *Yes.*

"How do you contain it?" she said. "I can't imagine feeling that kind of power all the time and holding back."

It's what I am, his thoughts spoke. *I know no different.*

"What now?" she said. "Why are we here?"

Speak with your mind, he pleaded. *Please, it's easier for this. I will hear you.*

Alright, she thought. *What's out here?*

It's not what's out here, he said, eyes still unblinking. *Do you trust me?*

Not really, she said. *But I trust no one.*

She didn't mean to think that last part. An unspoken thought she'd normally leave unsaid.

"Oh god, this is hard," she said. "Didn't mean to say that."

It's alright, he said. *Your lower dimensional body makes it a struggle to speak to the heart and mind. But I ask again, but reframed: can you trust me?*

A surge of his power, keeping her afloat, surged through her. She felt it deep within her; he meant her no harm. She was safe. *I can.*

Then watch, and see life anew.

A rush around them, and they submerged beneath the surface.

Chapter 25: Murphey's Wrath

t should've been you... IT SHOULD'VE BEEN YOU! The memories screamed at Ren as he saw the Xyelex wrap its elongated fungal arm around Michael's left forearm.

His right leg ached.

"Do you remember?" something whispered over Ren's shoulder. A whisper with the sound of a thousand voices within it. "We s-s-see what you remember s-s-so des-s-speratly."

Ren couldn't move. His blood iced and his legs numbed.

The whisper of the Xyelex right over his shoulder.

"Join us-s-s," it continued to whisper in his ear. "We forgive your crimes-s-s. Join us-s-s. We s-s-see you."

A memory rushed through his mind.

Time froze.

They say that human minds take in information at ten billion bits per second. Neurons transmit, sending pulses within mere microseconds.

And it took only microseconds for Ren to remember everything. The day he went too far, the day he broke his leg, the day he regretted more than anything.

The day he was told Michael died on his behalf.

It's a bad idea, Ren, he remembered Evie telling him. *Didn't Michael say you can get seriously hurt if something goes wrong?*

Ren's memory brought him back to the fully functional hab unit. He and Evie were sitting in the common room. Low, somewhat cushioned chairs surrounded a small circular table. Humble by all means, everything was a dull gray industrial color from the alloys used to create the hab unit. Everything simple, to be picked up and moved at a moment's notice. The room was domed with a single porthole window at the top center, revealing Triton's cold, stormy outer surface. Industrial lights circulated the room, poorly imitating natural sunlight. Nothing expensive for the UNSF. Economical and efficient, conserving resources for other endeavors.

But it was home.

"Nothing will go wrong," Ren said, taking a bite of rehydrated meat, or what he thought was meat. With UNSF food, you could never be sure of what you really had, only that it was nutritious, kosher, and edible. Even the term 'meat' was debated as its source was never revealed. A coagulated mush, firmed like tofu with a mealy texture.

As for the water used to rehydrate their food, all of it was recycled. Nothing wasted. Reuse and recycle. He kept his thoughts away from where a good amount of their water was recycled from lest he hurl his supposedly edible food.

"That's rather confident of you to say," Evie said, also eating the same fare.

"Mind if I join the fun?" Asa approached the table carrying a small industrial tray of glop.

"Not at all." Evie gestured to the open space. "And maybe you could talk some sense into this one while you're at it."

"Sense?" Asa looked curiously at Ren. "I don't know if anything I'd say would be of use to an engineer."

"Not an engineering issue." Evie crossed her arms, giving Ren a maternal look.

Ren wanted to laugh. "It's fine." He waved off Evie's look. "Everything's fine."

"No," she said. "*No,* it's not." She turned her attention to Asa. "He thinks he can do the repairs on the cargo transport."

The cargo transport. A spaceship of immense size, meant to take payloads of supplies every travel rotation, and able to go between orbiting ships and planets. It wasn't able to do anything interplanetary, but the hab unit depended on it all the same to receive and send payloads. During their last maintenance check, it failed, unable to start completely. Even under the protection of the hab unit, the Triton environment was more than they predicted it would handle.

"He's smart enough," Asa said, inspecting the food on his tray. "You always figure it out." He poked it with his fork.

"And completely against regulation," Evie said. "He's going to get hurt or killed."

"Wait," Asa set his fork down. "How?"

"He wants to repair it *by himself,*" Evie gave Ren a withering look. "*Tonight.*"

"Not worth it," Asa shook his head. "Wait for your team."

"Come on," Ren shrugged his shoulders. "Everyone else is off doing maintenance on," he held his hands up in air quotes, " *'necessary life functions.'* I guess you all like breathing and stuff. No one's available. And if it doesn't get fixed tonight, we miss the next payload transfer and have to wait another entire rotation." He put on his best charismatic smile. "Don't you all want those packages of fresh, delicious treats?" He gestured to their dehydrated mush. "Or keep eating this rot for weeks on end."

"Eat to live," Asa said. "We have enough supplies that it's not necessary. We and the rest of the crew will be fine for the following rotation after the repairs are completed properly with a team, not you single-handedly."

Ren tossed back his hair. "I'm flattered that you know I can fix it single-handedly, but it's not just food. It's all the other things that make life less miserable in this frozen prison. Waste not, want not, but everyone still seems to enjoy things like toilet paper."

Evie didn't look convinced. "What are you waiting on?"

"No idea what you mean."

"What did you order?" She leaned over the table slightly. "You really want this payload to arrive on time. What are you smuggling?"

Evie, the older sister he never asked for but still enjoyed having. Nothing got past her. "Not much," he said. "And smuggling's a bit of an overstatement. I just procured a few things to make life a little less boring. Some cheese... a little champagne... maybe a lot of something similar to champagne but stronger. . ."

Asa shook his head. "I don't hear any of this. Oh god, I'm not hearing any of this."

"Boring?" Evie rolled her eyes. "We're on an ice planet next to Neptune!"

"Moon," he corrected. "And my point exactly. Boring."

"Ren," Evie rubbed her temples. "You know she'll find out. She always finds out."

"What?" Ren grinned. "You mean Lilith?"

"You're on a first-name basis with her now?" Evie said disapprovingly.

"Not officially," he leaned back, hands behind his head, completely relaxed. "But *I am* her favorite."

"And *her favorite* isn't worried what she'll do to him if she finds out what you're planning?" she said.

"She'll congratulate me after she gets the spoils."

Asa refused to look at either of them. "I don't hear this."

"Come off it, Asa, you'll be fine," Ren said. "Relax, no one's getting hurt. I bet I could tell her everything and she'd tell me what a hero I am for ensuring the entire hab unit has their payload and more."

Evie leaned back in her chair. "Fine. Now's your chance."

"I still hear nothing." Asa took an oversized bite of glop.

"Huh?" Ren suddenly felt a heavy hand hit his shoulder.

Lilith's hand.

The weight of it almost made him fall over the back of his chair.

"Enjoying a lovely meal together," Lilith said, standing over them. In such a confined space, her stature seemed even more imposing. She put her fists on her hips. "And what's our engineering prodigy saying that's got our astromedic so worked up?"

Evie crossed her arms again, resigned. "Nothing. Nothing at all."

"Just discussing the next payload rotation." Ren scooped some of his food. "It'd be nice to have something other than undefined meat."

"I know," Lilith said. "But we can't receive anything till that transport's up and working. We'll just have to make do with what we have."

Ren gave a slick smile at Evie. "Exactly what I was saying. Right, Asa?"

"Oh god," Evie rolled her eyes.

Asa kept full attention on his food and didn't say a word. Ren knew he hated direct confrontation, which was why it was so funny to ask him on the spot.

"Not to worry, all," Lilith said. "If our rising star of an engineer has any say in it, he and his team will get that transport up and running sooner than expected."

"Already on it, Commander," Ren nodded. "I have a plan in action as we speak. I'll have it going in no time."

Lilith smiled approvingly at him, and something within that approving smile made his chest swell with pride. He won more than her approval; he'd won her favor. Something he held onto dearly.

"That's what I like to hear," Lilith said. "And why do we have your genius here. Michael did well choosing you."

"Thank you Commander."

Lilith nodded to the rest of them. "Cunningham, Baramba, always a pleasure. I'll be seeing you."

"Of course," Ren flashed a plastered grin.

Lilith walked away, leaving the common room.

"Asshole," Evie said. "She clearly knows."

"Ah," Ren held up a finger. "But an asshole who's still the commander's favorite."

"She's right," Asa said. "You are kind of being an asshole. She's just trying to look out for you."

"It will be fine," Ren clapped his hands together. "I promise, you'll be thanking me by tomorrow night when the payload's delivered."

"Staying up far past your night rotation to repair a transport alone so you can get your smuggled goods on time," Evie said.

"Doesn't sound even slightly irresponsible to you? And we have that survey mission coming up. What if something happens to you?"

"It'll be fine."

"You said that already," Asa added.

"Really, it will be," Ren reassured them. "Plus, if something were to happen, not that it will—"

"It will," Evie said. "Murphy's law."

"—Michael will cover me for the survey," Ren brushed off the comment. "He's good like that. No harm, no foul. Everything's good."

Evie slumped her shoulders, defeated. "I can't force you not to do this, just think about what you're doing, okay?"

"*I am*," he emphasized. "Let's talk about something else, please? Something fun. Oh, don't you guys look at me like that. Nothing will happen. Nothing will."

Nothing will happen.

It won't.

It can't.

But Murphy's law insisted on being known.

Ren mostly remembered the sheer pain. An unprecedented accident, one that could have been prevented if another set of eyes were on the inner turbines. If Ren were physically stronger, he could've stopped it. If a spotter had watched, Ren would've avoided the very area of the transport where the turbine came loose.

And crushed his right leg.

The injury made him due to leave for Earth on the next rotation.

But Murphy's law struck again.

Michael covered the survey just as he promised, as any good superior would for an injured subordinate.

And fell through the ice to his death.

"It s-s-should've been you," the Xyelex whispered to him, interrupting the memory. "We hear it. You know it."

He remembered the looks on everyone's faces. From prodigy to pariah, they all blamed him. Lilith hated him for what he did. He prayed for relief from their looks, their ostracism. To escape the mission, to move on.

No one rivaled Michael's brilliance. His photon accelerator kept the hab unit running, the epitome of harnessing energy in the depths of space. His brilliance died with him. No one knew how to maintain or run it.

Except Ren. The one who helped build it alongside Michael. The engineer to the experimental physicist.

And so he stayed despite the loathing from 4020. Despite the pain of his injury.

Despite hating himself.

"It s-s-should've been you," the Xyelex repeated. "Thes-s-se are your words-s-s, not theirs-s-s. Know yours-s-self and join us-s-s."

The words screamed in his mind: *IT SHOULD'VE BEEN ME!*

"It should've been me," he gasped aloud. He watched as the horror of this Xyelex creature assimilated its newest victim: Michael.

Instead of him.

Michael cried out, trying to tear his arm away. The fungal tendrils pulsed and began to spread up it.

"Join us-s-s," the one beside his shoulder whispered. "We s-s-see you!"

And a pain hit his chest. *Not the guilt,* Ren thought. *Not the guilt! Can't handle the guilt again. Always an answer—always a solution!*

All the answers were there, always there. One just had to look.

His eyes locked in on Olena, her dead body beside Michael, and the Xylex.

There was the answer.

Like flipping a switch, another part of his mind activated. The part he used when he built, when he problem-solved. His engineering mind.

He would not let history repeat itself.

Ren's terror faded.

Automatic, mechanical, his body reacted. Nothing in the way of the solution. He turned around to the Xyelex that whispered over his shoulder. It stood over him, outstretching its arm, its face so consumed in the fungus that its host was no longer identifiable.

He dodged the elongated fungal arm.

"Join us-s-s," it shrieked at him.

Another arm reached toward him.

He dove and felt air rush past his face as the Xyelex's finger tips fanned past him.

He rolled onto the shoreline, right beside Olena's body.

And beside the other Xyelex, consuming Michael's entire arm.

Michael cried out, fighting futilely against it. "No!" he begged. "Not like this!"

Ren only had one shot for this, no margin of error. A slim chance, but if his hypothesis proved true. . .

He stood up, two snapped poles, one in each hand. The ones Asa brought. Broken from the chaos that ensued from the Xyelex's attack.

And sharp.

The Xyelex was bigger. It was stronger.

He only had to get the right angle.

Michael bent to his knees, succumbing to the Xyelex.

The one that whispered in Ren's ear jumped onto the shoreline beside them.

"Join us-s-s," both Xyelex hosts said in unison.

No more guilt. No more blame.

Only a solution.

It didn't matter if one of the Xyelex grabbed Ren. He didn't care. Because all that mattered was if his solution worked, he wanted it to work.

It had to work.

With all his strength, he lunged at the Xyelex gripping Michael.

And shoved the sharp end of a tainted pole between its neck and jawline at an acute angle.

It screamed. Not any earthly screech. Not even one of an ethereal banshee. But an unholy screech of the thousands of voices it projected. As though it felt pain for the first time in all its existence. It arched back, continuing its piercing shriek. The fungal tendrils pulsed rapidly, turning a sickly orange and sulfur yellow across its host's body.

Michael's Vita-8 scar glowed as the fungus receded down. The tendrils that touched the scar frosted over, crystalline shards forming protectively around them.

Michael pulled his arm away, slipping out of its grasp like a slick glove.

Just as Ren stabbed the Xyelex, the other one reached for him.

As I predicted.

He held up the other pole in time for it to wrap its appendage around it instead of him.

And let go before it reached his flesh.

He pulled Michael to his feet. "Let's go!"

They ran for the Community, the moment's distraction of the Xyelex just enough for them to stay ahead.

The last to make it into the caves, they sealed the entrance behind them, entrapping all of 4020 within its dark depths.

Chapter 26: Primordial Submergence

Tholins.

The ingredients of life.

They're only known to be found on two celestial objects within the Sun's solar system: Pluto and Triton, brothers in creation. A dirty garnet colored substance, tholins are not much to the eye upon first sighting. From a distance, they are merely red patches, their pattern creating the unique outline of Pluto's icy heart.

But a deeper search into the chemical composition tells another story.

Long ago, before Pluto and Triton were separated, methane reacted to ultraviolet light from a young Sun. The sun's light began producing a tar-like material from the methane, the basic elements of life coming together in a soup of organic compounds.

While the reaction on Earth continued to evolve to create life, Pluto and Triton stopped. Their distance and gravitational separation paused their evolution, trapped in a state of stasis. Too cold for the sun to have any more effect, the tholins never evolved beyond the tar-like consistency.

That was until the sun expanded to a red giant, melting Triton's icy surface. Warming the compounds allowed for the process to resume. Like water to a plant, the tholins drank the warmed water and expanded. They grew, changing into something else. They released gases and erupted elemental compounds. Atoms bonded, molecules formed, and a living cell came into being.

And that cell was the long-awaited child of the sun, the first life to appear on Triton.

The process by all means should've taken another eon or more. But Triton's first child caught the eye of a watcher—an overseer by name. The process of life quickened beyond the natural as the overseer manipulated time's perception. Triton blossomed.

And Evie submerged beneath Triton's salted sea with that overseer.

She felt his power erupt from his hands through hers as they plunged into the dark depths. He watched her carefully. She instinctively tried to pull away, a panic to swim for the surface.

Don't let go, he said in her mind, tightening his hands around hers. *I've created a time loop around us. You will not perish while remaining in this loop.*

Evie expected the weight of the water to put pressure around her, but it didn't. She still felt as light as she did floating above the surface. She looked beyond Isaiah as they sank deeper, the sun's warm red light fading into a deep violet. She looked up, seeing a rainbow of colors much like the day she emerged. The temperature around her dropped, but still remained uncommonly warm. Not what she expected from the sea depths.

Time loop? she thought.

Yes, Isaiah said. *You are exactly as you were above the water. And will remain so until the loop ends.*

They continued their downward plunge. Evie marveled. Time loops? Defying laws of physics? What had she gotten herself into, seeking out Isaiah? What else could he do? Better yet, what couldn't he do? She shuddered to think what power he suppressed for her benefit. And why did he even care to show her any of this? He'd said he was the overseer of Triton, charged with cultivating it, and humans were the key to his goals. But why her? She was no one exceptional or any different from other humans he could assist. She wasn't anything special.

Still doubting yourself? His smirk stretched across his face, more naturally than it did before. His facial expressions were catching up to his thoughts.

Heat flushed to her face in embarrassment. *How did you know?*

Seriously? Our thoughts are connected, and you're asking me how I know?

Yeah, her embarrassment continued to rise. *Kind of a stupid question, I guess.*

Interesting choice of words, he said. *And ones you should choose more carefully when speaking about yourself.*

They continued the plunge, sinking deeper. All warm light dissipated, and only hues of violet and purple surrounded them.

Evie looked down and saw their shadows descending, fading into depths far below.

And become a part of something else entirely.

Although the cool light was dim, she could see the seafloor appearing. Like mists clearing, it came into view.

And it wasn't empty.

Elongated copper leaves sprouted from green mounds. Such a vibrant moss green, they seemed to glow along the floor. Between the copper leaves, all manner of small sea animals flitted among them. An array of bizarre yet colorful creatures. Arthropods, cephalopods, annelids, and mollusks all striking with vibrant yellows, oranges, and reds. Both familiar and foreign to life Evie recognized from Earth.

Their feet carefully touched the seafloor between two of the green mounds, sending a plume of sand around them. The mounds towered over their heads, each a living ecosystem of sea life swirling around them.

A reef, Isaiah said. He let go of one of Evie's hands, but held tight to the other. He gestured to one of the mounds. *Teeming with Triton life.*

But this can't be a coral reef, Evie walked forward. *This is something else.* A forest of green mounds surrounded them. Isaiah stayed beside her, keeping his hold on her hand.

There's chlorophyll. She remembered back to early school lectures. Life sciences are something all medics are required to know. They learned of Earth's earliest life to present today, with the hope that a better understanding of how life came to be, they'd be more capable at treating those in need. *Cyanobacteria. These are stromatolites. God, of all the things I remember, it's this.*

If that's what you want to call them, Isaiah said. *This was once the site of one of Triton's many tholins. It became this shallow sea and birthed these lifeforms.*

Shallow. Evie laughed at the idea.

By planetary standards, yes, Isaiah said. *But deep enough that these creatures and their early ancestors have been able to escape the eclipse and thus have thrived in harmony with one another. I cannot say the same for the surface life.*

Except where you've intervened, Evie said.

More or less.

The sand shifted where Evie stepped, and suddenly a long creature erupted from beneath. An eel, no more than a foot long. Mouthless, it had a suction cup where its face should've been, and stripped a vibrant crimson and yellow to match the rest of the sea life. It wriggled, its ribbon body dipping up and down to swim away.

They fear me, Evie said.

They've never encountered something like you before, Isaiah said. *Friend or foe? Prey or predator? They sense the latter of each in you. And they should.*

How can they? Evie said. *I could be the former.*

Isaiah pointed to the eel that swam from them. *Look.*

The eel was up one of the stromatolites. Its suction face opened wide, pulling tiny shrimp-like creatures into it.

That creature feared for its life a moment ago, and now it takes on pleasure in satisfying its hunger, Isaiah said. *And those that it consumes also fear for their lives as it takes life from them. Fear and pleasure, a never-ending cycle continuing.*

A tentacled cephalopod emerged from the copper leaves and darted at the eel. It pulled in the eel, consuming it within its tentacles.

Energies of another giving new life to many, Isaiah said.

Evie noticed a bulge on the side of the cephalopod, an enlarged sac.

Ah, you see it, Isaiah said. *She has yet to lay her eggs. She needs more nutrition before she can.*

She? Evie said.

It's what she is, Isaiah said. *She is making life for this sea, for this planet. The sun gives its energy to be consumed for the benefit of all lifeforms. How it is consumed differs for each creature, but it is essentially the same need. For life to continue, the energies of others must be given.*

It seems hardly fair.

Isaiah stopped. *Is it fair for her to let her children perish because of the guilt of killing another? She values their lives and her species' continued existence, for if she didn't, she and her species would surely perish. It is more than mere instinct that drives life to continue.*

He turned and looked Evie in the eye. *What truth are you willing to accept?*

He blinked, and everything suddenly changed around Evie.

They were back on the foreshore bordering the grove.

"What?" Evie looked back and forth. "How did we get here? Did that even just happen?"

"It happened," Isaiah said. "I took a shortcut back."

"You could've blinked us there and back the entire time?"

Isaiah looked confused as much as he could with his unpracticed expressions. "But you had to see? How else would you've seen if I did that?"

She realized Isaiah was still holding her hand. She quickly let go.

The moment she did, it was like something tore from her. Ripped from his energy that coursed through her, it dissipated in an instant, and she felt the weight of her body. She stumbled back.

"Careful," he said calmly, folding his arms and tucking his hands into his flowing sleeves. "Those unpracticed with coming out of a time loop can sometimes—"

She vomited.

"—eject their inner biles."

Evie wiped her mouth with the back of her hand. "Gee, thanks for the warning."

She knelt and cleaned her face at the water's edge.

"What shall you do?" Isaiah said.

"What do you mean?" Evie finished rinsing her face and stood.

"You've seen what it means to survive," he said. "What it means to value life. Are you going to do what is necessary?"

"If this is your way of telling me I need to hunt and kill for food, I get it," she said.

"It's more than that," he said. "Evie, taking life to obtain sustenance is one thing. I have no doubt you can do that. But your Community, if you can't do what's necessary to survive, you will perish. The Xyelex is more dangerous than any of you can comprehend."

"What do you know about it?" she crossed her arms.

"It's dangerous," he said. "So much so, I couldn't be with you in the hab unit the day it discovered you. It's relentless once it discovers the energies of another life form. Do you really think it will stay put? After witnessing what the earliest patterns of life do to one another, what do you think this highly evolved communal being is going to do?"

Evie remembered the look on Dennis's face as it infected his body. The indescribable fear that his life was no longer his own. A fear she'd have to face if she came face to face with the Xyelex again.

And if it ever made its way to the Community.

"The life in the reef was balanced," Evie said. "It had purpose in both life and death. But the Xyelex doesn't seem to respect that. It conquers everything it touches."

Isaiah nodded. "You finally understand."

"It can't suppress its power, it—"And it hit Evie.

Being with Isaiah, feeling his power, it was so far beyond anything she could imagine. And yet he never manifested all of it. In the blink of an eye, he could change the laws of their three-dimensional space, utilizing the laws of his dimension in theirs. He could feel their thoughts, emotions, and memories without the bounds of the physical.

Just like the Xyelex.

"The Xyelex is not native to Triton, is it?" Evie said. "It's not even native to this dimension."

"No, it isn't."

"It's—oh god, it's like you," Evie's heart pumped. How could Isaiah hide this from her?

"Yes, it's like me," Isaiah said. "But ignorantly took on a perverted physical form. It did not study or watch humans as I did, and took on the first form it saw befitting to this world."

"And now it's out of control." Evie felt her blood pressure rise. "And if you can't stop it, how are we supposed to? If the eclipse doesn't kill us, then we're doomed by the Xyelex."

Isaiah pulled his arms from his sleeves, reaching for her compassionately. "Child of Earth, please don't think—"

"Don't touch me," Evie put her hands up. "You hid this from me."

"I…" he looked thoroughly confused, as though he didn't know which emotion to express. "… couldn't tell you."

"Why not?"

"Earth child," Isaiah bore his unblinking gaze into her. "You think I'm all-powerful, but even I am bound by the laws of my dimension. Some things cannot be spoken; they must be discovered. I've been at war with beings like the Xyelex longer than humankind has called any planet in your system home. There are things I know and it knows that cannot be told to lower dimensional beings without it consuming their entire being and destroying them. It bound my words long ago, and I hoped you would discover its secrets from your savvy, for there are many more secrets it has that I cannot speak, as much as I wish to. It's survived eons for a reason. It's found a new dimension to try and conquer."

"Ah-ha," Evie pointed. "So it tried to conquer your plane. How did it get here? And why was it in our hab unit?"

Isaiah stayed silent.

"You know, don't you?"

"Some things, Earth child, you must discover on your own," he repeated. "Those walls in your head are there for a reason."

Evie closed her eyes, thinking to her mental wall. If she would only remember everything, then she'd have the answers she needed.

"I see what you're doing," Isaiah said. *Don't try it*, his voice echoed in her mind. *You saw what happened the last time you tried to force your walls down.*

You helped me before, her thoughts spoke. *It hurt, but I'm better for it. I have to remember.*

I merely guided, he said. *You remembered on your own. But the wall still stands; your will wants it up for a reason.*

Then guide me again. She saw a foggy memory. It unfolded, but too dim to make out.

"I have to remember," she said aloud. *I will.*

You cannot force amnesia away, Isaiah warned.

"When I first saw the Xyelex, I was in restricted Area E," she said. "But that wasn't the first time I'd been there. I was there when something happened... and that something has to do with the Xyelex."

Stop, Isaiah pleaded.

She pushed her thoughts through the mental fog and saw it all again: the fully functional hab unit before it sank, making her way down to Area E. Michael was gone, and she'd taken his passkey from his effects. No one questioned a mourning wife going through her late husband's effects. She had to go there—the restricted section, off limits to all except the head physicist and those who worked directly under him. Too dangerous. But why was she going?

Present Evie pushed her thoughts to remember.

Stop!

Pain, like a gunshot to the head, tore the memory to shreds, slipping away.

And she fell backwards, flat onto the beach.

She opened her eyes and looked up at the Triton Sky, Neptune watching.

"What the hell?" She sat up. "Did you do this?"

"No," Isaiah hadn't moved from where he stood before on the foreshore. "But you certainly had a momentary lapse in judgment. This episode was entirely your own doing, Earth child." His voice had an edge, like a parent scolding. "Am I expressing disapproval appropriately?"

She brought herself to her feet.

"I take your silence as a yes," he said.

"This is ridiculous." She rubbed the pain away on her temples. "Why does it have to be so hard? I just want things to go back to how they were before. I want things to be like they were on Earth. I hate this world—I hate that it has to be my home if I want to survive. And I hate that I can't even remember who I really am, or who I was."

Isaiah stepped close. "May I?" He held out a comforting hand.

Evie was mad. But not enough to reject comfort.

She let him clasp her hand between his.

"Earth child," he knelt with a soft voice. His expressions shifted between stoic and concerned, trying to take on the correct one. "There are no absolutes. One of the greatest lies of humanity is that there are absolutes. Anything worthwhile is hardly ever easy."

They took a moment and watched the sea.

"If I were paid a nickel for every time I watched water since coming here," Evie scoffed at herself. "Old Earth saying."

"Amusing," he said. "And now," he let her hand free of his comfort. "Not to downplay your human emotions, but you have physical needs, Earth child. You must take in substantial sustenance before your body weakens. Vita-8 no longer sustains your body. Will you?"

Evie swallowed away her frustrations. She marched into the water. She was no more than ankle deep when she felt the rough shell of the crablike creature beneath her foot.

She reached in and dug her nails into the sand and picked it up. Just as before, it curled in protectively, fearful.

I want to live, she thought.

The small creature squealed.

And she silenced it forever.

Chapter 27: The Physicist's Ruminations

Trapped.

Cornered prey, waiting to be caught.

The whole of 4020—or what was left—were closed off in the caves beneath the Community. Gathered in the antechamber, they mourned the loss of those taken by the Xyelex, terrified of its next attack.

Michael was among them, wondering why he was still alive.

It let go, he thought as he absentmindedly grazed his fingers along his arm where the Xyelex grabbed it.

He remembered his horror when he first encountered the Xyelex, the hopelessness at his inability to stop it from consuming Rami.

And he'd never forget the look on Rami's face.

One of his subordinates, a fellow experimental physicist like him. Rami was there along with him and Ren when they built the hab unit's power source. Someone he trusted with confidential research, and in turn, Rami trusted him inexplicably.

And that day in the hab unit when they found the Xyelex haunted him like an unending nightmare.

Rami's curious nature, something to be respected, got the best of him.

"What's this?" he remembered Rami asking when they first saw the fungal veins creeping along the hab unit corridors. He got close. Too close.

Seemingly out of nowhere, it reached for Rami, grabbed his arm, and consumed him.

"Help me! Michael, *don't let it—*" It drowned his voice, choking away all sound, as it exploded through his body. The fungus stabbed through his skin, taking away all that he was.

And his final look: betrayal. Eyes wide with shock, his mouth slightly open, trembling. It was only a moment that he faced Michael, the look on his face, realization that someone he trusted could not help him.

That split moment was all it took to break him.

"I can't think of that," Michael said to himself. After all, Rami was dead. And more were taken by the Xyelex. The eclipse was coming, and they were no better than entombed in these caves while the Xyelex rampaged the surface.

He knew it from the beginning. It was only a matter of time till they all... *until they. . .*

He shook his head. He didn't want to admit it. He failed to get what they needed from the hab unit; the Xyelex ensured that. There was no way they'd be able to retrieve or guarantee *it* still worked.

His photon accelerator.

A whimper from the corner of the antechamber distracted him. Voices echoed words of comfort. The people around him were losing hope.

Think, think, think! He leaned against the cool cave wall and angrily chastised himself. *You're better than this. You can think of something!*

You're better than this, son, he remembered his father's voice. *Don't make this harder than it has to be.*

Shivers ran up Michael's spine, and not from the chill of the cave wall.

"Report," he heard Lilith's voice echo.

Across the antechamber he saw Lilith with Asa, meeting with three of her scouts.

"No sign of the Xyelex trying to infiltrate the caves," a middle-aged woman said. "Scouts have looked out, and they have us surrounded. They're just standing there; a bit unnerving if you ask me. Those taken are fully assimilated."

"Damn!" Lilith swore. "Why isn't it trying to get into the caves? There has to be a reason."

"Easier to wait it out," Asa said. "Wait for us to weaken so they can take us with ease."

Lilith looked thoughtful. "A plausible assessment, maybe. But still, why not take the caves?"

Michael felt a tingling go up his arm into his scar. She didn't know about his arm and the Xyelex retreating after touching his Vita-8 scar. No one saw it except Ren. And Ren was scarce from the moment they entered the caves.

"Commander," he said as he approached.

"Dr. Smith, good, I need to talk to you," Lilith said. She turned back to her scouts. "Keep watch on rotation. I want to know if the Xyelex moves even a single blade of grass. Got that?"

Her scouts nodded and scurried away.

"God," she rubbed her head. "I need to meet with you both, in private. And with Tanaka—where's that god damn engineer when you actually need him!"

Asa shrugged. "I don't know. No one's seen him much since we entered the caves."

Michael couldn't tell if he imagined it, as it was only a millisecond, but there was a flash in Lilith's eyes; a flash of something venomous.

But it was gone as soon as he noticed.

"Please find him," she said, sounding defeated, tired even. "And meet me," she hushed her voice low, "at *the place*."

*　　*　　*

Michael walked with Asa and Ren through the narrow tunnels that led to the cathedral chamber with the Vita-8 reservoir.

"I'm gonna die, I'm gonna die—oh god I'm gonna die," Ren kept repeating.

"Will you knock it off?" Michael said, leading them with a torch, the same way he did when he first brought them down there. "You've been here before."

"Oh, it's not that Vita-8 shit that's going to do me in," he said. "I'm just going to turn back, before you all witness my untimely death."

Ren began to shuffle away. Asa grabbed the back of his collar.

"You're not going anywhere," Asa said.

"You big brute, let go of me!"

"That's the first time anyone's called me a brute," Asa said, amused. "But I guess compared to you."

"Let me go!" Ren pulled away. "I'm not going."

Michael stopped. "Do we have to do this drama all over again?" He faced his torch toward them. "We agreed, you're coming. The commander needs to speak to us, and it's urgent. Whatever it is could save 4020."

"Come along." Asa guided Ren to the center of their marching order. "Play nice and let's go."

"I'm nuts," Ren said as they continued. "Only a crazy person would go back into the line of fire. Crazy—you know—doing the same thing over and over again expecting a change?"

"What are you on about now?" Michael huffed, slightly irritated. He worked closely with Ren since the beginning of the mission. Most of the time, he found Ren's neuroticism refreshing from dull day-to-day routines. But right now it was vexing.

Ren bit his lip.

"If you want to say something, get it out," Asa said. "We've heard enough of it just getting this far."

"You won't believe me," Ren said indignantly. "But please, you guys, don't leave me alone with Lilith. And be careful around her—she's dangerous."

"We know," Michael and Asa said together. Michael didn't mean to say it at the same time as Asa. The unison of their voices made it firm, apparent in a way that widened Ren's eyes.

"You guys know?" He sounded surprised. "You really know?"

"I tried to warn you not to mouth off to her," Michael said. He knew Lilith's short temper; something most didn't see. Especially with those who exasperated her or stepped in the way of her plans.

It was easy for Ren to do that without trying.

Michael knew him well enough that it was best to talk it out. "So," he gestured for them to continue walking. "What did she say to you this time?"

They squeezed through a narrow passage. "Say?" Ren sounded offended. "She didn't say anything. God, we can barely fit in here."

"She didn't say anything?" Michael didn't believe him. "After that display you made?"

"After the display *I* made?"

"You got up in her face," Michael said. "It looked like you were about to attack her until the Xyelex showed up. If you wanted to poke a bear, you did."

"I didn't get in her face," Ren defended. "She was the one who... well, she. . ." Ren trailed off, exasperated. "*She tried too—*"

"Tried what?" Asa asked.

Ren huffed. "Never mind. You're both all buddy-buddy with her and won't believe me."

"No," Michael said. "She's our superior, and I respect her authority, and you should too."

Ren still sounded resentful. "Evie had the right idea to get out of here when she had the chance."

Michael stopped. Ren and Asa bumped into one another, almost falling on him.

"Don't," Michael said. "You said enough already."

Evie. Always on his mind, one way or another. She left. *She left him.*

He had to face the Xyelex alone.

He remembered the day of their first separation, back on Earth. He hadn't planned it for that moment; he'd premeditated on leaving, but it always seemed like an escape fantasy born of frustration. To make it a reality was entirely another level he never considered Tred. But the Triton mission was coming, time was short, and there was only so much more he could take. *I left her first,* he thought to himself. *It's only right she leave me this time.*

His internal thoughts suddenly changed, and he heard his late father's voice: *Not good enough, son.*

He remembered the day he introduced Evie to his family. His brother Benji, of course, welcomed her with open arms.

He couldn't say the same for the rest of his family.

"I told this would happen," he overheard his father say to his mother in their kitchen, away from everyone else. "Going out of state to that corn-cob school—"

"Cornell dear," his mother corrected.

"Doesn't matter," his usual steady father sounded unhinged. "And he brings home that bitchy tramp?"

"She's not a bitchy tramp!" Michael interrupted their conversation.

"Michael, sweety," his mother reached to comfort. "Why don't you go back to the dinner table? Your father and I will—"

He brushed it off. "No. Evie's just in the other room, and you come in here to talk shit about her?"

His mother looked like she'd faint.

"*You* don't use that language in my house," his father pointed at him. "I thought I raised you better. I thought you were strong. But that out-of-state school of yours has put degenerate ideas in your head, and that bitch you brought home is proof of that."

"How can you say—"

"There's nothing more to say, son," his father's indignant face glazed over into stoicism. "Disappointed. So disappointed. Thought you were better."

The silence that followed was worse than arguing. The refusal to validate.

He never told Evie what they said about her. But that moment told him everything he needed to know: he wasn't good enough, and never would be. Not even for her. That's why he had to leave. She deserved better than him.

And why Evie left him this time.

Ren stumbled over his words, interrupting Michael's meditations. "I'm sorry, I didn't mean—"

Asa put his hand on Ren's shoulder, shaking his head.

"We shouldn't keep the commander waiting." Michael continued on his way, not looking back at either of them.

The narrow tunnel finally opened to the cathedral chamber, the deep blue of the Vita-8 pool still and untouched. Lilith stood as still as the pool, her back to them a frozen statue of perfect attention.

Michael's torch sizzled as cold drips from above caught the flame.

Lilith's torch lay on the ground beside her, unlit.

"Was she just standing there in the dark?" Ren whispered to Asa. "God, I need to get out of here."

"You're not going anywhere," Asa whispered decisively. "Don't worry, Michael and I will stay with you."

"Yeah, the friend of the enemy."

"Stop being dramatic."

Michael ignored Ren's ramblings (sometimes it was best to do that with him) and cautiously approached Lilith.

She didn't move.

"My father was a great leader," Lilith said, her voice calm, tranquil. "Antarctica was not the strength people saw it as before my time in the UNSF. In fact, people hated us. We were the bane of united society, whining pests to be squashed. One more thing they didn't want to deal with or acknowledge. Genetic, inbred freaks."

Michael's curiosity piqued. He knew about Antarctica's sudden change of standing in the UNSF, but little else of how it happened. And why was Lilith telling them about it now, when so much was going on?

"What changed?" he asked.

"We did." She turned around, the shadows of his torchlight increasing the dark circles under her eyes. The shadows crept into unseen crows' feet and folds on her cheeks. Pressures of leadership aging her a decade or more.

"We were passive, on the defensive during the Poaching Wars," Lilith continued. "And we were going to continue staying on the defensive until the day we die and the next generation takes the burden. We were bleeding; not sustainable. The status quo needed to be challenged. And we did."

"How?"

"We took matters into our own hands." She lifted her hands before her face, staring at them as though they played a memory from long ago. "Literally. I was fifteen the day I dragged the frozen bodies of the poachers into Ronne. The visiting ambassador and emissaries were supposed to plead our case, but they had already decided the verdict before arriving. But even they couldn't ignore the poachers' bodies, not with so many witnesses from the UN watching our broadcast. I took the offensive that day, as did the rest of Antarctica. And we were finally validated. That was the beginning of our victory. And how we're going to win this."

The hero of Antarctica. Lilith's much-deserved title. The historic day she stood before the UN and won their favor, and started the end of the Poachers War. She herself, at a young age, led troops aided by UN forces against the foreign invaders. No more were Antarcticans genetic mistakes; they were powerhouses of strength, bred to perfection. Lilith the epitome of that strength.

Better. Stronger. Smarter.

"How exactly are we going to take the offensive against these things?" Asa asked. "Nothing can hurt them."

Michael guarded his actions, careful not to touch his scar. For some reason, he felt deep in the pit of his stomach that telling her about the Xyelex's reaction to his scar was a mistake. No logical reason. If anything, logic dictated that he should tell. But intuition stayed his voice.

A slight smile twitched at the corner of her mouth. "We have the leading experimental physicist, engineer, and chemist from Earth. You three. I have no doubt in my mind you will find a way."

She picked up an object hidden in the shadows.

Michael's sling gun, the one he used when they found him.

He thought he'd hidden it well. He wanted no one in 4020 to know about it yet, other than those who saw it. There was no telling how they'd abuse it in their heightened state of fight or flight while they rebuilt civilization. Even he, in a state of panic, almost shot the people he cared most for.

The *person* he cared for most.

"How did you?" Michael was at a loss for words. He should know. She was Antarctican. Stronger. Better. Smarter. If she wanted something, she'd find it.

"I want more of these," Lilith said. Water dripped from the cave ceiling onto her face, like a tear falling. "But with firepower. For our scouting team. And they won't be the scouting team any longer. They'll be a militia. The first for Triton."

"How?" Asa said. "We don't even have gunpowder."

"Oh, Dr. Baramba, don't pretend to be ignorant," Lilith said. "Igneous intrusions run everywhere in these caves. Evidence of volcanic activity. And evidence of the elements needed to make it. You said it yourself when we first arrived." Her eyes glided to the Vita-8 pool. "And maybe more."

Asa looked like a scared deer.

"Um, Asa?" Ren nudged him. "Do you have something to say?"

Asa took a deep breath. "Gun powder and Vita-8 are not a good mix," he said. "That concentrated form is far too volatile to utilize. And for all we know, the Xyelex could grow worse or feed upon it. After all, it's a parasite of this world, and Vita-8 originates here too. We don't want to create a more deadly enemy."

So Asa hadn't figured it out. Michael looked nervously at Ren.

Don't say anything, Ren's eyes screamed at Michael.

But Ren didn't know all of it either. None of them did. Only he and Lilith knew the true origins of the Xyelex.

"Wait," Ren furrowed his brows. "So essentially, we're making guns for your newly named militia, purely under your charge. If we want to defeat the Xyelex, shouldn't we make guns for everyone to fight the Xyelex? There aren't many of us left, and we all have to contribute and defend ourselves."

"And open a door to abuse by those less responsible?" Lilith was unblinking. "And we're not defending. We're attacking. Plans are already underway. Tonight, we announce the militia and name our generals. We are not going down without a fight."

"And you decided this without the rest of 4020-A?" Ren said. "Without us?"

"Ren?" Michael saw what was coming. The glare in Lilith's eye, the unsettling nervousness of Ren. This wouldn't end well. "The commander is looking out for us."

Asa said nothing.

"All three of you are indispensable," Lilith said. "Your intelligence is unique. But you're not soldiers, and we need soldiers to fight this thing."

"And if it doesn't work?" Ren said. "What if the Xyelex just absorbs bullets? It already showed nothing can permanently harm it."

"It has?" Lilith's mouth turned to a slight smile. "That's an interesting development."

Ren looked like he could hit himself in the head for saying so much.

"Gentleman, I'll leave you to it," she continued. "Make us strong, build the hope of our people to continue." She looked at Michael. "Talk some sense into him, will you?"

"Of course, Commander," Michael said.

"What materials do we even have to make it?" Ren said. "It's not like we can just pop open a crate and pull out what we need."

"Have faith," Lilith said. "Our medical team has created a surplus of materials for the eclipse. Use it as necessary."

With that, Lilith lit her torch and left.

"This is bad," Ren said. "Really bad."

"Provoking her won't do you any good," Michael cautioned.

"Do you not realize what she's doing?" Ren said. "This has nothing to do with the Xyelex."

"We have to defend ourselves," Asa said.

"She doesn't care about defense; otherwise, all of us would become the militia," Ren waved his arms at the Vita-8 pool. "And we have this!"

"She doesn't know." Michael's words made them pause.

"Know what?" Asa sounded confused.

A smile stretched mischievously across Ren's face. "*You* didn't tell her? Mr. *'I respect authority'* didn't tell her?"

"She doesn't need to."

"Know what?" Asa looked between the two of them, still confused.

"The Xyelex doesn't like Vita-8," Ren said triumphantly. "So your little chemical theory doesn't hold."

"How did you find this out?" Asa asked.

Ren folded his arms. "Ask him."

Michael recounted what happened when the Xyelex touched his scar.

Asa nodded, following along.

As Michael finished, Asa leaned in close, inspecting his scar.

"Vita-8 did this to your skin after you experimented with it," Asa said analytically. "Not as a pure substance. Still, what could it do as a pure substance, pulled straight from the pool? And the Xyelex pulled away from the scar after Ren stabbed it. Maybe Lilith was onto something, combining firepower with Vita-8."

"Bad idea," Ren said. "Bad-bad-bad-bad!"

"Why didn't you tell her?" Asa asked Michael.

"I don't know," Michael sighed. "I know it sounds strange, but it just didn't seem right to tell her."

"Are you going to?" Asa's eyes were something to contend with. When he looked at people, they pierced deep, reading a soul.

It made Michael uneasy. "I don't know. Something's changed." He thought back to his father, steady and calm like Lilith, to the point that it was abnormal. "Lilith's not the same. She's changed since the hab ruins. I just don't know."

"Strange hearing you say 'I don't know,'" Asa said. "And so repetitiously."

"Because I honestly don't know."

Not good enough, Michael heard his father's memory say to him.

"So we know firepower probably won't work against this thing," Asa said. "Based on Ren stabbing it."

"It hurt," Ren said. "But only a moment for us to get away. Nothing more."

Asa nodded. "So, what do we do?"

"We make guns and give them to everyone," Ren said. "And—"

"Speaking of bad ideas, that's one," Michael said. "Whatever you're thinking, Ren, it won't work. 4020 loves Lilith. And her scouting team—her new militia—has undying loyalty. We make the guns and look into utilizing Vita-8, like she ordered."

Ren looked shocked. "And I thought you were going to be cool. Boring."

"But," Michael held up a finger. "No one said how long it should take. She has no idea how long this will take. She wants haste, but research takes time. And we will use Vita-8 against the Xyelex. And safely utilizing it will take time."

"But-but-" Ren stuttered. "She—"

"Give him a minute," Asa said.

They waited for Ren.

And like a brick hitting him in the face, Ren's expression changed. "Ah—Michael, I love you! We're saved!"

Better, the memory of Michael's father spoke. *But still not good enough.*

"So, now that you're being cool," Ren said. "I should probably, how do I say it without sounding stupid... sorry for bringing up Evie like that. And for blaming you for not standing up for her back at the lake."

"I..." Michael felt blindsided. But then again, when it came to Evie, he always felt blindsided.

He felt the warmth of the torch. "Thank you. I've thought a lot about what you said. God, with everything else going on, I'm thinking about you calling me out. It shouldn't bother me, but it does. But when I saw Lilith just now, a change in her. You were right. I should've said something when she gave her speech. Evie was right to leave me." Horror gripped his chest as he realized his slip-up. "Us —*leave us*—leave 4020."

Asa and Ren said nothing to it. Michael took it gratefully.

"As for more time," Michael said. "I'll give you all my research."

"Why give it to us?" Ren's eyes widened. "We can just as easily— *no!* You're not going to—"

He was. He was leaving.

"It will give you the excuse of more time with me gone," Michael said. "And I'm going to do what I should've done. I'm going to find Evie. But I'm not abandoning you. She's out there with this thing running loose."

"How do you know it hasn't assimilated her?" Ren said.

"Four attacked us," Michael said. "The same four from the hab unit. Their numbers have grown only from those they've taken by the lake. She's out there, and I'm going to find her."

"Why now?" Asa said suspiciously. "You didn't care to go before. You're administrative and on Lilith's good side; you could easily order someone more skilled than yourself to track her down. You're my friend, but so is she. Maybe she's safer wherever she is. I will not see her hurt."

Michael understood. Asa didn't mean physically harmed.

"You need time, I will give it to you," Michael said. He handed his torch to Ren. "Save the Community. Save 4020. Utilize Vita-8. And I'll find Evie."

Not good enough, son, his father's voice continued to echo in his mind. *I'm disappointed.*

But I want to be good enough.

Chapter 28: The Hero Falleth

Imposter.

Fake.

Liar.

"They need their hero," Lilith said. "I want to save them. Save humanity. And elevate their potential."

She was alone beside the Vita-8 pool. The only time she could talk to *it*, the voice she heard from the moment she awoke in this new world. The one who spoke to her in the lab unit ruins.

But you're not a hero, the slick voice in her mind spoke. *I know the truth of what you are. A child parading in a hero's cape. It's only a matter of time till they see through it.*

"And you're a nuisance," Lilith said. She refused to speak to it except aloud. She'd never acknowledge it in her mind.

You want to be their leader, it said. *You want to save humanity from extinction and make it better than it was. I promised guidance. I vowed to hold them in place while you make good on your plans. What have you given me?*

"You will have what you want," she said. "You've already taken your fair share of hosts."

That engineer sees through you, it said. *I know his mind. Dispose of him!*

"Almost did," she said. "But the Xyelex showed up. Now I need him."

Almost isn't the same as doing it.

"I will," Lilith said. "As soon as he fulfills his purpose."

And that chemist sympathizes with him, the mental voice continued. *Expendable. Dispose of him, too, once he has served his purpose for you.*

"He has model traits that will contribute well to the gene pool," Lilith sighed. "I want him to build up the next generation in your name. He's wishy-washy enough I can convince him to consummate with someone to bear children, despite his aversion to women."

No, the voice said. *He won't. He's too virtuous to be with anyone he doesn't care about. I, too, know his mind. Dispose of him! He will challenge you.*

"Sad," Lilith sighed. "I could've used his traits. But I want to keep the physicist. His brains and physique are also ideal for our vision."

Yes, they are, it said. *But be wary. Remember what your mother said.*

And she did—the day of her father's funeral.

It's easier every time, she remembered her mother saying.

The memory unfolded. She was brushing off her Antarctican uniform in front of the mirror. She was in a windowless dressing room, small, compact for heat efficiency. The Poachers War ended, and her father was hailed a hero. She too, an unquestionable hero at the young age of twenty.

The door to her dressing room opened.

Her mother in it.

Dr. Farina wore a mourning uniform, dark, but still embroidered with Antarctican pride.

She closed the door behind her.

"My, aren't you a picture of perfection," Dr. Farina ogled at Lilith. "You've become more than I ever hoped my dear."

"Dear?" Lilith laughed and continued making minor adjustments to her uniform. She straightened her collar.

"Why not?" Dr. Farina said. "Is that not something I can call my daughter?"

"Sure, I guess," Lilith was indifferent to the term. "If it suits the occasion."

Dr. Farina smiled proudly.

"What do you want?" Lilith asked. "I want to finish getting things just right before the broadcast."

"Just checking in," Dr. Farina said. "You're going to announce it tonight, will you not?"

"Yes," she said, brushing back stray hairs.

"And?"

"And what?"

"What will you say?"

Lilith rolled her eyes and turned to her mother, perfect smile intact. "For the memory of my father, and I will keep his will alive by accepting the offer to join the United Nations Space Force."

"Good," she said. "I like the added detail of keeping his will alive."

She shrugged. "Why not?"

She turned away from her mother and began pinning medals to her uniform.

"It gets easier every time, doesn't it?" Dr. Farina said.

"Going to broadcasts?" Lilith looked for the back of the pin on her counter.

"Disposing."

Lilith pricked her finger on the pin needle. The blood pooled into a bead on her fingertip, and she sucked on it before it stained her uniform.

"We dispose of what is no use to us," Dr. Farina said. "I get it. He was weak and outlived his usefulness with the war over. I'm glad you took my advice. The Antarctican trial went better than expected."

An Antarctican Trial. A brutal challenge to authority, created during a dark time within their history. When the scientists who united them were long gone, people lost hope. A physical challenge that highlighted the genetic strengths of the Antarctican people. A tradition that should've died along with the people who created it.

But people rarely change, and the tradition lived well beyond the generations that used it and did well among those with a solely survivalist mindset.

A challenge that claimed the life of Chomar Amulius.

Dr. Farina mused. "Just like those insufferable poachers years ago."

So her mother knew. She suggested disposing of her father, Chomar, but she thought Dr. Farina had no idea about the poachers. When Lilith defied everyone and went out to bring the proof the UN ambassador wanted, she brought back frozen bodies.

She replayed it in her head every day to keep the memory fresh. She went beyond the Ronne shelf and found them in an inland cave. Two were dead, frozen to death. The last was at the back of the cave and begged for his life; her fifteen-year-old body was already stronger than that of an average man. The twinge of disgust twisted in her stomach at seeing a grown man in a fetal position. Were these really the poachers they warred against for generations? These pitiful goons were the ones whom she was taught to fear and hate. She'd known good people who laid down their lives on the hunt for these kinds of people, never to be seen again after seeking them inland. And this thing was dying before her, giving way to the elements that she called home. "Pathetic, miserable, weak creature," she told him, right before she shot him in the head with one of his own guns. She brought them back and reported—one shot by his own comrades, the other two frozen to death.

The first time she killed in cold blood. And hailed a hero for it.

"Are you sure his weakness will not show in me?" Lilith asked her mother.

"I made sure you only got the best genes from him," Dr. Farina said. "You are the most perfect specimen that humanity could ask for. You and all the others like you will go far. I'm proud of you."

Lilith smirked. Her mother wasn't proud of her. Lilith wasn't naive enough to think her mother loved or cared about her as a person. She was proud of her science experiment. Her mother wanted the perfect progeny, and she got it. But eugenics was taboo, so no one else in the world would ever be like her and the Antarcticans.

"The truth in learned behaviors and innate origins," Dr. Farina mused. "How easy it is to do something once you've done it before. Good luck at the memorial broadcast."

Imposter.

Fake.

Liar.

Present Lilith sighed deeply, taking in the cool air that emanated from the Vita-8 pool.

"Stronger. Better. Smarter." She recited.

Imposter, the voice said to her. *If you don't do what is necessary, they will find you false. And you will fall. Child of ice and winter, your heart is cold and will never melt. Keep it so. Ready yourself, those you summoned near!*

Lilith heard the footsteps and idle chatter of Michael, Ren, and Asa approach. She continued to watch deep into the Vita-8 pool. Its swirling blue, so much like the southern aurora borealis she once admired long ago.

And missed.

Chapter 29: Atop the Mountain

And Hesiod wrote about creation.

From the void, there was chaos. Then Gaia emerged, mother of life and the Earth itself. She gave birth to the heavens, who was so named Uranus. Then came the Titans, children of the earth and sky, and immortal parents of the gods. It was only Gaia who could breathe life into creation, and only she who could create life anew, for she was creation itself.

*   *   *

Evie looked up the cliffside.

"There's no way on Triton I'm climbing up that monstrosity," she said.

She stood at the foot of a mountain cliffside bordering the grove. The thick vegetation of the grove prevented her from noticing it before, just like the sea, until Isaiah told her to seek it out.

"No absolutes," he said. He appeared next to her, hands tucked into his sleeves, unblinking. "This is necessary. Just as you feed yourself, you must build your strength. You must climb."

"Here's an idea," Evie said. "How about you zap me to the top?"

"No."

"You said there's something up there I need to see," she said. "If you want me to see it so badly, zap me like you did out of the sea."

"You were encompassed in my time loop before," he said. "And I didn't, as you say, 'zap' us out of the ocean. I folded time and space and transferred our essence through a fourth-dimensional passage, which is only possible for you to withstand while in my time loop. And I don't think your body can withstand another transfer so soon. You may not notice it, but you are still recovering at the molecular level. I will not risk it."

"I can risk it," Evie said. As a resident, there were times when she was forced to make educated guesses and take risks to save a life. "What's the worst that could happen?"

"Your DNA will reorganize as it attunes to existing in another dimensional space and melt all your cells."

"Wow," Evie said. "Certainly doesn't sound good for my health." She looked up the cliffside again. "I think I'll climb."

"Wise decision."

Isaiah disappeared.

Evie searched for a footing, or any possible way up. In perspective, the mountain wasn't massive; a foothill in comparison to those she witnessed in the Catskills she visited often. Yet scaling to the peak would be no small feat. Her well-worn shoes offered little protection despite the skill of those who made them for 4020. She hoped the calluses she developed since awakening were thick enough to subsidize where her shoes lacked.

Twenty feet away, the cliffside turned gradual, trees mangled at distorted angles as the grove ascended the mountain.

"I guess that's where I'll start," she said to herself.

The pressure of walking uphill took its toll quicker than Evie wanted. The incline increased, and her calves stretched. She kept a rhythm as she walked, using the mangled trees as a support.

She picked up a branch, thick as a quarter and chest height. An optimal walking stick. She dug it into the wet soil, pushing her weight on it as a third leg. The slope increased, forcing her onto her hands and knees to continue uphill without falling.

Look only a few feet ahead, not to the top. A psychological trick to avoid discouraging her climb. If she made it those few feet, she'd make it a few more.

Her thighs burned, her lungs heavy, and her heart pumped. Sweat beaded all over her body, soaking her bodysuit in its sticky dampness. She exerted her efforts forth, her hand melting into her walking stick.

On Earth, this hike would've taken her out. She never imagined taking on a physically monumental task of this level. Residency and long hours in medical institutions made her soft.

She tasted salt in her mouth, and satisfaction elated her. Fatigue tugged, but she pushed through. She was not who she was on Earth. She'd become stronger. Entering a space program demanded a minimal level of physical strength, but she never tested how strong she'd become since joining the UNSF. More so, Triton did something to her. Was it during her cryogenic sleep? Or had the demands of survival increased her physique?

A downwind breeze drew her gaze ahead. The trees cleared, and she saw the peak.

She forgot all her pain and fatigue as she hurried herself to the top.

The peak plateaued into chalk-colored flat rock, the tips of tree tops brushing against its edges.

She pulled herself onto it.

She lay flat on her back. The warm rock soothed her muscles, and she closed her eyes, breathing fast.

"Slow your breath," she heard Isaiah say over her. "Give the oxygen time to penetrate your lungs." She felt his fingertip touch her forehead, but did not feel the crackle of energy from him like she did before. "Breath deep."

She opened her eyes, and he looked down at her, his colorless face outlined by the burnt coral sky behind him.

He removed his finger from her forehead, and she sat up.

Cool air brushed through her hair.

And Evie stood in wonder.

She planted her feet firmly into the stone ground beneath. The cold wind nipped at her cheeks, and her hair brushed against her cracked lips. She shivered and condensation floated from between her teeth, but she did not feel weakened by the mountain's breath. She was awake, energized by its chill. She'd come this far, her second wind pumping strength into her limbs.

"I've made it," she said.

Isaiah stood, hands tucked into his flowing sleeves. He looked neither proud nor disappointed in her achievement. He simply turned his head, observing the landscape that stretched before them. Neptune's semi-circular arch peered above the horizon, slowly sinking, its ever presence never truly passing away.

Evie's chest burned at Isaiah's disregard for her. "Have you nothing to say?"

He continued to look upon the landscape.

"I did it," she stepped toward him. "I've done all you've advised me to do. However, I don't know why in hell I did. But I did."

He said nothing.

"Why?" she demanded. The cold began to penetrate Evie's skin, the heat of the climb wearing off. "Speak to me! Why?"

They stood in silence, the mountain's howl like haunting words. Why had Evie done this? If all he'd told her to this point was true, then there was reason to be here, in the grove, and at the top of the mountain.

He turned his gaze upon her once again, his silvery, deep-set eyes focused. His brows furrowed, and he held out a hand.

"Come," he said. "And I will show you this new world."

Evie held her breath. She didn't want her cells to melt

Your climb has strengthened and healed you, his soundless voice spoke. *Feeling my power for a short time will not harm you.*

She reached and took it.

It was like static touching his hand. The energy hummed within it, sending a startling shock through her system. Was that him, or was it her own insecurity? He led her to the ledge, guiding her gently.

Look, he spoke inwardly.

The mountain wind shook them.

Evie stopped before approaching the edge. "I'll fall."

I will not allow it, he continued. *Come.* His other hand touched her elbow to continue guiding her.

She stepped with him to the very edge of the mountain ledge.

Step down.

Another ledge, about two feet in diameter, was right below them.

Evie didn't move. Vertigo told her it wasn't safe.

Trust, Evie, Isaiah's inner voice sent a sensation of unnatural calm through her. Was his emotion somehow being translated to her? How was he so calm? *You must learn to trust.*

She did trust him, even if every fiber told her not to. How could she not? She pushed against her natural instinct and wanted to trust this being that had listened to her sorrows, advised her in survival, and to whom she confessed her innermost secrets. 4020 doubted her and her sanity, and Isaiah validated her.

Together they stepped onto the ledge.

Look at this young world, Evie. What do you see?

It was awe-inspiring. Anxiety did not allow her to admire the landscape before, but Isaiah's touch and calming inner voice dampened her doubt.

It was like Earth, the greenery and stretching shadows against patches of rocky landscape. Clouds and sky, the crimson sun ever present, with the watchful eye of Neptune almost completely below the horizon.

And genuine. All of it natural Triton, untouched by human hands. The cold mountain wind turned sweet as a warm updraft came up, carrying the scent of rock and vegetation. She'd never known such a pure, untouched scent. Earth always had a scent mixed with some kind of human creation, be it food or industrialization. This truly was a newly living world, with young life ripe for reaping.

"It's beautiful," Evie gasped. "It feels beautiful. What you've done here—"

What I've done?

"Yes," Evie looked at his face. "What you've created is a marvel."

His face remained unchanged. *That's where you're wrong.*

"Wrong?" Evie said, confused. "I think, my friend, I'm right this time. What could possibly be wrong with this world?"

That's not what I mean—it is a marvel. You're mistaken about how it came about.

"But you made it happen," she said.

I had a hand in jump-starting the process, he said. *Just like I told you before, I only sped up the process.*

Isaiah dropped his touch from her. The static of his power faded gradually, draining without tiring.

His gaze turned to the distance. *The truth is, I've created nothing. In all my existence, I've only manipulated what was already present. The ability to create something from nothing; that is truly the power of a god. I've only known of one creature in this universe to naturally hold such a power. Life persists—even here.*

"But you made this happen," Evie said. "Triton would be nowhere near its evolutionary state if not for you, not with the eclipse freezing everything. When I emerged from the lake, I saw all the plant life, and none of it made sense. I wondered how it could be there without all the other symbiotic connections life needs to survive. It was you who made it exist, made it possible."

Isaiah smiled. *Didn't I tell you I cannot lie when I speak to your heart? I cannot create life, Evie. I'm utterly and innately incapable of such a thing. It's a part of my nature. Like I said, I helped life along to evolve to this point, but I didn't make it. It happened as the natural order of the universe. But your nature is entirely another matter.*

"My nature?"

Your nature. A pensive look shadowed his face. *The nature to bear life.*

"You mean—"

I do mean it, Evie. I've merely expedited the process of life on Triton, changed the perception of time on this moon. Nudged it along. Triton is born of the sun. And you, too, are born of the sun. You can create life, will new cells into existence by having them appear from unrelated ones. That is a power I can never hold. But the real question is this: are you, child of Earth, willing to wield that power here on Triton? Will you lead your people to raise a future generation that will save your Earth race from extinction and build a persevering civilization?

Lead the people. Raise a new generation to an unforeseen destiny on a world other than Earth.

And in the simplest terms for her: have a family.

Was he really discussing this with her? It was something Evie wanted long ago with someone she once loved. But that had passed. And a dream she gave up the day Michael left.

"This is stupid." She crossed her arms. "You brought me all the way up here to lecture me on the repopulation? 4020 is well aware that's eventually needed with Earth gone. Bottom of the priority list for now."

It is the natural order of things.

"It's stupid."

You said that already.

"The view is beautiful, it's amazing," she said. "But the Xyelex is out there, and I cannot think of those kinds of things. I can never think of those things. Not anymore. It's for other people in 4020 to worry about, when the time is right."

The time is never right! Isaiah's inner voice rose within her mind. *And it never will be. Your people have strange qualms and taboos about discussing such matters, but humankind will die out if it is not done. The Xyelex will win if your people refuse to do what is necessary. It's already taken members of your team. Your numbers dwindle as we speak, and will continue unless future generations are fostered.*

Evie's heart stopped. "Dwindle? What do you mean? Do you know what's happening to them?"

The Xyelex's power grows, Isaiah said. *Your Community is in danger. See.*

Isaiah placed his hand on her head, and a vision opened before Evie. The Xyelex, bigger and elongated. Those who assimilated by them unidentifiable. More assimilated, their cries screaming for freedom, doused by the Xyelex. Flashes of familiar faces: Lilith... Asa... Ren. . .

Michael.

Isaiah released her from the vision.

"They were supposed to be better off without me," Evie gasped. "Safer, better chance to survive!"

Don't lie, Earth child, Isaiah said. *You left because you feared their persecution. Your mental wall is still up, but it weakens as we speak. Take it down, and you might save your people. Remember what you are.*

"I can't!"

Remember.

"No!"

Awaken... remember what it was to be loved. . .

And she felt her heart open.

All the moments flooded to her mind, of a time when her soul and mind were in sync with Michael's. When she poured out her dreams and vulnerabilities to him, and he, in turn, trusted her with his. A time when she felt they were truly bonded together, when a single look told the other everything they needed to know. Closeness that they declared and consummated in matrimony.

Closeness she was feeling for him again.

She closed her eyes. In her mind, she watched another piece of her mental wall crumble. She stepped through it.

And found herself reliving the day they arrived at Neptune.

*   *   *

The new administrative members of 4020 were aboard a UNSF long-term transport.

Long-term transports provided travel to outer moons and planets. When the Mars colonies failed, and the Venus air cities defunded, the UNSF looked to the far reaches of the solar system to extend their efforts. Artificial gravity from centrifugal force gave humans the illusion of steady walking. Intense exercise decreased the rate of muscle atrophy, and homely quarters gave a sense of tradition on their long journey.

Evie and Michael stood alone outside one of those quarters, a narrow corridor lined with bars and straps in case the artificial gravity failed. The narrowness forced them to stand closer than felt acceptable. Something she hadn't done since they split their respective ways.

"I know it hasn't been easy on either of us," Michael said. "But, what I'm trying to say—well, um—thank you," he stumbled over his words. The same as always when he was nervous.

"Thank you?" Evie was confused. What did he have to be thankful for? She did her duty, and he did his since starting this mission. She stuck to their agreement.

"Yes," Michael continued. "Things were hard before we left."

"We don't need to talk about it," Evie said coldly. "Like you said, that's the past. We need to look ahead. We know our place on the mission, and that's what's most important. Right?"

"Right," Michael bit his lip. "But still, thank you."

Neither of them wanted to lose this career opportunity, that much they still respected in one another. A tacit agreement that the job came first. There wasn't time for anything else before leaving. And Evie lived up to that agreement and would continue doing so. She did her job and she did it well. She'd been cordial and professional to Michael, and he in turn. But nothing more beyond that.

But maybe there was more.

A glimmer of hope surged through Evie, like a spark flickering from her chest down to her fingertips. And she reached for Michael's hand, hoping beyond hope that he, too, would feel that same spark from her. The slight touch of the back of his hand against her fingertips made her feel a familiar affection she thought was all but drained from her.

She searched his eyes for reciprocation, his face holding steady.

"Michael, I—"

A sudden rumble hummed through the transport.

We're beginning de-acceleration to prepare for transfer to UNSF Neptune station, Ren's voice boomed over the intercom. *It should be gradual enough that you won't need to strap in, but I highly recommend looking outside if you can. Lovely stars this evening, don't you think?*

As quickly as it happened, it fled; the familiar spark went out. Evie, to her chagrin, pulled her hand away, crossing her arms.

Asa and Olena ran in excitedly.

"You need to see this," Olena said. "Best view is at section B. Hurry, before it's out of sight!"

Michael smiled politely. "Shall we?" He gestured to their colleagues.

"Of course," Evie said, uncrossing her arms and standing straight. "Wouldn't miss it for the world, literally."

They all chuckled as they left the section. Evie glanced at Asa. His expression said it all to her. He knew her joke was empty, a cover for what just happened.

The window in section B filled their vision as they entered. No longer a pale blue dot in the distance, Neptune finally looked like a planet. A pale teal orb with hints of green, the ice planet looked nothing like the enhanced cerulean photos they were all accustomed to.

Ren was already standing in front of the window, looking at the planet. "It'll still be just a couple of Earth days before we make it to the station," he said.

"Look!" Michael burst with enthusiasm. "You can see the moons!"

Everyone gawked at him. Their lead physicist, the calm, demur gentleman, raised his voice in excitement.

All, but Evie. This was the Michael she knew. He finally looked truly happy for the first time on this mission.

"Well look!" He pointed out the window. "And see, if you look at the angle there. . . and at that moon... and you'll see Triton... one thing to look through a telescope, but see with the natural eye. . ."

Michael went into a swarm of explanations, talking faster than any of them could keep up. Ren jumped in, being the only other one to keep up with him in conversation. Olena and Asa just admired the planet in silence with Evie.

Though Evie couldn't help but be distracted, fluttering her gaze between the planet and her estranged husband's ramblings.

No, she told herself. *Don't. I can't ruin this once-in-a-lifetime moment for myself because of him. Seeing Neptune in person is just as special for me as it is for him.*

But seeing him, excited for Neptune, talking without animosity and beyond blind professionalism, reminded her of one thing she wanted to forget: she still loved him.

The memory closed.

*   *   *

Evie opened her eyes.

She stood alone on the ledge, the landscape of Triton stretching before her, the long shadows from the red sun expanding the vast landscape.

Evie felt a tendril of Isaiah's presence, although she could no longer see him, as he spoke to her in parting. *Save your people.*

Chapter 30: Quiet Voices, Loud Whispers

Asa scanned the landscape from the cave opening. "This is suicide!" Ren's whisper rasped from below. His grip tightened on Asa's ankles, holding him steady against the cave wall. "Plain old stupid suicide!"

The cave opening was near the chamber ceiling, and just big enough for a head and shoulders to fit through. One of the many unknown entrances only Michael knew about. Asa found that Michael mapped out much more of the caves than he initially let on, keeping 4020 at bay with the volatile Vita-8 pool.

Asa squinted. It felt good to feel the fresh, open air after being stuck in the musty caves. All was clear in the warm dusk light.

Except for the looming humanoid silhouette, the Xyelex.

"Michael's clear," Asa said in hushed tones. "And one of them is no more than a hundred meters away."

"By god seal that opening and get down." Ren sounded more exasperated than usual.

"You can let go of my ankles," Asa said. "You holding them is doing little, you know."

"It's keeping you from running out like that maniac," Ren said. "He'd better bring Evie back like he promised."

"It's just standing there," Asa continued, staring at the Xyelex. Like a statue, it kept its stance. Still and unmoving. "It knows we're in the caves. Why isn't it attacking?"

"Just get down," Ren said. "I'm barely holding it together, man."

"We need that sample." Asa pulled his head back in and looked down at Ren. The dark cave shadows made his face look more desperate.

Ren's clutch on Asa's ankles tightened. "I know."

"Then let go?" Asa shook his foot. "And get the Vita-8 spears."

Ren didn't move. He rolled his lips inward and furrowed his brow.

"Go," Asa said. "Haste before the sun is down. Now is the opportune time. I have the other tools I need in my pack."

" *'Now is the opportune time,'* " Ren mimicked in a high-pitched voice. "Fine!" He let go of Asa's ankles and slumped away to the Vita-8 chamber.

Asa slid down the inclined cave wall.

He sat on the cool, moist floor, resting his arms on his knees.

What have you gotten yourself into? Asa thought. *Waiana, what would you think of me?*

He remembered his mother's kind face. Dark eyes aged before their time with crows' feet, and beautiful, looking down at him when he was a child. She was the most beautiful thing he'd ever seen. *Bubba, why didn't you say something?*

I couldn't, he remembered his childhood voice before it deepened. *It happens every time. I freeze up and can't talk. I want to, but can't.*

I know it's hard, she had told him. *But you have to speak up sometimes. You have to fight it, push through.*

What if people get mad at me?

Then let them be mad. He remembered her warm embrace, the same as when she gave it. What he wouldn't give to hug her like that again.

"Got them," Ren scampered in, carefully holding thick poles in each hand. The tips were bound with sharpened, hooked spearheads and reflected cool blue. Tips dipped in the concentrated Vita-8.

"Don't let it drip on you," Ren said. "Hold it at an angle. Unless you want a scar to match Michael."

"Maybe." Asa stood. "He messed with it before it injured him. This is the pure substance. Hand them up to me."

He climbed the wall, up to the opening. He poked his head out, one last check.

The red sun was almost set, the jade green of night closing in. The Xyelex still in position. If he was to do this, it was now or never.

Using his upper body strength, he pulled himself out. "Hand them up."

Ren handed the thick poles to Asa.

"Break a leg," Ren said. "But not how I actually did."

Asa smiled. He could always count on Ren for some relief and humor. "I'll be careful."

He kept low, using tall grass and evening shadows for cover.

You have to speak up sometimes. You have to fight it, push through... let them be mad. He continued to think of her words as he remembered a time he did speak up.

What do you want to be when you grow up? He remembered his primary teacher when he lived in Sydney as a child.

He'd been working on speaking up, talking to people who weren't his family or friends. Although academics came easily for him, simple social cues weren't so simple. He'd worked weeks on building up the stamina to present in class for careers day.

I want the memory of his young voice, the admiration he felt for his mother, *to be a dad when I grow up.*

The entire class laughed, and some jeered. *She means jobs, stupid! That's not a real job!*

The burning love for his mother, her kind eyes, awoke something in him. He felt his small voice reverberate: *Being a good mom and dad is a real job! Harder than any job your lazy parents did!*

Boys, that's enough, his teacher had put a hand on his shoulder. *Asa, finish your presentation, please. And this time the class will mind their manners.*

He never did finish that presentation. And he never spoke up again for all of primary school. Speech therapy helped him speak up for respectable conversations by the time he was in secondary school, and he communicated well enough in chemistry studies and graduate school. Never an unkind word, and nothing oppositional to authority. A trusted friend and advisor to many.

And his current silence was key to staying hidden in the tall grass. The Xyelex still hadn't moved.

Fifty meters, he thought. Its looming presence seemed unreal, not even swaying with the twilight breeze.

He crept closer. From what Micahel told him, the Xyelex sensed emotions and evoked feelings in its victims. Did it sense him? Was it ignoring him? If so, why?

Trapped, he thought. *It's keeping us trapped. It has its numbers, but wants us to stay put. Why?*

He continued his approach.

A hiss floated over him. "Child of the sunburnt country, you've sought us-s-s. . ."

It sensed him, but he stayed low, hidden.

"We s-s-see your grief," its thousand-voice hiss continued. "Join us-s-s and we s-s-shall take away your grief... You will connect and belong."

He saw a flash of a vision in his mind. Of someone he once cared for on Earth. A person with kind eyes like his mother, and a gentle laugh that warmed his heart.

Charlie.

"We s-s-see what you mourn." The Xyelex turned its head in his direction. The blackened eyes and mouth wide. "It is-s-s not this-s-s person. But the promises-s-s unfulfilled."

Time seemingly halted as Asa remembered his last conversation before saying goodbye to Charlie.

*　　*　　*

I can't believe you have this opportunity, Charlie told him. His dark hair and eyes sparkled with pride against his pale complexion. "You, on an outer planet mission."

"I—" Asa wanted to say something to Charlie. He wanted to tell him what he really wanted. But as always, he froze.

"Don't worry, I'll be fine," Charlie told him. "And I'll still be here when you get back."

"It's not that," past Asa said. "It's just that I don't know if going is what I really want."

"What do you mean?" Charlie sounded shocked. "It's all you've ever talked about."

"I know, I know," past Asa said. "It's just that, what I really want—" he choked before saying it.

"Hey," Charlie put a tender hand on Asa. "It's okay if you're not ready to say what you want. Just know that I support you."

Asa sighed. "Yes, of course."

"And while you're gone," Charlie brightened. "I'll take care of it so everything's ready when you get back. I already have a list of willing surrogate mothers to carry." Scientific mitomiosis processes made it possible for them to have a child born from their DNA. "I'll take care of the rest of the red tape while you're away."

It's all he wanted, and didn't want. Asa wanted what his mother once gave him. The feel of her nurturing arms around him, he wanted to do that for another. He wanted to give all that he was to another person and love them unconditionally. To be open, completely himself, like he was around his parents. To share and teach, to give and foster.

He wanted to be a father.

But going meant that it had to wait. And that Charlie would handle much of the process without him.

He didn't want to wait to be a father and have a family.

"I—," his voice froze again. Charlie was doing so much, he didn't want to hurt or disappoint him. "I appreciate it. I'll be careful so I come back in one piece."

Charlie's comforting, bright laugh. "You'd better! And I promise, we'll have a family. We'll do the whole shebang when you return. I can't want to be a parent!"

"Can't wait too."

*　　*　　*

"You loved the promises-s-s" the Xyelex's legion of voices invaded Asa's memory. "It remains-s-s unfulfilled, and cannot be fulfilled with your Community the way you want. We will give you those promises. Join us-s-s and be connected. Join us-s-s and we will be the family you crave."

The Xyelex suddenly stood over him. He was no longer hidden, vulnerable, and open to the Xyelex.

It reached its elongated fungal arm toward him.

And for a moment, Asa almost considered it.

He lunged and stabbed its arm with the tip of his Vita-8 spear.

It screeched a shrill scream with all its voices. Its other arm whipped at him, but Asa caught it with his other spear.

"Not a chance in hell," Asa gritted through his teeth.

The screech of the other Xyelex was heard. He didn't have much time.

He twisted and tore one of the spears away, its hook taking a piece of the Xyelex's fungal flesh.

"Join us-s-s," it continued to screech. "As-s-similate and join!"

He ran. He heard voices from Lilith's scouts yelling that someone was out there and that the Xyelex was attacking. The stomp of the Xyelex behind him, its lumbering legs stretching in one stride the length of three of his.

The grass ripped at his legs, razors against his flesh. He had to be faster. It was bigger, but he had to be quicker.

He saw Ren's head poke out of the opening.

"Get in here, you idiot!" Ren yelled.

Asa pulled clay flasks from his side pack. Cold to the touch, he threw them on the ground surrounding the cave opening, breaking them open to spill the concentrated Vita-8—a mote against invaders.

"Move!" he bellowed.

Ren's head dipped down just in time for Asa to jump. As he did, the Xyelex's arm swung at him.

And he disappeared down the opening.

He slid down the cave wall.

Ren was already in position, sealing the opening with bound rocks and dumping flasks of Vita-8 on it.

"It could still break through," Ren said. "Hurry, grab more—"

"Wait." Asa heaved a breath.

They both paused.

No tumult. Not even a scratch at the entrance from the Xyelex.

It was leaving them alone.

"Just," Asa heaved another breath, "as I," another pant, "thought."

He lay on his back, catching his breath. "It won't attack us while we're in the caves. It wants us trapped. We're cattle."

"No way." Ren looked up the entrance he just sealed. "Did it work? Did you get it?"

"See for yourself." He held up his spear, a piece of the Xyelex's flesh on it, stained from Vita-8.

Ren snatched it faster than a bullet shot. "You got it! You actually got it! And you're alive, thank god."

"Careful," Asa sat up. "I think it could still infect you if touched."

A commotion from deep within the caves made them take pause.

Asa stood. "Who's that—"

Lilith entered the chamber, followed by ten people, holding torches high, sharpened spears in hand. All those sworn to Lilith's scouting team, the most physically fit and athletically inclined of 4020. They filed in orderly, surrounding Asa and Ren, pointing the sharpened, deadly spearheads at them, blades glinting in the firelight.

Militiamen.

Asa put his hands up. Ren did not drop his spear with the Xyelex's flesh.

Asa felt blindsided. "Commander?" What was she doing? He knew Lilith had a temper, but she always protected them. She is the hero of Antarctica.

"Quite a fuss you stirred up out there." She gestured to Ren's hooked spear. "Hand it over."

He held it out reluctantly. One of the militiamen took it.

"Careful, there's a piece of the Xyelex on that." Asa felt torn. He knew these people, felt the need to help, to warn. But familiar faces showed stern aggression, empty of the compassion he'd seen so many of them display. Who were they?

"So this is what you do while we've been researching," Ren's voice was in a partial snarl. "Building the weapons for your so-called militia, you turn and start—"

"Shut the hell up, Tanaka," Lilith spat. "I've had my militia long before we awoke on this god forsaken moon." She looked at them, dripping with disdain. "Where's Dr. Smith?"

Asa and Ren's eyes met. Neither spoke.

"I expected this from Tanaka," she relaxed her hands at her sides. "But Dr. Baramba, I'm disappointed. Getting pulled into one of his irresponsible schemes? Letting Dr. Smith run off after a traitor and leave behind 4020 when they need him most."

"Evie's no traitor," Ren said. "You are."

Lilith grinned. "Show Mr. Tanaka what happens to those who throw careless accusations at their superior."

Ren buckled over, a gut-wrenching shriek as one of the militiamen shoved a spear into his side—a former male chemist under Asa who idolized Lilith's Antarctican heroism.

"Ren!" Asa moved to help, but nine more blades closed in, warning him not to touch.

"Don't worry, the injury won't kill you," Lilith stepped closer, towering over them. "But it'll hurt for a long time. You're lucky the Xyelex attacked when it did; otherwise, your usefulness would've run out. And that's going to keep you alive—your usefulness. The Community does not need those who do not contribute to the greater good."

Asa smelled the sick metallic scent of blood, its stains spreading along Ren's side, and dripping through the fingers that held his wound.

"You sick bastard," Ren spit. "I'm not doing anything for you."

"Very well." She raised a hand, eyeing the one who stabbed Ren.

She was going to kill him.

"Wait!" Asa spoke up.

Her eyes didn't meet Asa's. "And what does our ingenious chemist have to say on the matter?"

He felt it —the stiffness in his throat, right before freezing.

His mother's voice rang in his mind: *You have to speak up... You have to fight it, push through... let them be mad.*

He tried to speak. No words came out.

"Nothing to say?" Lilith looked happy, delighted, a person who'd waited more than long enough for this to happen. "Suit yourselves. Can't say I'm not relieved to be rid of you, Tanaka."

"We'll do it," Asa blurted out. "I'll make sure he does, too. With Michael gone, you need his engineering mind. I can't do it alone. Ren, you have to do this. For the Community, for your own good."

Ren's face twisted in anguish, still clutching his side. "Fine!" he gritted through his teeth. "For—the—Community!"

Lilith released her gaze and slowly lowered her hand. "Very well. I want two of you on guard at all times with these treacherous snakes. I want them working day and night until we get what we want. And dispose of that sample; it's dangerous, and they don't need it. Throw it into the Vita-8 pool."

"No—" Asa reached for his sample of Xyelex's flesh. He was met with a spear under his neck.

"Tsk, tsk," Lilith shook her index finger. "Only as long as you're useful, Dr. Baramaba. And make your work quick; the people wait for their protectors to have sufficient weapons against the Xyelex to calm their fears. I'd hate to see what happens if they're disappointed."

Lilith walked away, taking one of her militiamen with her.

Torchlight sizzled from the cave drippings. The remaining militiamen pushed Asa and injured Ren forward.

"You're making a mistake," Ren winced. "All of you. She's crazy, she's using you. The Xyelex's no danger to us while we're in the caves. We can beat it with science, not with aggression."

"*Silence inferior,*" the one who stabbed Ren said.

"Inferior?" Ren smirked through his winces. "Did Lilith teach you that?"

"We protect the Community," he said. "From the Xyelex and those who bring disorder."

"Stop, Ren," Asa shushed him. "Just do what they say."

They continued, spears at their necks, down dark cave chambers they thought once hidden.

Asa knew Ren was right. With the Xyelex at bay, one thing was clear: the weapons Lilith wanted weren't meant for the Xyelex.

Chapter 31: A Price Paid

Evie thought about the memories she regained atop the mountain.

They're finally coming back, she thought. *After all this time.*

It was midday, when the oversized red sun was partway to setting, and Neptune was a quarter of the way through its daily cycle. She created a small fire-pit in a clearing within the grove, roasting her morning's catch. A mid-sized fowl, the color of earthen soil. Since Isaiah persuaded her to kill for food, taking life while hunting became easier with each catch. Even in the few days she'd been in the grove, the variety of land animals increased; more fowls, small reptilians, even some creatures that looked neither fowl nor mammal but a mix of both.

Isaiah's been busy, she thought. Although she knew it'd been a few Triton days, the growth of life was beyond centuries. Was his time manipulation affecting her, too? He swore it only affected that which he desired it to, but she still held her suspicions deep.

And in her solitude, she pondered her regained memories.

I can't believe I still felt that way about Michael, after all that time. She prodded her fire-roasted meal. *Was that why I didn't remember we weren't together? Everyone made it sound mutual—but it wasn't. I should be relieved, right?*

But she wasn't. She felt its price.

The pain she wanted to forget was at the forefront. She pictured her mental wall; it was crumbling, only small pieces remaining. Did she want those remaining pieces if it meant more heartache? Was her amnesia truly a blessing and not the curse she thought?

There are still parts. She prodded her foot, checking its wellness. Still raw. *Parts my mind is refusing to acknowledge. How bad are they that I can't will myself to them?*

"That's for you to decide." Isaiah suddenly blipped into existence across from her, the fire smoke distorting him.

Evie grabbed her chest. "I don't think I'll ever get used to you doing that."

He tilted his head curiously. "I announced myself this time."

"Before you blip in," Evie said. "Before is key."

"Before, during, after," Isaiah said thoughtfully. "So linear. So—" he paused, as though thinking of the right word, "one-dimensional."

Evie shook her head. He wasn't going to get it.

He clutched at his shirt over his chest, gripping something underneath.

He noticed. "You're curious as to what I'm holding, are you not?"

He spoke it before she had the chance to put it into spoken words. "Um, yes. I saw you do that before, over the sea."

Isaiah's bright eyes blinked. Was that the crack of a smile from the seemingly emotionless creature? "You want to see." It wasn't a question; a statement of her curiosity.

He reached into his shirt, pulling a dainty chain that hung from his neck. Delicate, it sparkled like white gold. Attached to the end of it was a small fist-sized pouch. The pouch was as white as he was, iridescent strands reflecting like smooth water over glass.

Evie blinked, and he blipped out of existence.

And reappeared next to her.

He held it up to Evie. "I've been saving this for the right time." He put out his palm and tipped the pouch over it.

And out dropped the most peculiar of objects.

Evie immediately felt a pulse of energy as a rounded object dropped into his hand, as though the pouch was not only concealing it, but its power. Isaiah cradled a round, crystal-like stone that shone like a star. It gave a subtle glow, white light that pulsed like a heartbeat.

Evie felt like she was beside a power station, the hairs on her arms standing from invisible static. She felt a wave from it, trying to touch her inner self—her soul.

Just like when he brought her deep into the sea.

She leaned away from its beauty, wrapping her arms around herself.

"What is that?" she asked, unable to take her eyes off it.

"This is a celestial stone," Isaiah said, holding it closer to her.

"Radiation!" Evie cried. "I can feel it. Get it away from me! I know it probably doesn't affect you the same way, but radiation kills humans."

"It's not radiation," Isaiah said. "And this will not kill you." He eyed it, then put his gaze directly on her. "A celestial stone is the rarest of all things in this reality, for they are mined within the fifth dimension. You could say they are a physical manifestation of the fifth dimension. In this stone is the power to progress humankind forward, to restore it to what it once was and more."

Evie eyed the stone. It was enchanting, hypnotizing to look upon. It had an air of presence, stronger than that even of Isaiah.

This is my celestial stone, his inner voice said. *My companion; given to me when I became an overseer.*

"What does it do?" she asked.

Watch and learn. He held his hand out toward her roasting food. Pink flesh turned golden, and her fire died.

"Your sustenance is ripe for consumption." He lowered his hand.

Evie felt her mouth open wide and quickly closed it. "You-you sped up time."

"No," he said. "Manipulated the perception of time around it, no more, no less. We are still in what you perceive as the present. The bubble, per se, I put your sustenance within changed relative to what I desired.

"This stone keeps me connected to my realm, my dimension," he continued. "And it is imprinted on myself, so it can never be lost or removed from me."

"That's the answer," Evie said. "You can use that to save us from the eclipse. You can move things along, and we can skip it all and—"

"You cannot skip," Isaiah said. "That's not how time works. I know, coming from a realm where time is literally one of the dimensions. If I were to do that, all would wither and appear as it was, even if I stayed relative to your perception. No, it is not an easy fix. But it has allowed me to evolve things within their perceptions to give you the resources you need to survive. Even my abilities have their limits, as you well know."

Evie was still amazed at the stone's beauty, drawn to it. As though it weren't her own, her hand reached to touch it.

"Careful," Isaiah pulled it away. "Its influence is addictive to those not familiar with its power." He covered it with the pouch and slipped it under his shirt. "Your people are not the first in your system to tamper with such power."

"Tamper?" Evie's curiosity piqued. "Who else tampered with it?"

"A sorry people," he said. "Ones I once hoped to help, but became lost in their own lust for power. A once sister planet to your Earth race." He looked at her, narrowing his gaze. "What would you do if I gave it to you?"

The question caught her off guard. "What?"

"Would you accept such a majestic thing as a celestial stone?"

"That thing?" she pointed to where he hid it in his shirt. "You said it imprinted on you and can't be lost."

"I did," he said. "Would you still accept such a powerful thing? You enjoyed the freedom you had with me above the sea. Would you take such a thing to always feel that way? It'd free your mind, cure your amnesia. You'd have everything."

" I-uh—" What would she do with a celestial stone? If it was as powerful as Isaiah said it was, she could do anything, be anything she wanted. She could grow Triton as she wanted and feel free of the things that bound her.

But with the recent regaining of her memories, such things didn't come without a price.

"Balance," she said. "All things must be balanced. No one can wield such a thing without the price it'd take to balance, and I don't think I'm willing to pay that price it demands."

Isaiah looked pleased, as pleased as someone like him could be. "Child of Earth, you finally understand. Your restraint serves you well, unlike others in your Community. It is preferable."

"Preferable over what?" she asked.

Something unseen caught his attention. He stood, looking into the distance.

Evie stood to, trying to see what he saw. "What is it?"

"Someone comes," he said. "Not near yet, but I feel the intention." He looked at her. *I cannot reveal myself to this person. This is someone you must face on your own.*

Evie remembered the hab unit; Isaiah couldn't help her then. "The Xyelex?"

No, he said. *This is someone whose mind would unweave at seeing my presence. You've grown accustomed to my presence. You must confront this person.*

Evie picked up one of her makeshift spears, which she used for hunting.

Weapons are not needed, he said. *But be wary. You can be harmed in more ways than one.*

She nodded. "I'll go."

*   *   *

Evie trudged through the vegetation of the grove, swiftly to its edge. She continued as the vegetation lessened to the hills and grasslands she traversed along the lakeside. She saw no sign of anyone.

Come on, Isaiah, she thought. *Who's out there? You couldn't just tell me?*

But then again, his motivations never made sense to her.

Her mind ran through all the people from 4020 that'd make their way out here. Ren? Asa? Certainly not Olena, and Lilith had too many duties as a leader. A scout?

She refused to think of anyone else, lest her hopes be let down.

Evie heard whispers in the wind. *Remember. . .*

Wishful thinking, she thought.

She saw a figure along the horizon, the setting sun drawing out long shadows.

The wind blew through the grass, a wave of warmth flowing, the wind speaking to her, as though the voice of Triton begged:

Remember... reconcile... acceptance. . .

The figure drew closer, and she was able to make out features.

And her heart dropped. This was the price to pay for remembering.

Michael.

Chapter 32:
Rectification

Some say that love is the natural instinct for social species to come together for resilience. To ensure the continuation of their DNA, impulses created by chemical hormones surging through the body to create sensations of attachment and comfort. An illusion of emotions willingly created by the human brain to safeguard survival.

And others say it's like lightning. A phenomenon transcending three-dimensional understanding. Far more beautiful and mystical than any human can hope to fully grasp. For if love was as simple as natural instinct, then would we not attach so easily?

Some say the greatest of sins are ones that cannot give back.

Murder cannot give back the life it took.

Fornication cannot give back virtue.
Abuse cannot give back innocence.
A broken heart will always have scars.

*   *   *

Evie stood dumbfounded. How was Michael here?

But he was. In the gentle breeze, grass swayed, the warm sunlight stretching smooth shadows, and Neptune cast lush jade across the plain, adding a sense of familiarity with wide Earth fields.

He was tattered, his 4020 jumpsuit stained and torn. Days of stubble made his face rugged, and dark circles under his eyes aged him beyond his years. Yet, his face radiated relief and bewilderment, both solace and disbelief at seeing Evie.

He was still the Michael she knew, but also someone changed by Triton.

Unable to contain herself, she ran toward him.

He, too, picked up speed, running toward her.

Just as the rush of wind hit her face, so did everything else rush back to her.

Memories of firsts.

The first time they glanced at one another and pretended not to notice. The first time she approached and greeted him. When she heard his voice, his laugh, and saw him smile at her. The first time their hands instinctively entwined, and their lips touched. The first time they made promises, hoping for the future.

And the first of many broken promises.

Visions of the red door—opening it to Michael's packed suitcases. The pain and heartache of that moment as her home and world came tumbling down. The fighting, yelling, and arguing. The first time they spoke harsh words that cut deeper than knives. The unspoken words of insouciance, that injured even more so. The look in his eyes before he turned away from her for the first time, and every time thereafter.

All of it lay before her.

Many imagine reunions as grandeur. The embrace of loved ones, holding tight, speaking sweet words, and forgetting all past wrongs.

But in reality, past wrongs are rarely forgotten.

They stopped when they reached one another. No embrace, no sweet words, nothing forgotten.

"Michael?" Evie was lost at words to say. "Are you okay? How did you get here?"

Michael leaned forward, holding his hands to his knees. "I could," he panted, "ask the same thing." He caught his breath, and stood straight. "I'm fine. Thank God you're alive."

Silence, neither willing to break it. They stood before one another, plain and simple. Nothing else. They were just as they were.

And more than anything, Michael was here.

Evie felt the urge to hold him, jump into his arms, cling to what they once had. But the sting in her chest kept her from doing so.

Because she didn't want what they once had. She wanted better.

"You came," she said.

"You left," he responded. His lips pressed together tight, as though to seal a flood behind them. He breathed deeply, eyes shimmering, looking directly at her.

Now you know how it feels! She wanted to scream. Yell it to the heavens, justify all her decisions since the time he left. Take recompense from the pain he caused her all this time from his absence in her life.

But what good would it do?

People too often wait for the other to make amends. Truth tells us this is not so. It is not one waiting for the other, otherwise waiting will take an infinite circle. It is the mutual desire of both wanting the same, and both willing to take what the other has to give.

"Please, before you tell me anything," Evie put her hands up. "I want to tell you something I didn't think I'd ever get to tell you, and you being here, it can't wait. Something I thought you knew, so I never said it. And I should have, and I'm sorry I didn't. I want you to know: you're enough. And I've always thought that, even if I didn't say it. And I'll always think that."

Michael looked stunned. "Wow, I, um," he scratched his shoulder nervously. "That's one way to start things off."

"I know, I should've prefaced it, or waited for the right time," Evie said. "But there isn't time. Waiting is completely and utterly stupid, and I've done nothing but think about things, and I don't want to go without telling you." She gulped. They promised not to utter certain words again, to be professional. She had to be brave, defy what hurt them. "I love you. I've always loved you for who you are. You're enough."

She had uttered the damning words. There was no going back.

Michael's face stayed stoic, his voice silent.

"Michael," Evie reached for his shoulder. "Say something."

Michael curled his lips. "Evie, um," he took on his proper stance and expression, manners taking over. "Thank you."

He turned away, brushing her hand off his shoulder.

"Oh." Evie's heart sank in disappointment. She'd told him, begged him countless times before, on the premise of love. It never persuaded him to believe her. She hoped this time he'd believe her.

She felt a tinge of it, deep in her chest. *He always did this,* a past memory called to her. *He did this and I hated it—hated him for it!* A spark to a flame of anger. The rejection, pouring her soul out to him.

And he rejected it.

She heard her memory scream—her screams of anguish, yelling at him for the hurt he caused her.

But sparks cannot cause fires if they aren't fed.

No, Evie thought. *Not anymore.*

And the deep spark in her chest doused, turning to an ember and fading away.

"Sorry to make you uncomfortable," Evie said. "You came all this way, and I guess I blindsided you first thing. That was not my intention. I just wanted you to know. And I'm okay with you not feeling the same about me. I'm really okay with it. I can accept it. And—"

She paused.

Michael's body trembled.

"Are you alright?" Evie's medic brain kicked in. Seizure? Muscle spasm? "Michael, I—"

Like lightning striking, fast and unexpected, Evie was suddenly pulled in. His long arms wrapped around her, his face buried into her shoulder.

"I'm so sorry," he said. "Oh, Evie, I'm so sorry. You left because of me—I wasn't good enough to say something when Lilith pushed the inquiry. And should've been—I should've been better. The entire time I should've been better!"

Evie was stunned. He thought it was his fault? Warmth coursed through her, and her stiff body loosened, welcoming his embrace.

"I'm sorry I abandoned everyone," she said. "It was selfish, I was scared and didn't want to admit it, so I ran. I never should've left the Community."

"*I*," he emphasized, "never should've left you."

Were his words true? Or was this one of Isaiah's twisted visions lacking tact or human understanding? No, this was real. He was here, they were both here, speaking the same reparating confessions.

"You couldn't control falling through the ice," Evie said. "I don't blame you for—"

"No," he lifted his head, looking into her face. "I mean on Earth, at our home. I shouldn't have left."

She looked into his eyes as he spoke. The same eyes she looked into when he first said goodbye.

And for the first time, she saw something she'd missed before. Her own eyes reflected in his, and they were identical. The eyes of two individuals, both equally hurt and broken, yearning for love and comfort, easily mistaken for apathy and indifference.

"If only—"

"If only—"

If only indeed.

And they comforted one another.

Intertwining arms touched one another, a soft caress of solace. Softer than a warm breeze, cheek brushed upon cheek; lips whispering regrets, unloading the weight of encumbering burdens. But pain can only last so long as it washed away from their hearts. Clean slates carved from what felt like a lifetime of trials together.

"I wish—"

"I wish—"

And when words could no longer confess their desires, they felt the warmth from one another, familiar and reassuring.

"Do you remember?"

"I remember."

Their lips came together like delicate petals. And as familiarity took over, so did their passion.

End Part II

PART III: Sancti et Serpentes

Chapter 33: Leave Taking

**W**hat was Michael thinking?

I should've said something, he thought as he slipped his tattered clothes back on. *4020's in trouble and here I am with her—and we—*

Sunrise on Triton. He looked at Evie, sound asleep beside him. The tall, sweet, verdant grass and paradisal warm temperatures were their bed as he held her all night, afraid to let go lest she disappear. Silly? Childish to believe such a thing? Maybe, but the assurance of her in his arms gave him comfort he didn't realize he much needed.

The overwhelming emotion of the moment silenced him, made him forget about 4020, Lilith, Ren, Asa, everyone. Even the Xyelex. It was only he and Evie that mattered. But now that morning approached, the anxieties of their situation came flooding in. He found her; against all odds, he found her. And it was time to go back.

He leaned over her, curling his arms around her bare skin, kissing her cheek. "It's morning," he whispered in her ear. "Time to get dressed."

Her chestnut eyes fluttered open, and he brushed a dark hair from her face. A smile sparked across her face when she looked up at him

Not good enough, he heard the haunting remnants of his father's voice in his memory.

She thinks I am, he told himself. *I came all this way. Maybe I am finally good enough.*

His father's voice faded. *I am good enough.* He repeated, looking at his wife.

The memory diminished.

"I think I lost my clothes," she laughed. "Help me find them?"

"Easy," he said. "They're in better shape than mine."

After they were both fully attired, Michael mulled in his mind how to tell Evie what was going on.

"Come with me," she took his arm. "I have food stowed for a decent breakfast."

"Um, Evie," Michael scratched his head. "There's something you should—"

She put a gentle finger on his lips. "Eat, first order of survival. Get some glucose to your brain."

Glucose? One of the things he missed about her. He kissed her finger and pulled it down. "You win, eat first."

He wanted to extend his escape from what was happening back at the Community, but he knew he couldn't. Lives were on the line— he'd have to tell her.

She led him across small foothills, vegetation growing thicker and diversifying. Soon, vegetation cleared as the shade of deciduous trees took over.

"Trees," he gasped. "I never thought I'd miss seeing them." After living on Triton for so long, he was no longer accustomed to such lush forests. He missed the greenery of the eastern United States, the region around his experimental physics lab at Cornell.

Still, these trees gave a sense of home. And at the same time, had something unfamiliar about them that made him uneasy.

"It's a welcome sight for sure," Evie said. She gently pulled down a branch. "But look, these leaves are not of any tree I know of. These are purely Triton's."

Michael glanced as they passed by. The shapes, the serrated edges. The way the branches grew, not in any pattern of trees on Earth.

"This place gets weirder and weirder," he said. "How are these trees even here? Evolutionary-wise, compared to what we've seen on the planet, this is far beyond what should be here."

Evie stayed silent.

He got a feeling she did know.

They arrived at a clearing with a small unlit fire pit and a patch of woven branches.

"Here." Evie lifted a patch of woven branches. Beneath it was a hole filled with smoked fish. Was it fish? They were not any he recognized.

She handed him a few. "It's not what we're used to on Earth, and it's really salty. But it has the necessary nutrients, and it's better than plain root vegetables. To me, it's good. Since I started feeling hungry again, things aren't the same. I don't crave what I used to."

Michael gladly accepted. After no seasonings for god knows how long he was solitary on Triton, salt never tasted so good.

"You did all this?" When they lived together on Earth, Evie barely cooked, let alone catch and create surplus. She was always so busy, so focused on her schooling and residency. No time for anything but the goal. No time for people.

No time for him.

Who was this person?

"That sea I told you about that the lake drains into," she took some bites of food and swallowed, "is on the other other side of this grove. Has more abundant fish than the lake, and it was simple enough to sift and boil water to get the salt. Took some time, but there's been plenty to forage in the grove in the meantime while I made this. There's also a spring with clean water that drains off a mountain—I guess more a hill—just that way. Can't really see it through the trees from here. Um, why are you looking at me like that?"

His mouth hung open, and he closed it. "Sorry, it's just impressive what you've done. I didn't know you knew how to do all this."

She shrugged, looking embarrassed. "It's just science. I didn't know a lot of it, but I used science to figure much of it out. You need certain fats and proteins for your body to function, and thinking how cells work, you'd need salt to preserve. . ."

She went off on a tangent. He listened, enjoying it.

"People in the Community could really use this," Michael said.

She paused, face dropping.

"Evie, let's sit," he said. "There's more than one reason why I came looking for you."

They sat on a bed of leaves, and he recounted everything. The Xyelex's siege, the deaths, Lilith's plans to take control with her militia, all of it. Evie listened calmly, taking it all in as he spoke. He surprised himself, stating it all collectively. He hardly wanted to believe it himself.

"My god," she shook her head when he told her Olena's fate. "Olena—I can't believe she's gone. We worked so close for so long. I know we both had reservations for one another, but I never wanted this to happen. Not to her, not to anyone."

Evie didn't say anything else when he finished. He figured she needed to process, but she looked strange. The way she turned her head, the way her face perked, as though she were listening to someone else speak to her.

"I can't tell you how I know," Evie said. "But the Xyelex, I know what it is."

Michael held his breath. She knew the Xyelex was his fault?

And he was a dead man if 4020 found out.

"The Xyelex," she continued. "It's not from Triton. It's alien to this world, more so than us. It's from a higher existence. It sounds crazy, but the Xyelex is from a fourth-dimensional plane. It's only trying to survive the way it knows how in a three-dimensional world."

Michael gulped even though his throat was dry. "I-I know." He said nervously.

"You know?" she sounded surprised.

"It seems you figured it out." He crossed his arms, as though it'd stop him from spilling out a confession. But guilt ripped at him, tore at his insides. No amount of holding could stop it from spilling.

His father's echo spoke. *Not good enough, son.*

I want to be good enough.

"This Xyelex," he continued. "I knew what it was from the moment I saw it. Where it originated from. It's my fault, and I'm going insane because of it. If they knew, they'd crucify me. There's only one place that thing could've come from, one thing it could've used."

"My photon accelerator."

Evie's eyes widened.

"Don't you see?" His confession kept spilling. He couldn't stop it. "It was me who gave it a way to come here."

Stop talking. Not good enough, son.

I WANT TO BE GOOD ENOUGH.

If he didn't tell her all of it, then he'd never be good enough to be with her. "My photon accelerator. That's the real reason Lilith had us go on that scavenging trip to the hab unit ruins. We hoped that it was preserved like us. I thought if we could get it up and running, it could save us from the eclipse. But seeing where the Xyelex originated on the hab unit and how it behaves, I knew it came from the accelerator. It's the only reason the Xyelex is here. All I can conclude is that remnants of the Xyelex must've come through when we were living on the hab unit, before all this. And it must've grown in power while we were in cryostasis. It's the only answer as to why it's here—my machine tampered with particles from higher dimensions to give us the power we needed to run the Triton mission. And now we're paying the price. We're all paying the price."

He dropped his head in his hands. The guilt didn't leave, but he felt a wave of confessional relief. "I created this mess. I understand if you hate me for it. Everyone else will when they find out."

Evie put a hand on his back. "Michael, I know you. You didn't do know, and you'd never bring something like that on purpose."

"It doesn't matter if it was on purpose!" How could she show him sympathy? He didn't deserve it after what he did. "It was my negligence that brought it here."

They were quiet. Words unable to comfort others express the revelation.

"There's nothing I can say that will change what you feel," Evie said. "Somehow, I know this isn't entirely on you. It can't be."

He shook his head. "I don't know how to fix this."

Evie's hand gently stroked his back, fingers caressing. "Maybe it's not about fixing it. There's only one thing we can do: make it right."

I want to be good enough. "What would that even be?" he said.

"I don't know," she said. "But to begin, and I can't believe I'm saying it, but it starts with us going back."

She stopped stroking his back, pulling her hands in around herself. "I don't want to go back." She took a breath. "I know what we should do. But there's what we should, and what I want. I want to stay here, start our own homestead. Just the two of us together in this grove, with everything we'll ever need. A peaceful life away from it all." She looked at him with her warm, chestnut eyes, a longing in them. He knew too well that longing.

"It is tempting." He reached over and grasped her hand.

"I left for a reason," she said.

"I know," he said. "So did I." He observed the grove, its resources, its lush life. Everything they ever needed was here and more. They could stay if they wanted.

But he knew they couldn't. The doom the eclipse promised; all of this would be dead in a day when it came. And they both had their oaths, things they owed the Community. And if they were all that was left of humanity, just the two of them could hardly rebuild their species alone; lack of genetic diversity meant they'd die out within a generation.

And they had to do the right thing by humanity.

He squeezed her hand. "It's not going to be easy."

She reciprocated the hand squeeze. "I know."

"We'll have to be ready for anything when we arrive," he said.

Evie gave a tense laugh. "Does this make us idealists?"

He gripped her hand tighter.

She nodded. "Yeah." She leaned in and kissed him. "Let's take what we can and say goodbye to this place."

*   *   *

Evie heard Isaiah's voice as they prepared to leave.

I cannot go to where the Xyelex resides, his inner voice said. He did not appear since Michael arrived, keeping only to mental conversation.

She also felt pressure, a warning not to reveal him. Isaiah didn't want to be seen just yet, and she respected the request.

I understand, she thought to him.

You'll be facing the Xyelex and Lilith, Isaiah said. *I can't directly help you.*

I know. She packed only what food they'd need for the journey back.

Let me leave you with one last thing, he said. *One thing that could help you. The Xyelex is formidable, but it won't be the first thing you face. You have Lilith to contend with. She will lead your Community to doom if you allow her to lead them. Be wary, she has the love of 4020, she has a strong force to defend her. You won't be able to take her on with physical strength alone. You have something she doesn't.*

And Isaiah's voice whispered to her. A secret both terrifying and beautiful.

Evie's heart dropped and burst all at once. Could it be so?

Speak of it to no one until the right time, Isaiah cautioned. *Show them who she really is first. Be smart. If done right, this will be Lilith's undoing.*

Evie looked at Michael, busy with preparations for them to leave.

Go, child of Earth, Isaiah's voice faded. *Save your people. Save humanity.*

Chapter 34: The Matriarch's Ultimatum

They made haste as they journeyed back to the Community. Resting only when they needed, and walking for long hours, from sunup and well into the night, Neptune ever watching from above. Evie didn't realize how far she'd come as day and night passed, cycling. However, she finally saw how Michael found her. Little clues here and there; unnatural pathways she carved through grassland, rest areas she created along the way. Following the shoreline of the lake also kept them on their path.

Eventually, they came upon the hab unit ruins. They kept their distance, but the thoughts of those lost within its corridors weighed heavily on her conscience.

She'd have to answer for them when she arrived back.

Within a day and a half of reaching the ruins, they saw the Community along the horizon, and the shadow of the Xyelex surrounded it in the evening light.

Evie felt horror fill her being as they crept in the tall grass, concealing their presence. There were a number of figures it assimilated, each elongated in size from consuming their hosts. Was this truly what this creature had become?

"Shit," Michael swore. "They've grown bigger since I was last here."

"Bigger?" Evie gasped. "It must grow when it assimilates people."

"Fortunately, it looks like it hasn't infiltrated the caves," Michael said. "It's strange. It could easily go in and just take everyone."

Evie felt like she knew the answer. "There's a specific reason it's not going in."

Michael looked at her curiously.

"It doesn't want to assimilate everyone, not yet," she said. It sounded memorized, something she knew without knowing she knew. "It wants to contain, hold everyone. It's saving them for something else, keeping them all in one spot. It wants them gathered."

"It's a theory," he said. "But can we really know?"

Evie shook her head. "Not a theory. This *is* what it's doing. I know it."

"How do you know?"

Evie knew without a doubt this was what the Xyelex was doing. Just at the tip of her tongue, like a fleeting dream. Gathering the people, the Earth creatures, containing them in one space. To see something, witness something. She pictured her mental wall, almost completely crumbled, bits and pieces of it remaining, staying strong despite her tearing most of it down. The answer was behind those last crumbling pieces.

But how could she explain it to Michael?

Her silence was enough. Michael just nodded and put a hand on her arm. "I see. Just like how you couldn't explain the grove. It's okay, I trust you."

I trust you.

Trust.

He shouldn't trust me, she thought. *Why do I feel he shouldn't trust me?*

She put her hand over his reassuringly. Despite everything around them, her heart fluttered. He trusted her? He never said that once during their marriage on Earth.

But here on Triton, he did.

She looked at him. He was the same Michael she loved. But something about him changed.

Or had she changed?

They continued creeping within the evening shadows under the cover of the tall grass. Hiding behind varied rocks along the terrain, evidence that they were above the caves beneath.

They stole far too close to one of the Xyelex. Evie smelled rotting flesh carried downwind. It didn't move, still like a statue of revulsion. Only the squirming of its fungal tendrils gave way to its living presence.

And a thousand voices speaking in Evie's head.

You've returned, she heard the voices speak in her mind. *We are pleas-s-sed.*

"It knows," Evie grabbed Michael. "I hear it."

He paused, looking in the direction of the Xyelex closest to them, no more than ten yards away.

It did not motion or make any move to acknowledge their presence.

Michael gestured. "The entrance is over there."

We await for you to join us-s-s, the voices sang in her mind. *Join us-s-s.*

Their pace quickened, no longer concerned with concealment. They stopped at a small gathering of rocks, Michael kicking into the ground.

Evie followed suit, also kicking in, trying to break up the ground.

"He sealed it too well," Michael gave an angry strike with his heel.

Then the screech.

A sharp, ear-piercing screech of a thousand voices. All the Xyelex that surrounded the Community cried out in unison.

Welcome back, the Xyelex's words stabbed Evie's skull, and she held her head. She saw flashes of when she first saw it in the hab unit ruins, it growing, writhing. *Welcome back...* She relived her teammates swallowed into its assimilation. *Join us-s-s... join. . .welcome. . .*

"There!" Michael exclaimed. A hole, just wide enough for a head and shoulders to fit through, crumbled open. "Through here!"

The voices. The screeching. Evie couldn't move. She fell to her knees. "It's doing something to my head!" She yelped.

Join us-s-s.

Michael grabbed her shoulders and shoved her through the opening.

She, followed by Michael, slid down a gradual wall into darkness.

A final whisper in her mind. *Welcome back. . .*

The voices stopped when she hit the ground, although she could still hear the screeching outside.

"It's around here somewhere," Michael's voice said beside her. It was too dark to see. "I left a torch and flint. "It's—"

Like a crypt lit for mourners, the cave suddenly flooded with fiery light, followed by numerous footsteps.

Evie and Michael stood, facing Lilith.

Behind Lilith were fifteen or more members of 4020, holding torches and spears tipped with sharpened blades.

Pointing at them.

Lilith clapped. "Our prodigal astromedic has returned." She sneered. She glanced at those holding spears. They too sneered, as though they communicated an inside mock Evie wasn't privy to.

She snapped. "Take the traitors. Let them face judgment with the others."

Michael's face dropped. "Wait, commander, no—"

But Lilith was already gone.

Evie and Michael were swarmed, their hands bound behind their backs.

*   *   *

They were led to the cave antechamber, to the place where they first counseled and the Community was born. The table slab was still in the center. Lilith stood on one side, the whole of what was left of 4020 behind her, whispering and murmuring nervously.

Evie and Michael were placed across the table from them. A barrier separating them from their colleagues.

"You've gone too far," Evie cried out. "How dare you—"

"Bring the others," Lilith waved her hand. She didn't even acknowledge Evie's words.

"Don't you ignore me!" Evie spat. "All of you. What do you think you're doing?"

Lilith shrugged nonchalantly. "Rooting out those that would feed us to the Xyelex."

"Feed to the Xyelex?" Evie couldn't believe what she was seeing and hearing. "That's insane." This was far worse than Michael told her. What happened during the time he retrieved her? What began as a simple inquiry had somehow become an outright, total inquisition.

With Lilith at the head of it.

More members of 4020 with spears dragged a bound Asa and Ren out. The torchlight made them look all the more worse for wear. Thin, bruised, and weary-eyed. Ren was abnormally pale, with a massive dried blood stain on his side.

"God, what happened!" She tried to jump to them, her medical muscle memory taking over. Only the tip of a blade at her chest stopped her. "Can't you see they're sick? Ren, how much blood have you lost?"

"Shut her up, will you?" Lilith waved her other hand. "Or she will be held in contempt."

Unseen hands grabbed Evie from behind, a blade at her throat.

Asa and Ren were placed beside her and Michael.

"Much better," Lilith said. Her towering figure turned to 4020. "Friends, teammates, my community—

"As promised, our protectors, our militia, have rooted out the dangers we feared. Traitors, defectors, deserters—those who allowed the Xyelex to rise in power—are brought to justice before you today."

A trial? Evie thought. *What the hell is she holding a trial when the Xyelex is on our doorstep?*

But then again, this had nothing to do with the Xyelex.

"Of course, this will be a fair trial," Lilith said. "With the authority given to me by the UNSF, I will conduct this trial, with the assistance of our self-sacrificing protectors. You will all serve as the jury, witnesses to the proceedings of this court. We will begin proceedings by hearing out what each defendant has to say on their crimes."

She turned to Evie, Michael, Asa, and Ren. Her shadow loomed over them. "You've been accused of treason and negligence. Abandonment of assigned duties and insubordination, resulting in the various casualties of UNSF team 4020. How do you plead?"

They stayed silent.

"I repeat," Lilith's domineering figure seemed to grow. "And I don't like repeating myself. How do you plead?"

None of them answered. Someone coughed in the crowd behind Lilith.

Lilith's lip curled. "See their continued insubordination, evidence of their guilt. I hold you four in contempt of court."

Evie felt a punch to her gut, and the wind was knocked out of her. The other three in unison were also struck, Ren crying out in the most pain.

"Not guilty," Michael spoke up, his voice breathy from the punch. "We're not guilty."

"And the others?" Lilith said. "They must speak for themselves."

"N-not guilty," they responded.

Lilith smiled her faux smile, the one Evie recognized all too well. The one who always garnered sympathy from those around her. "We shall see." Her emerald green eyes blazed, zeroing in on Evie. "Let us hear first from the prodigal astromedic."

Evie was pushed forward. The rest of 4020 stayed behind Lilith. They didn't move or speak, listening intently. Why weren't they doing anything? Saying anything? Did they fear Lilith and her militia? Or did Lilith own their hearts?

"Ms. Cunningham," Lilith locked her gaze on Evie, her eyes stabbing. "Your negligence has resulted in the deaths and overexertion of duties on members of your community. One that you helped form, and then abandoned."

No one spoke up. No one said anything to defend. Evie was on her own.

Lilith *did* own their hearts. Evie had to win them over. And it would take more than words to do so.

And she knew Lilith already decided their fates and guilt.

She will lead your Community to doom, Evie remembered Isaiah's words. *Be wary, she has the love of 4020, she has a strong force to defend her... Show them who she really is. Be smart.*

"You've abandoned your leadership," Evie spewed at Lilith. "This is a sham of a trial, and you've become nothing more than a bloodthirsty inquisitor."

"Hypocrite!" Lilith pointed. The members of 4020 murmured behind her, 'hypocritical' slipping from their lips. "You abandon your duty, and come here challenging my authority when the Xyelex is about to take us all. Hypocrite!"

The murmurs continued, leery eyes bearing down on Evie.

"What you're doing is wrong," Evie said. "Where's *our* protection?"

"I'm protecting us!" Lilith yelled. "My duty! Which is far beyond what you've done. Where were you when the Xyelex attacked? Where were you when it took those we cared for? Gone—that's right —*gone!* You betrayed us, abandoned us. You did nothing to prevent the Xyelex from taking our team in the hab unit, and you were gone when it attacked at the beach. You did this to us!"

Arms raised, shaking fists taunted. Yells of grief, cries of anger. The whole of 4020 rose against Evie, only Lilith standing between them and her.

Logic and sense will not save me, Evie thought. *I have to outsmart her. But her words have such a hold on them.*

"You're right, I did leave," Evie said. "I shouldn't have, but I did. What justice would you demand I pay for my absence? What would it have me do in place of my omission?"

Evie's admittance of guilt surprised Lilith. Perplexed, she paused.

The crowd too mirrored, also perplexed by the admittance.

"Death came because of her," someone yelled out. "It should fit the crime."

The crowd erupted in partial agreement. Some yelled in agreement, while others stood strong against it. But one thing was common: Evie had to pay.

The crowd emboldened, stepping beyond Lilith. Yelling, pointing at Evie.

Evie stood her ground.

"No one answered my question," she said. "What does justice demand of omission?"

Lilith sneered at Evie, a silent word to her. *Let them take you.*

She motioned to step back, to allow the emboldened crowd to take Evie.

But she stopped. All quieted.

Asa stepped forward, spears at his neck warning him not to walk further.

"Enough's enough," Asa said. "This is Evie Cunningham, our astromedic. Not a monster. You all know her, and you have worked with her. Do these accessions sound like her?"

They all looked shocked. Asa, who never spoke a word for or against anyone, stood with Evie.

A flush of gratitude ran through her. "Asa, you don't need to—"

Ren also stood with Evie. "Not sure if my say will do any good, but if Asa says something, we'd better listen."

Michael stepped up.

"No," she whispered. "Don't."

"There's a process to everything," he said. "And it isn't this. We're all scientists, the best Earth ever had to offer. We do things by the process, by the laws we agreed to. We are still 4020, on Earth, on Triton, or anywhere."

The tension lessened. People quieted, their expressions softening.

But Lilith's goons stood strong.

"Mutiny!" One yelled. "The entire administrative team. Where's their loyalty?"

"For our commander!"

"For our leader!"

"Our savior!"

Just as the yelling began again, Evie lifted her head high. "I will take justice from the commander herself!"

Lilith raised a hand. All silenced.

"Cunningham," she declared, "will you accept total accountability on behalf of those who fell?"

"I accept the commander's judgement," Evie said. "And will accept her verdict, all of it on behalf of those accused with me. But she, too, must stand accountable for what's happened here. A judgment can only be as good as the leader who's allotted it."

She had them, 4020. They listened intently.

Show them who she really is.

"I, on behalf of myself and those accused, challenge Commander Lilith Amulius to an Antarctican trial."

Awe filled the chamber and disrupted their unison.

Their chatter mingled:

"I've heard of an Antarctican trail. . ."

"It's brutal. . ."

"It settles debates and serves justice. . ."

"Is that really what she wants. . ."

"The commander's brave enough. . ."

"I've always wanted to see one. . ."

Lilith looked nervously at the militia.

Evie had her. Lilith couldn't back out of the challenge; it discredited her leadership and her heroism.

Lilith masked with a pleasant smile. "Fine, as you will. I accept your challenge. Let us have an official Antarctican Trial!"

Everyone moved to the edges of the cave. Lilith's militia created a clearing, a circle twenty feet in diameter, and surrounded it. Evie and those with her were pulled back.

Lilith jumped on the table slab and leapt over to the clearing the militia formed. An unseen blade suddenly appeared in her hand. "Challenged chooses the weapon. Give her a dagger."

Evie was forced into the circle across from Lilith. Those against the cave walls stepped away, pressing against the militia that surrounded the clearing. She was pushed onto her hands and knees, and a stone dagger, six inches long, was thrown before her.

She looked up.

Lilith waited, holding her dagger defensively. "Let this trial decide your guilt."

Chapter 35: Secrets Foretold

Triton, the false moon that it was, did not behave as a moon should. For one, out of all the remaining celestial objects in the solar system, it developed complex organic life. A once unique quality only found on the planet Earth. And unlike its lifeless moon siblings, Triton followed a different path.

Most planets, moons, and satellites within the Sun's solar system follow a prograde orbit. Meaning, objects caught in the orbit of a primary celestial body follow it in the same rotational direction. Looking down upon Neptune from its northern pole, it would appear that the planet and its surrounding moons rotate and orbit counterclockwise.

Except for Triton.

From the moment it was stolen from its independent planetary orbit, Triton did not concede to follow all the other satellites in Neptune's orbit. Against all odds, it created its own retrograde orbit, taking a clockwise approach to its rotation. Although the ice giant's gravity field was great, it couldn't fully grasp the power of the dwarf planet; it never dominated Triton into becoming a true moon. No, Triton's gravity was too great, its independent power too strong. It would never be an ordinary moon.

For Triton's true power lay in tholins, a power of feminine nature. And Neptune would never—*could never*—handle the true power of Triton.

*　*　*

Lilith stood across from Evie, her slanted emerald eyes locked in, unblinking.

Spectators surround them in a perfect circle. How had it devolved to this? Spectators? They were supposed to be her team—scientists of the highest caliber—and the very people that she depended on.

And yet, she no longer knew them, or at least not this side of them. The primal instinct seemed to have infected them all, even her. They were no longer people of high intelligence and discipline. They were beasts trying to survive and desperately trying to retain a sense of order. Thirsting for leadership, for dominance and subservience, as all wild animals do.

She glanced beyond Lilith's domineering stature. Some of the spectators seemed to shift closer to her side of the circle; an unspoken display of alliance.

She looked behind her for only a moment. Michael, Asa, and Ren were there, held by Lilith's militia. Bound and forced to watch.

Show no fear, Asa's nod told her.

She was not alone.

Evie took the dagger from the ground and stood. "We don't need to do this," she called over to Lilith.

Lilith rolled her shoulders back in offense, a taunting smile grew across her thin lips. "Really? I very much believe we need to do this. Remember, *you* chose this." She held out her hand, not taking her eyes off Evie. "More than ready when you are—unless you want the other option. It's still on the table."

Evie felt the growing fire in her chest. Lilith was right; she did choose this from her own ultimatum. There was no room for other options.

There are no absolutes, she heard Isaiah's voice within her memory. *One of the greatest lies of humanity is that there are absolutes.*

"No absolutes," she breathed to herself. She still had a hard time believing that. But she had to put it from her mind if she was going to survive this. Think outside the absolute.

Lilith was bigger than her.

She was cleverer.

The perfect specimen of a human. Everything refined to what a human should be

Evie was none of those things.

They circled one another. Lilith holding her weapon exactly as intended; dagger in fist, pointed out the bottom and facing her opponent. Evie copied, holding defensively.

Evie thought of her oath. *I will maintain the utmost respect for human life...*

But there was no more UNSF. This was about survival and protecting those she loved.

"Tell me, Cunningham," Lilith continued her circling. "Have you ever witnessed an Antarctican Trial before?"

"Only from virtual histories," Evie said.

"They hardly do it justice." Lilith stepped inward, making their circling smaller. "The last Antarctican Trial I witnessed killed my father."

"I'm sorry to hear that," Evie said, leery of how close Lilith was getting.

"I don't need your sympathies," Lilith said. "It was his honor. You see, much like our dear Community, Antarctica was a sovereign nation founded by scientists." Lilith stepped closer. "Smartest, best, and brightest just like us. And in their isolation, they were wise enough to realize that when there are differences, sometimes, rather than sacrifice the whole," she stepped closer, "there is a simpler way to resolve problems."

She lunged at Evie. Her wide strides made her fast, too fast for Evie to dodge. She was able to grab Evie's dagger arm and pull her in close. "You see, not only did I witness that Antarctican Trial that killed my father, I participated. And won."

Evie knew Lilith could've ended her right then and there.

But she didn't.

She punched Evie's face. The impact was like an explosion, knocking her senses away. Lilith threw her aside, and Evie dropped her dagger, catching herself before falling.

"Stand and fight," Lilith said.

"Your father never should've made you fight him," Evie said. "He should've—"

"You don't get to say that." She pointed her dagger at Evie. "A fair trial is a fair trial, as this one will be. Stand and fight." She kicked at Evie, and Evie dodged it.

"Someone stop this," Ren yelled from the crowd. "She's going to massacre her!"

"No, Ren," Michael said. "Trust Evie."

"But—"

"I got his guys," Evie called to them, wiping blood from her lip. She picked up her dagger and mimicked Lilith's offensive stance. She knew the basic UNSF self-defense training. Still, that was nothing compared to Lilith's military prowess.

Show them who she really is.

I just have to make it a little longer, Evie thought. *Hold her off, long enough so they see the monster she's become.*

Lilith lunged again, and Evie deflected. Lilith's strength could've easily broken through Evie's defense, but she somehow deflected it away.

She's playing with me, Evie thought. *She wants a show.*

They began circling again.

Evie lunged for the offensive.

Lilith deflected and grinned like a child playing in a school yard. "Is that all you got, Cunningham. I thought I trained you better than that."

Evie did a faux jab this time, and Lilith immediately picked up on it and deflected.

And that was how it went. Both of them exchanging blows, deflecting, and circling. Every blow Evie gave grew weaker and weaker, her strength weening.

And Lilith's smile disappeared, a look of boredom taking over.

"This needs to end," Evie said.

Lilith nodded. "You're absolutely right."

In one fell swoop, Lilith had Evie on the ground, pinned down, dagger above her throat.

Triumphant stoicism filled Lilith's eyes, jaded and jeering at Evie. Her mouth twitched. "Any last words, guilty one?"

Show them who she really is, she repeated in her mind.

"Yes."

Evie remembered Isaiah's last words to her. *You have something she doesn't. Speak of it to no one until the right time. Show them who she really is. Be smart.*

"You kill me——" Evie made her voice loud, decisive. She was afraid, more afraid than she was of the Xyelex killing her. But she couldn't let that stop her, not let her voice show it. If this wasn't played right, Lilith had her life. " ——you kill two of us."

Lilith's triumphant face dropped into confusion.

"Will you have killing a pregnant mother and her unborn child on your conscience?" Evie said sternly. She dropped her dagger defiantly. "I will maintain the utmost respect for human life, from the time of conception, even against the possible violation of the law."

Someone yelled from the onlookers: "She's pregnant?"

Another cry: "She dies, then the baby dies?"

Voices rose from the spectators, their continued yelling staying Lilith's hand:

"It's just a fetus. . ."

"But it's alive. . ."

"Does it count. . ."

"You can't punish a fetus for the mother. . ."

"There's hardly any humans left. . ."

It was true that all of 4020 were scientists. The most knowledgeable and brightest Earth had to offer. Unlike the general public they served on Earth, every single one of them knew the significance of Evie's oath. The meaning of new life on a place such as Triton, humans on the verge of extinction, and the unique opportunity it posed.

All Evie had to do was remind them of that.

"Hold the trial," someone yelled.

"Stop the violence," another called out. "She dropped her weapon."

"You can't kill her," someone else bellowed. "You'll kill her child!"

"This is wrong—"

"Stop—"

Lilith gritted her teeth, still holding Evie down. "She lies!" she relented. "Lies to save her own skin!"

"No," Michael stepped forward. No one stopped him. The militia no longer held him, Asa, or Ren. "She doesn't. I'm the father." His loving eyes met Evie's. She felt guilty for him finding out this way. Isaiah told her the morning after her time with Michael that she had conceived. The secret he warned her to guard until the time was right.

The crowd burst into an uproar. Lilith's militia held them back.

"No!" Lilith snarled. "She is guilty, and her child is as guilty as she is and will pay!" Lilith stabbed her dagger downward.

Evie looked up, bracing for the killing shot.

Some say life passes before your eyes when you're about to die. Your brain looking profusely for anything to help it survive, to avoid death. The memories are overwhelming for some, and for others, a peaceful moment to comfort them before entering the beyond.

None of that happened to Evie.

Instead, she heard the sickening sound of a blade plunging into flesh.

Ren's flesh.

He shoved himself between Evie and Lilith, her dagger digging deep into his stomach. Evie sat up as he fell backward. She caught him in her lap, warm blood spilling from his abdomen all over her legs.

"You little shit!" Lilith screeched.

More screeches sounded along with Lilith's.

A thousand voices like the Xyelex. But they weren't from the Xyelex.

It was from 4020: murderer... murderer... *murderer!*

"Please," Lilith pointed. "That fool intervened in a trial. Militia, take Evie Cunningham and execute her for—"

None of her militia moved.

"I said—"

"They heard you," Michael stepped forward. "But none of them want to assist in murdering a mother and her child. *My* child."

"Murderer… murderer… " The echoes gradually increased, their volume dancing off the cave walls. "Justice for murder—justice for murder—"

"No," Lilith looked around frantically, the whole of 4020 closing in around her. "I uphold justice, I uphold order, I am your commander! Insubordination! I'm your—"

Hands grabbed at Lilith. She screamed a gut-wrenching scream as her hair was pulled, and her clothes were ripped. "Murderer— justice," 4020 continued to chant. Even with her singular mountain strength, she couldn't resist the strength of the many.

"Stop!" Evie yelled. They ignored her.

"Do something Michael!" Evie said. "It can't end like this, not for her. You're next in the line of authority. They'll listen to you."

Michael stood on the table, waving his arms. "Listen!" He pointed to Lilith's militia. "Take her, bind her, and we will have an UNSF trial worthy of her crimes. She doesn't get off this easy."

They nodded, pushing through the crowd that ripped at Lilith. Half of them were able to push the crowd away from her, while it took five to hold Lilith down.

"Imbeciles," she cried. "You'll all regret this—ALL OF YOU. MAY THE XYELEX TAKE YOU, AND IT WILL! YOU'RE GONERS, ALL OF YOU!" She laughed manically as her own militia dragged her away to an empty cave chamber, screaming and gnashing at them.

Ren coughed in Evie's lap, blood splattering. She cradled his head.

Michael and Asa were released from their binds and stood on either side of her. One of the militia cut Ren's bindings, bringing his hands over his chest comfortably.

Those who remained in the antechamber watched in silence.

"Was I responsible?" Ren looked up at Evie. "Was I brave?

"Sure's hell wasn't responsible," Evie choked, smiling comfortingly down at him. She felt the need to shed tears, and held them back. "But it was brave. So very brave. Thank you."

He cracked a smile. "I told you all Lilith would do me in." He laughed, but it turned to a gurgling cough, blood dripping from the corners of his mouth. "It doesn't hurt anymore. Hey, I'm okay, it doesn't hurt, it doesn't—" A final breath left his chest, and his eyes glazed.

Chapter 36: The Commander's Reprisal

Asa mourned all those who had perished.

News came quickly to 4020. The Xyelex was gone. Within days of Evie's confrontation with Lilith, the Xyelex disappeared from the Community. All that lay in place were their hosts' corpses.

Asa helped retrieve the bodies with the newly reinstated scouting team—Michael dismantled Lilith's militia. Hairless, naked, human bodies stained with blue iridescent lines where the fungal tendrils once encased them. Mouths gaping, eyes gouged out of sockets, they were almost unidentifiable.

Asa took samples for research and for Evie's newly reinstated medical team. Things were starting to come back together, people acting with logic and sense again. But Michael had that effect on those around him. The way he spoke, his calm nature. A natural leader, despite being a reluctant one. But maybe that's what made him a better leader than others.

The Community moved much of what they had into the caves, fearing that the Xyelex would make another appearance. They also needed to prepare for the oncoming eclipse and have everything established before they sealed themselves in for the long winter ahead.

Unfortunately, there was nothing of use from the hab unit ruins. With the disappearance of the Xyelex, the ruins wore away as though years were held at pause and finally caught up to it. But with Evie and Michael's mapping of the region, they were able to direct teams to where the lake drained into the sea, and send teams to hunt for more sustainable food.

Nothing was the same without Ren to lighten the mood. Asa missed him profusely. At times, he forgot Ren was gone, thinking of things to tell him. His heart sank every time he couldn't.

Many things still weighed heavily on Asa's mind in those following weeks; things he just couldn't let go. He wanted closure before the memorial service they planned for Ren and the other victims of the Xyelex.

There was one person who had no choice but to listen to him.

The day of the memorial service kept everyone busy with their daily tasks and the additional ones for the service. They decided it was fitting to host it in the cave's cathedral chamber before the Vita-8 pool, given it was Vita-8 that brought them to this world. Because Lilith's former militia knew about the pool, there was no use in keeping its location concealed anymore.

As people busied themselves, Asa slipped away.

He carried with him a clay pot of food: mashed reed root with salted fish. He wove through the marked cave passages. Lilith's trial was not scheduled until after the memorial service, and they had time to form a proper committee to run the trial fairly.

He wouldn't have another chance once that happened.

He came upon two members of the scouting team, standing guard. A brawny woman and a slender, fit man in their mid-thirties.

"I'm here to deliver the commander's meal," Asa said simply.

They looked at one another nervously.

"Better you than me," the brawny woman said. "Last person who did the meal almost had his finger ripped off."

"Well, I'm confident I can be successful," Asa smiled. "The commander and I have a bit of a different relationship than those who normally deliver food."

"Commander," the slender man scoffed. "Not worthy of that title."

Asa sighed. "Once a commander, always a commander. Please allow me through."

They pulled Asa aside, patting him down and checking the food pot.

"Sorry, Dr. Baramba," the brawny woman said. "We trust you and all, but check everyone and everything before entering."

"I understand," he said. "I'd be worried if you didn't." Once they were done checking him for contraband, Asa started through the passage, with them following.

He stopped.

"If you'd please, I'd like to speak to her privately while she eats," he said. "I'd like to think we still respect privacy even for prisoners."

"No," the slender man said. "She's dangerous."

"This is Dr. Baramba," the brawny woman said. "He knows what he's doing. Sorry, sir, go on. Holler if you need us."

"I will." Asa entered a small chamber, lit modestly with clay bowls converted to oil lamps, thanks to the fish oil they now had access to. Light from outside shone down from a small opening dug out of the ceiling to give natural light and circulation. In the center was a raised rock.

And the once towering commander sat low on the floor. Her hands were bound behind her and around the rock. Her hair was a scraggly mess, hanging over her face. A smell emanated from a lack of hygiene. It wasn't as though 4020 didn't try; they brought her on an outside excursion, but it resulted in one of her escorts gaining a dislocated shoulder, and another with broken fingers. With her massive strength, she was too dangerous to be unbound. No one could come wash her as she took on a maniacal nature when they tried. Even feeding her was a chore.

"Look who's finally come to visit." Lilith lifted her head. Her emerald eyes were sharper than a sword, a hungry, and rabid. She looked more like a sick, starved cat than the commander he once respected. "One of the saboteurs."

Asa stepped cautiously toward her. "Time for food."

Lilith spat at him. "I will not be fed like an animal. Not by you or anyone."

"Suit yourself." He set the clay pot just in reach of her. "You can eat whenever you like. It's easier if I help you, rather than digging your head into it like an actual animal."

Lilith chortled. "Oh my, Dr. Baramba, you've gained such a mouth, haven't you?" She kicked the pot away. "I liked you better when you were quiet and didn't say much."

Asa eyed the smashed food on the floor. Food was much harder to come by than on Earth. An insult and sign of Lilith's defiance at being captive.

"They normally have one of your underlings do the dirty work of feeding me," Lilith's crusted, dry lips smacked as she spoke. "Why are you here?"

"The memorial is today," Asa said. "You're going to have to answer for all those deaths. And I figured it out—you killed Olena. She was onto you, she knew. You killed Benson and Theo in the hab unit, didn't you? Threw them to the Xyelex to save your own skin as you ran like a coward. As if your life was more deserving than theirs. Evie and Michael trusted you too much to see it. And you did something with the Xyelex—controlled it somehow, I know it! You're the one who kept everyone trapped in the caves, using the Xyelex. That's why it's gone when you're bound."

"So that's what inspired this little visit." Lilith's eyes thinned. "Seems that I know why you're really here, but do you?"

His mother's voice: *You have to speak up sometimes. You have to fight it, push through.*

What if people get mad at me?

Then let them be mad.

Lilith was going to be mad no matter what happened.

"I have some things to say," Asa said. "Things that you need to hear, whether you want to or not. Things I want heard aloud."

"Closure." Lilith spat. "Save it for the trial."

"It can't wait."

"Everything can wait!" Lilith lifted her chin high. "Be disappointed, sir, because whatever closure you're looking for, you're not getting it with me. You want to hear something? I'll oblige. I'm glad that irresponsible idiot Tanaka is dead; he dragged down 4020. I only regret it wasn't that slutty bitch that took my blade. She's going to drag you all down even more than him, and you'll be begging me to fix everything when the eclipse freezes you out and the Xyelex takes you. I hate every last one of you for what you did to me, after all I sacrificed to save you all."

"Evie saved you!" Asa felt his fists ball up. "You should kiss the very ground she walks on because without her, 4020 would've torn you to shreds after you murdered Ren!" The fury expanded within. The part of him that froze when he spoke melted under the righteous anger. "It's no less than what you deserved. What she sees in keeping you alive, I don't know."

"Me neither." A cold fury emanated from Lilith. "Waste of resources." She smirked, looking at him as though she saw something he didn't. "Is that all, traitor?" She said traitor the way she used to call him chemist. "You know, you could've saved humanity with me. Made it better, made it stronger, made it smarter. I worked closely with you—trusted you. And you threw it away like the fools you all are."

His fury continued to spread. It was as though years of holding back were spilling out, breaking under pressure. Lilith didn't know what he truly wanted. He wanted a family, but it didn't have to look the way he imagined it would be on Earth. Triton didn't have the technology to make that possible. Humanity was literally starting from scratch, and he was a part of it.

"I may not be able to have the life I thought I wanted," he said. "But humanity *will* be better. What you were building wasn't going to be its second chance; it would've destroyed what was left. We would live, but we wouldn't be human anymore. And I think it's worth being a fool if it means we keep our humanity."

He felt his face turn warm, tears at remembering what he could've had. But that no longer mattered. Because he finally realized it was a dream, and reality needed him more. Mourning it forever did not serve it. He gave himself to this new world.

"Nothing else?" She smiled a knowing smile. "You know what's more dangerous than a bound prisoner? One with nothing left to lose."

In an instant, Asa was flat on his back, Lilith on top of him, free of her binds.

He tried to yell for help, but she covered his mouth. He bit it, and she didn't react, like it was nothing. She lifted him and held him against the very rock she was bound to.

Her slanted green eyes hissed at him. "You don't think I could break out of my binds any time I wanted? You're all idiots while I sit in here biding my time. I asked for you, all of you, Michael and Evie too. But not one word, no one sent them. And now you've come, and I'll get my retribution for what you did to me!"

Asa felt her hot breath on his face. He struggled to pull away, but her strength was too much. He felt her knees digging into his middle. She truly was stronger, better, and smarter. He shouldn't have come.

She held a shiv to his throat. "You could've saved humanity with me."

Her eyes shifted, glancing at something just beyond Asa. Seeing something he could not see.

And her eyes changed. They sank. "N-no. You can't ask that— no!"

She was still, shiv against his throat, unmoving.

Her voice whispered. "*I* wanted to save humanity. *I could've* saved humanity."

And the sensation of warm blood spilled down Asa's chest.

But it wasn't his.

Lilith's eyes glazed, her hold went limp, her dead weight falling on him.

Her hand slipped from his covered mouth.

"*Help*—someone help!" he yelled.

The two scouts he met previously ran in.

"What the hell!" The brawny woman's jaw dropped.

Asa pushed Lilith off him with the assistance of both scouts. Blood poured from her neck, from where she slit her own throat.

"What happened?" The slender man helped Asa to his feet.

"I don't know." Asa shook his head. "She was on me, and the next thing I know, she slit her own throat."

"She did?" The slender man raised an eyebrow.

"Please," the brawny woman rolled her eyes. "Screw privacy, we should've gone in with you. Dr. Baramba, I'm so sorry this happened."

Asa knelt beside Lilith, her frenzied eyes frozen in time. He pulled them shut. An overwhelming sense of grief and relief. His leader, his tormentor, all that she was was gone. "I am too. Dear god, I am too."

He mourned Lilith. He mourned Ren. He mourned all those who passed. He mourned his dreams. He mourned who he used to be and what Triton turned him into.

But he also hoped. He'd help Evie and Michael with their child; they were his family. And never again would he stay quiet or benign, not when those he loved needed him.

As Asa mourned, he did not notice who else watched. Nor did he see what Lilith saw. He didn't hear the whispers that spoke in Lilith's ear. The same whispers that spoke to her mind when she conceived of killing Olena, and plotted to conquer Triton and 4020. The things she spoke aloud to herself in her isolation. The very thing that stood beyond him, watching and persuading Lilith to take her own life.

The very last thing Lilith ever saw.

A man in white.

Chapter 37: The Xyelex's Last Stand

The pain of losing Ren was unbearable for Evie. Holding him, comforting him in his final moments, stung. Thinking of his sacrifice felt like venom, a bitter taste constantly in her mouth.

Word of the Xyelex's retreat after Lilith's confinement both shocked and consoled Evie. Making burial preparations for multiple graves didn't lessen the weight of Ren's departure, but it brought comfort. He hated being alone, and in death, he wasn't. Post-humorously, he'd be honored alongside the others, just as he would've wanted.

And the Xyelex's departure also meant Evie could feel Isaiah's presence once more.

She waited, expecting to hear his voice. So accustomed she was to his anecdotes and inputs, she privately meditated to connect to him.

But she didn't hear him.

She thought she'd be relieved, the mental silence giving her solace. She felt brushes of his thoughts feathering against her mind, as though he checked up on her. But not once did he speak or appear in physical form.

On top of everything else, she wondered if her pregnancy was real. It had to be, Isaiah told her himself. It was too early for her to physically determine its legitimacy. Either way, real or not, it saved her from Lilith's wrath and gave her the heart of 4020.

Indeed, their hearts she had. Moreover, with resuming her medical duties, people also laid other roles upon her. Roles of responsibility. She found herself attending to more than medical needs. Michael, next in line of 4020's administrative authority, managed much. But he wasn't alone; she and he co-managed the Community, taking on responsibilities beyond their previous administrative roles. Heading new committees, organizing teams, and delegating new tasks to those trusted in leadership roles.

This was not what she intended or wanted. But she did it.

The day of the memorial service for those who fell to the Xyelex and Lilith's ire was underway. Evie and much of 4020 gathered in the cave's cathedral chamber. Plants woven into infinite symbols and beautiful, rounded models meant to represent fractals were set around the chamber. Bowled oil lamps accented and lit everything. A fitting scene for those they wanted to honor.

"Not long till sundown," Evie said. "All of you, take a break, get a meal before tonight's service."

People nodded, separating into groups to chat; others departed.

Evie didn't feel much like talking. She hated socializing to begin with. She only did what she needed for her bedside manner. She went toward the Vita-8 pool, feeling its cold emanate.

She heard familiar steps echo. "Don't get too close." Michael's voice floated to her. "We have to follow the rules too, you know."

He stepped beside her, putting his arm around her shoulders.

Those who remained in the chamber were far enough away that they wouldn't hear what Evie and Michael spoke about. A rare moment alone since taking on their new roles.

"How are you feeling?" he asked.

"Physically?" Evie shrugged. "I'm fine. No morning sickness. Makes me wonder if this is really happening. Feels like a dream I can't wake up from."

Michael nodded in agreement. "I think dreams would be much kinder than what we've had to live through recently, the stuff of nightmares."

She waited for Isaiah to say something to her mind. It didn't come.

"What are you thinking about?" he asked. "You're awfully quiet."

"Nothing." She brushed it off. Had she become too dependent on Isaiah's words? She hated to think so. "Are we doing the right thing? Handling Lilith, the Xyelex, the bodies, the memorial service? I feel utterly underqualified to make these kinds of decisions."

"It's not a matter of qualification at this point," he said. "We just have to."

"Who's to say they won't turn on us?" Evie said. "Just like they did on Lilith?"

"They could," he said. "It comes with the territory. But that's the risk to save them. And the right thing to do." He tightened his arm around her. "I'm just glad neither of us has to do it alone."

"Yeah." Evie waited again for Isaiah's voice. "Too many risks."

"Speaking of risks," Michael put a gentle hand on her stomach. She put a warm hand over his. "I've been meaning to talk to you. You knew you were pregnant, why did you risk fighting her?"

She wasn't surprised by the question. She knew he'd ask eventually.

"Someone taught me recently that you have to be deliberate with every decision you make," she said. "Even the small ones. They ripple, take effect on everyone, whether we see it or not. I didn't intend for you to find out the way you did. Hell, I'm still not even completely sure, it's so soon since we—you know—"

Michael nodded. "Yes, I know."

"Saving 4020 was always a risk," she continued. "And I had to take on an equally monumental risk. Lilith had them. She conquered them. They were hers.

"They had to see the monster she is. If I said anything earlier, it gave her the chance to sway 4020 against us; it wouldn't have had the impact it did. No, they needed to see concrete evidence of who she is. I had to conquer their hearts to take her out."

"Conquer?" Michael laughed nervously. "Take her out? Kind of a strange thing to say. Doesn't sound like you. Wait—what's that on your hand?"

Something glinted on the back of her hand holding Michael's.

A sudden commotion erupted.

Asa came running into the cathedral chamber.

Evie's attention turned to him, as well as those who stayed behind after her dismissal.

"Evie, Michael, I found you." Asa was out of breath. "Everyone," he panted, "back away from the walls *now!*"

"Asa, what's wrong?" Evie marched toward him. "What's happened?"

"It's everywhere," his voice panicked. "Lilith's dead, and now it's everywhere!"

"What?" Michael's urgency pulled in the attention of everyone around them. "Lilith's dead? Why, how? Asa, get a hold of your senses, what's happened?"

He didn't need to answer for Evie to know. She felt it, its presence increasing.

"The Xyelex," she gasped. "It's here."

Someone yelped. Others cried out.

"Let's stay calm," Michael said. "We can do this. We have preparations this time. We can—"

Everyone in the cathedral chamber silenced. Wide eyes stared at Evie.

"What's everyone—"

Asa pointed. "It's—it's—"

"My god!" Michael's face looked as though his soul was crushed within. "Evie—it's all over you!"

Evie looked down at her arms.

And dread settled over her, fear gripping her chest as her stomach churned.

Iridescent blue and purple webbed veins reflected down her arms. She tore at her clothes, ripping away at the cloth on her stomach and legs. They, too, were covered with the writhing fungal tendrils.

"No—" she continued to rip at herself. "No, no, no—oh god, how long have I been infected?"

Oh, child of Earth, Isaiah's voice slipped into her mind. *You already know the answer to that.*

Fungal tendrils grew from the top of the cathedral ceiling, climbing down the walls, toward the people in the chamber. They pulled in close together.

Evie felt Isaiah's elation. *Time for us to conquer.*

Help us! Evie's mind called to him. *Where are you?*

"About time she died." Did Evie say that? It wasn't just her voice. She heard it spoken from her body, but it was mixed with Isaiah's. "Her final moments tried my patience."

She was appalled by what she said, yet at the same time felt satisfied.

Michael looked at Evie with a face she hoped to never see again. A face of horror, looking at her like a stranger.

She stepped toward him and the others, the fungus growing from her feet, closing them in along with those that spread along the walls. Nowhere to run.

What's happening? Evie spoke with her mind. *Isaiah, where are you? Help me stop this, please!*

I never left you, he said, snide triumph in his voice. *We're doing exactly as promised.*

She saw him. Isaiah stood by Michael and Asa, but neither took notice of him. He walked among them and the others, looking pleased at their terror, their fear.

As he spoke, she spoke.

"Earth children, hear the voice of your conqueror," they said together. "Join us, and reclaim this realm."

Evie tried to back away, tried to stop herself. But she didn't feel in control anymore.

Stop it, she begged. *You have the power to stop the Xyelex, you can—*

It dawned on her.

He wasn't going to stop it.

Because he was the Xyelex.

She'd been infected the entire time.

She harbored the Xyelex. Isaiah and it one—in the same. She was his thrall.

He wanted this world for himself.

"That's right," she and Isaiah both continued to speak in one voice. "This new world is mine, and you all are my worshippers. Join us, and you will find peace as my subjects."

The room heated up, and the fungus changed, turning to blood red and flaming orange, like hellfire.

Her body stepped closer, tendrils growing, extending from the walls, the floors, grabbing at people. They screamed, they shrieked, they howled. Enough to make anyone retch from their terrified cries.

And Isaiah continued to walk among them, looking at them lovingly like pets.

No! Evie fought against herself. *I cannot step closer. I can't do this! I don't want this—*

"But you do," her and Isaiah's voice said. "You always wanted this. This realm, all for your own."

The fungus reached Michael.

One grabbed at his scarred arm, flicking away when it touched his scar.

That's it! Her head throbbed as she fought against the urge to take everything for her own.

She was able to take one step back.

She looked at Michael one last time. The fungus grabbed at other parts of his body, engulfing him. The others, too, were engulfed.

She loved him too much to put him through such pain.

She knew what she had to do to free herself and them.

It would surely kill her when she did it.

I'm sorry, she told herself for the sake of her unborn child. *I'm sorry.*

You'll regret your existence if you try, Isaiah's colorless eyes jeered at her. *And I will persist either way.*

Not if I cut you, she projected her thoughts defiantly, *and myself off from them.*

There was only one answer, one solution.

She ran.

And plunged herself into the gelid Vita-8 pool depths.

Chapter 38: The Photon Accelerator

Evie did not stop falling.

Infinite darkness surrounded her.

The rush of the fall made blood surge through her body.

Faster. She continued to accelerate, picking up speed. She was no longer in the cathedral chamber or in the Vita-8 pool. She was in an infinite space, beyond her comprehension.

She existed in four dimensions.

She spiraled downward into the pit of darkness; she persisted. An endless whirl of plummeting, lurching into a great nothingness. Gravity's fist was gripping her as she twisted and contorted in free-fall. No wind, no air biting at her skin as it should in fall. A weightless existence, churning her deeper into its depths.

Visions flew by her. Reflections of her first fall on Triton. A glimpse of the geyser erupting, the ammonia ocean swallowing her whole. The visions began to swirl around her in the downward plunge. She saw the Vita-8 chemical mine Asa discovered, a plentiful well greater than they ever expected, fueled by Triton's tholins. It penetrated her body after she and the others fell into the ammonia ocean so long ago, saving her from instant death, and put her in cryogenic sleep until the planet warmed and bloomed with life.

"That can't be me!" she cried out when she saw the vision of her frozen body deep beneath Triton's surface. But her voice sounded strange. An echo within an echo, her voice inside itself. "Isaiah, where are you? Why are you doing this?"

"Naive Earth child," Isaiah's voice hissed from all around. "You did this!"

She felt her fall continue to pick up speed. "I thought we were friends! I know you!"

"Friends?" Isaiah's voice sounded amused. "This is my realm. Nothing is hidden here. I warned that you'd regret your existence, Earth child."

Another vision materialized, and she saw Michael, but he didn't look right. A shade his memory. "There are theories," his voice was haunting, chilling her spine, "evidence that suggests the possibility of fifth-dimensional intelligences existing in a fourth-dimensional plane."

And she was suddenly standing upright, no longer falling. His shade disappeared.

His voice continued to echo: "I wouldn't think them benevolent. Given how the universe always gives way to domination and survival."

The darkness was gone. She was in the fully functioning hab unit, standing in restricted Area E corridor, wearing UNSF loungewear, bundled in her coldsuit. She frantically looked at her arms, her legs, any part of herself she could. No sign of the fungal tendrils. This wasn't her present self; she was in the past. "How did I get here?"

"This is my realm," Isaiah's voice laughed, but he was nowhere to be seen. The laugh was maniacal. Unhinged, it continued to mock her. "Time itself. Past, present, and future all existing at once. Try to escape if you can, little Earth child. This is your eternal prison for defying me. Just try!"

The lights around her flickered, and she ran down the hab unit corridor. Downward it sloped, warning signs of Area E being restricted. She ran until she came to a sealed entrance.

Large read letters spelled out: AREA E: ENGINEERING—RESTRICTED, AUTHORIZED PERSONNEL ONLY.

Evie couldn't stop herself. As though her body weren't her own, she reached into her pockets.

God, I can't stop. Evie's stomach churned. *I'm reliving my memory.*

She pulled out Michael's passkey, the one he used when facial recognition programming was down. She'd stolen it before his effects were confiscated upon his supposed passing. She scanned it before the barrier.

Isaiah's unsettling laugh continued around her. "Nothing's hidden here, little Earth child!"

The barrier opened.

She walked in.

And stood before a massive, cylindrical machine, crackling with energy.

Particle accelerators. On Earth, such a device would've taken up an entire warehouse. But Michael and his team built something magnificent, one that could fit within the confines of their hab unit. It was why he was chosen for this mission; his research into the use of particles for unlimited energy, and application into devices beyond Earth made his genius unparalleled. Ren's engineering paired with Michael's experimental mind created something spectacular. Specifically for photons, light particles.

Light energy. A photon accelerator.

Above the cylindrical machine arose a hatch, hooded by a hollowed frustum. Wires and tubing show beneath it, encased by the clear metals.

Evie felt the things she felt back then, fully immersed in her past self. The draining hopelessness to emotional apathy. Everyone in 4020 moved on from Michael's death, but she hadn't. She didn't want to. She gave up long before he died. And with his fall through the ice, he was gone forever. The photon accelerator was his machine, his glory. The last piece of him left.

Sometimes the solitude of space travel drove people to madness. The isolation on outer worlds more than even the most stable could handle. She didn't want to handle it anymore. She just wanted to see him.

Beside the photon accelerator was a clear cabinet of radiation suits. She slipped one on.

If I can see him, her past self thought. *Just one more time.*

She pulled over a ladder from the corner of the room. She climbed it, remembering words Michael spoke to her long before they separated.

You see strange things when working with the micro, he had said. *Converting them to the use of the macro. Sometimes I imagine seeing into a higher-dimensional space. If you can speed up the protons just enough, our minds look into it.*

Evie already felt the hum of energy as she stepped onto the top of the accelerator. She stood beside the hatch and frustum.

My patient, her past self thought. *From my Earth residency, the one who saw ghosts. A higher dimensional space, a place where time doesn't matter; you can see ghosts of the past. If I go in, maybe I can go to that place. I could see him, even if it kills me, I just want to see him one last time.*

Her radiation suit would do little once she entered the accelerator. It'd only extend her time with seeing Michael if the photon accelerator really did what he told her it did. Light energy, harnessing power from a fourth-dimensional space within its particles

She used Michael's passkey to access the control panel on the hatch.

The hatch opened.

The energy hum turned to a crackling when it opened. Beneath it, light glowed bright white, heat emanating like a sun.

The frustum above began to lower.

She thought of Michael. *I'll see him again.*

And jumped through the hatch. The frustum sealed around the hatch, holding her in the accelerator.

She felt no physical pain as the very protons in her tore apart. Grief, anger, emptiness, and apathy amplified tenfold. She tried to think of Michael, but the pain from her consciousness gripped at her greater than any physical ailment. Colors beyond her eyesight spectrum turned everything colorless and gray. Tendrils grew from her, iridescent, writhing like worms. They became strings and webs that connected her to other consciousnesses. But she was caught between planes of existence, unable to see exactly where they led. Only that they stemmed from her grief and emptiness, fueling them and pulling her apart in all directions.

She felt a presence stroke her mind.

"Child of Earth, how did you come into this space?" a slick voice of the past spoke to her consciousness.

Evie did not speak, for she no longer could. Instead, one of the iridescent tendrils from her tightened into a string, connecting her to this voice. She felt transparent; she could repress nothing. Her anger and grief surged; she felt mental images of Michael and the photon accelerator course through the string.

"Ah, Child of Earth, you come seeking me," the past voice said. "I see."

"I've not sought anyone." How did she speak? A moment before, she couldn't.

"You have," the voice said. "In this space, the truth is never hidden. You've come seeking retribution. I can give it to you. For someone as clever to ascend into a higher space, they will get what they seek."

Retribution.

The truth finally revealed itself to her. She saw it pulse from her string, beat like her heart. Yes, retribution was what she wanted. In her deepest self, this was what she sought.

The truth finally revealed.

"I see through you a race of beings as numerous as stars in the infinite," the voice said. "As much as mine are. Your anger and grief have found me. Delightful."

Evie felt this being's presence. An intelligence of maliciousness and apathy beyond comprehension, feeding on the very things that led her to enter the photon accelerator. Humans were mere pests, unnoticed by it. To be smashed when they became an irritation.

"I will give you what you seek," the entity spoke. "If you give me what I seek."

"What do you seek?"

"A conduit," the entity said. "As your race has struggled to ascend, it is just as difficult to descend. But a hand reaching for hand—yours to mine, will give us both what we desire."

Evie saw it—the entity's consciousness reaching through her, placing a foothold in their three-dimensional reality.

"Why does a being like yourself want to descend?" she asked. "I can see you care nothing for humans."

"What reasons would your race want to ascend?" it asked in return. "Curiosity. A chance to explore only what we can observe."

And conquer.

The intention came as clear as its words. It could not hide it in this fourth-dimensional plane, even as slick lying words spoke. Like a whisper, it rang around her, slipping through hypothetical ears.

The whispers continued: *conquer... conquer. . .*

But even as the intention reached her, Evie considered it. This entity would give her the means to gain all she wanted.

I will make you a leader. Its consciousness delved into hers. *I will make you stronger where you feel weakest. I will make you respected by all those who would seek your downfall. I will give you back the one you've bonded your soul to. And you will have all the Earth things you've ever desired with him. The things that children of Earth so crave.*

Time had no relevance as visions flew in and out of her. Visions of Triton, the expansion of the sun, holding in her hands life anew, Michael beside her through it all.

She herself, reborn as a leader among people.

Against such a force, Evie wasn't prepared. After all, she was human and wanted all the things that humans wanted. Her heart's deepest desires considered it.

And in her moment of weakness, in that moment of consideration, the deal was struck.

Her hand reached for the unknown entity, the iridescent tendrils around her taking a physical form and gripping her hand.

And a face, one she thought she'd never forget.

One bleached by light, deep-set, colorless eyes, a thousand eons showing through them. Flowing hair slicked back.

And a name, like music.

She could not understand it, but it spoke to her consciousness, forming a word to his being.

Isaiah.

Forget, he said. *Forget and live on. A promise given through consciousness cannot be revoked. Let us meet again when time has deemed it so. Tomorrow you sleep, until the time of your retribution. And I will be unleashed into this existence. Until we meet again, child of Earth.*

Hands sealed to one another.

Then Evie suddenly felt herself pulled away.

"Goddamn it, Evie!" Ren's voice yelled. "What the hell are you doing!"

Her past eyes opened. Ren was kneeling over her in full radiation gear.

She was on the floor of the proton accelerator room, still in full radiation gear as well.

"I can't believe you got her out!" she heard Asa say from across the room. "What's all that on her!"

Evie couldn't move. All the energy was drained from her. She just stared into Ren's terrified expression behind the glass on his radiation helmet. The helmet was a mirror of what she looked like.

Her face, her entire body, covered in the iridescent fungus.

"Hell, she's awake!" Ren exclaimed. "But I don't know what that stuff is. Oh god, it's eating her. Don't die, please don't die."

Relief stretched across Asa's face. "Look, it's fading. We have to get her up to medical."

"And say what?" Ren said. "The commander will crucify her."

"We were, I don't know, doing routine maintenance," Asa said. "You're ahead of engineering and physics, you can do that."

"Ah-ho, with an astromedic and a chemist, like she'll buy that," Ren rolled his eyes. "Clearly, Evie's out of her mind. We have to get her back to Earth without Lilith doing something horrible to her."

A sudden flush of understanding came between them, unspoken.

Return Evie to her quarters, Isaiah whispered through her. *You will not speak of this to your leader or anyone. You will forget. Tomorrow you sleep for an Eon.*

Asa and Ren suddenly disappeared. The photon accelerator and the room Evie was in dissipated into darkness.

The memory ended.

Present Evie stood up in the darkness. The memory was gone, and she was in control of herself again, no longer replaying it.

"Me," Evie gasped. "It was me. I did this. I brought this on us, all of it."

"And now your wall is gone," Isaiah's voice mocked. "Only now do you understand—you serve me. You always have. Throwing yourself into the Vita-8 pool? You think you can be rid of me so easily. I own you!"

"You shouldn't be here," Evie said wearily. "You can't be here! You have no business among us!"

"My business is whatever I make of it!" Isaiah's voice boomed.

It'd be like us taking an interest in insects, a distant memory of Michael's voice said to her. *We'd be nothing more than pests to them. If there are intelligences beyond us, I wouldn't think them benevolent.*

"You invited me in," his voice dripped with venom. "And I do not let go easily of what is mine."

A glowing string suddenly appeared in front of her, stretching far beyond her sight. It pulled taut, and she was pulled with it.

Right to Isaiah.

Chapter 39: The Snake and The Saint

Isaiah held the string, wrapping it and pulling her in closer.

But the string changed. It became a chain.

The chain snaked around her, binding her limbs. He looked at her in disgust.

"This is my realm," he said. "You cannot come here without being bound by my power. Everything is under my dominion."

"Get out of my head!" Evie struggled against the chains

"This isn't your head, Earth child," Isaiah tugged on the chains. "Your pathetic race can't think of anything beyond three dimensions."

Everything changed around them. No up or down, no left or right. They were on Triton, but not in the sense familiar to her. The whole of the moon was present to her all at once, nothing hidden. The atmosphere, the surface, and its core folding in and out on itself.

The magnitude of an entire planet growing around her, and an insignificant grain within it. She did not move. She did not need to move. She was in a transparent reality, the time-space beyond the bounds of three dimensions.

"You don't own me!" Evie seethed.

"Do not speak!"

Evie's mouth involuntarily clamped shut. She couldn't speak.

"Much better," Isaiah smiled menacingly. "You know, I half considered making Lilith my conduit. But her rash lack of control was irritating, and you proved so much more useful when you rejected the power I offered. Something she never would've been able to do. And I had a promise to keep to you. Moving forward, you're going to behave like the obedient little Earth child you're supposed to. You're going to hold up your end of our deal. You're going to continue as my conduit and lead your Earth race. You and your people *will* create generations to worship me, and know nothing other than me. This world is mine, and you humans will cultivate it as I see fit. I am your master—*your god.*"

Evie pulled against the chains, clenched her jaw to break the invisible binds that held it shut.

Isaiah held up a finger. "We'll have none of that."

Evie was forced to her knees.

"Bow," he said unblinking.

Pressure pushed against her back. She fought it. The moment she bowed, he'd forever have his hold on her. The gesture, a sign of her forever subjugation to him.

"Come now, this will all be easier when you realize my assimilation of you has made this futile," he said. "I said bow."

The pressure pushed against her, and she lowered slightly.

No, she thought. *I can't. I won't!*

"Your thoughts are not shielded here," Isaiah said. "Try as you might, this is my domain."

Evie thought of anything to free herself.

"I see what you're doing," he mocked. "I know everything you're thinking. I know everything about you. You chose this—and you reap what you sow."

I'll kill you, her thoughts screamed. *Unbind me!*

"I'd certainly like to see you try." He pulled the chains and forced her inches from his feet. "Bow, and give in to my word."

No! She tried to pull her jaw open to speak.

"You will," he said. "They always do."

A series of chains appeared in his hands, all stretching forth and connected to other humanoid beings, so distant Evie didn't make out their features. But she felt them. Felt their pain, their grief, their hopelessness. All such emotions thickened their chains, connecting them to Isaiah.

"My subjects," Isaiah said. "So much like you. They sought me, just like you did. And I gave them what they wanted in exchange for dominion of their worlds. Some resisted at first, just like you. But in the end, it's futile. The laws of my dimension are not to be trifled with."

She felt an itch all over her body. The itching increased to irritation, and then erupted into boiling pain. She tried to scream, but her clamped mouth kept it shut.

Isaiah's subjects echoed in unison: "All things must abide by the laws of the dimensions it's within, or be utterly destroyed. Such is the nature of existence."

"Your very particles dissociate," he said. "Fight it all you want. Time makes no difference here. I shall wait for as long as it takes for you to break. I kept you in cryostasis for an eon till your sun turned red. I can do it again. *You* are my subject."

Unbearable. The pain erupting through her body made it impossible to function, let alone think.

And the pressure on her back increased. If only she bowed, the pain would cease.

Isaiah's subjects continued to repeat in cult-like unison: "All things must abide by the laws of the dimensions it's within, or be utterly destroyed."

A fifth-dimensional being like him could not die, not when it existed in all time at once.

But she didn't need to kill him.

In this realm, thoughts and emotions have power. Names, identities, the very essence of someone are powerful.

She remembered words she once spoke, in another time and space long ago: *And really, when you think about it, we as humans have electrical currents running throughout our bodies as a fourth-dimensional phenomenon. Which truly makes us fourth-dimensional intelligences, existing and perceiving a three-dimensional plane.*

She felt her jaw loosen, Isaiah's power on it lessening.

"I am not just a pathetic human," she said, finally free to speak vocally. "None of us are. We are so much more than that."

Isaiah relented, tightening her chains. "You are forever connected to me."

"Connected to *them,* too."

Evie thought of *them,* all the things that connected her to her three-dimensional life.

All the painful memories, all the pleasant ones. They all mattered as they linked her to those she connected with.

Threads of white light suddenly spread from her, fragile and delicate.

A strand to a former patient, once forgotten. A line toward a former mentor who taught her in her younger years. Another to an acquaintance she met in residency.

The connections continued to grow, like vines from a root.

A connection for Lilith, one for Olena, and another for Dennis.

Thicker strings emanated. One for Asa and one for Ren. They branched, outstretching beyond sight.

From those strings, another appeared, brighter than the rest. A lifeline to Michael.

The darkness around her lit with the white light of the strings. Blurred visions of people and events, from riveting to mundane. World lines, connecting and intersecting like a web—all crossing at specific times and locations. Memories of unreachable pasts and unknowable futures.

The strings that tied the universe together on all levels of existence.

"My chains are thick." Isaiah shook his head. "You cannot break them."

The chains tugged on Evie, forcing her lower. Her strings pulled back, preventing her from fully bowing.

I do not belong here, her thoughts spoke calmly. *No more than you belonged in my dimension.*

Isaiah's chains lagged.

"You—Earth child—"

The strings wove the fabric of space. Not only did Evie perceive all that she was connected to, but she also saw her home, Earth, in all stages of its life. Creation, living, and its destruction by the red sun. And with the sun, she saw all; its beginning, how its particles spread through the entire solar system to create the planets that orbit it, including the life that was born on Earth. The very particles that resided in her body and anyone else who came from Earth.

"I *am not* an Earth child." She stood, the pressure on her back lessening.

They say that everything in the universe came into existence all at once. All things living and nonliving in the solar system born of the particles contained within its mother star, the Sun. Its warmth and gravitational mass creating a cradle for life.

And the power of the sun was in all things born of it, confined to its space.

Evie decided to release it.

A sudden light struck her vision, although nothing blurred it. The chains around her shrank, and she pulled her right arm out. She pointed at Isaiah and realized the light was emanating from her— from her very skin. A cool emanation pulsing with her heart. Her body felt light, and she no longer felt the ground.

She fixated her eyes on Isaiah, his face indignant, vexed. However, she felt the terror he felt. He knew what she was becoming. "Unlike you, we humans are descendants of the sun, and we will endure. *I* will endure."

Plasmic energy radiated from Evie's skin, but did not burn her. She *knew* that this was only possible because of this dimensional plane. She felt the ions and electrons that moved through her body, that made her matter alive, and they became hers to command.

And the chains that bound her burst.

All things must abide by the laws of the dimensions it's within, or be utterly destroyed. . .

"I will not be defied!" Isaiah snarled at her. "You sold yourself to me! Your realm; it's rightfully mine—they took it from me, and it's mine!"

And suddenly, Isaiah was transparent to Evie. She knew everything about him.

Once an overseer charged with maintaining life in this solar system, he squandered his role with his lust for power. A sister planet to Earth suffered at his hands already. As punishment he was revoked of his role, and blocked from entering existential spaces below four dimensions. Imprisoned for his treachery.

Until he found Evie and used her as an anchor to escape his dimensional prison.

All things must abide by the laws of the dimensions it's within, or be utterly destroyed. . .

Striations and electrical arcs danced around Evie, emanating from her very presence. Her entire body was still humanoid, but it took its true form from solar creation. The energy within her broke the bounds of her three-dimensional body, no longer bound to the physical laws of their realm.

A daughter of the sun.

She reached and grabbed hold of Isaiah's celestial stone, right through his shirt. The last relic of his time as an overseer, bonded to him. A living gem of immense power. He tried to peel her fingers away, but they simply passed through her like a ghost.

She brought him to her realm; it was her responsibility to return him to his prison. One word escaped her lips: "Banish."

And with her final word, plasma arched from his celestial stone and struck Isaiah.

Wailing and gnashing of teeth followed as flesh peeled from bone on Isaiah. His physical form coming apart, his sub-atomic particles breaking their bonds within their three-dimensional counterparts, and reorganizing so that they could never appear again below the fourth-dimensional plane.

Pieces of Isaiah flaked away before her.

The strings that connected Evie to her realm pulled.

And her perception shifted, whisking her away from the fourth dimension.

She opened her eyes.

She floated under water—*no*—in the icy depths of the Vita-8 pool.

The thick viscosity of the substance made it difficult to move. She looked up to the surface. The distorted faces of those she cared for were on the other side: Michael, Asa, and the members of 4020.

You cannot escape me, the last remnants of Isaiah's voice whispered from beneath. *Do not deny what is mine. If I am banished from this realm, you too shall fall with me.*

She felt him lash out with hatred and anger, his empathic powers trying to grab hold of her once more. But they were beyond reach as she felt his essence slowly dissipate.

The frigid Vita-8 slowed her muscles, and she felt as though she'd drift away.

That's right, Isaiah's voice whispered in her mind. *Sleep, and die with me.*

But the light from above drew her gaze.

She reached her hand up.

And it broke the surface.

Many hands reached for hers, and she was pulled out of the Vita-8 pool.

"Bring fire," she heard Michael's voice order. "Warm her up. Her body's literally frozen. Asa, what's it done to her skin?"

"I don't know," Asa's voice sounded. "But look!"

Evie felt warmth, and her vision cleared. Her muscles loosened. Just like the day she first awoke on Triton, she sat up, coughing, retching up the blue substance.

Warmth from the surrounding firelight made it evaporate immediately.

Michael held her in his arms, and 4020 surrounded them.

"A miracle," Asa knelt across from her. "The concentrated substance, it didn't kill her. It freed her from the fungus, from the Xyelex. It was the cure all along."

Evie forced breath into her lungs. It felt like she was learning to breathe again. "It's over." She took another deep breath. "The Xyelex, all of it's gone. It won't haunt us again. It'll take power equal to a star, and countless more, before it would consider descending from its plane again." Evie knew words held power. Her curse would follow Isaiah—the Xyelex—forever.

Burning came to Evie's eyes, as it did so many times before. The dry, itching burn that yearned for sorrow, to cry, but she always held it back.

But this time her eyes welled.

Evie wept.

Epilogue: The Long Night Cometh

Nine Earth months later. . .

Evie cradled her newborn in her arms, her daughter comfortingly suckling on her breast.

Michael's arms wrapped around her, and he kissed the top of the child's head.

They were in the cathedral chamber, everyone around them making preparations.

Asa approached. "It's time. You ready?"

Evie smiled. "As ready as I will ever be."

She looked down at her newborn's eyes; stone grey, not yet adjusted to their color. But their shape were that of Michael's.

The more time she spent with her newborn, the less she thought of everything that happened those months prior. They seemed so distant, becoming memory in the back of her mind. Would she really have chosen differently? And if she did, would humanity have it's second chance? She thought decided to think little of it, for it no longer mattered. It was the past.

Michael touched his infant's cheek. "Do you think she can do it?"

"She can," Evie reassured. "She's strong enough."

After months of preparation, the cave system beneath the Community was unrecognizable. It was a town, a network of people striving to survive. They had their domestics, they had their troubles. But they were living.

They stocked the supplies they needed, took in living creatures, and raised them to their means.

But even with all the preparation, the eclipse still dawned, and there wasn't enough to survive the entire long winter. Not with the harsh surface conditions. Yet, the answer was under their noses all along. Triton produced life, and it produced the very thing to preserve its life.

Vita-8.

Evie lifted her free arm and put it on Asa's shoulder. "We'll be alright. I promise."

"I know you will," Asa said. "I ran the numbers and tested myself; I know it will. It's just, well…" his words trailed off.

Evie smiled. "I know." She saw his eyes drift upon the child. "Would you like to hold her?"

Asa's face lit, elated. "Is it safe? I won't make her ill or anything before?"

Evie laughed. "No, Asa, she'll be alright. Here, she's done nursing, just comfort suckling."

She gently pulled the child from her breast, her soft, petal lips still suckling in the air.

Asa took the child in his hands, holding her as delicately as melting ice.

"You won't break her," Michael said.

Asa pulled her in close, closing his eyes.

And the hum of a long-forgotten lullaby emanated from him, swaying as he kissed the top of her head.

"Oh little one, what name shall I call you?" Asa asked. "We have not yet recorded it."

"We had a few in mind," Michael said.

"I think I know," Evie said. "With all of us here, I think I know."

They all looked to her.

"Eliana," she said. "After my grandmother."

Evie felt an affectionate squeeze on her shoulder from Michael.

"Ahh," Asa gently rocked the child. "Eliana—first child born on Triton."

"Don't get too sentimental on me," Evie said musingly.

Eliana cooed, then released an infant cry.

"And she wants her mommy." Asa handed Eliana back to Evie, the child immediately reattaching to her breast, cooing as she suckled.

"I will miss you, my friends," Asa said. "We all will."

As Asa escorted Evie and her family to the Vita-8 pool, the others of 4020 gathered. All of those who agreed to enter the Vita-8 pool for the eclipse. They, too, were dressed down in only what they needed for modest comfort. The few who would upkeep the colony during the cryogenic sleep were the only ones bundled against the cold.

Evie and Michael's feet came to the edge, the still liquid like a mirror of cerulean blue; waiting, calling.

Together, they stepped into the infinite pool.

And walked, deeper and deeper into its depths. Hand in hand, child in arm, immersing themselves in Vita-8.

And it was a promise that drove them forward. The promise of the awake team, that they would reawaken the colony after the eclipse winter, after the long night was over. After they spent a season farming enough supplies to sustain everyone. A promise of tomorrow, a promise of hope.

And it was this promise that Evie dreamt of as others followed, immersing themselves into the infinite pool.

Asa watched the Exodus of people entering.

"We have our work cut out for us," a young man by him commented.

"You could say that again," Asa said, continuing to watch.

"I won't," the man said. "Redundant."

Asa turned his gaze to the young man. He had that smirk, that same smile his old friend Ren used to have. He put a hand on his shoulder and gave him an approving look.

"Young sir, redundancy is just a pattern," he said. "Patterns make the universe. And ultimately, life. The coming months are the next great pattern to rebuild humanity."

The young man nodded in agreement. "I guess we'd better start."

THE END

Afterword

What would you do with humanity's second chance? That was something I asked myself when I first came up with this thought experiment. What would happen if people had to start over, knowing what they currently know? Would they choose differently? How would society grow and organize?

And I remembered the hubris of people. The seven deadly sins: pride, greed, wrath, envy, lust, gluttony, and sloth.

As well as the seven heavenly virtues: humility, charity, chastity, kindness, temperance, patience, and diligence.

Ideas of sin and virtue are prevalent across much of classic Western literature, heavily influenced by the ruling beliefs of their historical time periods. When I thought about what I wanted this book to be about, I researched heavily into these ideas and how they not only influence literature but also human behavior.

Throughout the novel, all seven sins and virtues are represented. Not to by any means judge or condemn others, but to bring about a wider understanding of human nature as a whole. Evie faces each of those sins and rejects them all before she is strong enough to embrace her full potential. All other characters are each a representation of a sin and a corresponding virtue.

As for the thought experiment, what virtues would humanity choose to embrace? And what pitfalls would they face when the only accountability is their own self-consciousness? Is it the altruistic or the inartistic that will thrive in a world without modern means?

Those were some of the things I thought about while writing this novel. In the end, my thoughts begged more questions than answers. Questions about the very nature of existence and the physics that make up the known universe. If humanity had to start over, would they be alone? Or does life follow patterns like all other things in the universe, and appear in the far reaches of space? And if life persists beyond Earth, does it also persist beyond what we can perceive? Thus was born the idea of utilizing a fifth-dimensional intelligence from a fourth dimension in this novel. Sometimes life is tricky, and doesn't look the way we think it does. It was hard to imagine something like Xyelex, what form it would take if thrown into a three-dimensional space, and how it would react to other beings considered lesser than it.

In the end, this was a labour of love. What started as a short novella based on a thought experiment grew into something much more. And I'm happy I wrote it.

About the Author

H.B. Nuttall is a writer and educator, working professionally for over a decade. She's published previous works and written and presented entire course curricula on writing. She completed her graduate studies at *Grand Canyon University.*

Raised in the Finger Lakes region of New York, she now resides in central Arizona with her husband and children. She is a member of the *American Night Writers Association.*

Connect:

Website: www.hbnuttallwriting.com
Instagram: hb_nuttall_writer
Facebook: @H.B. Nuttall
X: @HBnuttallwriter